PRAISE FOR GREG RUCKA'S

SMOKER

"With *Smoker,* Rucka moves to a new level of confident writing and plotting. . . . The pace is greyhound-quick, the characters skewed enough to avoid stereotypes and, as always, Kodiak's compelling sadness makes him one of the more empathetic characters in contemporary thrillerdom. . . . This is by far the best of a series that always has had remarkable promise." —*The Dallas Morning News*

"Engaging . . . suspense-filled . . . *Smoker* is one of those books that unfolds so vividly, it will give the reader the feeling that they saw the movie."
—*Milwaukee Journal Sentinel*

"*Smoker* seals Rucka's status as a rising star whose books crackle with energy while examining current issues. . . . [He] designs a true modern hero . . ."
—*Sun-Sentinel* (Fort Lauderdale)

"*Smoker* blazes full-speed ahead. . . . A fast-paced and skillfully written novel. I give *Smoker* a rousing thumbs-up." —*The Knoxville News-Sentinel*

"There's lots of action and a few surprises at the end, which is always satisfying. Atticus Kodiak and his creator Greg Rucka make good companions on a dreary afternoon." —*The Orlando Sentinel*

"Kodiak is a highly likeable antihero with plenty of smart-alecky humor and charm."
—*Booknews* from The Poisoned Pen

"The third Kodiak novel is an incredible tale. . . . The characters are poignant and real. . . . The storyline is filled with action and twists. . . . There can be no doubt that Mr. Rucka is one of the leading authors of genuine tales of suspense."
—harrietklausner@bookbrowser.com

FINDER

"A top-notch thriller . . . Rucka makes superb use of crisp understated prose, complex and enigmatic characters, highly charged emotions, breakneck pacing, and a brilliantly original, cleverly engineered plot. A powerhouse of a story that will leave readers gasping." —*Booklist* (starred review)

"A memorable novel, dark as a moonless night."
—*Mostly Murder*

"As grit-gray and compelling as real life. A-plus."
—*The Philadelphia Inquirer*

"Rucka blends Spillane's 'tough-guy' private eye with Chandler's noir insights and Hemingway's spartan expression. . . . Once you've picked up this book, chances are you'll just keep going. And want more."
—*Statesman Journal,* Salem OR

"The action is nonstop."
—*The Boston Globe*

"If you're looking for a private eye with hard-edged skills and a soft center, try *Finder*."
—*Alfred Hitchcock Mystery Magazine*

"Fine cliff-hangers, well-executed violence, and skillfully sketched characters. Superior." —*Kirkus Reviews*

"A fast-paced and very contemporary thriller with a plot, as they say, that will not let you go. Suspense fans will finish this in one satisfied sitting, only to find themselves impatient for Rucka's next offering."
—*American Way* magazine

KEEPER

"Impressive . . . *Keeper* is one to hang on to." —*People*

"Crisper, tighter, and tougher . . . A keeper as a novel!" —*San Francisco Chronicle*

"Riveting . . . *Keeper* is full of surprises."
—*Houston Chronicle*

"*Keeper* is no ordinary thriller. It pulls at the heartstrings and brings tears to the eyes. . . . A remarkable first novel." —*The Orlando Sentinel*

"The book is a keeper." —*The Boston Sunday Globe*

"A few top crime writers—Robert B. Parker in the Spenser series for instance—have wandered into bodyguard territory. Rucka has the talent to make it his own." —*Publishers Weekly*

"A real contribution to the genre. *Keeper* combines compelling plot with right-now subtext. Greg Rucka is going to make his mark. . . . Stay tuned!"
—Andrew Vachss

SMOKER

GREG RUCKA

BANTAM BOOKS

NEW YORK TORONTO LONDON SYDNEY AUCKLAND

SMOKER

A Bantam Book
Grateful acknowledgment is made for permission to excerpt from
"East Coker" in FOUR QUARTETS, copyright 1943 by T.S. Eliot
and renewed 1971 by Esme Valerie Eliot, reprinted by permission
of Harcourt Brace & Company, and from *Four Quartets*,
COLLECTED POEMS 1909–1962, by T.S. Eliot, reprinted
by permission of Faber and Faber, Ltd.

PUBLISHING HISTORY
Bantam hardcover edition published November 1998
Bantam paperback edition / September 1999

ISBN 0-553-57829-4

Published simultaneously in the United States and Canada

Bantam Books are published by Bantam Books, a division of Random
House, Inc. Its trademark, consisting of the words "Bantam Books"
and the portrayal of a rooster, is Registered in U.S. Patent and Trademark Office and in other countries. Marca Registrada. Bantam Books,
1540 Broadway, New York, New York 10036

This is for the last of the White Hats:

N. Michael Rucka

my hero, my father.

ACKNOWLEDGMENTS

Giving praise where praise is due:

Evan Richard Franke, for having a brain worthy of picking, and the drive to research when the Bar is bearing down—may Ian always know how blessed he is to have you and Laura.

Nunzio Andrew DeFilippis, for a sharp eye and a good point, and everything spilled forth from there.

Gerard "Jerry" Hennelly, President of Executive Security and Protection International (ESPI), Inc., for taking the big puzzles apart piece by piece. Thanks for covering my back.

Daria Carissa Penta, for finding the drama; Alex and James Gombach, for NYC and NYPD accuracy; Joan Warner, for the insulin shock; Kalon, Laura, Stuart, and Wes at Em City; Kate Miciak, Amanda Clay Powers, and the rest of the Bantam crew, for their continued support; Sycamore Blaine, Claire Thayer, and Joaquin, for being damn good in a fight; and Corry Rucka, for clippings galore.

Long overdue thanks to Robert Irvine, a hell of a writer; you showed me the way, and I am forever in your debt.

And, at the end, there is always Jennifer, who stole my heart and has yet to give it back.

The only wisdom we can hope to acquire
Is the wisdom of humility; humility is endless.

—*T. S. Eliot*

I'd been waiting for forty minutes in the Oak Bar of the Plaza Hotel. Outside, coachmen smoked cigarettes and made jokes about the weather while their horses shifted in the heat, anticipating the order to drag another tourist couple around Central Park. I was wearing blue jeans, white sneakers, a white oxford shirt, a gray and blue tie, and a dust-colored linen jacket. My glasses were clean, and the two small surgical steel hoops in my left earlobe sparkled. It was the fourth day of July, and instead of fighting my jetlag or enjoying a holiday barbecue, I was nursing a club soda and wondering why Elliot Trent was late.

For the most part, I like the Oak Room. It stirs cultural memories of the alcoholic idle rich, the Roaring Twenties, and makes me think of literary giants like F. Scott Fitzgerald and Hemingway's moveable feast.

But after a while I start to think about the rest of it—the complacency, the arrogance . . . basically, everything that Fitzgerald talks about in *The Great Gatsby*.

My watch agreed that I'd been waiting forty-two minutes. I figured to make it a round forty-five before calling it quits. Trent hadn't said why I should meet him, only that it was "extremely urgent." That, in and of itself, was barely enough to draw me out. But there was a chance he wanted to talk about Natalie, and although I didn't think Elliot Trent knew the extent of my relationship with his daughter, I'd been wrong before.

I was reaching for the check when Trent arrived. He looked unhurried and cool, his summer-style business suit marking him overdressed, even in the Oak Bar of the Plaza Hotel. It may have been the Fourth of July, but according to Trent's clothes, this was a business day like any other. He made me in my booth and took his time heading over, even stopping to order drinks from the waiter by the bar. If Trent thought he was late, you couldn't tell by looking at him.

He had company, too, a man in his mid-twenties who followed a few steps behind. The man was very pretty, strong featured, with dark eyes and black hair cropped and styled in the same fashion almost every man had worn in prime time this last television season. The combination of looks and dress made him seem familiar, the way, after a while, every magazine model seems familiar, and I decided I didn't like him on principle. I also decided I was in a bad mood.

"I ordered you another of the same." Trent reached my table and waited for the other man to take a chair before seating himself. "I hope that's all right."

"It might go to my head," I said. "I've been drinking for a while."

Trent frowned. He has a good frown, with creases in the right places and the silver hair above it to make it all look distinguished. The other man smiled. The smile, too, was out of a magazine.

"Carter Dean," Trent said, "Atticus Kodiak. Atticus, this is Carter Dean."

"Of the Greenwich Deans?" I asked.

Carter Dean looked vaguely alarmed. "No," he said.

"Good. Can't stand the Greenwich Deans." To Trent I said, "I've been here for forty-five minutes."

"I was held up at the office," Trent said, and that was all he was going to give me by way of an apology. In one sense, it was an adequate explanation: Elliot Trent runs Sentinel Guards, one of the biggest security firms in Manhattan. Over sixty men and women on the regular payroll, with an additional stable of part-timers for when the going gets really rough, covering everything from personal protection to corporate security. Trent himself is ex–Secret Service, and had worked the presidential detail for Carter and, briefly, for Reagan.

The waiter brought our drinks. When he had gone, Trent said, "I've been trying to reach you all week. Erika said you were out of town."

"I got back today," I said.

"Working?"

"Yes."

"Not local," Trent declared.

"Los Angeles. I know a couple people out there."

"I didn't think it was local." Trent reached for his drink. "What were you doing?"

"Auditing. A Saudi princess is starting at UCLA in the fall. You know the story."

"So you weren't actually guarding."

"Nope."

"I'd imagine business has been rough. Not a lot of work."

"There's been enough."

"Really?" His creases went a little deeper in concern. "Even considering everything that's happened?"

I just looked at him, wondering what he was playing at. Pulling this shit in front of a client—if that's what Carter Dean was—made no sense.

"That whole SAS business, I mean." Trent shook his silver head. "And before that, the doctor, you remember. The one whose daughter was murdered."

"I remember."

"You were guarding them both, weren't you? The doctor and her daughter." He kept his gaze on me as he spoke, kept his voice wrapped in fatherly tones. His eyes are hazel.

I looked at Carter Dean. Carter Dean looked out the window. Out the window, one of the coachmen was tucking an octogenarian couple into his carriage for a ride around the park. The couple were holding hands.

"You know damn well I was," I told Trent. He also knew the rest, that one of the guards in the detail had died, and that the guard in question had been his daughter Natalie's lover and my best friend.

Elliot Trent took a sip of his drink, then wiped his fingers on the cocktail napkin. He glanced at Dean. Dean took that as his cue.

"I'm looking for some protection," Carter Dean said. He said "protection" like he was Al Pacino and Trent was Marlon Brando. I didn't want to know who that made me.

"Why?"

Trent answered for him. "Mr. Dean has just ended a relationship with a woman several years his junior. Of legal age, but young nonetheless. The lady in question has brothers. Irate brothers, who are unhappy with the disposition of the affair."

Dean made a face, probably at Trent's choice of words. "They feel I should have married her," he told me. "That just wasn't going to happen, and Liz understood that. They didn't. They don't. They're pretty angry right now."

"Wonder why," I said.

"I've told Mr. Dean there's probably nothing to worry about," Trent said, commiserating with me. "But he is insistent. Apparently, both of the Thayer brothers own guns."

"You're offering this to me?" I asked Trent.

"We're short-staffed at Sentinel right now. I can supply guards for Mr. Dean, but I have nobody free who can run the detail. So, yes, I'm offering it to you."

"It's not a detail," I said. "It's babysitting."

Trent stood up, and I thought the interview was over, but instead he just moved out of the way to let Dean pass. "Will you give us a few minutes alone?" Trent asked him.

Dean nodded, and I watched him head to the bar.

"I know it's babysitting." Trent sat down again. "You know it's babysitting. The threat is minimal, at worst. Neither of the brothers—Joseph and James—has a record. I've already tried to dissuade Dean, but he's after the peace of mind, and he's willing to pay for it."

"You can't really be so busy at Sentinel you don't have anyone to spare," I said.

"We're running a major operation upstate, and it's taking all of my resources." Trent leaned back in the booth to appraise me. I don't imagine he liked what he saw, but I couldn't argue with that; lately, I didn't like what I saw in the mirror either. It wasn't just the need for a haircut, or the scar that ran along my right cheek from temple to jaw. It was the suspicion that the whole

Atticus Kodiak looking back at me wasn't much of a package.

"It's an easy job, Atticus. We plant Dean at the Orsini Hotel, button him up there for two weeks, tops. Two thousand dollars for the work, and you don't even have to sit on him twenty-four/seven. I'll supply three or four other guards to make him feel safe, you'll all keep him company, and everyone will be happy."

"I'm wondering if I should be insulted," I said.

"The word is out." Trent said it gently. "Some people in our business—in this city, at least—don't want anything to do with you. After the death of that little girl, after the death of Rubin Febres, after the whole mess this last winter with the SAS, they figure you're dangerous. It's not hard to see why. You've had gun battles in downtown, for God's sake."

"Just the one," I said.

"There have been similar situations, but all right. Just the one." He smiled again, and I decided this smile was more condescending than paternal. "But the fact remains that another mishap will get you blackballed in our business. Right now, you're poison. If you do this job for me and you do it right, I'll see what I can do about restoring your reputation. I'll send more work your way, help you get back into the fold."

I stood up, found my wallet, and dropped a couple of bills. "I'll pass," I said.

"Atticus, don't be stubborn."

"I'm not interested."

"You owe me. I could call in my marker."

"If you want to waste it on this, go right ahead. But remember, I'm poisonous and I'm dangerous, and you probably don't want a man like that around the lovely Carter Dean."

"That's your answer?"

"My answer is no," I said, and headed for the lobby. At the bar Dean shot me a smile and I shot back with a glare and pushed my way through the revolving door and onto the street, wondering if Trent would have called that last exchange a "battle."

And in the Oak Bar at the Plaza Hotel. Nick Carroway would've plotzed.

It was just shy of six when I got back to my apartment, unlocking the door to hit a wall of industrial music blasting from the stereo. I fought the subwoofers down the hall and lowered the volume, then doubled back and found Erika leaning out of her doorway.

"You get a job?" she demanded.

"Passed on it."

"You serious?"

"Perpetually."

"Yeah, I noticed that." She made a little grimace, then added, "I made plans to go over to Bridgett's tonight, to watch the fireworks. I can call her and cancel."

"No, don't do that," I said, but it took me a second, and she caught it.

"I didn't think you were getting back until tomorrow," Erika explained.

"It's not a problem."

"You're certain?"

"Absolutely."

Erika shook her head at me, then turned and went back into her room, leaving the door open. "You should phone her," she called, sounding fifty instead of sixteen.

I followed, watched as Erika stuffed clothes into her

backpack. She was wearing olive shorts, sneakers without socks, and a black tank shirt with a silver ankh stenciled on the front. When she straightened, she smoothed her hair reflexively to cover her left ear. Her hair is the gold of unstained oak, and her left ear is missing most of its cartilage and lobe from where a man named Sterritt had cut it off just to prove he was serious.

When Elliot Trent referred to "that SAS business" he was referring to Erika, to her mother and father who had gone to war over her. Her father had died in the spring, taken by AIDS in the form of viral pneumonia. Her mother had died in the winter when I'd shot her four times.

That was almost nine months ago, now, and in that time Erika and I had rebuilt a relationship I'd all but destroyed five years back. Technically, I'm Erika Wyatt's legal guardian, but neither of us see it that way; we're like siblings, and after squandering my first chance at being her big brother, I'm grateful for another try.

Erika doesn't talk about what had happened with her parents—at least, not to me, and most likely not to Bridgett. She'd been seeing a therapist twice a week until her father died, and then it had become once a week, and now only once a month. We'd attended Colonel Douglas Wyatt's funeral together, and when his ashes were scattered on the Hudson River opposite West Point, she'd cried. But that was all.

Erika repeated, "You should call Bridgett."

"I can't."

"You're both being really stupid about this."

"Probably."

"The longer you avoid each other, the worse it gets, and you're not fooling anyone into thinking it doesn't matter. I mean, you haven't spoken since November, and you're still hung up on each other."

I nodded, but couldn't add anything more.

Erika hoisted the backpack onto one shoulder, cocked her head. "You want me to stay?"

"It's okay, I've got plans. You should hustle if you want to get there before dark." I moved out of her way, followed her down the hall. If she knew I was lying, she gave no sign of it. "When should I expect you back?"

"Tomorrow afternoon, probably," Erika said, opening the door. "I'll call if I'm going to be late."

"I'd appreciate it."

She gave me a hug, pressing her cheek to mine. Her face was soft and warm, and smelled of Noxzema. "You want me to tell her anything?"

"There's nothing I can say."

"Yes there is," Erika said. "You can call her and say 'I love you and I'm sorry.' That's what you can say."

"No," I said. "I can't."

I fixed myself a dinner of pasta with a homemade pesto sauce, then decided I was masochist enough to bake a loaf of bread. My sourdough starter was still alive, the yeast thriving in their earthenware home, and I pounded and kneaded and worked myself into a sweat for a bit. I took a shower while the bread rose, then sat back with a book and a beer. From my window I could see the flashes of early fireworks, glowing airbursts that made brief halos in the darkening sky. It wasn't full night yet and the effect was lost, but it's always that way on the Fourth of July; somebody always loses their patience, and the result is an unsatisfying and depressing show.

Wherever Bridgett and Erika were, I hoped they were watching a better spectacle.

At ten I picked up the phone and called Natalie Trent's apartment, knowing that I shouldn't, and hoping that she wouldn't answer. When I got her machine I hung up without leaving a message. It was probably just as well.

The phone rang almost ten minutes later, and Carter Dean said, "Mr. Kodiak, why won't you protect me?"

I said, "How'd you get my number?"

"I asked Trent for it. Answer my question. Why won't you take the job?"

"You don't need me," I told him. "I don't think you need Trent, either. If you're worried about angry brothers, take a two-week trip to France. It'll cost you less than what Sentinel is charging."

"I don't have a passport."

"Go to Canada, then."

Dean thought that was funny, and gave me a chuckle. Somebody on a nearby roof set off a string of firecrackers. They sounded a little like gunfire, but not much.

"This is what I'm thinking," Carter Dean said. "I want protection, and Sentinel is going to provide it. They're getting my money whether you're on the job or not. Given that I don't much like Elliot Trent, I'd prefer to give some of that money to you."

"If you don't like Trent, use another firm."

"Would another firm hire you?"

"I doubt it."

"I want you."

"Why?"

He was silent for a second. "I'd prefer to be dealing with someone closer to my own age, frankly. Trent's too old for my taste—I think he resents me being both young and wealthy."

Not to mention pretty, I thought. "So you're wealthy."

"I got lucky. Designed a computer game while in college, and the game was a hit. *Ferocious*. Maybe you've heard of it?"

"No."

"Well, trust me, most people who own a PC have," Dean said. "Look, I don't know what's going on between you and Trent, what that whole conversation at the Plaza was about. But you seem like a fair guy, a nice guy, and if I'm going to be spending two weeks locked up at the Orsini Hotel with bodyguards on me the whole time, I'd like at least one of those guards to be a fellow I can get along with."

"You don't need to get along with your bodyguards," I said. "All you have to do is listen to them."

"Then I want to listen to someone I respect," Carter Dean said. "I'd like that person to be you."

I almost laughed at him. Respect was something in short supply on my end. If Carter Dean had it for me, he hadn't been listening very closely to Trent.

"Please," Dean urged. "It would give me peace of mind."

I thought about it. The only reason I'd refused is that Trent had gotten me sore. I wasn't desperate for cash, but there was no question I could use the money. Erika was looking to start college in the next year, and as it was, she'd be traveling on student loans all the way. Two thousand dollars would lessen the burden just a little bit more.

A couple of booms like distant thunder went off overhead, and falling lights of red, white, and blue. Then another salvo, and another. One of the big fireworks displays had started.

"All right," I told Dean. "I'll do it."

CHAPTER TWO

"I don't think I can bear much more of this," Corry Herrera said to me. "I think I may start shooting people just to relieve the boredom."

We were standing in the hall outside of Dean's rooms at the Orsini. Through the door we could hear the television playing, another rented movie on the VCR. Occasionally, we would hear Dean or the guard posted inside make a comment or a joke. When things got really exciting, someone would laugh. Then room service would come.

It had been exactly this exciting for four days now.

"If it comes to that," I told Corry, "I'd like you to shoot me first."

Corry grinned, adjusted his Kevlar vest. He has a great smile, entirely honest, and the temperament of a man who likes to use it. Of the five Sentinel guards assigned to the detail, Corry was the only one I knew, and I was grateful for his presence. We ran two twelve-hour shifts, day and night, of three guards each. Today it was Corry, myself, and a man named Philip Fife. Fife, like all the other guards except Corry, watched me as if I had some potentially virulent disease. Corry at least made me feel like it wasn't communicable.

"He made you wear the Kevlar?" I asked.

"It's SOP," Corry said. "Trent wants all of his people wearing body armor while on an op. How'd you get out of it?"

"Reminded him I don't work for him."

"Vest's not so bad in the hotel, with the air conditioning. I'd hate to be working outside in it, though."

"You don't think it's paranoid? Body armor at all hours?"

Corry shrugged. "It's Trent's firm, his rules. He says he doesn't want any of his people getting hurt on the job. It's no more paranoid than putting six guards on Dean, or registering him here under a false name. Speaking of which . . ." He checked his watch. "You think 'Mr. Pugh' is ready for his daily excursion?"

"I hope so," I said. "It's the most scintillating part of my day."

Corry grinned.

I knocked on the door, waited for Fife to let me into the room. He checked me out through the spyhole before unlocking the door, and he kept his hand on his gun when I came inside. At least he kept his gun in its holster.

"How we doing?"

"Everything's clear," Fife told me, as if I'd accused him of sleeping on duty.

"You're a good man, Philip," I said.

Dean was lounging shirtless on the sofa, watching the television, an empty room-service tray on the table nearby. Also on the table was the *Complete Riverside Shakespeare*. I had yet to see Dean actually open the book, and wasn't certain if he was intellectual, pretentious, or honestly enjoying Shakespeare.

"Atticus," he cried. "Going to keep me company?"

"Just checking to see if you're ready to head down."

"Give the word. Will you join me today?"

"Like I told you, I can't while I'm on duty."

Dean pounded his washboard abdomen. "Women love a flat belly, Atticus. You've got to work at it if you want to be a chick magnet like me."

I didn't tell him that my abdomen was fine, bullet scar and all. I didn't tell him that I had no urge to be a chick magnet, either. I just said, "I'll make my sweep, then radio Corry and Philip to bring you down."

"Affirmative," Dean said.

I went back into the hall.

"Did he say 'affirmative'?" Corry asked, after the door had been shut and locked once more.

"Yup."

Corry shuddered. "I really don't think I can take much more of this."

"And we've only got ten more days to go," I said.

The sweep consisted of walking the route from Dean's suite on the eighth floor down to the health club on the first. Once at the health club, I'd check the weight room, the men's changing room, and the pool—every place Dean would visit while working out. From a security standpoint, it was during his exercise that he was at his most vulnerable, and so the sweep was simply prudent. But the fact was that Dean was making this job very easy on us—unless it was to go to the gym or the pool, he just didn't leave his room. He was religious about his workout, though, spending two hours in the weight room daily, then finishing with a half hour of laps in the pool. One of the things I could say with certainty about Carter Dean was that he kept himself fit.

I took about twenty minutes to clear the route, checking and double-checking, looking for anyone who might resemble one of the brothers Thayer lying in wait, and finding nothing to arouse my suspicions. I spent an extra few minutes at the pool, admiring the different bathing suits and the ladies who wore them, then keyed my radio.

"It looks clear," I told Corry. "I'll be up in five."

"Confirmed."

"Don't you mean 'affirmative'?"

"I hope you drop a hair dryer in your bathtub," Corry radioed back.

Our relief arrived just before six, and I sat them down and went over the day's activities. It took under ten minutes, at the end of which Corry, Philip, and I all said good night to Dean, that we'd see him in the morning, and headed our separate ways.

It was a nice night, in the high seventies, and the streets seemed cool and subdued after the fierce heat of the day. I took my time walking home, shaking off the headache I'd earned watching Dean, and wondering how I was going to survive tomorrow. It takes more concentration and effort to focus on a job when there's nothing to do than most people realize, and I wondered if Trent hadn't suckered me into some sort of slow torture.

Erika was in her room when I got home, working on her computer. She'd put a new poster up above her desk, a photograph of a man in latex briefs and thigh-high boots, with glossy black bat wings spread out against an upholstered wall. Over his head was the word "Spanky," written in a Gothic font.

I asked how her day went and she told me that she'd spent most of it writing. "I'm almost done," she said.

"Story?" I asked.

"Maybe."

"Do I get to see it?"

"No. How was work?"

"Hell, actually," I said. "There's nothing to do."

"You can talk to the other guards, can't you? You can talk to Corry."

I shook my head. "That's a distraction."

"But you said there's nothing to do."

"Yeah, but I have to be ready just in case."

"The old just-in-case clause," Erika said. "I remember it well. Oh—Natalie called."

"What'd she say?"

"That she wants you to call her back. Are you gonna?"

"Yes."

"If you make plans, I don't want to know." She turned her chair around, and began tapping on her keyboard once again.

I stared at her back for a few taps, then decided that she'd taken the exit line. From the phone in the kitchen I dialed Natalie Trent's number. After three rings she picked up.

"I've been trying to reach you for the last few days," I said. "Where you been?"

"Massachusetts," Natalie said. "Smith & Wesson. Taking the night-sniping course. I thought I told you about it."

"You probably did and I probably forgot."

"You have plans for tonight?"

"Not as such."

She clicked her tongue a couple of times. "Dinner?"

"That'd be fine."

We picked a French place in her neighborhood, agreeing to meet there at nine, and I hung up. Erika came into the kitchen then, heading for the refrigerator, and I watched her pull out a container of cottage cheese. She found herself a spoon and began eating, standing by the sink.

"You should use a bowl," I said.

"You're meeting her?" Erika asked.

"You didn't want to know."

"That's a yes."

"We're going to have dinner."

Erika took another mouthful of cottage cheese, licked the spoon clean, and dropped it in the sink. The metal made a sound like a broken bell. She closed the container, replaced it in the fridge. Then she stared at me.

After ten seconds, I said, "What?"

Erika shook her head, fixed the hair hanging over her left ear. "See you in the morning," she said, and went back to her room, letting the door close softly behind her.

The restaurant was quiet and mostly empty. We had a table near the front, and both of us positioned our chairs so we could keep our backs to the wall, out of habit rather than need. Natalie had salad and rabbit, and I had salad and duck. She had most of a carafe of wine, and I killed a couple beers. It'd been three weeks since we'd last seen each other, and we played catch-

up in our conversation. She told me about the sniper
course and I told her about the job for her father.

"You need any help?" she asked.

"I don't think so. It's a total of six guards including
myself, and that's probably six too many. The principal
just sits in his hotel room, watches videos, and flexes in
the gym. It's redefining boredom for me."

"It does sound terribly exciting," Natalie said, not
meaning it at all.

"Has your father said anything to you about me?"

"No."

"When I first got his message, I thought he might be
calling to talk about you."

"He doesn't know," she said firmly.

"I figured that. Otherwise, he wouldn't have offered
me work."

"Considering how image-conscious Dad is about
Sentinel, I'm surprised he offered you work at all."

"It's that bad?" I asked.

Natalie nodded. "You are not a popular man in our
community."

"Oderint dom metuant," I said, softly. "Let them
hate, so long as they fear."

"The bodyguard's mantra." Natalie took another sip
of her wine. With the light shining through the glass,
the wine was the same crimson as her hair. She let her
fingers rest on the stem of the glass, then sighed heavily,
and I knew exactly what she was thinking. I was thinking it, too.

We soaked up our silence for almost a minute
longer, and the silence felt lonely rather than compan-
ionable. Natalie's twenty-eight, a beautiful woman, tall
and striking, with red hair that falls straight to below
her shoulder blades and eyes the green of fresh pine

needles. She was wearing a silk shirt four shades darker than her eyes, and black twill pants, and she looked extremely elegant, her hair drawn back into a loose ponytail. The restaurant light made her look either tired or sad, but I couldn't be certain which.

The check came, and we split it down the middle, and without saying anything we got up and left the restaurant. We walked across on Eighty-fourth Street to her apartment building on East End Avenue without holding hands. She greeted the doorman when we entered the building, and he offered a cheery "Evening, Miss Trent" in response. I got a nod of recognition, or maybe disapproval.

We stayed silent in the elevator, and we stayed silent into her apartment, and Natalie didn't turn on the lights. I waited until she had locked the door, and I followed her in the dark into her bedroom, where we undressed. She didn't pull back the covers, and we had sex on the bed, and there was nothing to it. No urgent need. No desperate passion. The air conditioner had been left on while we'd met for dinner and the apartment was cold. Natalie had placed a condom on her nightstand, where I knew it would be, where it had been every night I had spent in her apartment since Bridgett Logan had told me we were no longer lovers, since Bridgett Logan had told Natalie that they were no longer friends.

Afterward we lay on the bed not touching, listening to the air conditioner, to what little the city could offer us from seventeen floors below. Natalie had a digital clock/compact disc player combination on the nightstand, and I kept my eye on it. When it read a quarter past midnight I rose carefully and dressed quietly, going through the motions of trying not to disturb her sleep, even though I was certain she was awake.

But she let me do it, fostering the illusion until I was almost out of the room before she said, "Make sure you lock the door on your way out."

CHAPTER THREE

Philip Fife leaned out of Carter Dean's room and said, "Trent's on the phone for you. He's pissed."

"Don't grin so wide," I told him. "You'll crack your icy façade."

Fife gave me an eloquent look that spoke in four-letter words, but he moved out of the way to let me pass, then took over my post in the hall. I shut and locked the door, ignored Dean's wave—he was still on the couch, and still without his shirt—and picked up the extension by the bar.

"Kodiak," I said.

"Who the fuck do you think you are, recruiting Natalie without asking my permission?" Trent exploded. "I want her off your detail, and I want her off now, do you understand? You don't go near Natalie, no one on your goddamn crew goes near Natalie while you're on this job."

I kept my calm. I made my voice even. I said, "Elliot, I don't know what you're talking about."

"Bullshit," he shouted. "Bullshit! Are you so fucking incompetent I need to bring in another team? You deliberately went behind my back and recruited my daughter and—"

"I did no such thing," I told him. "Natalie offered to help, but I specifically did *not* take her up on that offer. Now stop yelling at me."

Trent stopped yelling at me, but I could hear his breathing, a rapid and ineffective attempt to block his fury. "You get her off scene immediately."

"She's not here, Elliot."

He gave me more breathing, maybe deciding if I was lying or not, then said, "Natalie tries to come on-post, you damn well better send her home. I don't want her around you, Kodiak, understand?"

There was a knot in my gut, trying to reach my throat, and I knew if I let it up, there would be shouting. Part of me wanted to let it up anyway, wanted to bite back, and hard. But Carter Dean was sitting on the couch, looking at me with curiosity brimming in his eager eyes, and Philip Fife was standing in the hall, probably listening with a drinking glass against the door. Even if everything Elliot Trent thought about me was true, even if I was no damn good at my job, I was still a professional. I wasn't going to lose my temper in front of my principal.

"If Natalie comes here, I'll tell her you called," I said.

"Don't fuck this up," Trent warned me. "You fuck this job and you're out for good. I'll see to it."

She showed up about forty minutes later, coming down the hall dressed for work in black jeans and a white T-shirt, a navy blue windbreaker to cover the Glock she wore on her hip. She had a small tactical-gear bag slung over her shoulder, and she moved it into her hands as she approached, smiling at Corry and me, saying, "I figured another warm body couldn't hurt."

"Well, not yours, at least," Corry said. "How was Smith & Wesson?"

"Worth every penny."

"Your father called," I told Natalie.

Her smile went away like steam and she looked at me, then at Corry. "Give us a minute?" she asked him.

Corry shrugged and tapped on the door. Fife did his precious business with the spyhole, then opened up, and Corry slipped past him into the room. Fife saw Natalie and said, "Hey, Red."

Natalie stared at him, and Fife shut the door without another word. "He shouldn't have called you," she told me.

"Did you tell him that I'd asked for your help?"

The anger in her eyes turned solid. "I told him that I'd talked to you and was going to lend a hand."

"Well, your father tore my head off," I said. "He thinks I solicited your help. He thinks I went behind his back. He thinks it's dangerous for you to be around me, and he told me to send you home."

Natalie leaned against the wall opposite me. She was wearing dirty white Filas, and they sank a fraction into the hall carpet. "That son of a bitch," she murmured.

"I'm not in a position to say."

"Are you telling me to go home?"

"Hell, no," I said.

"He doesn't like being opposed."

"Maybe it should happen to him more often."

"Maybe it should."

"Maybe you should."

"Maybe." Natalie turned her hands into fists a couple

of times. "Probably." She put her fists into her pockets, looked at her feet. "I'm thinking of moving to Boston."

I took a moment. "It's closer to the Smith & Wesson Academy."

She shook her head. "No, it's not that. It's just . . . I think I need to get out of here. . . . I think I need to get away from him." She looked from her shoes back to me. "You know something? I don't think I've gone longer than two weeks in my entire life without seeing my father. Certainly not since my mother died."

"That happens when he's also your boss."

"Even while I was in college. Even while I was in France during my junior year."

"Maybe you need some time off."

"Maybe I need out of this business," Natalie said, and sounded like she was spitting out a mouthful of used motor oil.

At one that afternoon I walked the route down to the health club. The halls were mostly empty all the way to the first floor, the tourists and business travelers currently in residence all out and about in the city. I saw several members of the housekeeping staff, all diligent in their work, and on the fourth floor passed three kids playing tag in the corridor.

The weight room was empty but for the attendant who was reading the new issue of *Premiere* at his desk. When I came in, he grinned and said, "The rock star's coming down, huh?"

I nodded and continued to the men's changing room. I saw four discarded towels and an abandoned athletic supporter, but no people. All of the maintenance doors were shut and locked. I took a peek at the pool deck, counted four heads, and then went back to the weight room. The attendant pushed his log book at me and I checked it over, signed Dean in as Jeremiah Pugh and gave his room number, then keyed my radio.

"Bring him down," I said.

"Confirmed," Natalie said.

It took them six minutes, during which time the attendant went back to his magazine and I kept my eyes on the doors. They arrived with Corry leading, Fife in the rear, Natalie providing the close cover on Dean. He'd put on a shirt for his walk through the halls, but I was certain he'd given Natalie a good chance to see his flat belly before covering up. As they came down the hall, I went back and checked the access through the changing room once more. No one was lurking.

We took up position around the room, and I caught the attendant grinning and shaking his head, and I wanted to tell him that, yes, I agreed, I thought this was silly, too. Dean's protection was more ornamental than functional. Trent had all but said that was what Dean was after. But I felt awkward; there were too many of us just for show, and not enough of us for actual work.

Dean grunted and groaned and worked himself into a lather. He was flexing a tad more than usual today, and I put that down to Natalie's presence, but otherwise his workout was identical to those of the previous five days.

"I'm exhausted just watching him," Natalie murmured to me after an hour. "He does this every day?"

"A man's body is the temple of his soul," I said. "Mr. Dean is obviously clergy."

She went to check the hallway again.

•   •   •

At a quarter of two Dean began his last set of leg presses and I went to check the changing room once again, and the pool. It was hot and sticky by the water, sunlight falling through the curved skylights that roofed the space, chlorine heavy in the air. The pool was large, though not Olympic size.

A mother-father-son combination frolicked in the water, splashing and laughing and noisily having a hell of a good time. There was a woman in a black one-piece lying on a lounge chair near where I had come in, too, drying off with her eyes closed. She was long and healthy, with hair that might have looked blond when it was dry, and the suit fit her very well. She opened her eyes and caught me looking. I grinned and she shut her eyes once more.

I walked down to the opposite end, checked the doors to the lobby and the pool supply closet. There was a table stacked with fresh towels, and a bin to hold the dirty ones, and I poked through them, then doubled back to the men's room.

"Three in the pool, one on the deck," I told my radio. "Otherwise looks clear."

"Be right there," Natalie said.

I pulled the door to the men's changing room open and swung it back against the wall, holding it in place with my foot. The trio in the pool had squirt guns, and dad and son caught mom in a crossfire. When she shrieked, the sound echoed along the glass and the water and the tiled deck.

They came through the changing room in the same formation as before, and I heard Dean saying something to Natalie about how she should have gone through the ladies' changing room rather than the men's. I didn't hear her respond. I waited until Fife passed me, covering the rear, then swapped places with him, leaving him on the door. He scowled but didn't hesitate, and I appreciated that.

Corry picked a lounge chair not too far from the lobby exit, and Dean dropped his towel on it, then sat down and began removing his sneakers. I motioned Natalie and Corry to post, and each spread out, covering the doors from the lobby and the women's changing room, respectively.

Dean stripped off his sweatpants, revealing a pair of red Speedos, then pulled his swimming goggles into place.

"Lane 10," I said.

He looked over the pool. The lane I'd requested was farthest from the lobby entrance. "Sure," he said. His goggles were tinted green, and made his eyes seem buggy. We walked down to the end of the lane, where Dean took a couple of deep breaths, then slapped me on the arm and said, "I'll try not to splash you."

"Thanks," I said, and then he was in the pool, starting his laps, and my pant legs were suddenly sodden. I followed alongside on the deck, keeping pace until I reached the end of his lane, where I stopped to watch. The family was climbing out of the water near where Corry watched the lobby door. The woman in the one-piece had gathered her things and was passing Natalie on her way back to her room.

Dean took ten minutes to warm up, lazy laps, during which time the family left and two teenaged boys arrived, followed by a pool attendant pushing a laundry cart. The boys were loud, almost obnoxious, and entered the pool with sloppy cannonballs that shot water all over the deck. They followed that with a contest to see how much water each could remove from the pool in the shortest amount of time.

"Punks," Fife radioed. *"You want me to remove them?"*

"Negative," I said.

"They're creating a distraction," Fife told me.

"Watch your door," I said.

Fife glared at me from across the room and I went back to watching Dean swim. He had finished another lap and was flipping in the water to push off the pool wall when the woman in the black one-piece returned. She stood in the doorway from the hall for a moment, towel wrapped around her waist, looking around. She settled on Natalie and headed her way, and I keyed my transmitter.

"Nat, heads up."

"Got it," Natalie responded. Over her mike I could hear the woman in the one-piece asking if Natalie was security, if she worked at the hotel.

Dean was merrily swimming away, and I scanned the perimeter again. The pool attendant was shoving a lump of wet towels into his cart. One of the kids was climbing onto the deck, preparing for another dive.

"We've got a complaint," Natalie said softly over the radio. *"This woman says the pool attendant has a gun."*

In my peripheral vision, I could see the attendant, now placing fresh towels out on the table. I couldn't get a clear look at his hands. Corry had moved in slightly, and Fife was moving off his door. They were waiting for orders, waiting for me.

I pressed the tiny button in my left palm. "Nat, check it out. Corry, Philip, let's button up."

"Confirmed," Corry responded.

I saw Natalie nod. Fife was already moving to the edge of the pool to grab Dean when he finished the lap.

"Sir? Excuse me?" I heard Natalie ask the attendant. She had her hand back and at her right hip, covering her weapon.

The man was anywhere between twenty and forty, with black hair and eyes set wide apart. He was dumping another armload of dirty towels into the cart, and they fell away to reveal black plastic and metal, a wild-looking design, like a log married to a crazy straw. He had pivoted, the submachine gun in his hands already ripping the air, spilling a ribbon of brass from beneath the weapon's grip. Natalie dropped to her flank, her weapon all ready to bear. Fife was on the deck, and I prayed that his Kevlar had held. There was no way to get Dean out of the pool in time. I tried anyway, went down and caught him in the water, feeling my shirt soak through. I was reaching for his arm and feeling the pool deck shred its way to me, and then there were the shots, five of them, a string of firecrackers that ended in the pinging of spent brass bouncing on the blue tile.

Dean came out of the water and onto the deck hard, and I rolled back and came up with my weapon out, but it was already over, and a piece of me knew that, just as a piece of me knew Natalie had put the assassin down.

He was on his back, one leg bent beneath him, the submachine gun discarded by his right thigh. Blood and brain matter spattered the wall behind him, staining the towels. More blood puddled on the tile, flowing through the grooves. He'd been hit with at least one head shot, and his skull rested two inches lower than the rest of his body.

Corry was pulling Fife to his feet, dragging him

oward where I was standing over Dean. Fife was saying that he was all right, that he'd only slipped, that the deck was too fucking slippery. He was trying not to shout, repeating himself, over and over. I stowed my weapon and yanked Dean up, using both of my hands to propel him past Natalie, to the lobby door.

She hadn't moved, still on the ground, her Glock in both hands, muzzle pointed at the body.

"Evac," I told her.

"Yeah."

"Now," I said.

Natalie snapped her head back, scrambled to her feet, and went to the lobby door. Corry stayed right behind me, still guiding Fife. In the water, the two teenage boys clung to the side of the pool. The woman in the one-piece was now covering her mouth with both hands, shaking her head from side to side.

"Thanks," I told her.

The woman scrunched her eyes closed and doubled over, holding her stomach. We were out of the room before she could begin throwing up.

There were people in the hall, and they got out of our way, and I was hearing shouting. Guards, probably, maybe the police, but that didn't matter right now. They'd find us in time, and the priority was getting Dean to a secure location, back to the room, before another attack could be launched. I didn't know if another attack would be launched, but then again, I hadn't really believed in the possibility of the first one, and I wasn't going to be caught stupid twice in the same day; at least, not if I could help it.

Natalie got us into an elevator, and the four of us stood around Dean, who was shivering violently. It wasn't the air conditioning.

"Jesus fucking Christ." Dean's voice sounded raspy, like he'd been crying. "He tried to kill me. That guy tried to kill me."

There was no way for any of us to respond to that.

It took another ninety seconds for us to clear the hall and get Dean back into his room. Corry went immediately to the phone and called down to the front desk while I led Dean to the bedroom to get him changed. He slumped on the bed while I got some towels from the bathroom.

"Dry off," I told him. "Get some dry clothes on. The police are going to be here in a couple of minutes and we're going to have to go with them."

"That wasn't supposed to happen," Dean said. "He assured me that wasn't going to happen."

"Was that one of the Thayers?" I asked.

"I feel sick, I feel really really sick. I feel like I'm going to puke."

"You're in shock. It'll pass in a few minutes."

"Thank you, Doctor! Shock? You want shock? I'll fucking give you *shock*! I'm going to sue Trent's ass like there's no tomorrow, I swear to God I'm going to fucking—"

"Carter," I said. "Calm down."

"I'm not Carter!" Dean spat at me. "There is no Carter Dean! I'm not goddamn fucking Jeremiah Pugh, either, okay! My name's Nathan, Nathan d'Angelo, get it?"

"Nathan d'Angelo," I repeated. "Got it." Outside, I heard the door opening and Natalie's voice. NYPD, probably.

"No you don't." Dean said it quietly, his anger suddenly gone. He picked up a towel, rubbed it over his vet hair. "I'll explain it to you. Trent hired me, under-stand? He hired me to pretend I was some jerk named Carter Dean. He paid me two thousand dollars to spend two weeks in a hotel room with guards and all of this shit and all I was supposed to do was pretend I was a guy named Carter Dean and that I wanted protection."

I blinked at him.

Dean—d'Angelo—whoever—shot me a sour grin. "Now you get it," he said. "I'm just a goddamn out-of-work actor. I'm fucking nobody. I'm certainly nobody who deserves to get shot to fucking shit."

I thought about Elliot Trent, everything he had been saying to me, everything that had happened. I thought about how badly he had wanted me to take this job, about how violently he had opposed Natalie taking part. I thought about Corry and Fife and their Kevlar vests.

I thought about the weapon I had seen on the pool deck. The Fabrique Nationale P-90, a submachine gun that was impossible to obtain outside the military, a weapon I'd only seen in books and magazines. A weapon that can spit nine hundred rounds a minute, and pene-trate twenty-seven layers of Kevlar at thirteen hundred meters. A weapon that could only be obtained from black market sources in this country.

I thought of the blood trickling through the channels of grout in the tile.

Trent had known this was going to happen from the beginning. He had known from the moment he hired me—from before he had hired me—that an attempt would be made on Dean's life.

A professional's attempt.

Dean had finished drying his upper body and was

now watching me, towel in his lap. "I told you I didn't like Trent," he said.

"He told you this was a dummy op from the start?" I asked.

"He said this was a dummy op, that I was his decoy, and you . . . you . . ." He shook his head, ran the towel across the back of his neck.

I swallowed some of the cotton that was coating the inside of my mouth. "I want to know what he said."

"Dummyguard," Nathan d'Angelo said. "Trent called you his dummyguard."

CHAPTER FOUR

The last time I had spoken to Donald Harner had been after evacuating a hotel in Midtown, and despite all of that, we had gotten along well enough. Harner was over the half-century hump, a little underweight and mostly bald, with a strip of gray and black hair running around the back of his head. He wore glasses with safety black frames, and I thought he looked more like a high school chemistry teacher than a cop.

"Kodiak, right?" he said when he saw me.

"Captain," I said.

"What is it with you and the hotels in my precinct?"

"I'm drawn to the jet set," I said.

"Park it." He pointed a stubby thumb at the chair opposite his desk. I parked it and he looked through me for a moment, then began thumbing through the reports on his desk. The office was claustrophobic, on the corner of the building. The two walls that faced the squadroom had small windows, and through them I could see where Corry, Fife, and Nathan d'Angelo were seated. D'Angelo could barely keep still, and from body language alone I could tell he was getting on Fife's nerves. Corry stared complacently at a poster on the wall. The poster said, *If guns are outlawed, then only outlaws will have guns.*

Harner finished with the reports and cleared his throat, and I asked, "Where's Natalie?"

"Ms. Trent is having her statement recorded," Harner said. "We had to get the video stuff set up." He raised an eyebrow at me. "Don't worry, we stopped using bright lights and rubber hoses last week."

"Her father arrived yet?"

"Nope."

"So she's making a statement without counsel?"

"Is that a problem? All of you are backing up her story. If the detectives confirm it, it'll go down as a clean shooting."

"There were witnesses," I said. "Some kids. A woman."

"I know. We got statements from all of them." He leaned forward in his chair, put his elbows on the desk. On his left lens I could make out the smear of a greasy fingerprint. "Now, what's this about a decoy operation?"

"You've been talking to d'Angelo," I said.

"He's got a big hair up his ass about this," Harner said. "Are you telling me he's lying?"

"I don't think so."

"Trent hired him?"

"I don't know."

"You didn't know you were part of a decoy operation?"

"First I heard of it was when Mr. Nathan d'Angelo told me that he was Nathan d'Angelo, not Carter Dean."

"Or Jeremiah Pugh?"

"Or Jeremiah Pugh."

"Lot of fucking names," Harner said. "Is that common?"

"Well, you don't want to register your principal under his real name if people are trying to kill him," I said.

Harner curled his lips back like a growling dog. "I meant a decoy operation. Do you people do this often?"

"It's not uncommon. Especially if you have a high-risk principal and you're trying to move him or her around. You use decoys to confuse the opposition."

"Sounds like a dangerous way to live."

"Normally, the guards involved know what's going on."

Harner heard the bite in my voice and gave me a quick reappraisal. "You're pissed off."

"I think Trent manipulated me," I said. "I think he nearly got me, three other guards, and one innocent *schlemiel* who thought he was making easy money, multiply perforated. And, yeah, that pisses me off something fierce."

"Speaking of the devil," said Harner. I followed his gaze, looking to see Elliot Trent entering the squad-room, canary feathers practically jutting from his mouth. Trent was flanked by a gray-suited man on either side, and all three made straight our way. "This should be good," Harner told me, getting to his feet and moving to open the door.

"Donald, how have you been?" Elliot Trent said as soon as he'd crossed the threshold. He offered Harner his hand, and the captain took it. Trent shook it like it had been a long time. "Keeping well?"

"I'm under investigation by IAB," Harner said. "Somebody downtown accused me of beating a suspect pulpy."

Trent needed a moment. "I hadn't heard."

"It's my temper," Donald Harner said. "I have difficulty keeping my temper in check, you see. What the hell is this I'm hearing about a decoy operation?"

Trent looked pointedly at where I was seated. I waved at him. To Harner, he said, "Does my daughter need an attorney?"

"It couldn't hurt," the captain answered.

One of the gray-suited men quietly backed up, pivoted, and went in search of Natalie.

"Brought your own lawyers," Harner observed. "That's good preparation."

"What has he told you?" Trent asked. He hadn't looked away from me yet.

"Doesn't matter. I want to hear it from you. Your little girl popped the back of a machine-gunning nut's skull off at the Orsini Hotel this afternoon. The way things are looking, you set the whole thing up."

The remaining attorney said, "I hope you're not implying that my client conspired to have a man murdered?"

Harner turned his head to me. "Did I imply that?"

"Kind of," I admitted.

"Hell, what was I thinking? Talk like that, I'm not going to make any friends. Mr. Trent, why don't you and your lawyer and I have a little chin-wag, and we can sort this whole thing out."

"Is he staying?" Trent asked, still watching me.

"That a problem?"

"We'd like a chance to speak with you privately," the attorney said.

I got up, waited for Trent and Attorney Number Two to move out of the doorway. To Trent, I said, "I trust I get the explanation once all is said and done in here."

"Oh, yes," Trent told me, and he smiled, and I

started out of the room. He caught me by the arm and leaned in, saying softly, "I'm in a good mood right now. Things worked out. But if anything had happened to my daughter . . . you would have paid dearly for it."

"Lucky for me," I said, and pulled my arm free.

I resumed waiting in the squadroom with Corry, Fife, and d'Angelo. For the most part we were quiet, with d'Angelo occasionally muttering about how he was going to make Trent pay.

"Mental anguish," he kept saying. "That's what this was, this was mental fucking anguish, baby."

I kept my mouth shut and my eyes on the smudged window to Harner's office. Nobody's voice ever got loud enough for me to hear distinctly, but the body language was clear. Harner was demanding answers, and Trent was in full diplomatic mode, but whether or not that meant he was giving the captain what he wanted, I couldn't tell. They went around and around for twenty minutes, with the attorney acting like a referee, and then a Deputy Inspector from the Manhattan Borough H.Q. showed up, and all four left the squadroom together.

"Mental fucking anguish," d'Angelo repeated.

It was a minute before six o'clock when Harner came back, sour on his face and anger in his eyes. He stopped in front of our bench and said, "You can all go. Trent and his daughter are downstairs. You can get your guns from the desk sergeant."

Fife and d'Angelo rose at once and headed for the stairs, but Corry held up, waiting for me.

"She's being released?" I asked.

"She's being released," Donald Harner confirmed. "Though, in my humble opinion, her father should be locked up good and tight. Trent's got a lot of friends in this department."

"Is that why you're handling this?"

He nodded. "Case should've stayed with the detectives and their lieutenant. But Trent's got clout."

"IAB won't count this against you?"

He laughed. "You bought that line of crap? Jesus, I was just spreading a little piss and vinegar, trying to rattle cages. Normally it gets me pretty far, but not with the likes of Elliot Trent."

"What did he say?"

Harner shook his head. "You go ask him yourself. Just make certain you don't punch him in my station, or else I'll have to lock you up."

"The principal's name is Jeremiah Pugh," Elliot Trent said. "And all you need to know about him is that, until today, he was in the crosshairs. You've saved his life."

The desk sergeant returned my weapon to me, and I checked the breech and slide before slipping it back into my holster. The leather of the holster had turned from light brown to almost black where it was still wet from the pool. I turned back to Trent, who proceeded to head out the door. He put a hand on Natalie's arm, trying to guide his daughter by the elbow, and she shrugged the touch off angrily. I waited until Corry had taken his gun back, and we followed them out.

It was cooler outside than in the station, and still plenty light. Parked sector cars crowded the street on both sides of the block, and I figured the cops were

coming up on a shift change. I couldn't see d'Angelo or
Fife anywhere on the street, or the attorneys.

Trent had stopped by his car, a sleek blue Lexus,
and was now leaning in on the roof, writing something.
Natalie stood a couple feet away, her arms folded across
her chest, glaring at her father's back. Trent finished
writing, then tore the paper out with a flourish, and I
realized it was a check. He held it out to me.

"The balance of your payment," he said.

Natalie moved the glare to a point somewhere
beyond the East River.

I took the check. It was for the outstanding thousand dollars. I folded it and put it in my wallet. My
wallet was still wet, too.

Corry said, "I should head home."

"Report to the office tomorrow," Trent said. "I've
got another job I want you on. You did good work."

Corry offered me his hand. He wasn't smiling any
longer. "See you around."

I shook his hand. "Take care."

Natalie gave him a nod good-bye, and all three of us
watched him head down the street. When he turned the
corner of Eighth Avenue, I asked Trent, "What happened to d'Angelo?"

"One of my attorneys is speaking with him."

"He's planning on suing you," I said.

"I don't think he will. He's getting a bonus, and he
signed a contract with me before starting the work.
Legally, he doesn't have a hope in hell." Trent swiped
street grime from the side of his car, then leaned back
against the vehicle. I watched while the self-satisfied
look he'd worn into the station came back to his face.

"You're exceptionally pleased with yourself," I said.

"Yes, I am. The decoy worked brilliantly." He smiled at Natalie. "Almost better than I had hoped."

Natalie said, "It seems the man I killed today was in the Ten." Her voice was soft and composed and her look was anything but.

Trent's smile grew a fraction.

"Bullshit," I said.

Trent shook his head.

"You put us up against one of the Ten and you didn't even warn us?" I asked Trent.

"I wasn't certain until today what Sentinel was dealing with," Trent said. "Killers of that caliber don't advertise."

To Natalie, I said, "You're sure it was one of the Ten?"

"My father is sure," she answered evenly.

Trent stood straight and found his car keys in his pocket. He said, "A colleague at Justice notified me that Interpol had whispers of a professional in the U.S., on the job. The FBI confirmed it as best they could. You know how it is—the professionals are ghosts. There's no way to be certain until after the body's cold."

"Which one?"

"His name is unknown; *nom de guerre* of John Doe."

"You bastard," I said. "You arrogant bastard."

Trent moved his head slightly, as if not believing what he was hearing. That made two of us, but the difference lay in the fact that Trent managed to look a little hurt.

"I've done you a favor," he explained. "Yesterday you were nothing in our business, your feet were on the bottom of the barrel. Today you helped bring down one of the ten most dangerous contract killers in the world. You're back in business, Kodiak. With a credit like this, you can maybe find yourself some real work."

"You're a fucking philanthropist, all right," I said. "Never mind that you could have gotten us all killed, never mind that there were two innocent kids in the pool and a woman on the deck. Do you realize how close you came to having this blow up in your smug face?"

Trent closed his eyes with a sigh, then thumbed the button on his car alarm. The Lexus made the noise a bird makes just after a cat has pounced on it. "I knew the risks. I considered them, and I did what was necessary."

"Yes, you did, at least as much as you saw it. But don't pretend you did me a favor, Elliot. You used me precisely because you knew the risks, and you didn't want your own people getting hurt. You used me so, if it went wrong, you could say it was my fault and not Sentinel's."

"You are overreacting, Atticus. It could have gone wrong, but it didn't. Today Sentinel Guards neutralized one of the world's most dangerous men. That's a cause for celebration, not recrimination." He opened the passenger door for Natalie, then went around to his side. "I'm going to inform my principal of the day's events. I'd invite you for a drink after, but I'm afraid you'd throw it in my face."

"Maybe he wouldn't, but I probably would," Natalie said. She reached for the door and shut it firmly. "I'll talk to you later."

Trent shot a glance my way, and in it there was none of his previous generosity, none of his concern. Now there was irritation. "Natalie . . ."

"I don't want to talk to you right now, Pop."

Trent looked at his daughter, and she returned the stare without moving. I've been on the receiving end of Natalie's icy stare, and it isn't a nice place to be. Her father didn't seem to care for it, either. Maybe they were having a conversation without words, I don't know, but it lasted too long, and then Trent slid into the driver's seat. "We'll talk about this later," he said, and then he pulled the Lexus out into traffic, and I watched him disappear.

Natalie said, "I'm sorry."

"Don't apologize for him," I said. "He's not your responsibility."

"He waited until I was at Smith & Wesson before contacting you. He knew I'd want to be a part of the job."

"Well, he doesn't want you getting hurt," I said.

"No, but apparently getting you killed, that's okay. I don't know what's gotten into him. He didn't used to be like this."

"It's a competitive business."

"Yeah." She rubbed her hands together, using her thumb to massage her palm. "I'm going home."

"You want company?"

Natalie looked at me.

"To talk," I clarified.

"No. I want to be alone."

"Fair enough. Call me if you need anything."

"I will," Natalie said. "I'll call you if I need anything."

"I mean it."

"I know you do," she said.

I left her to be alone.

CHAPTER FIVE

"You're late," Erika said as soon as I came through the door. "If we hurry we can still make it."

"Not quite the warm and fuzzy greeting I was hoping for," I said. "Still make what?"

"Dinner, remember? I told you I'd made reservations at Portrero for tonight. Eight o'clock." She held her arms out as if signaling for a plane to land. "I even got dressed up."

I took off my windbreaker and hung it on the peg in the wall. Erika promptly took the coat off the peg and handed it back to me. I shook my head. "Tonight's not good, Erika. It's been a bad day."

She tried to hand me the windbreaker again. "What happened?"

"We had an incident."

"What does that mean?"

"Somebody tried to kill the man we were protecting. Natalie shot him."

She conjured a grin that said I was almost funny. "No kidding? Wow, that's a whole new kind of protection, isn't it? Now put this on, let's go."

"I misspoke," I clarified. "Natalie shot the man who was trying to shoot the man we were protecting."

"Nice try. Come on." She pushed the windbreaker against my chest.

"I'm not joking, kiddo."

Erika stopped trying to hand me my coat, and she lost some of the color in her face. I could see the bad memories coming to the surface as she said, "Is Nat all right? Is everybody all right?"

"Everybody's fine." I took my coat back from her. Dressed up for Erika consisted of a black long-sleeved T-shirt and black cargo pants that didn't have any holes in them yet. She was wearing dog tags on a chain around her neck.

The color was still gone from her cheeks.

"You look nice," I said. "Where'd you get the tags?"

She needed a second before saying, "They're yours. In case I get lost."

I hung my jacket on the peg once more. "Give me twenty minutes to shower and change, then we can go."

Portrero is in SoHo, in the snarl of narrow streets that look European rather than American. Erika and I rode the subway down to Spring Street, and we stayed silent on the train, Erika reading the new ad campaign for the Bronx Zoo, and me wondering about the day's events. I was preoccupied enough that Erika had to say my name twice before I realized we were at our stop. She got ahead of me as we were on the stairs, and I came topside to see two young men wearing torn cutoffs asking her if she wanted to join them and "dance the night away."

"I'll have to ask my dad," she told them, indicating me.

We had missed the rush hour crowd, and for the most part, we were able to walk side by side without having to play chicken with oncoming pedestrians. We were waiting to cross Broadway when Erika asked, "What's bullshit?"

"Sorry?"

"You said, 'It's bullshit.' What's bullshit?"

"Ah," I said. "That wasn't supposed to be out loud."

"Kind of guessed that. So, tell me."

"Are you sure you want to hear about what happened today?"

Erika patted my arm reassuringly as the light changed, and we resumed walking. "Go ahead."

"I don't think the man Natalie shot today was one of the Ten," I said.

"What is that, that the name of a band or something?"

" 'The Ten' is an industry term. It refers to an elite group of professional killers. The top ten in the world, the ten best, whatever. The Ten."

"Like in *The Day of the Jackal*."

"Kind of, except these people are not fiction. This is what they do for a living. No politics, no causes, no histrionics. Just contract killings for big money."

"And that's who Natalie shot today?" Erika asked.

"That's what her father thinks, yeah. He thinks that Natalie killed an assassin who goes by the name of John Doe."

"Stupid code name."

"Well, he probably didn't pick it. Somebody in some intelligence service somewhere figured out that person A, person B, and person C all met untimely or suspicious deaths, and, what do you know, person D was nearby each and every time. But person D is a pro, and whatever name he was using, it wasn't his real one. So whoever in intelligence decides to call him John Doe."

"Racer Dee," Erika said. "See, that's a good code name. John Doe. Ugh. No flash."

"That's the point. Assassins don't want flash. They are the *best* at what they do, they don't need advertising. Absolutely disciplined, absolutely professional. They don't make stupid mistakes and they don't take stupid chances. Hell, they don't take a leak without six alternate escape routes planned and six alternate identities ready for each of the routes."

"I don't understand what the problem is," Erika said. "Is it that Natalie shouldn't have seen this Doe guy coming?"

I tried to formulate my response, started to answer, when I saw the car. We had just made the turn south onto Wooster, and the restaurant was only six or maybe seven doors down. The car was parked on the opposite side of the street, maybe twenty feet from the restaurant. A Porsche 911 Carrera twin turbo, and even though the sun had dipped below the high-rises, I could make out the color.

"Erika," I said, stopping.

"What?"

I pointed to the car.

"I don't see anything," Erika said.

"I'm pointing at the green Porsche."

"Oh. Hey, that looks just like Bridgett's wheels, doesn't it?"

"Yeah, just like it."

"What a coincidence," she said. "Maybe she's eating at Portrero, too."

"Does she know what you're doing? Does Bridgett know that I'm supposed to be joining you two for dinner?"

Erika checked the hair over her torn ear, then put her hands in her pockets. "I just want you two to talk to each other," she said, after a moment.

Set up twice in the same day, I thought. A new personal record.

"Just talk," Erika said. "Just come into the restaurant, have a seat, and say hi. That's all."

"It doesn't work that way."

"Why not? Who says it shouldn't? All you have to do is come inside with me."

"She doesn't know I'm coming, does she?"

"No."

I shook my head, feeling the day catch up with me. There was a twinge from my abdomen, where I had been shot a while back, and I wondered if I hadn't strained something reaching for d'Angelo in the pool.

"You go on in," I told Erika. "Have a nice dinner. I'll see you at home."

"Tonight, you mean?" she asked. "Or tomorrow? Where are you going to go? To Natalie's again?"

"I'll see you later," I said, and headed back toward Spring Street.

"I hope you two have a good time," Erika spat after me. "I hope you have a good fucking time. Or maybe a good time fucking."

I walked for almost an hour, back uptown, stoking my anger. The last thing I had wanted was to see Bridgett, to poke that particular festering wound. I doubted Bridgett felt any differently about me; it didn't matter what I felt for her; all that mattered was the damage I'd done, the mistakes I'd made.

It was easy to burn hot at Erika, to resent the trick, but I hadn't gone three blocks before I realized I was focusing on the wrong manipulation. No, I was angry at Elliot Trent, and what Erika had tried to do with the best of intentions only served to feed that anger.

Trent had decided that I was expendable, and that was why he'd given me charge of the op. That John Doe hadn't completed his hit, that he hadn't killed d'Angelo and the rest of us, was nothing short of a miracle. We were alive because Natalie had been mistaken for a hotel employee, and because she was an extremely good shot.

Unless it hadn't been John Doe trying to mow us down beside the pool, but someone else.

I was at Forty-third Street before I realized I had passed my apartment about fifteen blocks back, and finally admitted where I was heading. Erika had done a good job of making me feel guilty, though, good enough that I hesitated. Before Natalie and I had begun sleeping together I never had to second-guess my desire to see her, to visit her apartment, even when she and I weren't getting along. Now it wasn't so easy.

I walked over to Park Avenue and flagged a cab, rode it up to Natalie's apartment building, and presented myself to the doorman.

"She told me she didn't want visitors." The doorman was missing three of his incisors, and blew a fine mist when he hit the *sh*'s.

"Tell her it's Atticus," I said.

"Yeah, I know who you are." He wandered over to the phone and flipped the switch for 17D. "You two serious?" he asked me.

"I beg your pardon?"

"You and Miss Trent, you serious about each other?"

"We're friends."

"Uh-huh," the doorman said, and then added, into the phone, "Miss Trent? Your friend Atticus is here. . . . Uh-huh . . . I'll send him up." He replaced the phone and said, "Have fun."

I went for the elevator, wondering how the doorman managed phrases like "see you later" or "she sells seashells by the seashore."

I'll take my triumphs anywhere I can find them.

She was waiting outside her door for me, and when I got out of the elevator, she said, "It's bugging you, too."

"Yeah."

"Come on in."

I followed her through her apartment and out onto her small patio.

"You want something to drink? Coffee?"

"Coffee would be great."

She turned and went back inside, and I took a seat, admired the flowers she had growing in long planter boxes around the railing. Natalie has a large apartment, the kind of place Manhattanites talk about killing one another for, well appointed and with a nice view of the East River and the lights of the Bronx off to the northeast.

Natalie took ten minutes, then came back with two mugs, an ashtray balanced on the top of one of them. I took my drink and she sat down, put the ashtray on the table between us, then dug a pack of cigarettes from her pants pocket. She lit one with a match, took a long pull, and then coughed a little on the exhale.

"When did that start?" I asked.

"About fifteen minutes after we parted company. I'm doing it to piss off my father."

"What'd you do, call him and say that you had started smoking?"

"Mom died of cancer," she said.

"Ah."

"It's a stupid way to lash out." She looked at the ember before taking another drag. This time there was no coughing. "So, what about this is bugging you?"

"I don't believe that one of the Ten would have neglected basic legwork. All John Doe had to do was a little surveillance and he would have known that d'Angelo wasn't the man he'd been hired to kill."

Natalie nodded her agreement. "That's one." She tapped ash. "I've been wondering how he thought he was going to get away with it."

"Me too."

"That FN-90, it's not a finesse weapon, per se. That's serious firepower. He was planning on taking all of us out. Planning on taking us out first, probably, and then, once we were down, finishing off d'Angelo."

"Which means he knew d'Angelo was guarded. And he planned for that."

Natalie nodded.

"But if he knew he was guarded, he had to have done some legwork," I said. "And if he'd done his legwork, he knew that d'Angelo certainly wasn't Pugh."

"Well, maybe Pugh and d'Angelo look alike," Natalie said.

"Maybe."

"But you don't think so."

"Do you?"

"No."

"It doesn't make sense," I said.

Natalie exhaled some smoke, and we watched it whip away past a bunch of red carnations that stood proudly in one of the planter boxes. I drank some of my coffee. It tasted like vanilla.

"There's another thing," Natalie said. "Why the pool? Why not the weight room, or in the halls? I mean, it's not like the pool was the only place in the hotel where we were exposed. Why not just take a room along our route, wait until we were moving him one day, and open fire then?"

"We never should have seen him coming," I said.

"No, we shouldn't have. If this guy was one of the world's ten most dangerous men, I'm thinking he got on the short list by mistake."

I put the mug on the table. I didn't much care for vanilla. Natalie finished her cigarette, pinching the cinder onto the ground, then snuffing it with her toe. She put the butt in the ashtray, beside the pack, and then lit another. It was pleasant on the patio, warm, but with a nice cooling breeze.

"Somebody should tell Pop," Natalie said after a while.

"I don't think he'll want to hear it. As far as he's concerned, Sentinel stopped John Doe, and that's that."

"That wasn't John Doe."

"I know."

Natalie crushed out her second cigarette. "Then whose life did I take today?"

CHAPTER SIX

Erika was still asleep when I rose the next morning, so I picked up some bagels on my way back to the apartment after my morning jog. I showered and changed and put the bagels in the oven to warm, then went to make my walk-through of the building. Bridgett had helped me find the apartment. She'd put me in touch with the property managers, who were willing to let me stay rent-free as long as I provided security for the building, and as long as they could advertise that they had a security consultant on the premises. There wasn't a whole lot for me to do, really, just check that doors stayed locked, and that no one was sneaking in to rob or vandalize at night. The apartment below ours had emptied out at the beginning of the summer, and was still unoccupied, awaiting a new tenant. The realtors sometimes forgot to lock it up after showing the space, so I'd added it to my rounds. It was unlocked again this morning. I did a sweep, shut and locked the door, and hoped that whoever rented the space would be a quiet neighbor.

When I got back, there was still no sign that Erika had stirred. I wrote her a note saying that I'd be out most of the day, and that there were fresh bagels in the oven, and taped it to the mirror in the bathroom. I took one of the bagels with me when I left, munched on it as I walked to the subway station at Twenty-eighth and Park. I rode down to Union Square and transferred to the express, got off at City Hall, and then walked back north through Foley Square to Federal Plaza. It was about a quarter of twelve, and the streets were beginning to fill with hungry civil servants. I found a working pay phone and dropped a quarter, dialed, and got the FBI.

"Scott Fowler, please," I said.

There was a click and a pause and a recorded announcement telling me that I, personally, could stop crime at no risk to myself. The potential of a cash reward was mentioned as well, and I was just getting interested when Special Agent Scott Fowler said, "Atticus? What's up?"

"You busy?"

"Depends on what you need."

"You heard about Natalie?"

"I heard she dropped an assassin at the Orsini yesterday, yeah."

"That's what I want to talk to you about."

"Where are you?"

"Right outside your office."

"Buy me lunch," he said, then hung up.

I trotted across the street and into the plaza. A couple of vendors had their carts set up, and I bought two hot dogs from one and a can of Dr. Brown's. Scott was coming out just as I got my change, and I waved the can at him. He stopped to put on a pair of sunglasses before approaching me.

"Incognito," I said.

"It's the glare, bozo," Special Agent Fowler said. "I'm wearing contacts and the sunlight hurts my eyes."

I handed him his lunch.

"For this, I wouldn't tell you who was on the Ten Most Wanted list."

"I'm on a budget," I said.

"I can tell. Let's find a bench, shall we?"

We parked ourselves with a view of the U.S. Court House across the square. Scott spread a paper napkin across his thigh, then began on the first hot dog. He's got four years on me, which puts him in his early thirties, but he looks much younger than I do. It doesn't matter how you dress him up—Scott always looks like he's fresh from some Southern California beach, surfboard no more than a short reach away.

"I can guess what you want to know," he said after the first dog had vanished. "And I'm not going to be much help. You want the boys in the NFIP. I only deal with the domestic stuff."

"But," I said.

Scott grinned. "But . . . I did some checking when I heard about it, anyway."

"Let's hear it."

"I don't know," he said, examining the remaining hot dog. "My information is certainly worth more than this."

"If you're good, I'll buy you a churro."

"How can I refuse an offer like that?" He cracked open the soda and took a sip. "Still no ID on the assassin, but it's only been twenty-four hours, so that doesn't really mean anything yet. The NYPD found his cache, or one of them, at a storage facility near Kennedy. Almost thirty thousand in cash, mostly American, about five thousand in deutsche marks. Also found some

weapons—two SMGs—an MP-5 and a Steyr TMP—
and two pistols, both clean. The pistols were P-7s, by
the way."

That surprised me, but only a little. Everybody who
works with guns has a favorite, and mine is the P-7, for
a variety of reasons. It's not an uncommon weapon,
but it's also not an extraordinarily popular one. In a
world full of thousands of models of firearms, I was
vaguely alarmed to hear that a professional killer had
chosen the same weapon I had.

Scott grinned at me. "You haven't misplaced yours,
have you?"

I pretended to check my pockets until he told me to
knock it off. Then I said, "Anything else?"

"Well, no more of those fancy FN-90s, if that's what
you're asking. There was also a half a case of con-
cussion grenades. U.S. Army issue." Scott licked his
fingers, then wiped them on the napkin, which was
starting to shred from his repeated attentions. "Bought
on the black market, probably. They also found two
sets of papers, good work, not cheap. One for a Mau-
rice Derveaux, French, and another for Jhonen Salvatore, from Spain." He spelled both names. "We ran the
names, and Derveaux came back legit, but deceased.
Died two years ago, November. I expect we'll find
something similar about Salvatore."

"Was anything found on the body?"

"Aside from the grenades and the key to the storage
place, about five hundred in cash, a pocket Glock. That
was it."

"No paper on him?"

"Nothing."

"Doesn't that strike you as odd?"

Scott fiddled with one of the studs in his left ear.

"Not really. He was performing a hit. Why should he carry any ID? He'd want to work clean, in case just what happened happened. He probably planned on heading to his cache after he was done."

"What if he had been stopped?" I asked. "Don't you think he would have wanted paper for that?"

"Maybe it was hidden somewhere nearby. Somewhere in the hotel." He was watching a group of women eat their lunches. All looked in their twenties, and all wore skirts. "It's what one would expect to find."

"I know."

"Is that the hint of suspicion in your voice?"

"I'm more puzzled than suspicious," I said. "Trent claims that the killer was one of the Ten."

"John Doe." Scott nodded. "Yeah, that's the rumor in the office. There's no way to confirm it."

"But John Doe exists?" I asked.

"The NFIP has a file compiled from different sources for a series of deaths they think were contract hits, and they think the contracts were fulfilled by the same assassin. That assassin is referred to as John Doe, but what we think means dick. It's a question of what can be proven, and that's one of the problems with these guys. They don't exactly claim responsibility for their kills, and they're good enough that they won't use a consistent pattern. Some businessman is poisoned in Italy, another gets blown apart in Rio, and a third falls from a tall building in Manhattan—the same assassin could be behind all or none of them."

"So what makes Trent so sure the one we dealt with yesterday is Doe?"

"Well, one of the Ten *is* supposed to be in the country," Scott said. "But it's just a suspicion. It's the same problem—there's never any proof. A couple of months ago an arms dealer that the CIA had been watching made a trip to Brooklyn, then left for Mexico after depositing over a million dollars at a Russian Mafia–controlled bank in Brighton Beach. A week later a paperhanger Interpol had a watch on flew into Boston, then disappeared in Providence. The million dollars vanished at roughly the same time. Two days later the same arms dealer showed up again in San Francisco, then headed for Japan."

"And these people are associated with the Ten?"

"They're suspected of being associated with the Ten," Scott clarified. "More likely their orbits sometimes coincide. It means nothing or it means everything."

"This could drive a person crazy," I said.

"Oh, yeah." Scott finished the last drops of his pop and then balanced the empty can on the arm of the bench. Someone had scratched a swastika into the paint. "Beautiful day," he said. "Good day to go to the beach. Too bad the waves on this coast suck."

"Take a couple days and go down to Florida."

"There's a thought. Did you ride any water when you were in Cali?"

"I don't surf. How'd you know I was in California?"

"Bridgett said something about it. Erika told her, I guess."

"I didn't realize you'd seen Bridgett," I said.

"We went to dinner last week."

"Sounds like a nice date," I said, and I thought I meant it innocently until I'd said it.

Scott took the pop can off the arm of the bench. "We've only been out five or six times."

It was the way he said it, as if he was apologizing,

that struck and stung. He and Bridgett had been dating, and I suddenly didn't want to be in the conversation any longer. I got to my feet. "Thanks for the meeting."

"It's not what you think, Atticus."

"You don't know what I think, Scott. It's none of my business in any case."

"It's not what you think," he said again, but by that time I was leaving the plaza behind and heading for the subway.

It was none of my business. What he did, what Bridgett did, none of my business at all. I had no claims on either of them; certainly no claim on Bridgett. If Scott wanted to pursue a relationship there, that was his call, and I knew that, and the knowing didn't make it easier to take. I couldn't even be certain which bothered me more; that Scott had been seeing Bridgett; that she had been seeing him; or that I still, after nine months, could get so worked up.

By the time I got off the subway and started walking home, I'd decided it ultimately didn't matter. There was really only one thing I knew for certain: Scott Fowler and I had probably had our last meeting, at least for a very long time to come.

CHAPTER SEVEN

"They've secured an estate outside of town, near the Amawalk Reservoir," Natalie said. "Looks like a converted farm or ranch house. High stone wall with cameras set up to watch the perimeter. Armed guards at the gatehouse and within the compound."

"How many?" I asked.

"At least thirty, maybe more. Pop's cleared out the office for this one. He's using almost all of the permanent staff and I'd guess another handful of stringers. The ones I saw are all armed, most with long guns as well as their sidearms. I've never seen anything like it."

"Sounds like a government operation."

"Or a military one." Natalie rolled the cigarette she was holding along the edge of the table. "Whoever Jeremiah Pugh is, he's getting the best Sentinel can give."

We were in a restaurant called Maria's Pizza, "The Best Pizza in Town," according to the sign. The town in question was Yorktown Heights. I hadn't had the pizza, and I didn't know enough about the town to disprove the assertion.

Erika had left for the day by the time I'd returned

home. A note on the kitchen table said that she would
be out until evening, and that she would call if she was
going to be late. She had also left the remaining bagels
in the oven, and left the oven on. The bagels were hard
as bathroom tile when I found them, and I'd dumped
them in the trash after turning off the oven.

Then my pager had gone off, and I'd called Natalie's
cellular phone.

"I'm in Yorktown," she'd told me. "Yorktown
Heights, more precisely. Outside of Maria's Pizza on
Saw Mill River Road. Can you meet me?"

"It'll take me an hour or so to get there," I said.

"It's route 118. I'll be waiting."

I'd gone down to the garage and done a quick safety
check on my motorcycle, then put on my helmet and
swerved around traffic until reaching the Henry Hudson. I'd bought the bike three months back, more at
Erika's urging than my own, her argument being that if
I wasn't going to buy a car, we should at least have some
means of ready transportation. She'd had a point, too; I
hate cars for a variety of reasons, most of them related
to security, and paradoxically feel safer on a motorcycle. On a motorcycle, at least you can maneuver.

It is also a hell of a lot more fun than driving a car.

Erika had lobbied hard for a Harley, but we'd settled
on a used BMW 850. It wasn't until after we'd brought
it home that she informed me of her intention to learn
to drive it. She's planning to get her motorcycle certifi-
cation next month.

Outside of Manhattan I'd caught the Taconic, and
the drive was easy and at seventy miles an hour the July
heat and humidity dissipated in the wind, and for
twenty minutes or so my mind cleared; I thought about
nothing but the drive and the day. Bridgett, Scott,

Natalie, John Doe, they'd all vanished in the smooth curves of the tree-lined road.

Yorktown Heights is in the northern part of Westchester County, almost exactly an hour out of Manhattan. Yorktown Heights refers to itself as a hamlet, part of a confederation of similar hamlets with names like Jefferson Valley, Kitchawan, Mohegan Lake, and Shrub Oak, and together they make up the township of Yorktown. As best as I can tell, they're mostly commuter communities, pleasant retreats from the epileptic frenzy of New York City.

I'd found Natalie at a table in the restaurant, most of a small pizza untouched before her. She'd offered me a slice and, when I'd declined, brought me up to speed.

"Have you talked to your father?" I asked.

"No." Natalie frowned. "He was out of the office when I arrived this morning. The whole place was deserted, with the exception of the receptionist and a couple of the PAs." Natalie looked at her cold cigarette some more, then lit it with a match from a book with a tiger cub printed on its flap. "Tina paged him for me, and he called me in my office and told me to come up. He wants me on the detail."

"Doing what?"

"He said I could work as a counter-sniper on the Perimeter Team."

"What'd you say?"

"I told him I'd give him an answer when I saw him." Natalie made a face and crushed out her cigarette. She had only taken two puffs.

"I thought you'd seen him already."

"No."

"How do you know about the set-up at the estate?"

"I went for a lurk in the bushes after I called you."

I didn't ask her why. She'd been pursuing sniper training for a while now, and one of the things that entailed was being a sneaky bastard. Lurking around the estate would have been good practice, and reasonably harmless.

"Did you find out anything else about the man I shot?" she asked.

"I talked to Fowler. The NYPD found where the assassin had been keeping his gear. Nothing out of the ordinary in the cache. Still no ID on the body."

"So he can't be certain I shot John Doe?"

"No. But the fact is, there'd be no way to refute that you had, either. The only person who could confirm it would be John Doe, and he won't do that, dead or alive."

"To shoot the Invisible Man."

"The more I think about it, though, the more I'm certain that yesterday we weren't dealing with a pro."

"The legwork," Natalie said.

I nodded.

"Pop's not going to want to hear that."

"No."

Natalie looked at the check, took some bills from her wallet and spread them neatly on the table. Her wallet was thin and sleek, soft-looking black leather, with a monogram. She rose and I followed her back out to the parking lot, pulling on my helmet. I fastened the strap and put my glasses back on while Natalie climbed into her car. She'd had a Lexus like her father's until I'd crashed it last year, and was now driving an icy-blue Infiniti. We went north on 118, and I followed her when she turned east outside the hamlet of Amawalk onto 35. After a few minutes she signaled a left, and we slip-streamed onto a two-lane side road. The houses became farther apart, mostly hidden behind the trees lining either side of the road. Almost all were fenced. The fences were made of rotting wood or stone, and the area reeked of history, of a time when soldiers in red coats marched through the countryside looking for men in rags.

History brings out the patriot in me, I guess.

After another four miles the Infiniti slowed, then turned onto an outlet road of fresh asphalt. After a hundred feet Natalie parked on the shoulder. I followed suit, went through the helmet and glasses routine again, this time in reverse. Natalie waited while I locked my helmet to the bike.

"It's about fifty yards that way," she said, pointing down the road. The road curved to the south, and I couldn't see where it led. Heat haze rose from the asphalt.

"Not a whole lot of visibility," I said.

"They've got cameras mounted in the trees at the bend."

"Panning or static?"

"Static. Probably on a random sequence piped into the command post."

"Nothing else?"

"Not that I could see."

That made sense to me. Using lasers or infrared or even ultrasonics would be problematic in an environment like this; just too many things could trigger an alarm, from an animal straying across one of the sensor lines to leaves blown in on a breeze. Trent would have his reaction teams running themselves ragged at all the false alarms. If it was my show, I'd have gone with static cameras, too.

Natalie began following the road. "You coming?"

"Sure," I said, and caught up with her. "Any particular reason we're walking?"

Natalie's mouth turned into a small, wicked smile. "To mess with the guards."

The estate was much as she described it, but the stone wall was lower than I had imagined. An iron gate blocked the driveway, and through its bars I could see the house, three stories, large, painted in a smudged pearl-white. The trim was gray. A small satellite dish jutted out of the roof over the front porch, but otherwise, I could have been looking back past the turn of the century.

The gatehouse stood on the left side of the gate, not part of the original architecture, and as we approached, a man emerged, armed. A second guard remained in the gatehouse, a radio in one hand. I couldn't see what was in the other, but I had a pretty good guess. Both guards were in the black Sentinel uniform, adorned with gold piping along the seams of their slacks and jackets. The uniforms looked unpleasantly hot.

The guard didn't stop us and didn't speak to us as we approached. He was larger than his counterpart in the gatehouse, my height, and heavier, with a nasty split in his bottom lip. Another camera was mounted on the wall, good placement, designed to give a view of anyone who approached.

Natalie and I were within ten feet of the gate before he called, "Can I help you?"

"I'm Natalie Trent," Natalie said. "My father's expecting me." She said "my father" so the guard heard "your boss."

"Who's he?" the guard with the split lip asked, pointing at me.

"I'm Atticus," I said. "Kodiak."

The guard in the gatehouse checked a clipboard. "She's expected," he said. "He's not."

"Kodiak's with me," Natalie said.

"We'll have to clear it," Split Lip said.

"You go right ahead."

Split Lip's eyes clouded for an instant, while he wondered if he had done something to get himself fired. He had, but not what he thought. He returned to the gatehouse and exchanged words with his counterpart. The counterpart got back on his radio.

"You know these two?" I asked Natalie.

"Never seen them before. Square badges, probably. Rent-a-cops."

"You want to tell them or should I?" I asked.

"We'll wait until their superior gets here."

Their superior took under forty seconds to arrive, jogging down the path. When he recognized us he slowed to a walk, began shaking his head. "Barbarians are at the gate," he said.

"Hi, Yossi," I said.

Yossi Sella held up his hands in greeting, looking delighted to see us. He's a *sabra,* wooed away from the Shin Bet's Executive Protection Squad in his homeland of Israel by promises of wealth and glory in Trent's employ. I didn't know if he'd found either of his goals, but there was no question he was having a hell of a good time trying.

"Do they have a checklist?" Natalie asked him.

Yossi motioned at the guard in the gatehouse, and to the left of us a motor growled on. The iron gate began to slide back. "What'd they do wrong?"

"They didn't check our IDs," Natalie said, slipping past the gate. I followed. The gate clanged, stopped, and reversed itself, closing again.

"Merle!"

The split-lipped guard returned. "Yes, sir?"

"Did you check their IDs?"

Merle gnawed on his split lip, pondering Yossi's question. "Winter had her on the list. How could she know who was expected if she wasn't who she said she was?"

Yossi nodded as if he agreed with both Merle's syntax and his logic. "You always check IDs, Merle. Someone walks up to the gate and wants inside, you check their IDs."

"I thought—"

Yossi waved his hand, and Merle cut himself short. Yossi said, "Trust me, there are plenty of ways for someone to find out who's on the access list. SOP is that you always check IDs. Also, you might ask whoever's waiting to step back from the gate. Twenty feet is good, gives you time to react."

Merle nodded.

"If this happens again, we'll have to talk about finding someone who can take over for you. Neither you nor I want that, okay?"

"Got it," the guard said.

"Good man. You tell Winter what I told you. And we won't have to worry about this anymore."

"It won't happen again, Mr. Sella."

"I don't think it will, either, Merle." Yossi looked at us. "This way, if you please."

We followed him along the driveway up to the house. Several cars were parked in front of the garage, among them Trent's Lexus, and a gray Mercedes-Benz. There was a lot of lawn, tended and healthy. The air smelled of the grass and the trees. Along the edge of the house were flower beds with blooms of red, white, purple, and yellow. Someone was putting a lot of effort into landscaping.

The security was thick, and perhaps impressive. I counted another three cameras, and four more guards. Two of the guards were in uniform, walking with dogs, a German shepherd and a rottweiler. Another two guards were traveling around the grounds in a Cushman cart. The guards wore headsets, and were dressed in tactical gear. They traveled heavily armed, with a shotgun and an AR-15 for each.

Not for the first time, I wondered about Jeremiah Pugh. The operation we'd just walked in on was expensive; somebody had to be footing the bill. And assassins like John Doe aren't cheap. Their going rate's rumored to be in the million-a-contract range. Both the offense and the defense seemed to have a lot of money to spend, and I had no idea who, let alone why. It wasn't something I could ask Yossi about, either; discretion is a professional watchword, and one bodyguard does not pry into another's business.

Yossi clapped me on the back. "Haven't seen you in a while, my friend. How's Erika?"

"Fine," I said. "Learning to ride a motorcycle."

"You're kidding me."

"Nope."

"She's going to have to beat them off with a stick."

"I hope not."

"Afraid of turning away her suitors?"

"If I can handle the candidates as well as you handled Merle back there, I'll be a happy man," I said.

"You liked that?"

"You were too easy on them," Natalie said.

Yossi shrugged. "They're security guards, they're not BGs. This way, they learned something and they still like me. Happens again, I'll fire them."

"Where are the regulars?" Natalie asked.

"Inside the house, mostly. Mosier took them for close work."

"Mosier?" I asked.

"You haven't met him," Natalie said. "He's the new golden boy. Pop recruited him last month."

"A boob," Yossi added. "But a published boob, and that's why Trent's so impressed by him. Couple books about his adventures in South Africa or some such. Had a piece in *American Handgun Journal* about how to secure your principal on the Concorde."

"I'll have to read it," I said.

"It's crap," both Yossi and Natalie said, almost in unison.

We reached the porch and Yossi knocked on the front door, then opened it. Another guard was seated just inside, another shotgun leaning against the wall. Another camera stared at us intently.

"They're with me," Yossi told the guard in the chair.

The guard looked at all of our faces. When he got to Natalie he said, "Hi, Natalie. How you been?"

"I've been good," she replied. "What about you?"

The guard shrugged. "Bored."

"Where's Trent?" Yossi asked.

"In the study."

"Thanks."

We went down the hall, passing a couple of closed doors on the left and right. An air conditioner was roaring away someplace nearby, fighting off the outside heat. The floor was hardwood, shiny with varnish, and a thin rug had been thrown down to protect the surface. We passed a staircase with another guard watching us from the landing. Like Yossi, the guards in the house wore casual clothes, not uniforms. Mostly jeans and T-shirts.

As we walked, Natalie whispered, "Who was that?"

"Lang," Yossi said.

"Lang, right."

The hall opened into a T intersection; Yossi led us to the right and into the study. It was everything a study was supposed to be, three walls of books and a deep oriental carpet that almost touched all of the walls. A desk filled one corner of the room, and chairs were positioned to afford comfortable reading positions. Trent sat behind the desk, a laptop computer open before him, a sheaf of papers stacked to his left. He was again wearing a suit, but the jacket was off and hanging tidily behind him.

Trent had been speaking when we entered. He stopped and started to smile when he saw his daughter. The smile faltered, then died when he noticed I was with her.

"Natalie," he said. "I was expecting you several hours ago."

The man Trent had been speaking with turned in his chair to look at us. He was a whip-like guy with dirty blond hair drawn back in a ponytail, sunglasses hanging from the collar of his denim shirt. He rose when Trent did, and I put him between five foot eight and five foot nine. He was casually dressed, a gun at his hip, and judging from the lump near his ankle, another on his leg.

"I was waiting for Atticus," Natalie told her father.

Trent came around the desk and gave Natalie a kiss on the cheek. She took it with a pinched smile and Trent stepped back, looking from her to me.

"I don't really think we need any more guards," he said.

"I'm not looking for any more of your work," I said.

The relief showed despite Trent's best intentions. He headed back to the desk. "Thanks, Yossi. You might want to check in at the CP. They're complaining about one of the monitors on the north perimeter."

"I could do that," Yossi said. "See you two later."

Trent sat back down and Yossi left, shutting the door soundlessly behind him. The man in the chair was staring at me. I stared back.

"Raymond Mosier," Trent said. "Atticus Kodiak."

"Hi," I said to the man in the chair.

"Yeah, I've heard of you," Mosier said. "Never when I was asking for a referral, of course."

Natalie's back went a little straighter at the insult.

"Ray is running the close work," Trent told us. "He's only been with Sentinel for a couple of months. Before that he was working in the Middle East."

"And Japan," Raymond Mosier added. "Did some work on the Côte d'Azur, too."

"No kidding?" I asked. "The jet set, huh? Ever have to take a principal on the Concorde?"

"Several times."

"I hear securing them is a bitch."

Elliot Trent cleared his throat. "Why don't you two have a seat?"

Natalie and I each found a chair. Mosier stared at me until I was seated, then turned his attention back to Trent.

"I assume this is about yesterday?" Trent asked.

"I don't think the man I shot was John Doe," Natalie said, and then she explained why, going from point to point clearly.

Trent listened while Mosier examined the spines of the books on the shelves. Every so often he shot a look my way, but I wasn't certain if his glances were contemptuous or sullen. Each seemed just as likely.

When Natalie finished, her father was silent for almost a minute, looking at us. I couldn't read his expression. Outside the study, I heard footsteps traveling on the hardwood floor.

"Doesn't prove anything," Trent said, finally.

Mosier nodded.

"Pop," Natalie said. "It means he's still out there."

"Our security is still in place."

"That's hardly the point. If I didn't shoot John Doe yesterday, who did I shoot? And why was he there? This guy didn't even verify his mark. I'm not even sure anymore that it was a pro's hit."

"The weapon, the technique, the—"

"I know, they're solid, they're perfect. But that's all window dressing—the mannequin is still naked, Pop. It looked like a pro's hit, because that's what it was *supposed* to look like. But it wasn't the real thing."

"You don't know that. You can't prove that."

"Of course I can't. And you can't prove that I killed the right man."

"It was John Doe," Trent said.

"Suppose it was," I said. "Why are you still running like you're in a war zone? This must be costing you a lot of money. If you're so sure the threat's been neutralized, why do you have a tactical team zooming around the compound in an E-Z-Go?"

"John Doe's not the only threat to our principal." Mosier squinted when he said it, maybe to make himself look tough. It made him look farsighted.

"You're expecting the remaining Nine to show up?" I asked.

"If they do, we'll handle them."

"The client is willing to pay for full protection," Trent said. "The principal is important enough to warrant the best we can offer. And Ray is right. There could well be other threats."

"Which you can't begin to locate, because you haven't dealt with the primary one," Natalie argued.

"John Doe has been dealt with," her father shot back, barely keeping his voice from climbing. "The word is already out that Sentinel took Doe down. The plan worked, and the primary threat to Mr. Pugh has been eliminated. There is nothing more to discuss."

"Except how I may have killed some dupe because you wanted a feather in Sentinel's cap."

Trent's face froze in pain from the verbal blow. "I never wanted you to have to draw your weapon. I never wanted you to take that man's life."

"No, you wanted Atticus to do it. You wanted to use my friend the way you used d'Angelo. It's just your rotten luck that I wouldn't go home when you wanted me to. It's just your rotten luck that I reacted the way you taught me to."

The room was suddenly quiet. Natalie was breathing hard, eyes locked on her father.

Trent said, "I didn't want you around him. I still don't. He's dangerous, Natalie. Violence follows him.

He can't keep his principals safe. I was afraid you'd get hurt."

"But you put him in the violence," she said. "What did you expect to happen?"

"Do you really think that was what I had planned?"

"I don't know. I don't want to think so. Maybe the only thing you saw was the chance to take down one of the Ten. But what you did disgusts me. Manipulation like that, it's only a step away from hiring an assassin to take a life. At least the person who buys a contract is being honest about what he wants done."

"Honey, you're just upset about what happened yesterday. That's to be expected."

"Of course I'm upset, that's not the—"

"You should take some time," her father interrupted, soothingly. Mosier nodded, looking at his boss. "A couple of days off, maybe. Why don't you head up to the house in Maine? Bring a couple of good books and relax."

Color rushed Natalie's cheeks, turning them scarlet. For several seconds she was too furious to speak, and then there was a knock on the door, the creak of its hinges.

The man who entered was big, well over six feet, with the body of a linebacker and the face of a rabbi. He was somewhere in his late fifties, with a fringe of black and silver hair around his head, and a mustache and goatee of almost the same hues, but lighter. He wore glasses with trifocal lenses, and a dusty blue seersucker suit. His shirt was striped blue and white; his bow tie green, blue, and gray. He wore red suspenders.

"Bad time?" he asked. The voice went with the figure, a big low rumble with an undercurrent of humor.

For a second there was more silence. Then Trent

said, "Just talking a little threat assessment. Nothing to worry about."

"Leslie Marguiles," the big man rumbled at us, offering his hand. "Pugh's my witness."

"Natalie Trent," Natalie said.

"A pleasure. Elliot, you didn't tell me you had such a lovely daughter." Marguiles released Natalie's hand and took mine. "And you?"

"Atticus Kodiak."

The grin was unbidden and honest. "Now, that's a good name! Named after Mr. Finch himself?"

"My parents had lofty aspirations for me," I said.

"Almost every attorney I know cites *To Kill a Mockingbird* as the reason they got into the Law. That and *Perry Mason*. Me, I'm decidedly in the Harper Lee camp. You here on the job?"

"Mr. Kodiak was just leaving," Trent said.

"I'm in the business, but not on the payroll here." I answered Marguiles without looking at Trent.

Marguiles nodded. "I can wait if you want to finish up in here, Elliot. I've got a little time before I need to head back to the city."

"No," said Trent. "We can talk now. As I said, Mr. Kodiak is leaving."

One of Marguiles' bushy eyebrows rose above his glasses, but he didn't comment. Mosier got to his feet and planted himself in front of my chair. "I'll walk you two out," he told me.

Natalie cast a last glance at her father, but didn't say anything. Her cheeks were still flushed, and the anger danced in her eyes. No one can enrage a child the way a parent can, I thought.

"Nice to meet you," I said to Leslie Marguiles.

"It was my pleasure, Atticus," he answered.

Then Mosier had us outside of the study, and was guiding us back down the hall. He walked behind us, as if afraid Natalie or I might try to make a break for it, try to double back and somehow corrupt Marguiles with our presence.

Once we were back out on the porch, he said to Natalie, "I'd listen to your father's advice and take a couple days off."

"You should listen to my advice and go to hell," she replied.

Raymond Mosier put his sunglasses on, sliding them up his nose with his middle finger, before adjusting his footing on the wooden slats of the porch. "You two might think you know what's going on, but you don't. The threat against Pugh is still active."

"No kidding," I said. "You're guarding him."

"And I'll keep him alive," he shot back. "I found a device on the road outside the estate this morning, a shaped C-4 charge fixed to a tree, faced to catch outgoing transit. We disarmed and disposed of it, but, believe you me, it was no cakewalk. Just because John Doe is dead doesn't mean the contract on Pugh is off."

"You better rush back to Marguiles and tell him what a hero you've been," I said. "He might think there are other guards on the payroll."

"You can see yourselves out," Mosier said, and he went back into the house.

CHAPTER EIGHT

Natalie stormed off the porch and headed across the lawn to the gate. When I caught up to her she began shaking her head, as if hearing a sound she couldn't tune out.

"That bastard!"

I didn't say anything.

"Did you hear him?" she raged. "Did you hear the way he spoke to me? Did you hear his tone? Bastard! How dare he talk to me like that, especially in front of Mosier? How dare he!"

I put a hand on her arm. "Take it easy," I said.

She spun around, her mouth trembling. "How is anyone supposed to believe I'm a professional when he does that? How am I supposed to keep any respect when he turns me back into his little girl?"

There was a wood and iron bench nearby, set up near a mound of earth rising out of the lawn. The mound was covered with zinnias inside a ring of marigolds. I headed over to it and took a seat. After a moment, Natalie joined me, but she didn't sit down.

"He didn't even listen to us."

"Not when he started hearing things he didn't like," I agreed. "He certainly didn't want us poisoning the well around Mr. Marguiles."

"I'm going back inside," she said.

I thought about suggesting she not, but the blaze in her eyes was all I needed to keep my mouth shut. Instead, I nodded and said, "I'll wait for you here."

"This won't take long," Natalie said.

After twenty minutes the dog patrol came by and asked what I was doing. I told them I was waiting for Natalie Trent. The guard with the rottweiler radioed to Yossi to make certain everything was kosher while the other guard and his German shepherd kept me under close surveillance. I knew better than to try and pet any of them—guards and dogs alike. Yossi confirmed that I was permitted on the premises, but cautioned the guards to check my pockets for "the good silverware." They almost took him seriously.

It was hot, and sitting on the bench only made the heat stronger. I thought about moving to some shade, but didn't want to deal with yet more guards as a result. Instead, I put my feet up and lay back with my head on the armrest, and shut my eyes. This way I wouldn't look like a threat, and could bake in peace.

I was listening to birds chirping and the distant sound of the Cushman's motor, getting drowsy, when someone said, "Got a cigarette?"

I opened my eyes. There was a man looking down at me, lanky and lean, skin like weathered parchment. In one hand he held an artist's portfolio by its handle.

"I don't smoke," I said.

He motioned for me to move my legs, so I righted myself and made room on the bench. The man sat slowly, as if used to arguing with gravity. He rested the portfolio carefully in his lap. He was in his sixties, with clean-cloud white hair that stuck straight up from his scalp and small watery brown eyes. A thick wedding band rested on the appropriate finger, and his hands were slightly discolored, like a tanner's, perhaps with ink.

"You like art?" he asked.

"Some," I said.

He spat on the grass, then nodded. "Heh. Know what you like, huh?"

"Something like that."

He unzipped the portfolio and handed me three sheets of heavy cardstock. "Take a look at these."

The sheets were laminated, bowed slightly from the tension of the glue. All three were collages, pictures assembled from cut-up ads, bright advertising colors and fragments of body parts from model layouts. A cowboy hat here, a woman's leg there, a slice of the San Francisco skyline, an ashtray. I took a moment to look them over, to see the larger pictures, while the man waited patiently.

The first collage was assembled in the shape of a death's-head, almost a Jolly Roger. The stub of a cigarette hung from its fleshless lips. The second was a guillotine, with a laughing child's head, severed and bloodless, at its base. The third was a graveyard, a field of precise headstones. It had a caption, "Come to where the flavor is."

All of the images were pieced together from cigarette ads, at least as far as I could tell, and skillfully assembled. There were no ragged edges, no broken

nes. The artist had cut precisely and glued with great
are, and the end result was gaudy, accomplished, and
isturbing.

I handed the three sheets back to the man, who
racked a smile. "What do you think?" he asked.

"I think they're good," I said. "Morbid as hell, but
ery good. You do them?"

He nodded.

"They're better than some of the stuff I've seen in
he city," I said.

"You're from New York City?"

"Yeah, live in Murray Hill."

"Don't know Manhattan that well," the man said.
He sighed and settled against the backrest of the
»ench, extending his legs. He wore alligator skin cow-
»oy boots, much scuffed, and his heels dug small divots
rom the lawn. "Used to take the wife shopping in
Midtown, sometimes, when we were on vacation."

"I'm Atticus Kodiak," I said, offering my hand.

"Pugh," he said. "Jeremiah Pugh." We shook hands.
His palms and fingers were hard, as if laminated like
his collages. "Haven't seen you around here before."

"I'm not on the detail," I said.

Jeremiah Pugh cleared his throat and spat again, hit-
ing the nearby zinnias. Eyes on the flowers, he asked,
"You going to try and kill me?"

"Nah, probably not."

He liked that, chuckling while he replaced the col-
ages in his portfolio, handling them gently as if they
vere made of glass. "Didn't figure you were one of the
guards," Pugh said as he ran the zipper closed. "Sleep-
ng on duty and all that."

The front door of the house had opened, and Mosier

was standing on the porch, looking around. He put on his pair of sunglasses again and leaned against the railing, master of his domain, and then he saw me and he saw Pugh. He turned back inside, saying something I couldn't hear.

"You've got a lot of protection," I told Pugh.

"Don't I know it, son."

The guard inside the door, Lang, had joined Mosier on the porch. They headed our way.

"Mind if I ask why?"

Pugh set the portfolio at his feet and pushed himself harder against the back of the bench. There was a creaking noise that might have been his bones, but was probably just the wood. He grunted when he stretched. "'Cuz I'm the smoking gun."

Another three plainclothed guards and the foot patrol with the dogs had joined up with Mosier and Lang. They were about fifty feet away.

I thought about asking Pugh why someone had hired a professional assassin to kill him. I doubted I had enough time left to get an answer.

"Hell, I'm busted," Pugh said.

"I think they're after me, not you."

Mosier stopped ten feet away, Lang and the dog patrol backing him up. Lang had brought the shotgun with him, a Benelli, but he looked embarrassed to be carrying it, and he kept the muzzle up.

"Mr. Pugh, you shouldn't be out of the house," Mosier said. "Lang will escort you back."

"Wanted some fresh air," Pugh said, mildly. "It's getting stuffy in my room. Smells like a corral, really."

"You know you're not supposed to be walking the grounds alone. Remember the bomb we found this morning?"

Pugh sighed, spat again, then rose, taking his portfolio. Lang nodded to me and moved to Pugh's side.

"Nice talking with you, Atticus Kodiak," Pugh said.

"Thanks for showing me your collages, Mr. Pugh."

"Jerry, son," he corrected. "Call me Jerry. You truly liked them?"

I nodded.

He smiled, and all of his wrinkles etched deeper. "I'll make you one."

Lang and another guard led him back to the house. We watched them go. The dogs watched, too. Pugh walked slowly, and I thought that he could use some spurs to go with his boots.

When the group reached the porch, Mosier turned his attention back to me. "I thought I told you to leave," he said.

"No, you said that I could 'see myself out.'"

He sighed, looked at the men around him for moral support, then said, "You may not be a threat, but you're sure as hell a distraction, and I don't want you getting in the way of my operation."

"I'm waiting for Natalie."

"Not anymore you aren't."

"Oh, pretty please?"

Mosier took a couple steps toward me, motioning for the plainclothed guards to follow suit. Suddenly, I was sitting in the shade. The German shepherd growled.

"Get this . . . loser . . . off the estate," Mosier ordered.

I looked at my reflection in Mosier's expensive sunglasses and saw it give him a smile. I started to get up. "I'll wait out—"

Mosier punched me in the middle of my chest, knocking me back to the bench. He hit me with the

knuckles of his right hand, and it hurt, and for a mo
ment I couldn't get air.

"What the hell was that for?" I asked when I could

"You fucking mess with my principal again, I'l
break your goddamn fingers," Mosier said. "I don'
need you here, understand? We've got a high-speec
operation running, and we don't want a hump like you
messing it up."

I started to get up once more, and the two guards
grabbed my arms. They needn't have bothered; I hac
no plans to rearrange Mosier's face. Both of the dog:
were growling, and their handlers were holding then
back on their leashes.

"We need to talk about your impulse contro
problem," I told Mosier.

"Pussy," he said.

I laughed. It hurt to do it, but he was funny, whether
he meant to be or not.

"Throw him out," Mosier told the guards.

I made it easy on them, didn't struggle and didn't
resist, and the guards were good about it. Their grip
was sure, but they didn't muscle me too much. Mosier
and the dog patrol followed us to the gate, where Merle
let us out.

As the gate was opening, Mosier told Merle, "You
see this asshole lurking around, you call me."

"We're supposed to report to Mr. Sella," Merle said.

"Listen, shithead, you like your job? You want to
keep it? Don't fucking talk back to me. You see him,
you let me know."

The guards on my arms deposited me beyond the
gate, then doubled back. The gate began to close.

"Yes, sir," Merle said.

Mosier looked at me one last time, then turned and headed back for the house. The guards followed him, and after a second, the dog patrol resumed their walk. Merle and I watched them go.

"Merle," I said.

"Yeah?" He hadn't looked away from Mosier's back.

"When Miss Trent comes out, tell her I went home."

Merle turned his head to me. He nodded. "I'll let her know."

"Thanks," I said, and headed for my bike.

I was grumpy when I got home, and my chest still hurt. I parked the bike in the garage, in the space that Bridgett had kept her Porsche when we were on better terms. It was almost five and Erika still wasn't home.

In the Yellow Pages, under attorneys, I found a listing for the law firm of Marguiles, Yonnemura, & DiFranco, with offices on West Fifty-seventh Street. According to the small ad, the firm specialized in personal injury and workmen's compensation cases. I gave myself thirty seconds to think about it, then dialed anyway, and got a receptionist who was way too peppy.

"I'd like to speak to Mr. Marguiles," I said.

"I'm sorry! He's unavailable right now! May I take a message?"

I gave her my name and my number, and said, "If he could call me, I'd appreciate it."

"I'll make sure he gets your message," the receptionist enthused. "Have a good night!"

"Not likely," I said, but she had already hung up.

.   .   .

It was past seven when Erika called from Bridgett's apartment. I'd been making dinner, pasta salad and gazpacho.

"I'm at Bridie's," Erika said. "She's invited me to spend the night. Is that cool?"

I looked at the dinner I'd prepared and said, "Sure, that's fine."

"How was your day?"

"That was fine, too." Suddenly, I was lying an awful lot. "How about yours?"

"I hung out on St. Mark's for most of the day. Then came over here. You want to talk to Bridgett?"

"No, thanks," I said.

She grumbled something I didn't catch. "See you tomorrow, then. Oh, hey, thanks for the bagels this morning."

"It didn't look like you'd had any of them."

"I ate one. Wasn't hungry. Talk to you later." She hung up.

I looked at the dinner I'd prepared. I got a Sam Adams out of the refrigerator and drank half of it. Then I called Natalie.

"What?"

"It's Atticus," I said.

"Thought you were my father."

"How'd that go?"

"I heard you had a problem with Mosier."

"He punched me."

"Unprovoked?"

"Well, my rakish charm may have set him off, I don't know."

"Been that sort of day all around," Natalie agreed. "What're you up to now?"

"Erika's spending the night at Bridgett's, and I'm looking at more than enough food for two people."

"You want company?"

"Yes," I said.

"Give me twenty minutes."

She arrived with an overnight bag and dropped it in my room beside the bed before using the bathroom to wash her hands. We sat at the table and started on the gazpacho. Natalie had a glass of merlot while I stuck with beer. Natalie doesn't go for beer, but that's okay, since I don't much care for wine.

"Did you get a chance to talk to Marguiles?" I asked.

"Pop wouldn't let me near him. I tried to explain what we're thinking, but he just won't listen. Doesn't want anything getting in the way of Sentinel's little triumph. Mosier's the same way, for that matter."

"I've got to tell you, I don't much care for Mr. Mosier."

Natalie pushed her gazpacho away and started on the salad. "He's wrong for our kind of work. Likes the hardware too much. Yossi says that he carries two guns, three knives, and a baton. He's looking for a fight."

"Yeah, I discovered that," I said.

"Why'd he hit you?"

"I think because I was talking with Pugh. He wandered over while I was waiting for you, showed me some collages he made, and we started talking."

"What's he like?"

"Pugh?" I thought for a second, conjuring the man again in my mind. "I'm not really certain. He seems like a nice enough guy. A lot older than I'd have thought, at least given d'Angelo. Has a cowboy thing going, that sort of laconic drawl. Boots."

"Big belt buckle?"

"Didn't see one," I said. "Anyway, Mosier accused me of 'messing with his principal' or something like that. I don't know what he thought I was doing."

"Maybe telling Pugh about John Doe?"

"Maybe. Pugh's got to be a witness for whatever Marguiles is working on, but I didn't get a chance to ask what exactly that was."

"He was walking around without bodyguards?" Natalie asked in horror.

"I think he ditched them."

"Idiots," Natalie said.

I started on my salad. "I called Marguiles' office, left a message asking that he call me back. Figure I'll tell him the same thing you tried to tell your father today."

"And then?"

"Urge him to get your father to reconsider the arrangements he's made for Pugh's security. Mosier was talking big, but if the principal is wandering around like he was today, that means Sentinel's let their guard down. And if John Doe's still out there . . ."

"Bang," Natalie said.

"What'd you make of Mosier's bomb story?"

"Yossi confirmed it. Said that Mosier had already disarmed it by the time he got there."

"And your father doesn't think that's proof Doe's still out there?"

"Yossi doesn't. Yossi thinks it was a fake and that Mosier planted it himself."

I stopped eating and looked at her. She nodded. I said, "Mosier's got a Superman complex?"

"That's Yossi's take. Let's face it, Mosier acts like the kind of jerk who needs a lot of limelight. I wouldn't be surprised if he's manufacturing situations to make himself look better."

"But, of course, your father doesn't believe this."

Natalie frowned. "Yossi hasn't told him. No proof. Doesn't want to create a schism between the different protective teams."

I watched her refill her wineglass. "You didn't tell me how it went with your father."

"Badly."

We finished our salads in silence. I cleared the table, began washing the dishes in the sink. Natalie offered to help and I told her to stay put. When I had everything washed and dried, I asked if she wanted coffee.

"No," she said, and she headed to my room.

The lights were off, but there was enough street light to see by, the blue night turning to black in the corners of the room.

When she spoke, her voice was hard to hear, and thick. "He offered me the counter-sniper position again."

"Did you take it?"

Natalie shifted on the bed, careful not to touch me. "No."

"Yossi could use you."

"I know."

In the hall outside the apartment, I heard a door slam, and then the creak of the floorboards by the stairs. Probably Ortega in 5F, headed for the bodega on the corner. He was an overweight man maybe ten years my senior, a nice enough guy, friendly. I had no idea what he did for a living. Out of milk, maybe, or in need of a quart of ice cream. And the bodega would have it, whatever it was he needed, and that would be that; Mr. Ortega would go back to his room and resume his life, content.

Natalie shoved the covers back and sat up, swinging her legs onto the floor. The street light turned her luminescent, like a ghost. She ignored her clothes folded on my desk, took her bag, and headed to the bathroom. After a minute I heard the toilet flush, and then the shower started.

She wasn't under the water long, five minutes at the most, and I didn't move. There was a spot of water damage on the ceiling, and in the darkened room, it looked like a hole to the sky.

When she came back she was wearing the clothes she'd brought in the bag. She put the bag on the end of the bed and tucked away her old outfit, then sat down on the desk chair and reached for her shoes.

"Why do we do this?" she asked, suddenly.

"Comfort," I said.

"And maybe for a minute it even works," she muttered.

I started to get up, reaching for my glasses and my robe.

"Don't bother," Natalie said. "I know the way."

CHAPTER NINE

"I can give you fifteen minutes," Leslie Marguiles said. "Sit down and tell me what I can do for you."

I took the offered chair and waited for Marguiles to resume his seat. His office seemed small, but that was an illusion brought on by the clutter. Mostly files, piles of them in blue folders with spears of yellow legal sheets jutting at all angles. They were stacked on the floor, toppled against the wall, and mounded on his desk. He pushed several out of the way to clear the line of sight between us.

"The cleaning lady comes on Mondays," he explained with a grin.

"Only one?"

He laughed, and then the phone rang. "Damn, hold on," he told me. It took another bleat of the ringer before he could find the machine. He stabbed a button with a finger. "Yes?"

"Caulinsky is on four," barked a voice from the speaker.

Marguiles glanced at me, then frowned. "Got to take this," he said.

"I can wait," I said. In fact, I'd been waiting two days, but it didn't seem the time to mention it.

Marguiles picked up the phone and began niceties with Caulinsky on the other end, and I went back to looking at his office. There were three chairs including the one I was in and not including Marguiles', all of them with leather seats and wicker backs. A bookcase filled the wall behind where I sat, packed with volumes of New York's Civil Code. On another wall hung a lithograph by David Agam, a series of diamonds in bright colors set one within the other, disappearing at the center to infinity. Beside the lithograph hung a couple of plaques, and Marguiles' diplomas. He'd gotten his J.D. at Columbia. To my right, a window gave a view of another building, taller than the one we were in, across Fifty-seventh. Marguiles was now into the good-bye phase of his conversation. A small plastic replica of the lumbar vertebrae sat beside the monitor for the computer on his desk. Two photographs stood in frames by the model section of spine. One was of a serious-looking woman with a very unserious grin. I took her to be Marguiles' wife. The other was of three children, two girls and a boy. The boy was the youngest of the three, it seemed. One of the girls was ruffling his hair, and he didn't look like he cared for that much.

"My family," Marguiles told me, hanging up. "That picture's five, six years old."

"Nice-looking kids," I said.

"Hillary, Shoshana, and Simon. Shosh and Simon are still in high school, but Hillary is starting college this fall, going to Yale. She's in New Haven right now, with her mother." He leaned back in his big chair. "Now, what was it you wanted to see me about?"

I ran it down for him quickly, because I took the fifteen minutes he'd said he could give me seriously. He'd been impossible to reach in the three days since I'd returned from Yorktown Heights, either out of the office or in a meeting. I'd finally shown up in person at nine this morning, and Marguiles' secretary had said Mr. Marguiles would try to fit me in. I'd waited nearly three hours till he did.

"So you really think an assassin is still trying to kill Pugh?" Marguiles asked when I'd finished. He was doing a good job of keeping the doubt out of his expression.

"I don't know," I said. "But I'm certain that the man Natalie Trent shot at the Orsini wasn't the man after Pugh. I only have Trent's word that an assassin is after your client at all."

"Witness," Marguiles corrected. "Not client. Pugh is not my client. And I do think his life is in real danger."

"Can I ask you why?"

Marguiles rubbed his beard. Today his bow tie was red with fat black polka dots. "Jeremiah Pugh is both an expert and material witness in a case this firm has brought against DTS Industries."

"DTS Tobacco," I said.

Marguiles nodded.

"This is about cigarettes?"

Marguiles nodded again.

"Isn't this old news?"

Marguiles sighed once more, the exhale rustling loose sheets of paper on his desk. "You're referring to the deal before Congress."

"I thought a settlement had been reached."

"No. It is a *proposed* settlement," Marguiles corrected, "one which will let Big Tobacco off with a slap on the wrist. And even with congressional and presidential approval, it will be in contention all the way to the Supreme Court."

"All the same—"

Marguiles shook his head, a move that reminded me of a bull preparing to charge. "No. The proposed settlement, among other things, grants Big Tobacco limited immunity in class-action and personal injury suits. It absolves them of their crimes. Damages would be capped at five billion dollars a year." He stopped shaking his head. "Sounds like a lot, doesn't it?"

"It is a lot," I said.

"To you, certainly. To me, absolutely. To them, it's nothing. Less than five percent of their annual revenue. And it doesn't begin to cover the collective costs of all those who have lost their lives."

"Still—"

"Let me finish," Marguiles said, holding up a hand. I shut my mouth. "You have to understand, Mr. Kodiak, that until this past year, no tobacco company had even hinted to the public that their product was lethal, let alone admitted that cigarettes kill. All such evidence was brought to light by independent sources, by the government. Never by the corporations themselves. Big Tobacco has, time and time again, stared down at the cancer-riddled lungs of a dead smoker and told his survivors, 'You can't prove we did that.' Proof to them would be the remnants of one of their filters fused into the lining of the same lung. And even then they would argue that their product was never designed to be taken internally.

"But for thirty years—perhaps even longer—they have known *absolutely* that they were committing murder, and they did nothing to alter their course. They fought every attempt to inform the public. They spent billions to discredit and vilify each and every person who spoke out against them. They spent billions more to ensure mega-sales with glossy advertising and a propaganda campaign that the Nazis could have taken lessons from.

"These corporations are liars. These men are murderers. And they are poised not only to get away with murder, but to continue getting away with it for generations to come. The deal they're angling for now gives these tobacco barons limited immunity against litigation, Mr. Kodiak. Do you know what that means? They want law drafted that will prevent a citizen from taking them to court. They want a chance to write one check, wash their hands of the whole mess, and then return to the business at hand, that of selling smoke and making money. More and more money. The richest corporations in the world, selling a product that kills, and they expect to get away with it."

"And Pugh can prevent that?" I asked.

"Jerry Pugh can prove the Big Fraud," Marguiles said, relishing the phrase. "He was head of R&D at DTS for twenty-two years. Aside from his actual work of cigarette design he also took part in discussions where policy was set. He was there when DTS said that, although they *knew* their product was taking lives, they would continue to publicly deny the same. He has firsthand knowledge of not only the chemical dangers that DTS knew about, obfuscated, and denied, but he can also testify about DTS's sales strategies. He can name the names. He can give the dates. You know Glory cigarettes?"

I nodded, but his question had been rhetorical. Marguiles was warmed up now, and could clearly go on for a while longer. But I was following him, and believing him, and responding to his conviction. If Robert Frost was right when he said that a jury consisted of twelve people deciding who had the better lawyer, Marguiles' opponents had better be attending charm school.

"Glory Juniors," Marguiles continued. "Introduced in 1982, designed to be sold to younger smokers. Incidentally, introduced when DTS's sales were at their lowest point in two decades. Mildest taste of any of their brands. Highest nicotine content. And for their ad campaign they took the Glory Soldier and turned him into a cute little tiger cub named the Glory Bee who chain-smokes. I guess the Madison Avenue folks thought that a tiger smoking a cigarette made more sense than some damn insect."

"It's easier to give the tiger fingers," I said.

Marguiles' face broke into that huge smile, and he began searching his pockets. "That's it exactly. 'It's easier to give the tiger fingers.' I'll remember that." He found a fountain pen in his breast pocket, and scribbled on the corner of a notepad.

When he had capped the pen, I said, "You haven't answered my question. Do you really believe DTS has hired a professional killer to silence Pugh?"

Marguiles scratched at his beard before answering. "Trial is scheduled to begin in three weeks. The case is a personal injury suit against DTS, filed in Federal Court on behalf of a woman named Gloria Brazzi. We're seeking three and a half million in damages. If we win, we'll set precedent in the Southern District of New York. That will in turn open up more suits by other injured parties, and in the long run will cost DTS billions of dollars.

"But more importantly, Pugh's testimony will become a matter of record. That testimony will be used in further suits, perhaps even in criminal proceedings. Remember that DTS engaged in a conspiracy to defraud the consumer. In essence, they committed negligent homicide on a national—no, global—scale.

"They'll kill to keep that conspiracy off-record," he concluded. I didn't say anything, but something in my face must have changed, because after a second for thought, Marguiles added, "You must understand how wide-reaching the results of a win would be."

"DTS would take a hit," I said.

"A possibly fatal hit. And we're not just talking about money. We're talking about the possibility of criminal action. I'll give an example—about three years ago the Senate held hearings on the tobacco industry, you may remember."

"I do."

"William Boyer, the Executive Vice President of Marketing and Sales at DTS, stood in front of the Senate committee, and was asked why DTS augmented the natural nicotine in Glory Juniors. His response was, 'Because it tastes like Virginia.' He vehemently denied that his corporation engaged in any practice to foster addiction."

Marguiles leaned forward to make certain I got his next point. "William Boyer lied to the Senate, and Pugh can prove it. Boyer was Pugh's immediate superior for seven years, and during that time they had no less than six conversations where Boyer explicitly instructed Pugh and the R&D division to make Glory Juniors the 'most effective nicotine-delivery system on the market.' They spoke in terms of 'dosages,' Mr. Kodiak. Of 'fixes.'

"Believe me, Pugh is in extreme danger. We're

speaking of men driven by greed, and they know they're on the verge of losing it all. They'll kill to protect their profits. They've been committing murder for fifty years, one way or another. Murder's second nature to them."

Marguiles' phone rang again. He picked it up, listened, and then told his secretary that it would have to wait.

"You may have a problem," I said, when he had hung up the phone. "Trent didn't stop John Doe."

"He said you might say something like that."

"Trent?" I asked.

Marguiles nodded. "Told me that you would probably try to harass me. Called it sour grapes. Is that what this is—sour grapes?"

"I don't think so. What else did he say I would probably do?"

Marguiles looked at me thoughtfully. "A few more things. Nothing you should concern yourself with."

I felt very small in the chair, suddenly. Small in the world. It's never nice to find out that people have been talking about you behind your back; it's hell with razors when you find out what they've been saying is, at best, unkind.

"Trent may be more concerned with his reputation than with your witness," I told Marguiles.

"He does seem to have an ego, I agree. But the fact remains, Trent's kept Jerry safe so far."

"I hope things stay that way."

"I do, too. Jerry's a good man. Conflicted, guilty as hell, but at heart a decent fellow. He needs protection, maybe not only from hired killers." Marguiles looked at the clock on his desk. He sighed. "I'm afraid that's all the time I have for you. I have work to do. Jerry's first deposition starts tomorrow."

"Good luck," I said, rising.

Marguiles got to his feet. "I'll need it. For a while there, it looked like they wouldn't try to question him at all, but that turned out to be a clerical error—a secretary forgot to file Notice of Intent. Had to have the trial court judge reopen the discovery phase."

Marguiles offered me his hand and I shook it. He led me to the door.

"I appreciate you coming by," he said. "I'll take what you said under advisement."

"Despite what Trent told you?"

"Trent called you dangerous, violent, and incompetent. I didn't see any sign of it today."

"Wait till you've known me longer," I said.

CHAPTER TEN

There's a five-hour time difference between New York City and Hereford, Wales. By my clock, that meant it was just after seven in the evening in the U.K. when I started dialing. There was a good chance that the man I was trying to reach would be unavailable; there was a good chance he was crawling around in the darkness somewhere, dressed in black, being a soldier. The man I was trying to reach was a sergeant in the SAS, and not the kind of fellow who lived a quiet life.

The phone rang four times before being answered. There was laughter as it got picked up, and the sound of clinking glass. "Hereford 3338, hello?"

"Robert? This is Atticus. Atticus Kodiak, from New York."

"Jesus, I bloody well know who you are," Robert Moore said. "Wanker. Think I don't remember you. How's the girl?"

"Erika's fine."

"Heard her father finally faded away."

"In April," I said.

Robert Moore made a grunt that acknowledged

what I'd said. "Why you ringing me up, then? Not planning on coming for a holiday?"

"Not for a while yet. I need some information, and you're the only person I can think of who can get it for me."

"Ah, you're after a favor. Should've known."

"Yes," I said.

"Hold tight," he said. The sound from the receiver became suddenly muffled, but I heard him shouting for everyone to get the hell out of the bloody room. "There, that's done it."

"I catch you at a bad time?"

"Party."

"What for?"

"Who needs a reason? What is it you want?"

"I need any information you can get me about a professional assassin, whose *nom de guerre* is John Doe. In theory, he's one of the Ten."

"Jesus, you don't hunt small game, do you?"

"You know him?"

"Reputation only," Moore said. "And it's a nasty one, at that."

"What can you tell me about him?"

"Not much. I'll ask around, see what more I can give you, ring you later. Fine?"

"I'd appreciate it."

"I'll call when I have it."

Erika had picked that night to stay home, so we ordered pizza and watched some television together, and then she disappeared into her room to "get back to work." She left her door open; I could hear the clacking of the keyboard at irregular intervals.

I figured Moore would wait until the next morning, his time, to find me my answers. There was no point in trying to stay awake until he called. The meeting with Marguiles had left me convinced, more than ever, that Pugh was in real danger. I didn't know why, a teasing at the back of my brain, maybe something that the lawyer had said.

Erika emerged from her room a little before midnight and found me on the dumpy couch in the living room, reading and listening to music. The couch had come with the apartment, the only piece of furniture to survive the previous tenant, and it was ugly and old. It was also very comfortable, and that was why it remained.

She cocked her head and listened for a moment, then asked, "Stan Getz?"

"Dexter Gordon. You're getting better. Both played sax."

She smoothed her hair, then asked, "If I make coffee, will you want some?"

"If you're making coffee, sure. I'm going to be up for a while longer."

"Me too. I'm on a roll."

"Do I get to read it when you're done?"

"No," she said, and went to the kitchen.

I'd been having a dream about my attorney, a woman named Miranda Glaser, when the phone woke me. Miranda is acerbic and pretty and very very smart, and she always gives me good advice. In my dream, she had been counseling me to take a plea, to confess my guilt for something I couldn't remember and wasn't certain I had done. Miranda wouldn't tell me what crime I'd committed, but she kept saying, "They've got evidence, Atticus. They've got plenty of evidence."

The apartment was dark, and I realized I was still on the couch. I got up and promptly kicked the empty coffee mug into the wall. There was no light coming from beneath Erika's door.

"You're lucky I fancy you," Moore told me when I picked up the phone. "I don't normally cancel my plans for an evening when just anybody calls."

"What time is it?" I mumbled. The sky had the hints of dawn.

"Half past ten, here."

I fumbled for the switch, winced as the lights stabbed my eyes, and turned them off again.

"I've got the mother lode, mate."

"Go ahead."

Moore cleared his throat. "Right, then. Understand that everything I'm going to tell you is off the record. Most of this I got through a bloke I know in the Foreign Office, and he got it through someone at Six."

"Understood."

"Almost none of this has been confirmed in the official sense. We're dealing with the Ten here—or one of them, anyway—so there's very little hard evidence. What I've got is based mostly on intelligence bullshit—hearsay, circumstantial evidence, informant reports."

"You're hedging," I said.

Moore chuckled. At least, I think he chuckled. He might have been clearing his throat again. "I just don't want you taking any of what I'm telling you as gospel."

"Give me the facts first."

"First official hit credited to Doe appears on radar about five, six years ago. Your DEA busted a crew of opium peddlers out of Laos. One of the arrests rolled over, started spilling names and dates, and in the course of things mentioned that he'd hired a contractor to help 'resolve' a conflict with the Wo syndicate. Apparently there had been a disagreement over profit sharing."

"That happens," I said. I flipped the light on again. There was a notepad on the table, and a pen, for when Erika or I had things we needed to remember when shopping. I reached for them.

"Upstanding, caring people, drug dealers," Moore agreed. "Nobody in Laos wanted to touch that contract—afraid of crossing one of the Triads, you know how it is—so they went looking abroad, and apparently found a taker for the Wo hit in Europe."

"The DEA confirmed all of this?"

"They checked it out, and lo and behold, two months after the hit was reportedly contracted, Lui Sun-yu of the Wo syndicate caught a bullet in his head while his yacht floated in Hong Kong harbor. Lui was sunning himself on the quarterdeck at the time. The DEA's guy said that the shot was at nine hundred meters, but HK police figure it was closer to five hundred."

"Shit," I said. A head shot scored at half a kilometer was terrifying to contemplate, and that had been the low estimate. In essence, it meant that Pugh couldn't be allowed out-of-doors. There's almost no way to protect against a sniper who can make a shot from that distance.

"Yeah, it's nothing to sneeze at, whoever's numbers you believe," Moore said. "The DEA's guy swore up and down that that was the hit he bought.

"Of course, when the HK police goes looking for a hard confirmation, all they can be sure of is that Lui Sun-yu is extremely dead. It went out on the wire,

Interpol, the CIA, the FBI, us. Nothing for a bit, then Scotland Yard cracks the Benny Harrison hit. You remember that one?"

Benjamin Harrison had been the CEO of International Petrol–UK, in his sixties and still living like he was in his twenties. He'd died on vacation in Cornwall almost three years ago. The telephone in his suite had exploded while he was making a call. Initially, the assassination had looked like a terrorist act, perhaps the IRA, but the police didn't let it go, and in the end arrested Harrison's wife of forty years, Catherine. She confessed to buying the hit, but the assassin was never caught.

"That was Doe?" I asked.

"Some DCI took a look at Cat Harrison's accounts, noticed a lot of money had been moving around. They brought her in for questioning, and she broke. When she mentioned the fee, the DCI just about sprayed her with the tea he'd been drinking. One point five million pounds. Everyone sat up and took notice, then. This bloke's not your run-of-the-mill hitter."

"Not for that kind of money," I agreed. There were places in the U.S. where a person could buy a hit for less money than it cost to have someone kneecapped. The logic was that, in a murder, the victim didn't survive to testify against you. Last I had heard, you could buy yourself another human being's death for about a thousand dollars, give or take a couple bucks.

"They spent six months trying to find the assassin, and all they came up with were the wire transfers to three banks in the Caribbean, accounts that had since been closed. Nothing else. They did some cross-checking, and found that the contact and recruitment procedures Catherine Harrison used were almost identical to those of the fellow in Laos. Conclusion: they were dealing with the same assassin, and that the killer could be anyone. Some smart-ass at Scotland Yard started referring to the mystery man as John Doe, and it stuck."

"Anything else?"

"According to the Mossad, a hired assassin capped the chief presiding justice of Turkey, and they think it's the same person who did the Harrison and Sun-yu hits, but they won't say why. Seems that His Honor found himself suddenly dead after agreeing to extradite three members of the Islamic Jihad to Israel for trial. Fifty-seven years old, died of respiratory arrest alone, at home, a week after the decision. Autopsy revealed no foul play, but it was awfully convenient.

"Then we've got four members of the FARC in El Salvador found hanging by their feet outside the convent where three nuns had been raped and murdered four months earlier. Rumor was that some upstanding member of one of the cartels in a neighboring country took his Catholicism seriously, and felt the FARC should repent with their lives. There's also an International Red Cross investigator who was looking into the sex trade in Thailand. His face got mailed to the head office in Geneva."

"There's no pattern."

"One of the Ten," Moore said. "Wouldn't let himself become predictable. There's two more. You want them?"

"Go."

"An American arms dealer named Nic Arnzen screwed some Syrians out of a shipment of red mercury last year. Took something like a million-dollar deposit, then didn't deliver. Same arms dealer got blown all over southern France while driving from Paris to Cannes when his Porsche suddenly became a rocket. Witnesses said the car went up about twenty feet when the bomb detonated."

"Messy," I said.

"Wait, this one's my favorite. David McCormack, while filming *Hard Law II*."

"That was investigated, put down as a suicide," I said. McCormack had shot himself in the head six months earlier with a prop gun supposedly loaded with blanks. "He had been in therapy, in and out of rehab, depressed, the whole wad."

"The film had also sucked up something in the neighborhood of one hundred million dollars," Moore said. "And the studio was looking at having to write the whole thing off. Then McCormack died, and suddenly Lloyd's of London is paying out almost one hundred and fifty million to the studio."

I pulled the chair out from the kitchen table, had a seat. The sun was rising, and light was starting to seep into the room. I flicked the switch and turned the overhead off.

"You still there?" Moore asked.

"I'm thinking," I said.

"Mostly circumstantial stuff tying these together," he said.

"What about Doe personally? Anything at all?"

"Best guess is that he's Caucasian, European, maybe former Soviet, maybe in his forties. Since the wall came down, the KGB has been more forthcoming about their covert and black ops work, but they won't claim this guy. Doe's rumored to use assistants for his legwork. Both the DEA's informant and Cat Harrison said they were contacted by different people at different times while setting up the hit. Harrison swore it was a man and a woman, and the DEA fella said it was two men. The Mossad thinks it's two women, but, as I said, they won't say why."

"Descriptions? Photographs?"

He laughed.

"So no one is on record as having met him face-to-face?" I asked.

"No one's admitted to it. I wouldn't. I'd be afraid to even tell the coppers what the hell his voice sounded like, just in case he decided to come back and slot me. Wouldn't want Doe mistaking me for a witness."

"You could take him, Robert," I said.

This time his laugh came over the satellite clear, as if he were calling from next door. "You're up against this guy?"

"Not personally," I said. "Someone I know." My mind was stirring, again, trying to track an idea.

"Tell your friend to duck. This is precision work. I don't think our bloke has ever had to fire a second shot. That all, then?"

"Yeah," I said, then, "Hey, Robert? What do you know about depositions?"

"Not a thing, mate. You take care. Give the girl a greeting from me."

I hung up the phone and headed back to the couch with the notepad. Moore had told me a lot, and he had told me nothing. He'd confirmed that there was an assassin named John Doe; I'd already known that. He'd confirmed that I should be worried; I already was.

I thought about the information he'd relayed, looked at my notes. Precision, he'd said. And planning, I thought. A lot of planning. None of the hits he'd described were easy jobs. Each would have required time—to observe the target, to track his movements, to build or purchase what was needed for the kill. An arms dealer, a Triad member, a judge, an actor, linked in death through rumors and nothing more.

Nothing was consistent. It could be the work of one assassin. Or seven. There was no way to tell. And the methods were across the board, but that didn't mean anything, either. People buy hits for different reasons; normally the big three of money, revenge, and sex. Sometimes they want to send a message, like hanging members of the FARC outside the scene of their crime, or mailing the face of someone who had been poking their nose where it was felt that appendage didn't belong. Sometimes, it's just business. A bomb beneath a car is a remarkably clean way to close an account.

But now I knew one thing for certain: John Doe never would have waltzed into the Orsini Hotel and started spraying bullets around the pool. It wasn't that the attempt lacked finesse; Doe could be subtle, or not, as it suited him; it was that it wasn't smart. Doe would have done his legwork. John Doe would have been damn certain that the man he was shooting at was the man he'd been paid to kill.

Whoever had died at the Orsini Hotel, it hadn't been John Doe, but a dummy. A dummy assassin, presented for the delight of Trent and his dummyguards. Part of a larger plan, a plan to get Sentinel to lower its guard.

And it had worked, and now the way was clear for John Doe to kill Jeremiah Pugh.

CHAPTER ELEVEN

It's a twenty-minute walk from my apartment to
Miranda's office, south of where Broadway crosses Fifth
and the Flatiron Building juts its ornate prow onto
Twenty-third Street. I cut through Madison Square
Park on my way, dodged a film crew shooting a segment on summer fun in the city's parks, and waited to
cross by the statue of William Henry Seward, that
esteemed New Yorker who, among other things, committed Seward's Folly, namely the purchase of the
Alaska territories from Russia. Someone had taped a
flyer to William Henry's nose, an impressive achieve-
ment considering that his nose was a good twelve feet
from the ground. The flyer advertised a rave taking
place Friday night in the meatpacking district on the
West Side. I figured I'd give it a miss.

When I reached the offices of Glaser, Ferenzo,
Doolittle & Glaser my watch said it was just past ten. I
presented myself to the man behind the reception desk.
He was young and well groomed, and he didn't look
up from his work as I said, "I'd like to see Ms. Glaser.
My name's Kodiak."

"Ms. Glaser is very busy right now."

"If you could just let her know I'm here. It'll only take a couple of minutes."

The receptionist examined me before activating his plastic smile. "I'll see what I can do." The line sounded plastic, too.

"Thanks," I said, and took a seat in the reception area with the other waiting clients. There were seven people in chairs and on the couch, a couple of them reading archaic issues of various magazines. I found a copy of *Time* that was three years old.

It took her fifteen minutes, but finally the glass door beside the receptionist's cubicle opened, and Miranda Glaser stuck her head out, looking for me. Miranda's thirty-two, slender, with short black hair and big brown eyes, and today I thought she bore a remarkable resemblance to Louise Brooks. She was wearing slacks and a blouse, and had a pile of files clasped to her chest with one hand. When I waved, she used her other hand to motion me over.

"Did you kill anyone?"

"Good morning to you, too," I said.

"Just checking. Follow me and make it fast. I'm supposed to be in court in twenty-two minutes."

With that, she set off down the hall. I had to rush to catch up to her. "I've got a question."

"Is this about your last bill? It was more than—"

"No, no, the bill's fine, and I've paid it already. I need you to explain depositions to me."

She kicked open the door to her office and dumped the files on her desk. The addition of the files to her desk caused a brief avalanche, and when it was over, she was crouched on the floor, gathering paper and swearing.

I crouched to assist her, but she said, "Don't touch a thing. Why do you want to know about depositions?"

"An academic curiosity," I said.

"And you couldn't go to the library?" Miranda muttered. "Depositions. Depositions exist to allow a witness's testimony to be recorded prior to trial in the interests of reciprocal discovery."

"Which means?"

"Each counsel gets an opportunity to cross-examine their opposition's witnesses before entering the courtroom. It's like a mini trial. It's what separates real life from *Matlock*," she said. "No secret additions to the witness list, no Perry Mason surprises. Both sides know what they're going up against in court."

"And they always happen?"

She sighed heavily. "If you have a witness that you're planning on using at trial, you have to disclose that information to your opponent during the discovery phase. It's up to your opponent to actually request a depo. Once the request is made, you must comply. Otherwise your opponent can go to the judge and basically say that you've withheld information during discovery. That usually results in the judge barring your witness from testifying. For that reason, you take your depositions as soon as possible."

"When? Specifically?"

She tapped the stack of papers against the floor and got up, set them back on her desk, and then reached for the barrister's briefcase resting on her chair. "Before discovery closes. Normally sixty days before trial begins."

"Not three weeks?"

Miranda shot me an exasperated glare, then began feeding a new set of files into her briefcase. The briefcase was old, scuffed brown leather. "Not unless there's been an error of some sort. Once discovery is closed, it's closed. Only the trial judge can open it again, and then only in special circumstances." She clicked the briefcase shut. "Is that all? I really have to go."

"What happens if the witness dies?" I asked.

That got her attention. She arched an eyebrow at me. "Are you in trouble?" Miranda asked.

"What happens if the witness dies? After the deposition is taken."

"If the witness has been properly deposed by both counsels, nothing. One of the things a deposition ensures is that the testimony will be heard at trial."

"Even in the event of death?"

"Especially in the event of death. It's one of the more sordid reasons for having a deposition in the first place."

It was like being hit on the head with a brick, except I felt it in my gut more than my brain.

Atticus, you are one stupid, stupid man, I thought.

DTS's attorneys hadn't rushed to depose Pugh because they'd been giving John Doe time to work. The clerical error had been a deliberate one. Marguiles had said that Pugh was being deposed today for the first time. But if Pugh's deposition was today, that meant he had to be silenced before he could speak. It wasn't about the trial, at least not only the trial; it was the deposition that mattered. Doe had to stop Pugh before he could testify in any forum.

Doe had to kill Pugh today.

"I need to use your phone," I said, already reaching for it.

"Oh, please, be my guest," Miranda said.

I dug out my notepad, found Marguiles' number.

Miranda had stepped away from her desk to give me room, watching me with a brew of amusement, concern, and irritation. At least, I'd like to think there was amusement and concern.

"Marguiles, Yonnemura, and DiFranco, attorneys-at-law," the receptionist said. It wasn't the voice I was used to; maybe the peppy receptionist had the day off.

"Leslie Marguiles, please," I said. "It's an emergency."

"I'm sorry, Mr. Marguiles is in a deposition right now."

"I know. This is urgent."

"He's unavailable, sir—"

"Is he there? Is the deposition being held there?"

"I'm not permitted to give that information out. If you want to leave your name and a message, I'll make sure he gets it."

"I'm calling from New Haven. It's about his wife and Hillary."

The voice on the other end of the line climbed three octaves and dropped half of its volume. "Has something happened?"

"There's been an accident."

"Oh my God," the receptionist said. "Hold on . . . he's at Lamia and Brackman, they've got an office on Chambers." She gave me the phone number. "The deposition is supposed to start at eleven but he should be there by now."

I hung up, dialed again, checking my watch. It read ten thirty-seven. After two rings, I got voice mail, telling me that all lines were busy. I waited, asking Miranda for a phone book.

"What are you trying to find out? What's going on?"

"I need the address of Lamia and Brackman," I said.

"Which one? They've got two offices in the city alone."

"The one on Chambers."

She reached around my legs for a desk drawer, came out with Bell Atlantic's latest edition. I snatched it from her, began tearing through the pages. The message on the phone had ended, and another kicked in, telling me to stay on the line. I found the listing, tore out the sheet, tossed the phone to Miranda.

"When you get someone on the line," I said, "tell them to cancel the deposition and to get Pugh the hell out of there. Tell them his life is in danger."

Miranda looked at me as if I'd suddenly stripped off my clothes and revealed a pointy tail and hooves. "What do I tell them about you?" she asked.

"Tell them I wish I could fly," I said, and then started running.

On a good day, it takes about thirty minutes to make it from where I was in the Teens down to Chambers Street. That's if the traffic is with you, if you've got a taxi driver that knows English, if you can catch a cab.

I didn't have that much time.

I hit the lobby of Miranda's building and tore out onto Fifth Avenue, trying to plot my route, deciding I'd head west for Seventh. It was ten forty-two A.M., business traffic snarling on the streets. I ran out onto Sixteenth Street, dodging one bike messenger, a delivery van, and a dented Jaguar. A black Saturn was pulling out as I crossed, and I went over it, leaving a nice print from my sneaker on the hood as I came back down onto the corner of Eighteenth. Someone called me a son of a bitch in Spanish. People were getting out of the way, looking behind me to see who was in pursuit. Nobody tried to stop me. It's New York, after all.

I'd already broken a sweat by the time I reached Sixth Avenue. The light was with me, this time, and I kept going, scattering a cluster of teens. They called me names. I ignored them. I had a block to go, and was praying that the next part would be easy. My shins hurt.

On Seventh, I began running south along the side of the street, watching the traffic, waving for a cab. From here it was a straight shot down to Chambers, the shortest distance between two points. The avenue traffic was heavy, but moving. Four cabs passed me, two with fares, two who didn't like what they saw. I kept going.

Just below Twelfth Street, a cab was dropping off a passenger, a stooped Hispanic woman with two net bags of produce. I dove in as she was paying the driver.

"Chambers," I all but shouted. "Just go straight down Seventh, and go as fast as you can."

The cabby was white and fat and he looked at me in the rearview mirror. I leaned up against the ballistic glass.

"Now!"

Whatever edge he had been balanced on, my shout pushed him over, and he floored it, yanking the cab out into traffic. He started the meter with his free hand, then hunched down and concentrated on the cars around him.

"Running from or running to?" His accent was Eastern European, maybe Ukrainian.

"To," I said, trying to catch my breath. "Definitely to."

He gave me another glance and went a little faster. It wasn't fast enough for me, but I kept my mouth shut. This was the risk; I'd given complete control of my journey to a total stranger. As useless as the running was, at least then I'd been able to feel like I was doing something.

We shot past King Street as my watch clicked over to ten-fifty. I dug out my wallet, discovered that I only had twelve dollars in cash. Seventh had turned into Varick, and the World Trade Center came into view in the cracks between buildings. We hit a string of red lights, fought with another cab to change lanes. I resisted the urge to look at my watch; it didn't matter how much time we were losing, there was nothing I could do now.

I didn't know how they organized a deposition, when which parties had to arrive, had to be present. If Mosier had an ounce of sense, they wouldn't be bringing Pugh in until the last minute, to keep the window of exposure to an absolute minimum. Yossi would have done a sweep of the area already, the outside, the streets, the ingress and egress routes. The security inside would have been handled by Mosier and Trent's advance team.

We merged onto West Broadway, and all of a sudden reason kicked me in the brain. What the hell did I think I was doing? There had to be at least twenty guards already on-site, Sentinel pros. Trent had pulled out the stops on this one, I knew that; if there was a threat, someone would have seen it already. Pugh was fine, he was going to be fine.

A ConEd truck was parked at the curb at the corner of Chambers, working an access grate in the ground. Traffic crept around the workers. My cabby tried to edge us through, but a brown-uniformed MTA worker waved us back.

"I'm getting out here," I said, dropping my twelve dollars on the seat beside me, and heading out the door.

More running, right, heading west, and now it was men and women in business clothes who were getting out of my way. A group of suits were clustered by the rotating door in front of 478 Chambers Street, all of them on cellular phones, and I shoved through and into the building.

The directory was encased in glass on the far wall, opposite the security desk. Lamia & Brackman were on two. A clock in the lobby declared that it was eleven, exactly. I had an option of elevators or the stairs. The guard at the desk shouted for me to stop as I headed for the stairs. I slammed the door to the stairway open and kept going.

There was a bodyguard in plainclothes at the foot of the stairs, and I'd surprised him. He was backing up, trying to speak into his radio and index his weapon at the same time.

"The deposition," I shouted at him. "Where's the deposition?"

"On three," the guard said, and I realized I was shouting at Lang. He had stopped going for his gun.

"There's going to be a try," I said, and went past him, taking the stairs fast. "Tell them."

Lang began speaking into his radio. Below me I heard the door from the lobby swing open again, and the furious shouting of the guard at the desk I'd ignored. Lang shouted something back, and I thought they were coming after me, but by then I was on three and coming out into the hallway.

They were easy to spot, a cluster of plainclothed guards at the end of the hall. When I stepped into the corridor, the guard posted on the door I'd just used grabbed at my arms, but I ducked him, resumed running. The guard shouted at me to stop; he could join the club.

"Friendly, friendly," I shouted my way down the hall, holding my hands out and up.

The cluster of guards had drawn their weapons. Mosier pointed a big black Beretta at me. I half expected him to start pumping off rounds.

"Stand down," he told the guards. "What the fuck are you doing here, Kodiak?"

The room they were guarding reminded me of a fishbowl, with glass walls facing the hallway. Inside I could see a large rectangular table, Pugh, Marguiles, and three others seated at it. Pugh sat near the end, Marguiles to his left, another man with a laptop computer at his right, attached to a stenotype machine on a tripod. The stenotype machine looked like an odd typewriter with big keys, and was just beginning to spit out paper. Trent stood against the wall behind Pugh, watching, his arms folded. At the opposite end of the table were a man and a woman in suits. The far wall was one large window, affording a view of Chambers Street below.

"Get him out of there," I said.

"No, they're about to start." Mosier holstered his weapon, putting his back to the door.

"Goddamnit," I shouted, "get him out of there!"

That got the attention of everyone in the fishbowl. I reached for the knob but Mosier caught my wrist, tried to torque it into a fancy martial arts hold. I punched him in the face with my free hand, followed it with a knee to his stomach. He doubled over and let go; I shoved him out of the way and into the three guards who'd stood at his side.

Trent was glaring at me, shouting at me to get out before I was even through the door. Everyone at the table was getting to their feet. I went straight to Pugh, grabbed him with both hands, one on his arm, one at his collar, and hoisted him up.

"Who in hell do you think you are?" Trent was yelling.

I was propelling Pugh through the door back into the hall. "I'd clear out, and I'd do it now," I yelled back.

Mosier slammed into me as soon as I cleared the threshold, almost knocking me back into the room. The other guards had grabbed Pugh, and were moving him away, but that was all I saw, because Mosier was bringing his fist around to meet my jaw, and I had to concentrate on blocking that. It didn't work, and I went against the doorframe. Someone pushed me out of the room. Mosier grabbed me by my shirt and pivoted, and I went into the opposite wall. He punched me once more in the kidneys. There was another blow, a kick, I think, to the back of my leg, and then I was on the carpet.

I rolled over to see Trent and a guard restraining Mosier. The fishbowl had emptied, and from where I was, I could see the angry faces of everyone who had been about to take part in the deposition. Even Jeremiah Pugh looked like I'd ruined his day.

"Motherfucker tried to coldcock me!" Mosier was explaining.

Marguiles glared down at me. "What the hell is going on here?"

Trent stepped forward and looked down at me. "You want to explain yourself?"

I took a couple of breaths and straightened my spectacles. My lower back was throbbing from Mosier's kidney punch. I looked at my watch.

It was eleven-oh-seven.

I opened my mouth, and then the table in the deposition room exploded.

CHAPTER TWELVE

"Suzy forgot to send notice," Neil Lamia was explaining. "I sent her a memo two, three weeks after we got your witness list, told her to set up a time to depose Pugh. She called Leslie's office, spoke to his secretary, they cleared four days on the calendar. But the notice never got sent, and it wasn't until three weeks ago that I even realized Pugh hadn't been questioned. Christ, do you know how much paperwork a trial like this generates? Suzy had to swear an affidavit so I could give it to the judge, have him reopen discovery."

He finished the scotch he was drinking and looked at Leslie Marguiles and me.

"Clerical error," he repeated, for the fourth time since we'd sat down. He looked at his empty glass. "I want another. Do either of you want another?"

Both Marguiles and I said we were fine, and Lamia leaned out of our booth and waved for the waitress to get him a refill. She didn't even come over this time, just nodded; this was his fifth drink, and she'd figured out the pattern by the time he'd downed number two.

After the device had gone off, everyone had gone into overdrive. Trent had ordered an immediate evac, and within seconds the hall had emptied of Pugh, Mosier, and those guards who were uninjured, leaving behind the hurt and the confused. Most of us had been fortunate and were out of the way of the glass wall when the device had gone off. One of the guards, a man about my age named Tony Lamond, had been bleeding badly, glass shards having lacerated his face, arms, and chest. The last any of us had heard, he was stable at St. Vincent's.

After the emergency crews arrived, I'd been able to find out a couple of things: the other occupants had been the court reporter and the DTS counsel. The court reporter, whose name I'd missed, was a soft-spoken and dignified man in his fifties who headed home without lingering after the police had finished with him. It was Neil Lamia—*the* Neil Lamia—who had been hired to spearhead DTS's defense in the current suit, and he'd been accompanied to the deposition by one of his associates, Claire Mallory, up from the firm's offices in Atlanta. Mallory had gone home as soon as the police had done questioning her, as shaken as the rest of us, but Lamia had stuck around, waiting for Marguiles and me to finish.

The police had been understandably skeptical when I'd told them the bomb had been planted by a professional killer named John Doe. Marguiles' word had helped, and probably kept me from becoming a suspect. He was still coming down from the trauma of the explosion during the interview; exploding tables didn't happen often in his line of work.

"Talk to Scott Fowler at the FBI," I'd told the detective interviewing me. "He'll confirm."

The detective told me he sure as hell would, and then told me to stick around. It took the NYPD another

three hours to get ahold of the appropriate people at
Sentinel to set the record straight, and ninety more
minutes before they were willing to let me go. The only
pertinent information I gleaned in that time was that
the device had been a shaped charge, disguised to look
like the segment of the table it had replaced. It had
apparently been activated by a timer. Had Pugh been in
his chair when the bomb went off, he'd have been cut
into two halves, and one of them would have stuck to
the ceiling.

The irony was that if Pugh had been in his chair, no
one else would have been injured in the blast. Pugh's
body would have absorbed it all.

It had been just shy of six when I'd headed back to
the street and been intercepted by Leslie Marguiles. He
looked better now, color having returned to his face.

"Neil and I are going to have a few drinks. We'd like
to buy you a couple, if you don't mind."

I'd agreed, used a pay phone to call home, and left a
message on the machine for Erika, telling her I would
be late. Then Lamia, Marguiles, and I had ducked into
the first bar we could find.

After Lamia got his refill, Marguiles asked, "Do you
think they're trying to kill him?"

Neil Lamia didn't answer. He was about Marguiles'
age, smaller and stockier, with black hair and brown
eyes, and a heavy five o'clock shadow that had grown
appreciably darker in the time I'd known him. The
watch on his left wrist shone with the blue-gray of plati-
num, and his fingernails had the luster of a man who
enjoys his manicures.

"Neil?" Marguiles asked, when Lamia didn't answer.

Lamia shook his head. "No, Les. My clients can be scurrilous bastards, I'll grant you that, but I can't believe they would honestly try to obstruct justice by committing murder."

"You believe it was mere chance that made the table we were sitting at explode this morning?"

Lamia looked into his glass. "You know I couldn't answer that even if I had an idea. Which I don't."

"You've got an idea."

"Maybe I'll just withdraw."

"If you drop the case, DTS will find another lawyer to fill your shoes," Marguiles said. "One not as ethical as you."

"I tell you what," Lamia said. "I'll look into it."

"If you don't mind me asking," I said, "why did you take the case in the first place?"

Lamia focused on me. "You think they're all murdering bastards, too?"

"Given what's happened, I'm leaning towards it."

"Anything is possible." Lamia shook his head. "Me landing on the moon tomorrow, that's probably not going to happen. Listen, you own a car?"

"A motorcycle."

"Even better. So, you own it, it's yours, and you've purchased it knowing the risks, agreed? You know that motorcycles are dangerous transportation, that you can die very easily riding on one, or at least get seriously hurt. You following me?"

"Go ahead."

Lamia knocked off half his drink. He didn't wobble. "So, one day you get in an accident. You fly over your handlebars and into the East River, who knows? And you die, or you live, it doesn't matter. What matters is that someone decides that Harley or Yamaha or whoever built your bike should be responsible for what happened to you. They sue the maker of the bike, even though you assumed the risk, even though you knew exactly what you were getting into. It was possible that you would have an accident. If you're saying it's probable, why'd you buy the bike in the first place?"

Marguiles was making a small shake of his head.

"Leslie doesn't think it's the same thing," Lamia confided in me.

"It isn't analogous," Marguiles confirmed.

"Find me one person in this bar who thinks smoking is good for you," Lamia told him.

"Hardly the point. The manufacturer assumes responsibility for the product. If they sell a product that causes harm, and withhold the extent of that harm from the buying public, the manufacturer is liable. Especially when they actively seek to addict people to their product."

"People can quit smoking. They do it all the time."

"And for very few of them it's easy," Marguiles said. "High rates of recidivism, most people struggle with it for years. That's the fault of firms like DTS, who doctor their product to create an addiction, while at the same time lying about the same practice."

"You're denying free will," Lamia argued. "You're implying that a smoker is a slave to his or her brand."

"So, going back to the motorcycle example, if I sell you a faulty helmet, it's your own damn fault for believing me when I assured you it was perfectly safe and sturdy?"

Lamia responded with something about how the

consumer has responsibilities, too, but I wasn't listening anymore. There was a woman at the bar I recognized from earlier in the day. Maybe in her late twenties, straight brown hair in a shell cut, jeans, short sleeves. She was seated on a stool, eating peanuts from a bowl and drinking a beer, and every so often she was looking our way.

I excused myself from the discussion and went over to her. Neither attorney seemed to notice my departure. The bar had become crowded in the last couple of hours, filled with off-duty cops, mostly, and the noise level was rising along with the alcohol intake.

She saw me coming and went back to her peanuts while I pressed myself in at the bar.

"Guinness," I told the bartender.

"On me, Bernie," the woman said.

The bartender nodded and drew me the pint. After he'd moved away, I said, "Thank you."

"I was thinking about buying you a drink anyway," she said. "Chris Havel."

I gave her my name and we shook hands. Her palm had salt on it from the peanuts.

"Saw me giving you the eye, huh?" she asked.

"Saw you at the First Precinct earlier today," I said. "You a cop?"

"Nope—reporter. Cover the crime beat for the *Daily News*. And you, you're a bodyguard, aren't you? Or shouldn't I say that?"

"I prefer Personal Security Agent," I said.

"I'll try to remember that." She smiled. It was a nice smile and she wore it well. Her eyes were hazel. "You one of the Sentinel crew?"

"No comment," I said.

"But you were with them today? You an independent? What's the deal over there with Lamia and Marguiles? Talking about the bombing?"

"No comment," I repeated, and took a sip of my pint.

"I think somebody was trying to kill whoever was in that deposition room today," Chris Havel said. She gestured again at Marguiles and Lamia. I looked over, saw that the two were still in a heated discussion. "I haven't had a chance to look into it yet, but I'm willing to bet that whoever the witness was, he's important to their case."

"I really can't talk about it," I said.

"Oh, come on, Atticus," she urged. "Can't you at least confirm that you're working for one of them?"

"No, I can't. It's a security operation, Chris. Even bad guys read the papers."

"It can be off the record."

I shook my head.

"Bombs going off in prestigious downtown law firms. Secret witnesses. Bodygu—excuse me—*Personal Security Agents* lurking in the city streets. Lamia and Brackman aren't known for defending small clients. I'm smelling money. I'm also smelling a story."

"Could be the smell of something else," I said. "Maybe a coincidence."

"Do I look stupid to you?"

"No," I admitted. There was more green than brown in her eyes, especially when she was amused.

"Then let's not bullshit. You help me out, I can give you terrific coverage."

"Not interested, sorry. Thanks for the beer."

"Maybe you'll want to talk later?"

I picked up my pint. "Maybe, but I wouldn't hold the presses for it."

Chris Havel's smile stayed, but a hint of anger darkened her eyes. "You're a riot," she said.

I went back to the booth. Marguiles and Lamia were still at it, but it looked like Lamia was beginning to lose ground.

"I'm going home," he declared when he saw me. "Going home and kissing my wife and kissing my kids and petting my dog and praying that tomorrow will be a better day."

"We'll get you a cab," Marguiles said.

We walked Lamia to the curb. I stood by his side while Marguiles hailed a taxi. Lamia was steady on his feet, but unfocused. I wasn't certain he was really drunk, or if he would just have preferred to be, but it didn't really matter.

A yellow cab pulled up, one of the new Honda vans, and we put Lamia in the back. He leaned out before Marguiles shut the door and said, "Les, I am sorry."

"It's not your apology to make, Neil."

"Bastards," Lamia muttered.

The cab pulled away, and Marguiles sighed. "Let's go back inside and finish our drinks. I have a couple of things I want to discuss with you."

We returned to our table in time to stop the waitress from clearing our glasses. I sat down opposite Marguiles. He took a gulp of his beer, and then undid the bow at his throat. Today, the tie was green and white, with black highlights. Some masonry dust still clung to his clothes.

He sighed. "How did you know there was a bomb today?"

"I didn't. But the whole John Doe discussion bugged me. So I made a call last night, found out what I could. This morning I asked my attorney to explain depositions

to me, and when she had, alarms went off. I couldn't
understand why Lamia would have waited till the last
minute to depose Pugh unless it was because DTS
wanted to give Doe time to make his kill."

"You don't believe there was a mix-up on the
paperwork?"

"No."

He frowned, thinking. I took another look around
the bar. Chris Havel's drink stood empty and alone at
the bar, and her seat was now occupied by a man
drinking something with an olive in it.

"I want you to take over security on Jerry," Marguiles said.

"I can't," I replied.

"Atticus, if Neil pulls out of this case, DTS will have
to retain new counsel. That means that we'll be starting
the whole process over again. That could take the better
part of a year. Maybe more. Jerry would never survive."

He had a point. With a year to work with, John Doe
would have no trouble completing his contract. It
wouldn't matter who was running the security, either;
with that much lead time, guards get dull, routines
become fixed, and an assassin can afford to be patient.

"Well, maybe Lamia won't withdraw."

"You know as well as I do that there's going to be
another attempt on Jerry's life. Even if Neil stays on the
case, the danger remains."

"I appreciate the offer," I said. "But it's not the sort
of operation I can run. I've got, at the most, three other
people I can call on to assist me. You need more help
than I can provide."

"If this is about Trent, I'll set him straight. I'm
paying his bill."

"As much as this hurts to say, Trent has a point

when he calls me poison. My track record hasn't been that good lately. In the last year and a half I've lost one principal and one friend while on the job, and almost added another to that total."

"And all that's your fault?"

It was a question I'd asked myself many times. I'd made mistakes, several, both personal and professional. Bridgett was, perhaps, the shining example of them, but the reminders were there in other things. Like every time Erika adjusted her hair.

"It was all my responsibility," I answered.

"I can't speak to that," Leslie Marguiles said after a moment. "I don't know enough. But I know what I saw. You saved Jerry's life today, and I want you working on this."

"There's nothing that I can do for you that Sentinel isn't doing already."

"Sentinel didn't go home and 'make a call.' Sentinel didn't yank Jerry out of harm's way thirty seconds before that bomb went off."

I set my drink down.

"You'll do it?" Marguiles asked.

"I could audit," I said. "Evaluate Sentinel's security, find the weaknesses, the holes, then inform Trent so he can patch them. He'd have to be informed in advance, but the other guards shouldn't be notified."

For the first time since I'd seen him that day, Marguiles' frown eased. "I like that."

"Trent won't." Mosier won't either, I thought.

"I'm paying Trent. If I want to hire an outside consultant to evaluate his security, he can't argue."

"He'll find a way," I said.

"Let me handle that. How much do you charge, and when can you start?"

I pushed my glasses up and rubbed my eyes, think-ing that I was about to uncork an industrial-sized jug of trouble. Marguiles was waiting patiently, smiling now. If only he knew.

"Two-fifty a day plus expenses," I said. "I can start tomorrow."

I passed blood when I urinated the next morning. It wasn't the first time it had happened to me, and it probably wouldn't be the last, and I knew it would stop in the next couple of days. It was disturbing nonetheless, and it gave me impetus for the work ahead.

Humiliating Mosier would be nice payback for the kidney punch.

Auditing another firm's security can be done a variety of ways, depending on the environment and the threat level. The one constant is that the audit *must* be thorough—if an attempt isn't made to spot every weakness, the exercise is completely undermined. I'd do my best to give Leslie Marguiles his money's worth.

Saddlebags on the bike loaded almost to bursting, with more gear held down with bungee cords over the backseat, I headed for Forest Hills, to Dale Matsui's house. He had a place south of Queens Boulevard in a quiet neighborhood of similar homes, sitting along a tree-lined street. Suburban, domestic, and peaceful. It was seven exactly when I pulled up outside of his house and cut across the tiny lawn to the front door. He'd be awake, I was certain; for as long as I've known him, Dale has been an early riser.

I knocked and waited, and after a minute the door opened, and a man I didn't know answered. He wore sweatpants and a Melissa Ferrick T-shirt, and held an enormous earthenware mug that resembled an artichoke. The handle of the mug was shaped like a curved tree branch.

"Can I help you?"

"I'm looking for Dale," I said.

"He's still asleep," the man said. "I'm Ethan."

"Atticus."

"Why don't you come in, I'll go give Dale a kick. There's coffee in the kitchen."

The kitchen was clean but for last night's dinner dishes sitting in the sink. I found myself a mug and poured some coffee and looked around. I'd only been to Dale's house two times before, the first to help him move in, and the second to drink his beer during the housewarming. He'd owned the place for over a year, and it wasn't that we didn't get along, or that I didn't want to visit; it was just that Forest Hills was off my beaten track. Normally, when we got together, we met in the city.

It took him six minutes, but Dale appeared in the kitchen, dressed in boxer shorts and looking blearily at me. Ethan got down another mug—this one shaped like a cactus—filled it, handed it to Dale, and then said, "I'm going back to the paper. Good to meet you, Atticus."

"Thanks for the coffee," I said.

Dale stood unsteadily, holding the mug in both hands. He's a great big Japanese-American, with a broad face and plenty of muscle, an old friend who's possibly the nicest person I know. Ethan gave him a pat on the shoulder before heading out of the room.

"How long you been seeing him?" I asked.

"Month," Dale mumbled, slurping his coffee. "Sweet."

I grinned. He didn't mean the coffee. "Seems like it."

"He's a stockbroker. Isn't this a little early for you?"

"I'm working."

"This a recruitment?"

I shook my head. Dale had gone through the same Executive Protection course I had at Fort Bragg, and we'd been assigned to the Pentagon at roughly the same time. Among his other protective skills, he was a hell of a driver. "I'm auditing Elliot Trent."

That helped him wake up a little. "Does Trent know?"

"He's been informed. I'm starting the site surveillance today, and I was hoping I could borrow some of your gear."

"What do you need?"

"Your camcorders."

"What happened to yours?"

"Mine got totaled in the fire. Haven't had the money to replace them yet."

"They're in the closet in the office," Dale said. "I'll go get them. The Watchman needs batteries, though."

"That's fine."

He set the cactus mug down and left the room. I waited. I could hear the sound of Ethan rustling the morning paper, and it made me smile. For the last year or so, Dale had been in a dry spell. Looked like that was over now, and I was happy for him.

Dale came back with a duffel bag and handed it over. I moved its contents to my backpack.

"Who you working for?"

"An attorney in Midtown. Trent's protecting a witness he's using in a civil case."

"How'd you get involved?"

I told him.

"Call me if you need help," Dale said when I'd finished.

"You can join me on the audit."

"I meant besides that. Didn't you get enough of crawling around in the dirt when we were in the service?"

"Yeah, but sometimes I miss it. For old times' sake."

"Me, I'm going to confine my crawling around in the dirt to my garden. You have fun." He walked me to the door.

"Tell Ethan I hope to see him again," I said.

"You really like him?"

"I hardly got to speak to him. Seems nice enough. Even for a stockbroker."

"He's a cutie," Dale confirmed, and sent me on my way.

It was chilly when I hit the Taconic, but the heat was starting to rise by the time I stopped at a convenience store in Yorktown Heights. I bought extra batteries for Dale's Watchman, two blank videotapes, a couple bottles of water, and some snacks. In a stand by the register were maps of the area, and I went through them, found one that showed the area around the Amawalk Reservoir in detail, and added that to my pile. I kept the receipt to include in my bill to Marguiles.

I left the bike in the bushes off the main road about

a mile and a half from the compound, locked the forks, and then changed into the camouflage I'd packed. I painted my face to match the pattern on my body, then checked my compass against the map I'd bought, and started walking. It took me almost another hour to skirt the estate, circling around to approach from the east. The trees were thick and there was a lot of cover, but for the most part I wasn't worried about being spotted yet. All the same, I kept my distance from anything that looked like habitation; one call to the sheriff and I'd have a lot of explaining to do.

Most guards have two modes—best behavior and same-old-shit—and they're normally in SOS. I'd fallen into the pattern while at the Orsini Hotel. If guards know they're being audited, they'll switch to their best behavior, which may save them a scolding, but doesn't teach them anything. My job was to catch their mistakes, to shake them up, see how they responded. There were limits to how I could accomplish this, of course; nothing that would damage the protective effort, nothing that could frighten the principal.

By now, Marguiles would have spoken to Trent, told him what I'd been hired to do. If Trent was playing fair, he would have passed that information on to the head of his Perimeter Team, Yossi, but would not have told Mosier, since the audit shouldn't have any direct contact with the close team. I was counting on Trent's ego to keep him honest; this was now a contest of skills, and I felt certain that Trent believed he could beat me.

By eleven I'd made a quick cache for my gear at the base of a tree, and, taking both of the camcorders and my entrenching tool with me, had worked myself around the perimeter enough to make an educated choice of observation posts. The trees were mixed evergreens, cedar, spruce, some pine, and they gave good cover, in some places almost all the way to the decrepit stone wall surrounding the grounds. There was a spot on a slope roughly sixty meters from the wall that I quite liked. The ground dropped off into a dip another forty meters down, and the lay of the land allowed a fairly unimpaired view of the house from the south, east, and even a portion of the north. I gave it a try, settling down under an ancient tree to watch the estate, and after eight minutes decided that I had, indeed, found my primary observation post.

I dug what is referred to in the Army as a hasty fighting position; basically a coffin-shaped scratch-out in the ground about twenty inches deep, just enough to lie flat in. I spread a space blanket over the hole, staked it down with some sticks, scattered some earth and brush on it, then started setting up the first camcorder. I double-checked its clock, set it to record, and then backed up a hundred meters or so, walking a box around the house until I reached the western perimeter.

As I was moving to place the second camcorder, I caught a glimpse of the wall, and realized I was a lot closer to it than I'd thought I'd been. I'd been working my way through a thick growth of laurel shrubs, hadn't checked my compass, and now realized the wall was five meters away, at most. I'd just started to retreat when the dog patrol came into view, the same unit of handlers and animals that I'd encountered four days earlier. The German shepherd that had growled at me stopped and looked my way, then gave its leash a tug.

"What's the matter, Max?" his handler asked. "What's the matter, boy?"

The German shepherd stared at my position.

Don't bark, I thought. Please don't bark.

I stayed very still. Max had caught my scent, and there was nothing that I could do about that now except pray it didn't worry him. The sun was almost directly overhead, and that was good, because it meant that there would be no glare from my glasses. I was pretty certain the handlers couldn't see me. Still, I found myself thinking I should invest in contacts.

"Squirrel," the other handler said at length. His rottweiler nudged Max with her snout.

"No, he's got something. What is it, Max? Someone out there?"

"You want to call it in?"

Max's handler looked my way, squinting. "I'm not seeing anything."

"It's a squirrel."

"We should check."

"You want to chase Max chasing some damn squirrel?"

Max turned his head, looking at his handler. His handler stared my way a moment longer, then patted the dog. "Nah," he said. "Let's go."

For twelve minutes after they had left I remained in the bush. My lower back ached from where Mosier had punched me. When I was certain they weren't doubling back, I quietly withdrew.

I set up the second camcorder, went back to move my gear from its temporary cache to a position about a quarter mile away from my primary observation post. It was a good site for a base of operations, in a cluster of old evergreens, and heavy with shade. From here I would be well out of sight and sound of the estate, and could move freely.

I unpacked and sorted my things, then checked myself for noise. There wasn't much on me that would alert a listener. I switched my pager from beep to the "excite me" vibrate mode, then jumped up and down a couple of times. Nothing but the sound of my feet hitting pine needles. In my backpack I kept my notebook, two pens, an extra roll of film for my camera, the binoculars, some toilet paper, two bottles of water, and the Watchman.

For a couple of seconds I stood still, listening and waiting, feeling like a commando member of the Audubon Society. Then, dressed to kill, armed to observe, I went forward, back to my primary observation post. When I reached it, I hooked the Watchman to the camcorder, rewound the tape, and then slipped under my blanket into my hole.

It took me fifteen minutes to review the videotape, fast-forwarding until I spotted movement, then pausing, rewinding, and viewing to identify what I'd seen. I recorded the time from the tape that each patrol made their rounds. At one point, a plainclothed guard emerged from the house to sneak a smoke. I recorded that, too.

For the next three hours or so, I remained in place, watching through my binoculars, taking a couple of photographs. This was grunt work, simple, boring, and requiring a fair amount of concentration. To find the holes in the security required observation, and that took time. And staying still is a pain in the ass, as any child will tell you.

Trent had doubled the number of walking patrols since I'd last been there, but there were still only two dogs. Every so often I caught sight of the Cushman buzzing about. Once I saw Mosier, in what looked like an argument with one of the uniformed guards, and twice Yossi walked past, checking his perimeter. The second time, he stopped and looked around at the tree line, right where I was lying. After half a minute, he continued walking his perimeter.

I took pictures and notes, and it was just after four when my pager started thrumming. I flicked it off, checked the number, started the camcorder recording again, and retreated to my base camp to call Marguiles.

"I notified Trent," he told me. "He told me I was wasting my money."

I took a drink of my water. "You can call me off anytime."

"You've already started?"

"I've been out here most of the day. I'll pack it in before too much longer. This is a light day. Tomorrow I'll be spending the night. I want to see what the night routine is like."

"Lamia filed his intent to withdraw," Marguiles said. "So far, I haven't been able to get in touch with him. I told Trent, and he thinks it's a mixed blessing."

"It is. Lessens the immediate threat to Pugh, but gives the assassin more time to work."

"That's exactly what Trent said."

"Nice to know we're agreeing on something."

"I also contacted the U.S. Attorney's office," Marguiles said. "Told them I was concerned for Pugh's well-being, that I had suspicions that yesterday's bomb might well have been an attempt to obstruct justice, as much as commit murder. They told me someone from the FBI would look into it."

"I assume NYPD is already working with the Feds about the bombing," I said.

"And some people from the BATF, I believe. Well, I'll let you get back to your work. Can I expect a call from you tonight?"

"Probably tomorrow. But I'll check in every day."

"Early morning or late evening is best. You have my home number. By the way, did you tell Adrienne that my wife and daughter had been in an accident?"

"Adrienne?"

"My receptionist."

"I had to find out where you were."

"Upset a lot of people."

"They have my apologies," I said. "Before you go, I need you to do a couple of things for me."

"Like what?"

"I need you to write me a letter saying that I've been hired for the audit, and if you could send that over to my apartment ASAP, I'd appreciate it. It doesn't have to be long, just needs to say that I'm supposed to be doing what I'm doing out here. That way if the guards catch me, I'll have a way to explain myself."

"I'll messenger it over before closing. What else?"

"I need you to have someone address a FedEx package to Pugh, at the estate. Make it a box, a small one, and throw in some papers, and something metallic, not too heavy. Just a box of pens, wrapped in tinfoil, something like that."

There was a pause, and then Marguiles said, "It's supposed to be a bomb?"

"Yeah. In fact, on one of the pieces of paper, write 'bomb' in big letters. If you could send it so it'll arrive tomorrow afternoon, I'd really appreciate it."

"I will. You realize that if I send it from here, it will have the firm's address on it?"

"That's half the point," I said.

"You think this assassin has access to my office?"

"Possibly. He certainly knows who you are. It'd be an easy enough thing for a professional to fake."

"I find that more than a little alarming," Leslie Marguiles said. "I'll have my secretary do it right away. Keep me informed."

I turned off the cellular phone and checked my watch, thinking that it was time for me to retrieve the tape from the second camera. A chipmunk watched me from a nearby log. When I moved, it followed me with its eyes.

It was gnawing on something shiny.

Bastard's got my lunch, I thought, and took a step forward. The chipmunk bolted, dropping its prize, skittering up a nearby oak.

It had been gnawing on an energy bar, the sort of food Yuppie hikers and weekend athletes use for quick sustenance. I picked up the remnants. The chipmunk had gnawed the wrapper open, taken a piece of the brown bar inside. Fresh food, I thought. Chipmunks are fussy—they won't eat anything they feel is dirty, that has had insects on it.

I hadn't brought anything like the energy bar I was holding. I'd brought a couple of Hershey bars, some jerky, and a granola bar, but no energy bars.

I took another look around, slowly, then started going over the ground, foot by foot. By the time I had finished it was starting to get dark, but I'd found enough.

I'd known all day that other people had come through the area before me, kids, hikers, perhaps some of the

Perimeter Team, probably even Yossi himself. I'd seen the signs, the odd piece of trash, sun-bleached or rusted, the broken twigs, the scuffed bark and torn leaves.

But thirty yards from where I'd made my little staging ground, I found signs of another base of operations. Through a thicket and in the well of three trees that had grown close together, I found a spot in the soil that sank slightly beneath my heel. I went to my knees and started digging, and the earth was soft, and I knew I was onto something. It took me another forty seconds to find the plastic bag, sealed. Two more bags were buried beneath it. Each contained human feces.

You crafty motherfucker, I thought.

Human waste attracts attention in the out-of-doors. Animals and insects. When special forces troops work covert in hostile territory, they're taught to relieve themselves into plastic bags that can be sealed, then buried. That way, no one can come along and get an idea of numbers or position or direction. One less track.

No hiker had done this. No amateur, either. Fecal analysis is not my forte, but I had to guess that what I'd found was less than two weeks old. It almost made me laugh, to think that I was holding proof of John Doe. Maybe I could send it to the FBI for analysis.

I dropped the three bags back where I'd found them, filled in the hole, and then headed back to my observation posts to retrieve the camcorders. I brought everything back to my base camp and covered the gear with camo netting. The chances of it being discovered before morning were slight.

The feeling wasn't rational, and part of it I had to put down to the night, to the fact that it was full dark by the time I reached the place where I'd left my motorcycle. But it clung to me as I wiped off my camouflage paint and hastily changed clothes, and for a moment I froze, feeling observed, feeling caught.

John Doe was watching.

CHAPTER FOURTEEN

Erika greeted me with characteristic warmth, saying, "Where've you been? You've got messages. What's that on your face?"

I dropped my helmet on the kitchen table and shrugged out of my jacket. "Westchester. What messages?"

"A letter got delivered around five. I put it in your room. Natalie called, and some chick named Chris. Chris called four times. Asked if I was your girlfriend. I set her straight. I told her I was your concubine."

"You're not too big to spank."

"Promises, promises. You hungry? I'll make you some Os," she said.

"A culinary treat. I'm going to take a shower."

"You should. You stink. And you've got dirt or something all over your face. You look like a chimney sweep."

"It's camouflage paint," I told her, heading toward my room.

"Of course it is," Erika responded. "Sing something from *Mary Poppins*."

The envelope was on my bed, from Marguiles. There were two letters inside, one generic and one written for me. Both declared that the bearer had been hired by the law firm of Marguiles, Yonnemura & DiFranco, to audit Sentinel's security of Jeremiah W. Pugh. I put the letters back in the envelope, then stuck the envelope on my alarm clock, so I would remember it the next morning.

I showered and put on clean jeans and re-entered the kitchen to find Erika had set out a bowl of Spaghet-tiOs for me, along with a tall glass of tap water. I thanked her and began eating, and she asked me what I'd been up to, so I told her.

"I'm not going to be home for the next two or three nights," I said. "Starting tomorrow I need to stay out there as much as I can."

"You're going to sleep out there?"

"It's not that bad. The worst part will be trying to stay awake for most of it."

"I could come with you," Erika suggested. "You could paint my face and teach me to creep around in the bushes. I could learn some fancy fighting moves and get a utility belt, and together we could fight crime. I would become Audit-Grrl!"

"You're deranged," I said.

"Hey, I'm not the one who's going to spend three nights in the woods with a face painted brown and green spying on people."

"*Touché.* You really want to help?"

"If I can, sure. It's not like I've got a crammed social schedule."

"Keep the next couple of days clear, then. I'll call you if I think of something you can do."

"Do I get to sleep under a canopy of stars?"

"No. But you might get to show some leg to some leering security guards."

She grinned. "Can I wear my fishnets?"

"They might be a little over the top." I reached for the phone. "I'm going to return my calls, if you don't mind."

"Why should I mind?" Erika said, mildly. She left the table and I heard the television click on in the living room.

I called Natalie.

"What are you doing for dinner?" she asked.

"Erika just made me SpaghettiOs."

"Oh. We need to have a chat about basic nutrition sometime. You want to get a drink?"

"I'll meet you at Paddy's in half an hour," I said.

She hung up and I took my bowl and spoon to the sink, washed and dried them. Erika was lying on the couch, channel-surfing vigorously, as if trying to race from one end of the dial to the other in the least time possible.

"There is dick-all on tonight," she complained.

"I'm going to meet Natalie for a drink," I said.

"Should I expect you back?"

"Yes."

She stopped her surfing and fixed a doubtful stare on me. After a moment she returned her attention to the screen. "I'll give Bridie a call, tell her I'm on my way over."

"I'd prefer if you stayed here tonight."

"Yeah, but I don't want to cramp your style."

I started for a comeback, then abandoned it. There wasn't any point. It didn't matter if Natalie would be coming back with me or not; Erika had made her decision, and I wasn't going to change it now.

"Call and let me know when you'll be back," I told

her, and headed for the door. I'd almost reached it when the phone started ringing. For a moment I considered ignoring it, but I've never been that good at refusing a call. Some people, I am told, have a relationship where they are the masters of their phones, responding to it only on their terms, when they please.

I am not one of those people. I am a slave of the Baby Bells.

"Kodiak," I said.

"Chris Havel," said Chris Havel. "This a bad time?"

"I was just on my way out."

"I've called four times tonight."

"I wasn't in."

"Busy busy busy," she said. "Wouldn't be protecting anyone, would you?"

"I might, rabbit, I might."

"I've got an article running tomorrow morning that you'll want to see. It's about the attempted hit on Jeremiah Wendell Pugh."

"I don't know what you're talking about."

"Oh, come on, cut the crap. Politicians can pull that shit, not regular Joes like you and me. From what I heard, you saved the man's life."

"That's an oversimplification."

"Fine, then fill in the blanks for me. Complicate it a little."

"I don't think I will. I've got enough complications in my life right now."

"Give me a break, here, will you? All I'm asking is for you to let me in a little, to tell me what's going on. There's a great story here—the struggle of those who protect against those who would do harm. Tell me that doesn't make good copy."

"It would make excellent copy," I agreed. "But you've got the wrong guy. I'm not on the detail. I suggest you talk to Leslie Marguiles. He'll give you a story."

"Yeah, in legalese. Snore. Okay. Fine. If you change your mind, call me at the paper, leave a message, something."

"I'll do that."

"Sure you will," she said, and hung up.

I found Natalie on a stool at the bar, drinking bourbon on the rocks and smoking. It was a rare night at Paddy's; quiet, and not much of a crowd. My stomach knotted when I crossed the threshold, saw the back of a woman who could have been Bridgett. But it wasn't, and I ordered myself a drink, then took the stool at Natalie's side.

"He's clearing me out," she began without a greeting. "He's fucking assigned me to some shit job in Miami. Two weeks I'm supposed to hold some woman's hand while she cooks herself at the Fontainebleu."

"Your father?"

"Who else?" she snapped. "He doesn't want me around. Instead of saying, 'I'm sorry, you were right, John Doe's still out there' and asking me to help, he sends me out of town."

"Are you going to go?"

"It's my job, isn't it? He's my boss, after all." Natalie rattled the ice in her glass. "My boss also mentioned that you're auditing him."

"Marguiles hired me yesterday."

"You've already started?"

"Spent most of the day setting up my observation posts, taking notes. Doe had been there already, probably doing the same thing. I found where he'd been burying his waste."

"He didn't carry his trash out?"

"Excrement," I clarified. "Sealed in plastic and buried a foot or so beneath a ceiling of pines."

"Shit," Natalie said.

I gave her a look that hopefully said she could certainly be wittier than that if she gave it half an effort.

"So why haven't you asked me to help?" she demanded.

"I didn't want to put you in a bad position by creating a conflict of interests. Given everything that happened, I figured if I even suggested it, it would make things worse between you and your father."

"Don't see how that's possible."

"Is it really that bad?"

Natalie didn't answer, just looked at a point over my shoulder while she finished her drink. Then she asked me a few more questions, about what I'd seen, what I was planning on doing to test Sentinel's security. She didn't say much else, and after I finished my beer, we got up and headed for the door.

"You've got to be up early tomorrow," Natalie said, as we were walking back up Second Avenue. Outside of a bodega on the corner, a Korean woman was dumping water from her flower buckets into the gutter.

"I'm going to try and get there by eight," I confirmed.

We stopped at the corner of Thirty-first, a block from my home. A couple was waiting at the light, a man and a woman, both very blond, holding hands.

After a moment's hesitation, Natalie said, "Can I come up?"

"If you like."

"Erika home?"

"She told me she was going to Bridgett's."

"She used to like me."

"She still likes you."

Natalie took my hands, then kissed me on the mouth. Her mouth was hard and sad.

It was the first time in months that we approached passion, and the fire came from Natalie's rage more than anything else. We stayed away from the bed, making love against the walls in the living room, using the furniture for support. She stayed until it was almost two in the morning, left me sitting on the desk in my bedroom, propped against the window, as she dressed.

"The farewell fuck before I'm off to Miami," Natalie said. "Thanks for a wild ride."

The bitterness hung in the air like tar after she was gone, and covered me like a blanket while I slept.

CHAPTER FIFTEEN

I was up before dawn, and after making my walk-through, I headed to the bodega on the corner for a cup of coffee, a muffin, and a copy of the *Daily News*. Fresh flowers filled the buckets out front. I didn't see the Korean woman.

Havel's article was there, with her byline, on page eight. She got two columns of about four inches, with a photograph running alongside of Tony Lamond being wheeled out of the building on Chambers Street on a gurney. The headline read, "Bomb Blasts Building Downtown," with a subhead that added, "Bodyguard Saves Star Witness's Life." My name was mentioned.

I reread the article while drinking my coffee at the kitchen table. She'd gotten the facts pretty straight, even if the headline had been an exaggeration. My name appeared at the start of the first sentence, which read, "Personal Security Agent Atticus Kodiak had only moments to spare when he reached the law offices of Lamia & Brackman at Chambers and West Broadway. . . ." The rest of the report was in a similar vein. She quoted me only once. " 'No comment,' Kodiak said after the attempt. 'Bad guys read the papers, too.' "

At least she hadn't misquoted me.

Havel took two paragraphs to describe the bombing and the "timely" save of the "anonymous" witness, then went on to talk about the security firms in the city. She was quick to point out that I was an independent, and that Sentinel was a great big firm. The David-versus-Goliath theme was reinforced when she added a couple of lines about "those men and women who lay down their lives for others."

I finished my coffee, then threw the paper, and the coffee cup, into the trash. The article annoyed me for a couple of reasons. I didn't need publicity. I certainly felt I didn't deserve it. I'd gotten lucky, and there's a world between that and being good.

Havel was going to stir up trouble, whether she meant to do it or not. My instinct told me she'd take the story as far as she could. Publicity and protection never mix well.

I went back to my room, put a few things into my backpack, and headed down to the garage to get my bike. When I pulled out, I almost hit Natalie, who was standing on the sidewalk.

"I hope you're getting paid well for the audit," she told me after I'd killed the engine. "Because now I'm on the payroll with you."

"What happened?"

Her smile was pure delight. "I quit. Called Pop at five this morning and told him that he'd have to find someone else to escort Mrs. Fat Ass to Miami, because I wasn't going to do it. Not today, not next week, not ever." The smile got a fraction wider. "So, all of a sudden I find my schedule is free, and I hear you're performing an audit for some high-priced shyster."

"It's a nothing job," I said. "Some fly-by-night security firm in the city thinks they know what they're doing. I've been hired to prove them wrong."

"Oh, now, *that* sounds like fun. Can I come?"

I feigned scratching the top of my head, which translated into scratching the top of my helmet. "I don't know. It's not exactly woman's work."

"I'm in such a good mood, I'll take that in the mirthful spirit intended," Natalie said. "Now, get rolling, soldier. We've got auditing to do and people to humiliate."

Since we were going to be "in the bush" for at least two days, Natalie and I decided a large breakfast was in order. We ate at a restaurant in Yorktown Heights called Gersky's, loading carbohydrates while we discussed our plans. Natalie was brimming with ways to "embarrass the bastards," as she delicately put it. She had packed her car with a variety of equipment, promising one or two surprises, but after five minutes of discussion, we decided more shopping was in order. It would be another hour before the shops started opening, though, so we each had another piece of a really tasty cherry pie, and some more coffee. I told her about Havel's article.

"Pop's going to love that," Natalie said. "He's going to say you deliberately made him look bad."

"Wasn't my fault nobody swept the room before they let Pugh inside," I said. "Mosier should have handled that."

"They did sweep the room, they just didn't check the chemical content in the air. Probably wouldn't have found anything if they had. The only way they could have prevented that explosion would have been to jam all frequencies coming into the room."

"I thought the bomb was on a timer."

"An internal timer activated the receiver just prior to detonation. Theory is that Doe was nearby, maybe even in the building, detonator in hand." She ate a bite of her pie. "Pop told me that the only reason he agreed to Marguiles' audit was because he figured it would make you look bad. He's trying to get you to quit the business."

"What did I ever do to him?"

"Nothing. It's what he thinks you're doing to the industry. You know what a bad reputation BGs have. Most people on the street think a BG is a muscle-bound heavy with mirror shades, undereducated and overarmed."

I picked at the crust of my pie. Nice, light and flaky.

"You're taking it personally," she said.

"Is there another way to take it? It's getting to a point where I have to wonder if I'm meant for this kind of work."

"You sound like me."

"Maybe it's something in the pie," I said.

When we reached my base camp, I went to set up the camcorders while Natalie separated and cached her gear. It didn't look like anything had been disturbed at either of the observation posts, and none of my hidden gear had been touched.

When I returned, Natalie was nowhere to be seen. I

took a couple of steps towards the camp, scanning for her. Her stuff was still there.

"Problem?" she asked.

I looked for the source of her voice. There was a rustle, and then she resolved against one of the trees. She had been only five feet away.

"Wow," I said.

"Made it myself." Natalie turned around slowly to let me get a good look. "I guess it works."

"Quite well," I agreed. She had changed into her Ghillie suit, her sniper camo. The outfit had started life as an olive-drab flight suit, but Natalie had stitched camouflage netting to the back of the clothes, down her arms and legs. Attached to the links of the net were cut strips of rubber camouflage. She had added a couple of local branches, too, weaving them through the links, to augment the look. Her boots and gloves were brown leather, a hue that matched the earth tones all around. She had a sniper's cowl over her head, hiding her hair, and a wraparound veil in the same pattern, concealing her face.

Unlike the camo I was wearing, hers could move. If a wind kicked up, if there was a rustling in the reeds, her camouflage would respond, moving independently of her body. The folds and layers of strips allowed light and shadow to fall naturally, and broke up her silhouette. Even in direct light, knowing where she was, I kept losing her edges.

We spent another ten minutes checking one another for sound, then moved to the primary observation post. Natalie dug herself in while I reviewed the tape that had been running. By the time I'd finished, she had her optics up and running. I slipped back under my blanket and she handed me her binoculars.

"I have a pair," I said. Sixty meters from the wall, it was safe to talk to one another, as long as we kept our voices low.

"Mine are better."

She was right. Her binoculars were powerful, clear, and incorporated a laser range finder.

"Nice to get the expensive toys," I said.

I played with the binos, watching the grounds and the house, while she set up the tripod for her spotting scope.

"Should have brought a laser mike," she murmured. "We could eavesdrop."

"You have a laser mike?"

"Pop does." She held out a radio scanner. "This'll have to do."

"I can't imagine what I'd do without you."

"You'd suck without me."

"Probably true."

We remained at post until dusk, dividing the work. I kept a log of the rounds, noting the number of guards, their beats, their patterns. Natalie watched the house, drawing a diagram of the interior based on what she saw from outside. We alternated listening to the scanner, an hour or so each, moving the headphones back and forth. There was a fair amount of radio traffic coming from the house, most of it mundane. Guards calling in to the command post, occasionally Mosier or Yossi giving an order to adjust the SOP.

At two-thirteen, as Natalie was listening to the scanner, she announced, "FedEx has arrived."

"That's us," I said, shifting the binoculars to get a view of the guardhouse.

"What are we delivering?"

"Fake bomb," I said. "From Marguiles."

"Sneaky," Natalie said, then added, "Okay, the gate has called for backup."

"Points off for using the radios," I said. "Pat on the back for calling support, though." The guards couldn't know how many people were actually in the van. In fact, they had no way of knowing if it was a real FedEx van at all. Therefore, more personnel was probably a good idea. However, if it was a bomb about to be delivered, a stray transmission could detonate it prematurely.

The Cushman came into view and parked near the gate. Both occupants got out. Merle emerged from the gatehouse.

"Gate has confirmation that nothing is expected," Natalie told me.

The FedEx driver climbed out of the van holding a medium-sized box and his clipboard. He approached the wall, then stopped. Merle was speaking to him, holding out a hand. A brief discussion ensued. Body language didn't tell me much more than the FedEx driver was growing irritated.

"The gate has been directed to identify the sender."

I watched while Merle relayed this request to the driver. The driver looked at the box he was holding, said something in response.

"Gate says, 'From Marguiles.' Pause . . . they're being told to wait. . . . CP is going to call for confirmation. . . ."

The driver leaned against his van. I couldn't see his face well, but I imagined there wasn't a smile. Three minutes passed, with another two guards approaching from the south, staying out of sight of the wall. Good support, I thought.

"CP is telling the gate that they cannot contact Marguiles," Natalie relayed. "They've spoken to his office assistant, and she believes that nothing was sent yes-terday. They're going to refuse it."

Merle broke the news to the driver, who looked at him in disbelief for a couple of seconds, then threw up his hands and went back to his vehicle, carrying the box. None of the guards moved until the van had turned and pulled away.

"Standing down," Natalie informed me. "I give them a C. Too much radio traffic."

"Maybe a B-minus." The guards were returning to their posts.

"We'll have to get meaner."

"All in good time," I said.

Around dusk, Natalie moved out to the second obser-vation post to change tapes and finish her diagram, and I withdrew. We met up at our campsite, broke out rations, and ate, while talking about how we wanted to proceed. Starting the next morning we'd begin with small disruptions and events, escalating as we saw fit.

"How do you want to divide tonight?" she asked.

"I'm easy."

"I'll take twelve to four, then. You can take four to eight."

I told her that sounded fine, and Natalie moved off with my shovel to dig us a refuse and waste pit while I called Marguiles and gave him the update. He asked how the fake bomb delivery had gone.

"They refused it," I said. "Didn't even make it through the gate."

"That's good?"

"It makes me feel a little better about Pugh's safety inside the house. Is he going out again anytime soon?"

"Shouldn't be. With Neil withdrawing from the case, the defense is on hold until DTS can retain new counsel. Whoever takes over will want to depose Jerry, but that may not be for several weeks."

"Then we'll stick with the estate work."

"'We?'"

"Natalie Trent's helping out. I'll pay her out of my fee."

I called Erika next, told her what I wanted her to do, and she agreed, saying that we could expect her between nine and ten the next morning. I gave her Marguiles' number, told her to give him a call and tell him what she needed. She said she would, then told me that Chris Havel had called several times during the day.

"She wanted to know what you thought of her article. Said she's running a series," Erika told me.

"Pick up a copy for me."

"Oh, sure. I'm keeping a scrapbook."

Natalie went back to post first, and I went to use the pit. Neither of us was going with the plastic bag method. I made a small fire afterwards and brewed some instant coffee, pouring it into a thermos. After dousing the fire, the thermos and I made our way back to the observation post.

We shared the watch until midnight, when I took off my glasses and hunkered down beside Natalie in our ditch. She gave me a pat on the head and wished me sweet dreams. It had become chilly, but the space blanket trapped our shared body heat, keeping us warm and preventing our thermal signature from being seen by any guards using infrared. I was out almost immediately.

She woke me at four with a poke in the ribs. I had

been having one of those dreams that mirrors the activities of the past day, and switched positions with her, haunted by *déjà vu*. John Doe had been in the woods, in my dream, a shadow following us.

Natalie unwrapped her cowl and used it as a pillow, then curled up with her body pressed into mine. I kept my log, illuminating the pages with the small flashlight Natalie had brought. The light could be worn on a finger, and the lens was amber, to preserve night vision.

I saw a couple of things that interested me, but nothing grossly incompetent. The dogs went to their kennels after dark, and another foot patrol was added. Motion-activated floodlights had been posted on the corners of the building and at a couple other points on the grounds. There was some movement behind windows, but the curtains remained drawn. The nocturnal animals were out to play, and I had to concentrate on ignoring them. They were more fun to watch.

I prodded Natalie awake a couple minutes before eight, telling her that I was going to activate the second camcorder, and that I'd meet her at the campsite. Natalie had heated water for both coffee and washing up by the time I joined her. I gave myself a quick field washing, dressed again, and reapplied my camouflage paint. We shared a breakfast of instant oatmeal and dried fruit, then headed back to post.

I was on the scanner when, at nine-thirty exactly, I heard the guard on the gate say, *"Incoming vehicle."*

"Tac team, respond to front gate," the command post ordered.

"Car coming in," I told Natalie. "Erika."

Natalie smiled, a flash of white teeth behind her

woodland veil. She tracked the binoculars around, and I followed with the monocular, so we both could watch.

Marguiles had got her the right car for the job, a Ford Mustang convertible, black. Erika pulled up to within twenty feet of the gate before stopping.

"Too close," Natalie muttered. "They keep letting people get too damn close to that gate."

Neither of the guards in the gatehouse were men I recognized, both nondescript, maybe in their thirties or early forties. Both looked fit. One of them emerged to speak to Erika.

The other guard, still in the gatehouse, raised his radio. Over the scanner I heard him say, *"Solo driver. Female."*

"No one is expected," the command post radioed back.

"Roger. We'll see what she wants."

The other guard was speaking to Erika through the gate, and she put a hand to her undamaged ear, as if trying to hear him better. The Cushman had come to a stop thirty feet or so from the gatehouse, and one of the foot patrols was jogging in from the south end of the lawn. Erika shook her head at the guard, not understanding his words, and stepped out of the car. She took a leather knapsack with her, holding it in both hands.

"Clever girl," Natalie said. "That your idea?"

"Hers," I said.

She was wearing one of my dress shirts, sleeves rolled up, unbuttoned, but tied above her midriff, a short skirt, and ankle-boots. Through the scope I could see her mouth highlighted in red. She hadn't actually gone with the fishnets, but she didn't need them.

She made it to perhaps ten feet from the gate before the guard got her to stop. She pointed back to the road.

The guard in the gatehouse radioed, *"She wants directions."*

"Get her out of there," came the swift response, and I recognized the voice as Yossi's.

"Come on, come on," Natalie was repeating. "Commit."

Erika now had the guard on the gate in a conversation, and had managed to close the distance between them to a very sociable five feet or so. The foot patrol was watching from a distance, but one of the occupants of the Cushman was getting out.

I watched Erika laugh, then point at the man in tactical gear coming from the Cushman. The guard turned his back to Erika when he looked.

Natalie groaned.

"Stupid," I agreed.

Erika kept it going for another six minutes, engaging the guard from the Cushman as well, before I heard Yossi saying, *"What's your status?"*

"We're giving her directions to the Caramoor Jazz Festival."

"Get her out of there."

"Affirmative."

"Yossi's getting pissed," I said.

"About time. How long she been at it?"

I checked my watch. "Eleven minutes since she showed."

The gatehouse guard had come out, perhaps to dismiss Erika, but now seemed to be part of the conversation. She had set down her backpack and was opening it. None of the guards were covering their weapons.

Erika came up with a pad of paper and a pen, and actually reached through the gate to hand them to the one in tactical gear.

"Status?" Yossi asked again.

"Just getting her out of here."

He muttered something, then went off the air.

"Yossi's coming out," I told Natalie.

"Time?"

I checked again. "Fourteen minutes."

"I'm giving them an F for this one. A big, fat F."

Erika had taken the pad back and was adjusting her hair.

"There he is," Natalie said.

I panned quickly, saw Yossi storming down the walk to the gate. I panned back and saw that Erika had seen him, too. She said something to the guards, waved, and jogged back to the car. By the time Yossi had reached the gatehouse, she'd begun backing the Mustang around the bend. I couldn't tell if he got a look at her before the car disappeared, but it was academic; he could have seen her from the surveillance monitors.

Natalie and I watched while Yossi gave all of the guards present an inspired scolding, sending them on their way. Then he began a walk around the perimeter, staring hard at the tree line.

"Ah, he made her," I said.

"Doesn't matter. He knows how to play," Natalie said. "Is she going to call?"

"She'll page me when she gets to a phone."

"Go."

"Yes, boss," I said, and slipped out from under the cover, making my way back to the campsite. My pager began vibrating within five minutes, and it took me another five before I got to my phone.

"How'd I do?" Erika asked.

"Brilliant," I said. "What'd you say to them?"

"I told them that I was meeting my boyfriend at the jazz festival in Katonah. I also told them that if he stood me up I was going to dump him. The one in all the heavy gear, his name is Marcus Van Holt. He wrote his phone number on my pad when he offered to draw me a map."

"Did you get any other names?"

"The first guy to talk was Arthur, and the other one in the gatehouse was Sean. That's all I got. Did Yossi recognize me?"

"Doesn't matter, you did exactly what I needed you to do, and you did it well. Leave the paper they wrote on in my room. I'll need it for my report."

"Is that it?"

"Depends. How much longer do you have the car?"

"Mr. Marguiles said I had it for the whole day. He's pretty cool, by the way."

"I like him," I said. "A little after noon, I want you to go to a place called Maria's Pizza, it's on 118, easy to find. Order a pizza to be delivered to the estate, and pay for it in cash."

She giggled. "Pizza?"

"Yeah."

"You know, some people might think what you're doing is mean."

"Mean is in the eye of the beholder," I said.

The pizza arrived at twelve-thirty, and took until almost one to sort out. Fifteen minutes after that, a van from the local cable service pulled up, responding to the service call I'd made after talking to Erika. The television van was replaced by one from a local florist an hour and a half later, delivering a dozen red roses to Arthur at the gatehouse. Last, around five, came a private ambulance.

"This is Dr. Rachel Mosier, calling on behalf of one of my patients," Natalie had told the dispatcher. "His name is Marcus Van Holt, and, sadly, he's suffering from testicular cancer. His radiation treatments have made him extremely weak. I need a transport for him from Amawalk to Cedars-Sinai in Manhattan."

We spied and took our notes and our photographs, and every so often giggled like kids, especially when Yossi wandered around to the back of the estate and gave the finger to the trees. He was facing ninety degrees off of us, but we got the message, and had to duck our heads to keep our laughter from carrying. We also got a hoot out of Marcus Van Holt's response to being summoned to the gate.

"You've got cancer?" I heard someone ask over the radio.

We learned a few things. The guards, all of them, were good about access. No one made it through the gate, no matter how much they yelled. The florist and the cable guy, for instance, yelled a lot, but gained no ground. Consistently, though, the gatehouse let strangers get far too close to the gate.

Most of these were minor mistakes, and fairly obvious distractions. We gave them really only one daylight challenge, an idea I'd come up with the previous day over breakfast.

I took a stick of gum, chewed it up pretty well, and after letting it harden in the sun, bundled it in its wrapper. A little after three, I used a wrist-rocket to launch the gum over the fence.

One of the dog handlers noticed it at a quarter to six, just as it was starting to get dark. Natalie, who was on the scanner, perked up, and murmured, "Oh, that's good."

"What?"

She held up a hand for me to wait, listening, turning her spotting scope to watch. I followed the action through the binoculars. The two dog handlers were sweeping their immediate area, one of them on the radio.

"They found the gum. One of them made a general query to see if anyone was chewing Wrigley's. Got a whole bunch of negative responses. They're going to sweep the estate. Now, that earns an A."

At ten-thirty that night, Natalie said, "Is it just me, or are the foot patrols walking a little farther out than is prudent?"

"They're avoiding the sensors," I said. Only twice since darkness had fallen had I seen anyone actually move into range of the motion detectors. When it had happened, the lights snapped on, bathing their quadrant of the lawn in halogen glare. I understood why the guards were steering clear of them; the lights were blinding—they'd destroy the night vision of anyone in range.

However, it meant that the close perimeter of the house was going unguarded.

"We ought to do something about that," Natalie said.

"Like what?"

"Like shoot at them." She drew her cowl tighter around her face and slipped out of our hiding place.

I sat in the darkness wondering if she was joking, and had decided she must have been when she returned, carrying a rifle that I didn't even know she'd brought.

"Natalie? You're joking, right."

"It's just a .22, nice and quiet," Natalie said. "Suppressed, see?"

The rifle was a bolt-action .22, with a bulge at the end of its barrel where the suppressor had been fitted. After I'd taken a look at the weapon, Natalie went down flat on her belly and used the finger light to check her optics.

"Pop got it for me."

"The suppressor, too?"

"Doesn't hurt to have friends in D.C."

"And what are you planning on doing with it?"

"I'm going to shoot out one of the lights. See how long it takes them to notice it's not working. You want to give me a range? I'm going for the one on the southeast corner."

I used her binoculars to find the bulb. The unlighted fixture wasn't easy to see in the dark, and it took me almost a minute before I was sure I had it. I keyed the laser, got a range reading back of one hundred and seventeen meters, and gave her the numbers.

She nodded and pulled down the bipod legs beneath the barrel, adjusted the scope on the rifle. Then she exhaled, calming herself, and began lining up her shot.

There was a pop, loud enough to cause a creature in the nearby brush to stir and run. Through the binoculars, I saw the bulb disintegrate. The broken glass would be hard to see in the darkness. There was a very good chance no one would notice the light wasn't working at all.

Natalie sighed, and took down the rifle.

"Nicely done," I said. "John Doe would be proud."

At two, Natalie skirted the perimeter to the west side. When she came back an hour later, she said, "Any time, now," and no sooner had she spoken when we heard a long string of bangs and pops off in the distance, the firecrackers Natalie had set on a time fuse.

"Explosions," one of the patrols reported. *"Western perimeter."*

"Roger. Post three, you seeing anything?"

"Negative."

More cracks of gunpowder, closer, a little louder.

"We heard that," said another unit. *"How do we proceed?"*

"Stand by."

Natalie looked at me smugly.

"That it?" I asked.

"Wait for it," she said.

The next series was a lot closer, a lot louder, and a lot more.

"All units, perimeter sweep," snapped the command post. *"Watch that fence."*

Inside the house, three lights blinked on, one after the other. I watched the lights move from a room on the ground floor upstairs, to a room facing the south side of the building. Then the light went off, and another one came on downstairs.

"You think they're moving him?"

"Looks like. Where's the hardened room?" Natalie asked, referring to the room Mosier would move Pugh into if the house came under attack.

"No idea," I said. "From the lights, I'd guess downstairs."

We watched the guards scurry around like ants.

. . .

We gave the guards a chance to relax for most of the next day. Yossi had posted a man on the roof, working with what looked to be some high-powered optics, so Natalie and I had to be more discreet in our movements than we had the days before.

Natalie had bought some fox urine at a hunting supply store in Yorktown Heights, and in the afternoon she moved off upwind and sprayed some. The canine unit had just come on shift, and when the scent hit them, the rottweiler began barking. Max, the German shepherd, stayed silent but alert, under his handler's command.

When the shift changed at three, we pulled back to prepare for the night's finale. I took down the camcorders. We broke camp and humped our gear to where we had parked. Tonight, they'd come looking for us, and to avoid capture we needed to travel light. There was an element of danger to what we'd be doing; the guards would be angry and scared, and they'd be carrying live rounds.

After we'd packed everything away, I pulled out the envelope Marguiles had messengered to my apartment and handed Natalie the generic letter. She took it with a smirk, saying, "They won't catch me."

"They're not incompetent, Natalie."

"No, they're not. But it's a matter of pride. I want to see Pop's expression tomorrow when he listens to our list of mistakes that his team made. What time are we presenting?"

"Marguiles said he'd meet us at the house at three."

Natalie folded the letter and slipped it into her Ghillie suit, and we slowly worked our way back to the primary observation post. I settled in with the binoculars while Natalie went to place our gags and prepare the few other devices we'd be using.

I was looking forward to being finished. The pleasure in performing an audit, for me, is the academic puzzle; finding the holes and then exploiting them. Like Dale, I preferred to sleep in my bed more than the dirt. A hot shower, a hot meal, and eight hours with my head on a pillow were now near the top of my list of priorities.

Natalie tapped me on the shoulder at a quarter past ten, surprising the hell out of me. I kept myself from yelping.

"Don't do that," I said.

"I thought you heard me coming."

"I didn't hear anything," I said.

Natalie handed me a paper bag and the thermos we'd been using for coffee. "Everything's placed. We've got fifty-six minutes."

"Get comfortable," I said.

She hunkered down beside me. There was the barest whine as her night vision goggles powered up. I stayed on the scanner and opened the paper bag. Inside were four bottle rockets. I positioned the fireworks, placed the disposable lighter she'd brought within easy reach.

At ten of eleven, Natalie said, "I'm going to take position. See you tomorrow."

"Don't get caught."

"They'll never take me alive."

She pulled back into the brush and disappeared. The scanner was on my belt, and I put the headphones back on, checked my watch. When it read eleven, I opened the thermos. A small cloud of steam rose in the

darkness. I emptied the hot water, then poured one of
the sixteen Super Balls that had been heating inside the
thermos into my palm.

I took the wrist-rocket and one of the Super Balls,
checked my watch once more, and let the ball fly. I was
aiming at the guardhouse when the Cushman came
into view, and so I chose that as my target instead. It
was too dark to see the ball actually hit, but a couple
seconds after I'd fired, the cart braked.

I reloaded and lobbed a heated ball at the house.

"Something's going on," a voice said on the scanner.
"I think something just hit one of the windows."

"Stand by. We'll get someone to check it out."

By "check it out," they intended to get someone
onto the roof wearing goggles not dissimilar to those
Natalie wore. This, as Erika would have said, was the
mean part. The heated rubber balls would show up as
bright streaks when seen with infrared. They'd look an
awful lot like tracer fire, or even bullets.

I waited another sixty seconds, then fired off three
back-to-back, aiming all at the house. As I was loading
the third, a voice came over the scanner, saying, *"Holy
shit! Someone's firing on us! I'm seeing shots, I'm
seeing shots—"*

*"Stand by, see if you can pinpoint. This is the com-
mand post, all units, you are on alert."*

There was a quick babble of voices, several trans-
missions cutting one another off. I heard Mosier order
that the principal be moved to the hardened room
immediately. He sounded worried.

Good, I thought.

I kept firing Super Balls, letting them rain down on
the house and the grounds. The radio traffic was loud
and busy, but no one was moving out yet. A point in

their favor; they were securing the principal before trying to identify the threat.

Yossi came on the radio. *"Tac Team prepare response. Everyone keep your head on, now. Team Two, secure the fence. Teams Three and Four prepare to sweep out. Three, take the north perimeter; Four, take the south. Canine?"*

"Canine, go ahead."

"See if you can get a scent. Don't loose the dogs."

"Ten-four."

A new voice broke in, frightened and swearing. *"There's something out there!"*

The strobe light Natalie had placed on a timer went off. The bright light was eerily disconcerting as it flickered on the perimeter opposite me.

"I want light," Yossi ordered.

There were two loud booms, explosions, and then a bottle-rocket salvo went off. More consternation, more yelling over the radios. I set off half of the fireworks from my paper bag, trying to angle them into the grounds.

The guard on the roof began launching flares, pumping them up and over the trees on every side, with an extra heading my way. The flares dropped on their tiny parachutes, glowing white, turning everything below to daylight. All of a sudden, my hiding place wasn't very good at all.

Time to go, I decided, and began unhooking the scanner. Three more bottle rockets went off, and another couple of flares. I could hear the dogs barking. They were loud. They sounded close.

I ran for it.

A new flare went up every twenty seconds or so, just as the previous one was burning out. The light killed the shadows, left nowhere to hide. The dogs were adding growls to their barks, and I was certain they had to be ten, at most fifteen feet away. I didn't bother looking. The adrenaline was flowing, and I was flying over the forest floor, and then I was tripping, tumbling, finding my feet again, and rushing on.

They were pissed, and, letter or no, Mosier would want to take it out on me.

I know they didn't chase me the whole way. Yossi would have ordered the guards to go no more than a mile from the estate.

I didn't stop running until I reached my bike, anyway.

Natalie had already gone, and it was quiet, very still. In the distance, I could see the flares being put up around the grounds.

I changed clothes quickly, stuffing my filthy camouflage into the saddlebags, pulling on a pair of jeans, a shirt, my jacket, all the while trying to catch my breath. I started the BMW, pulled out before the engine had a chance to warm up, and had to gun it to keep from stalling out. I took the road too fast, leaning hard on the curves, and then I broke out of the boondocks, and was on the highway, heading home.

I was almost back in the city before I could stop laughing. It wasn't funny at all, in a way; Natalie and I had given the guards a good scare; at the same time, I had a feeling of accomplishment I hadn't tasted in a while. We'd done a good job, a hard job, and I was proud.

I parked the bike in the garage, started upstairs, and then decided I'd earned a beer. At the corner bodega, I bought four bottles of Anchor Steam and a leftover

copy of the *Daily News,* leafed through it on my way
back home and up the stairs. Havel had another story,
and I saw Nathan d'Angelo's name. I folded the paper
and shoved it in my grocery sack, then did a balancing
act while I struggled for my keys. I was thinking about
how much I was going to enjoy shaving. Then I
planned to drink one of my beers while in the shower.

Erika had told me she was spending the night at
Bridgett's, so I didn't bother trying to be quiet when I
opened the door. I kicked it back with my foot, slipped
inside, used my butt to close it. The street light was
enough to see by, and I went to the kitchen, dropping
my sack on the table. I'd turned around to reach for
the light when I realized I wasn't alone.

"Hey, Erika," I said.

A shadow moved, raised a hand, and then my vision
exploded white, blinding, and I was caught under the
flares once more, with no place to hide.

CHAPTER SIXTEEN

"Taser," the woman said. "You'll be all right in a couple of minutes."

There was a white noise, and a lot of pain.

I tried to speak.

Failed.

Every muscle in my body had seized, spasming from the shock. I was aware of her moving, of her hands on my body as she frisked me. Out of the corner of my eye, I saw her discarding my pager and my wallet.

There was a tearing sound, like fabric being ripped, and the noise and the pain stopped. I urged my muscles to help me move, but they wanted nothing to do with any orders my brain had for them. I tried catching my breath, tried to look at the intruder in my home, and had a rush of true fear when I realized she was right above me. She was wearing black gloves, and the Taser had been replaced with a knife.

I couldn't move.

She went down on one knee. I felt the metal blade touch my throat. I closed my eyes. The blade moved, and I felt my shirt tear twice. The shirt came off me, now a rag. My shoes were next, then my socks. Then she unfastened my belt and yanked my jeans down and off my legs. She ran her hands up my legs, around, frisking my shorts.

There was something wrong with her face. Too big, half of it too pale, the other half impossible to see, melting into darkness.

She stowed the knife and brought out a pistol. It was a semi-automatic, silenced, and it targeted my head and didn't waver, didn't drop, didn't pull, even when she backed up to check the hall again. Once she was certain no one had heard us, she turned back to me.

"You're not carrying a weapon." Her voice was soft but slightly muffled. Her accent was Mid-Atlantic.

"No," I said.

"Up," she ordered.

I got up. I moved like cooling lead.

"Sit on that tragic couch," she said. "Indian style, if you please, hands in your lap."

I walked into the living room, sat as she had directed me. The floor was cold on my bare feet, and the walk seemed to take forever. I wondered if I was dreaming, if I hadn't wiped out on the Taconic, if I wasn't dead or dying.

Or about to die.

She sat in the chair that faced the couch, holding the gun on me. She crossed her legs at the ankles. Her outfit was black, sleek, the sort of thing cat burglars wear in John Woo movies. She was maybe my height, a little slighter. I saw a glimpse of hair, maybe brown. The cat suit was tight on her, with a pouch on the belt. She looked to be in excellent shape.

Her face was concealed by a plastic mask, one half

in marble white, Comedy, the other in pitch black, Tragedy. The cutout for her mouth was outlined, maybe in red. I couldn't be sure.

She let me look her over without comment, then turned the mask slightly to take in the room. She pointed with one hand to the wall above me. The other hand remained on the gun. The gun remained centered on me.

"Macabre," she said.

I nodded. She was pointing at a painting that Rubin had done before he had died. It was a piece in two frames that he had called "Gun 'n Head." The first frame depicted a hand firing a semi-automatic pistol at the second frame, complete with cone of flame and ejecting shell. Frame two was of a man's head, looking full on, with the bullet exiting on the far edge, trailing blood and gore. The piece had been done in acrylics, very cartoony, and yet managed to cross the line, to be both serious and flip at the same time. The victim's expression was more one of stunned disbelief than pain or rage.

I was identifying with that painting a lot right about now.

The woman in the drama mask said, "I'm an associate of the person you know as John Doe."

"Of course you are," I said. "Now what?"

"Now we talk," she said. "Think you can handle a little conversation?"

"You've got the gun."

"I do, indeed." If she thought I was funny, only half of her mask showed it.

The weapon in her hand was another H&K P-7, but the designation S model, made to be silenced. I'd never seen it outside of a photograph. The weapon was supposed to be used by counter-terrorist groups only, GSG-9 and the SEAL teams.

"You're not talking," she said, and mimed a mouth, her thumb the flapping lower lip.

"I was admiring your weapon," I said.

"It's a nice one, isn't it?"

"Lovely."

There was a muted popping noise, the sound of a shell hitting my floor, and the sudden smell of gunpowder in the air.

"Accurate, too," she said.

I looked at the new hole in my couch, this one only half an inch from my left shoulder.

"I'd appreciate it if you wouldn't do that again," I said. Somehow, I kept my voice from climbing.

"Guns don't kill people . . ."

"It's the bullets, yeah, I know," I said.

She used her free hand to indicate my abdomen, pointing at the scar with her index finger. "Recent?"

"Recent enough."

"Gut wounds are the worst."

"They are."

"I got shot, once," she said. "Through-and-through from a .38." She used her free hand to pat her left leg, traced a line along the outside of her thigh with her index finger. "Hurt like hell."

"How'd you get hit?" I asked.

The mask canted to a side briefly as she considered her answer. "When I was younger, before I met John, I did some work like yours," she said, finally. "And somebody didn't like me."

"Hardly seems possible."

"I know. Way I see it, I'm friends with the world."

"You can afford to be when you're holding the gun."

"Sarcasm," she said. "Aren't you friends with the world, Atticus?"

"No."

"Didn't think so. Neither is John."

"Nice that we have that in common."

"Oh, you have more than that, believe me. I've been researching you for him, ever since you kept the mark from getting killed during the Chambers Street deposition. Impressed him. Impressed me, too, but John's the man who counts, of course."

"I was in the right place at the right time."

"No, it wasn't just luck. You took that round on skill. John thinks you're good at this."

"John's in the minority."

"Don't be modest, Atticus," she chided. "You're certainly doing a better job than Trent. What the hell was that at the Orsini? Was it supposed to be an insult? Registering the guest in the mark's name. Did Trent expect that to work?"

"Yeah, I think he did."

"You saved him a lot of embarrassment, at least according to the latest article in the *News*. Have you read Mr. Havel's piece? He's building you up quite nicely."

"I haven't been keeping up with the papers," I said. If she thought Chris Havel was a man, at least there was something she didn't already know.

"Hard to get home delivery when you're in the bush."

"Been keeping tabs on me?"

"Don't flatter yourself. John's path and yours have crossed more times than you know, that's all. And, like I said, he's impressed."

"So you're just spying on me for the hell of it?"

"Not an entirely unpleasant way to pass the time."

"I'm glad I've got some entertainment value."

"Does it bother you, knowing that you've been under surveillance? Some men might be flattered, knowing they were the object of a woman's attention."

"If you want to ask me out on a date, go right ahead. Maybe dinner and a movie?"

"I don't think so. You could never just love me for who I am. You'd only say yes because I'm holding a gun, after all."

"You could put the weapon down."

"Not really."

"I'm not that dangerous."

"Don't insult me," she snapped, and the gun went a little more parallel to the ground. The opening at the end of the silencer was perfectly round, barely visible in the darkness. "There's no need."

"Depends on whether you're looking down the barrel or the sight," I said. It probably wasn't a smart thing to say. It could probably get me killed. I wondered if I'd get a shower and a six of good beer in the afterlife. Simple pleasures.

She didn't respond. Outside, I heard someone singing in Spanish as they walked past, voice cracking in sorrow. The song faded.

"We have to gather our intelligence, same as you have to gather yours," the woman said. "It's always good to know something about the man you're up against. You and John are a lot alike."

"Ironic," I said. "But wrong."

"How so?"

"Hmm, let's see . . . One, I don't kill people for a living. Two, I don't kill people for a living. Three . . . should I continue?"

"You're being simplistic. You can't apply an outdated morality to the actions and reactions of this day and age. I'd have thought you knew better."

"I somehow doubt we see the world the same way," I said. "In my world, killing people is wrong."

"You think John is crazy," she said.

"I think his wiring is faulty, yeah."

"And mine?"

"Jury's still out."

"What's your attorney think?"

"That I should take a shower and go to bed. How about yours?"

"That we should chat a little longer. Aren't you enjoying yourself?"

"Not really, no."

"And here I thought we were having such a nice time."

"The jury just came back," I said. "You're sprung."

She seemed to like my response, and leaned forward slightly. Her voice was friendly, easygoing. "No. John and I, we're professionals. This is our trade, like protection is yours. Trying to reduce either of us to lunatics with a death fetish is a mistake. John does a job, and he does it exceedingly well."

"An immoral job."

"You've never protected someone you didn't like? The mark is the mark."

"Not the same."

"Precisely the same."

My glasses were sliding down my nose, but I didn't adjust them for fear she would shoot me. Then I decided that she might shoot me anyway, and so I fixed them.

"You ought to wear contacts," she said. "You'd look better without the frames."

"Thanks for the fashion tip."

"Like your shorts, too."

"My silk ones are at the laundry."

"No, they're in your bureau. Upper left-hand drawer. Don't really seem your style, though."

"They're for special occasions. If it wasn't you who died at the Orsini, who was it?"

The mask bobbled for a moment as she reacted. "Me? You think I'm John?"

"I think everything you've said to me so far is a lie. No reason John Doe has to be a guy."

"You wound me," she said.

"I also think that he—or she—is smart enough to know that working alone is the only way to stay entirely anonymous."

"Working alone gets lonely."

"Is that what you are? Lonely?"

"Aren't you? The apartment was empty when I got here. Aren't you lonely, Atticus?"

"How could I be? I've got you."

She remained motionless for a couple of seconds. Our serenader had long gone, and there was only silence. "The Orsini corpse was nobody of consequence. Just a subcontractor hired by John."

"Lot of effort for a decoy," I said.

She shrugged. "Think of what would have happened if the hit had been successful. Trent would have had a lot of explaining to do then, wouldn't he?"

I didn't say anything. If Doe's hit had succeeded, Corry, Natalie, Fife, d'Angelo, and I would have died. The hit wouldn't have just embarrassed Trent; it would have destroyed him. He'd have lost his business, his reputation, and his daughter, and the security around Pugh would have gone out the window with us.

"You understand," she said. "John said you would."

"That John, he's a crafty bugger. Pity he couldn't oin us tonight, huh?"

"Well, he's a busy fella. And, frankly, I wanted a chance to talk to you."

"Why?"

"I told you. I've been doing my research. I've been watching you."

"And now you know all about me."

"Actually, yes. Want to hear?"

"Only if it's nice," I said. "I only like hearing people talk about me if they're going to be nice."

"I'll try. Let's see . . . you're twenty-nine years old and your birthday is October ninth. Your SSN's 550-02-0012. You have two accounts at Citibank, checking and savings. Total balance is just over four thousand dollars. You were born at the UCLA Medical Center in Los Angeles, but were raised in San Francisco.

"You enlisted in the United States Army at the age of nineteen. You received your professional training at the Executive Protection Center at Fort Bragg, North Carolina. Your record is clean, some insubordination issues, but several commendations. You left the service just prior to your twenty-fifth birthday, having worked as the OCBG for three ranking officers and having served in the CID.

"How am I doing?"

"Fine," I said. All of the information was available, certainly on computer somewhere, if you knew how to look. That she—or her employer—had discovered it was not surprising. That she felt the need to share it with me, that was annoying.

"I'll continue," the woman in the drama mask said. "You live here with Erika Danielle Wyatt, whose father

you protected at the Pentagon. Both of her parents are
dead. You're her legal guardian—"

"Don't try—" I started to say.

"Relax, Atticus. We're not going to leverage you
through Erika. We don't work that way."

"That makes me feel a whole lot better," I lied.

"Would you prefer if we did?"

"I'd prefer if you didn't work at all."

"But then you'd be out of a job. We *need* one
another."

"Bullshit," I said.

She paused, and again, I wished I could read her expression behind the mask. Even her eyes were invisible
behind the slits. I imagined they were brown, but that
was just a guess.

"Your parents are both college professors," she resumed. "Your mother teaches English literature, your
father Judaic studies. You have a younger brother, also
an academic, enrolled at the University of Oregon in
Eugene. Didn't have time to discover what his field is,
though."

"He's pursuing a Ph.D. in American lit.," I said.

"Really? Family of academics, you went into the
Army. Why?"

"I thought you'd have figured that out."

"I'm not the FBI. I don't do profiles. You want my
assessment of your personality, I can give you that. But
I don't read minds."

"You'd love what I'm thinking right now," I said.

"Is it dirty?"

"It's certainly obscene."

"Care to share?"

"Take off the mask."

"I do and I'll have to kill you."

"So I'm getting out of this conversation alive, am I?"

"That's the plan. In fact, I think I should be going. It's very late."

"I'm free for the rest of the night. Want to split a couple beers, shoot the shit?"

"Ooh, that's tempting, but sorry. People to do, things to meet, you know how it is." She got out of the chair gracefully. The gun stayed zeroed on me.

"What's the rush?"

"You haven't heard? Lamia reconsidered his decision to withdraw from the case. The trial will take place as scheduled. It's going to be an extremely busy two weeks."

She stood a few feet from where I sat, and her mask tilted as she cocked her head to study me. Again, I found myself wondering if I wasn't actually lying in a hospital somewhere, making this whole scene up.

If so, my subconscious and I needed to have a long talk.

"Let me show you out," I said.

"No, you can stay right where you are, thanks." She put her free hand into her pocket, brought it out again holding a small black box with two metal nubs protruding from its end.

"You don't need that," I told her.

She laughed softly. "You keep trying, I'll give you that. It was nice meeting you, Atticus Kodiak. Unfortunately, I don't think we'll be seeing each other again."

And before I could move, she put the stun gun to the base of my skull and flicked the switch.

Blackout.

CHAPTER SEVENTEEN

She was long gone when I came back. The clock on the VCR said it was almost six, and the sunlight filtering into the room agreed with the numbers. My head ached. On my chest, just over my left breast, were two tiny holes, perhaps three inches apart, where the Taser had hit me and broken skin. There was some redness, but no blood.

I straightened up and sat on my couch in my underwear for almost another hour before moving, wondering what the hell had happened here. Why would John Doe send me his regards? Why send his lackey to do it for him? Why believe any of it?

She had all but told me that another attempt on Pugh's life was imminent. Why do that when she knew I'd be obligated to try and protect him? Unless she—or John Doe, presuming they were two different people—didn't think that highly of me after all.

My mind raced, spat out theory after theory. There was no John Doe, there was only the woman in the mask, Drama. Or there was a John Doe, and Drama had nothing to do with him; she was a joke, a test, a gag. Mosier and Trent's way of getting revenge. Maybe they were auditing me in return for the job I'd done on them over the last few days. Or maybe everything she'd said was the truth. She worked for John Doe, and John Doe had been impressed, and wanted to say as much. It couldn't be that often that one of the Ten found their plans thwarted.

But I couldn't believe it. There had to be more to it than that. I was dealing with people who made plans about the plans they were planning on making. Drama, John Doe, whoever, they wouldn't do anything unless it worked for them, unless it forwarded their own goals.

My muscles ached, and my quadriceps nearly went out on me when I got to my feet. I used the wall to steady myself, waited until my legs remembered the principles of balance, and then I lumbered into the kitchen. I picked up the phone and dialed Marguiles at home.

"Atticus?" he asked.

"Is Lamia back on the case?"

"How did you know? I was only notified last evening."

"Why did he change his mind? Why did he come back?"

"No idea. He hasn't returned any of my calls since the bombing. My secretary should be hearing from his office today about scheduling the make-up depo."

"No way to keep that from happening?"

"None. Lamia has the absolute right to depose Pugh before we go to trial. If he doesn't get that deposition, he'll go to Judge Halendall and ask him to bar Pugh from testifying, and Halendall will grant the motion. Which means I'll be going into court without Pugh's testimony, and without Pugh's testimony, I have no case."

"They'll try again," I said. "John Doe will try again. That's what he's been paid to do."

"Maybe he doesn't know there's going to be another deposition."

"He knows," I said.

I hung up my phone, went into my bedroom. I lay down on the bed and pretended that I could sleep.

At a quarter to four I pulled up to the gate outside the Westchester estate. Merle was on duty, and his split lip was healing nicely. He asked me for my wallet, confirmed my identity and my presence on the visitor's list, and allowed me onto the hallowed ground. Natalie's Infiniti was parked in the driveway, beside Marguiles' Mercedes. I was late and I knew it.

The guard at the door directed me to the same study where Natalie and I had found Trent exactly a week before. She was waiting outside the closed door, impatient and irritated.

"Sorry I'm late," I said.

"Where the hell were you?"

"Overslept."

"Jesus, it's almost four."

"Long story. There was a woman in my apartment when I got home last night, and it wasn't Erika. She gave me a couple hundred thousand volts' worth of shocks, and told me John Doe liked me."

Natalie said, "The fuck you say."

"Swear to God. Wore a mask, and never gave me an opening at anything. Very professional, very cool. Slick."

"Are you all right?"

"Better now. Scared me."

"What did she want?"

"She said she worked for Doe, and that he wanted to pay his respects, some bullshit. Said I had done a good job saving Pugh from the bomb. Added some unkind things about your father."

"You're sure you're okay?"

I nodded. "Did you present already?"

"Finished fifteen minutes ago. Mosier was rude, Yossi was attentive, Marguiles was curious, and my father—" She shrugged. "They asked me to step outside. I assume they're discussing our findings right now."

"You have a copy?"

Natalie handed me several typed sheets from her satchel, held together at the corner with a metal clip. "Where's yours?"

"I didn't get to it."

"It's probably just as well. Pop would have gone through it with a magnifying glass, looking for a way to screw you."

"What have I done now?"

"You've been talking to a reporter."

"Havel?" I said. "No I haven't."

"That's what I told him, too. Neither of us has had time to be leaking to the press. But there was a story in yesterday's *Daily News* about the Sentinel operation at the Orsini Hotel, and it quoted both d'Angelo and an anonymous source inside the protective effort."

"Bad?"

"Bad for Pop. He comes off looking like a psycho. D'Angelo's still talking about suing."

The door opened and Yossi motioned us inside. He looked serious, but murmured hello to me when I went past.

Trent was still behind the desk, as if he hadn't moved in seven days. Mosier was standing behind him, and Marguiles was seated in one of the reading chairs. Yossi went back to his seat on the couch. Natalie and I remained standing, as if summoned to the headmaster's office for acting up in class.

"We've considered your report," Trent said. "And after discussion, have agreed it has some merit. We will follow your recommendations on several points, particularly posting a two-guard watch on the roof of the house to reinforce our counter-surveillance of the perimeter, and we'll add another foot patrol. We'll also be instructing the guards to keep their defensive zone at the gate to a minimum of thirty feet."

Natalie nodded.

"Why don't you two sit down," Marguiles suggested. "I'd like you to be here for the next bit of business."

Neither Mosier nor Trent liked that, but Trent was the only one to speak. "They're not part of the operation. They don't need to remain."

"All the same, I'd like them here." Marguiles' voice was mellow, asking for Trent's indulgence.

"Would you like more information being leaked to the press, too?" Trent asked him. "We should keep this meeting need-to-know."

Natalie looked at me, and I shrugged, took the chair next to Marguiles. Natalie sat on the couch beside Yossi.

"We can't discuss it if he's here," Trent insisted.

"I'm not leaking anything to the media," I said.

"You're lying."

I shook my head.

"So how's Havel getting his information?"

"First of all, Havel is a she, not a he. Second, maybe she's good at her job."

"She's quoting an anonymous source," Trent spat. "Someone who wants me to look bad."

"And you think it's me?"

"It is you."

I looked at Mosier. "I can understand that, Elliot. After all, your employees have been treated so well of late."

"It's irrelevant," Marguiles told Trent. "The article doesn't mention Pugh, doesn't give any details about what's going on here, now. It only describes your undertaking at the Orsini Hotel." There was an edge in his voice. "Neil Lamia intends to depose Pugh on Monday. We agreed to take the deposition at the Sheraton in Midtown. We'll get a suite, hold it until the depo is done."

"It's a bad idea," Yossi objected.

Trent said, "I agree."

Marguiles turned to me. "I assume you're with them on this?"

"You already know what I think," I said.

Leslie Marguiles nodded, rubbed his chin, making his whiskers rustle. He said, "I explained to Atticus this morning that there's really no choice in the matter. It's a question of discovery. Lamia must be allowed to question Pugh prior to trial. If he doesn't, he'll make certain Pugh never takes the stand. I recognize that the situation places Jerry in jeopardy, but there is no other recourse."

"All right," said Trent. "We'll work with it. Ray, take the advance team down to Manhattan immediately, do a work-up of the Sheraton, get an idea of where we'll be most vulnerable. Yossi, I want you—"

Marguiles cleared his throat. "Excuse me, Elliot, but I want your daughter and Mr. Kodiak to handle the security for the deposition."

"With all due respect, Leslie, you—"

"Is this a problem?"

"They're not qualified. They don't have the manpower, the support, or the expertise for this kind of operation."

"You misunderstood me," Marguiles said, mildly. "I don't want them taking over for you. I just want them protecting Jerry. Running the close work, I think is the way you phrase it."

Mosier glared.

"Absolutely not," Trent said, eyes locked on Marguiles. "There's a team assigned for the purpose, Ray is in charge of it. I won't switch my people in mid-operation."

"Why not?"

Trent paused, and I could see him thinking. There were several legitimate reasons for not wanting to follow Marguiles' instructions, and only one personal one. But Marguiles was paying the bills. That gave him the limited right to make requests, even ones as out of the ordinary as this.

Trent finally said, "They work independently."

"I expect your firm to help them," Marguiles said.

"We'll maintain the operation here and provide guards at the deposition."

"I want them protecting Jerry during the deposition, and during travel."

Trent's jaw muscles moved. "It's not standard operating procedure."

"It would make me feel better about Jerry's chances," Marguiles said, mildly.

Trent turned to Natalie and me. The way they had been talking, we might've vanished from the room, but now we were back, worthy of notice. "You can liaison with my people. I'm sure you know how to get in touch with them."

"Good," said Marguiles, rising from the chair. "I expect there's work you all need to do. Atticus, if you'll walk me to my car?"

I got up, looked at Natalie. "Meet you out front?"

She began to agree, but her father interrupted, saying, "I'd like to speak to you, Natalie. Alone, if that's not a problem."

"Fine."

I followed Marguiles out of the room, Yossi and Mosier behind us. Mosier slammed the door, then stormed off down the hall. Yossi patted me on the back and said, "I'll be around."

"I'll find you," I said.

Marguiles led me to his car. "I assume you can do this?" he asked.

"Protect Pugh? I can't give you any guarantees."

"Nor could Trent, he made that quite plain when I hired Sentinel. But he was optimistic. You, I think, are more realistic."

"No, I'm pessimistic," I said. "It's a bad situation. John Doe knows about the deposition. He's already planning something."

"Then I trust you to put a stop to whatever he's planning." Marguiles unlocked the door to his Benz. "When you prepare your bill for the audit, send over a contract that I can sign, retaining you and Ms. Trent."

"We don't have a contract."

Marguiles looked surprised. "I thought you had a partnership."

"No. We're just friends."

"Well, draw something up all the same. We want to keep the papers in order. For the lawyers, you know."

"We need to talk about the money," I said.

"Am I paying a flat fee or a daily rate?"

"Short-term job. Flat fee. Thirty-five hundred dollars for each of us."

Marguiles arched an eyebrow. "Seven thousand dollars?"

"We're probably going to get shot at," I said.

He took that in, then nodded once. "Send over a contract. I'll have the check cut to you as soon as it's signed."

I watched him go. After the gate had closed behind his car, I headed back to the house, asked the guard at the door where I could find Yossi.

"I'll call him for you, sir." The guard was about five eight, trim and in shape, with light brown hair. I put him a couple years younger than me.

"Thanks."

After he had used the radio, the guard asked me, "You're Kodiak?"

"That's right. Atticus." I offered my hand.

"White, Pete White." He shook my hand. "You're an asshole."

"Yeah, sorry about last night."

"We were finding those goddamn rubber balls all over the place once the sun came up. Maximum pucker factor, let me tell you."

"Let me guess," I said. "Army?"

"Yes, sir. I started out as a leg, went up to the Eighty-second Airborne."

"Paratrooper," I said.

He smiled with regimental pride. "Yes, sir. I'd done some skydiving as a civilian, so they put me on the Golden Knights."

That earned him a second look. You didn't get selected for the Golden Knight demonstration team just because you knew how to pull a rip cord. The Army prefers its show-offs to know their shit.

"White," I said, "what the hell are you doing here?"

"Well, after getting paid to jump out of airplanes for four years, going to work at Jiffy-Lube just isn't the same."

"Last night wasn't personal, you know that?"

"Yes, sir." His smile broadened. "But you're still an asshole."

Yossi led me to Pugh's room, saying, "It's sort of strange in there."

"Strange how?"

"You'll see."

We stopped outside the door, and Yossi introduced me to the guard standing post. The guard acknowledged me, then went back to watching the hall. He didn't have anything to say. Most of the guards, with the exception of White, didn't have anything to say.

If you can't say anything nice, etc.

I knocked and a voice hollered, "Who is it?"

"Atticus," I said. "We met last week."

"Hell, son, come on in. It's unlocked."

"See you later," I told Yossi.

"Maybe before you leave."

I stepped into the room. All the walls had been decorated in Pugh's collages. Cigarette ads cut to form mushroom clouds, raging infernos, tanks, guns, bombs, spikes, spears, knives, hung from each wall. The curtains had been drawn, and the light in the room came from an overhead fixture and three lamps, all shining without their shades. The naked bulbs made me wince.

Jeremiah Pugh was seated on the floor, wearing blue jeans that had faded almost to white and a black denim shirt, surrounded by piles of dirty clothes and cut paper. He was assembling another piece of art, cutting carefully with a pair of scissors around the head of a horse.

"Ever seen *The Godfather*?" he asked.

A jar of rubber cement was uncapped in front of him, resting on some cardboard, and I caught it in the miasma of scents in the air. There was also the smell of alcohol, body odor, and food.

"Don't they let you out?" I asked.

"They run me round the corral once a day, sure. But I'm just on a roll right now. Coming up on hour nineteen. Take a look at these." He used the points of his scissors to nudge a stack of collages my way.

I crouched and leafed through them. They were as bleak as the ones he'd shown me at our first meeting, but more accomplished and more alarming. His cuttings were gradually becoming smaller and smaller. One of the collages was of the Glory Bee, composed entirely of pieces cut from ads featuring the Glory Bee. From the mouth of the patchworked tiger cub hung a cigarette made of children.

"I wanted to say hello," I told Pugh.

"Give me a minute, almost done."

I nodded, set the collage I was holding back on the

stack, and took another look around the room. An empty bottle of vodka was sticking obscenely from a pair of brown slacks. I straightened up, feeling my back twinge again, and saw a syringe on the bureau. Pugh's cowboy boots stood neatly at the foot of the bed. There were several books scattered around, some paperbacks, some medical journals. All of the paperbacks were by Louis L'Amour. Three Hershey bar wrappers were crumpled on the bed, and beside the pillow, on the night-stand, was a photograph of a young man. He looked to be seventeen or eighteen years old, in a graduation gown of bright blue satin with gold trim.

"This your son?" I asked.

"Yeah, that's my boy." Pugh finished placing the clipping he'd been working with, and wiped rubber cement off his hands onto his thighs. He reached out to shake. "Glad you came by. Didn't get a chance to thank you."

I took his hand, and he used my hold to get to his feet. His grip was strong. When he was up, he slapped me on the shoulder.

"Thank you," he said. There was a trace of alcohol on his breath, and maybe the vestiges of his lunch.

"You're very welcome. Quite a place you've got here."

"You like it? I call it home. You want a drink?"

"No, thanks."

Pugh went to the bureau and pulled a bottle from one of the drawers. "Leslie doesn't need me right now, so I'm going to take my afternoon pick-me-up."

He poured himself an inch into a simple glass, capped the bottle and put it away. He sipped at his drink. "You think I'm an alcoholic?"

"Haven't known you long enough."

"But maybe I am?"

"Maybe you are."

"Here, take a sniff," he said, and held out the glass to me.

"Vodka," I said. "I saw the bottle."

"You'd think. Try a taste."

I took the glass, tilted it back. It was vodka, but severely watered down.

"People thought Winston Churchill was an alcoholic. Always had a scotch in his hand. Poured his first one at nine in the morning, honest. Read your Manchester, he'll back me up. But what most people don't know is that he watered the stuff down, nursed the same damn drink for hours. Some fool sees a glass in ol' Winnie's hand, says, 'That man drinks like a fish!' But he didn't. He just liked keeping people off-balance, liked being a character."

"And that's what you're doing?"

"Drives that ponytailed one crazy, that Mosier. Thinks I'm going to get blotto and do something stupid. No, I tell him. I've already done my stupid thing, did it for most of my life. Now I'm playing it smart."

"I wanted to tell you that an associate of mine— Natalie Trent—and I will be taking care of your security during the deposition Monday."

Pugh sat down on the edge of his bed. "Delighted to hear it. Feel safer already."

"We're going to need you to listen to us," I said. "It's more than likely there will be another attempt on your life."

"I will listen attentively, I will respond appropriately, and I will keep my sorry ass in one piece, you have my word. DTS won't even know what hit them by the time I'm done talking." He took a noisy sip of his play-vodka. "People got it wrong for so long. It's not about whether or not cigarettes are bad for you. It's about how DTS knew exactly how bad. You know, they had me working on a safer cigarette for five years? Then they pulled the plug."

"Why?"

"Son, think about it. How the hell could they sell it? They'd have to admit their other cigarettes weren't safe. And that would mean they'd have to admit that they'd known all along that what they were selling was a poison. No, it ain't about the cigarettes, it's about the men behind the smoke. Time for them to take responsibility. Time for them to stand up and admit what they did was wrong. Before God and country, they'll be made to pay."

His voice had stayed level throughout his speech, reasonable and calm, but near the end I had caught another tone. Guilt.

There was noise in the hall, and a shout, and I'd started to grab Pugh before actually thinking about covering him. I had my left hand on his arm and my right dropping to my hip when the door to the room banged open, and the guard from the hall came in and made straight for Pugh.

"We've got an evac," he told me. "Come on, sir, I need to get you down to the hardened room."

"What's going on?" I asked.

The guard had Pugh by an arm, tugging him away from me. I let him go. Pugh scooped up his cowboy boots. He looked alarmed, but not panicked. The guard began pulling him toward the door. Two other guards in plainclothes had appeared outside the room to help with the evac.

"They've found another bomb," the guard stopped long enough to say. "This one's on the grounds. And it may go any second."

CHAPTER EIGHTEEN

The bomb was in a cardboard box, and the cardboard box was nestled against the curve of the propane tank, where the metal met the ground. The box didn't look like all that much. Just an anonymous container, a couple inches high and couple inches wide, no markings, nothing to distinguish it. Except for its placement. It wouldn't take a whole lot of explosive to rupture the tank and start a hell of a fire.

The tank itself stood fifteen feet from the west side of the house, well within the perimeter of the wall. If it went, it would take the house with it. Maybe not in the blast, but certainly in the resulting flame.

I helped the three guards move Pugh to the hardened room—a makeshift bunker in the basement where Pugh could be defended from attack—then made my way outside to find Natalie, her father, Yossi, and another woman I hadn't seen before, staring at the tank.

As I approached, I heard the woman say, "He's out of his mind." She was tall, broad-shouldered, with blond hair and a face with strong lines, pretty.

Raymond Mosier was crawling his way along the

manicured lawn towards the propane tank. He crawled like a soldier, but slowly, as if by moving too fast he might detonate the device prematurely.

"Why are we standing here?" I asked. "Why aren't we getting the hell out of the area?"

"We're waiting," Yossi replied. "Could be a decoy, trying to draw us out."

"Mosier wanted to take a closer look," Natalie said. "Chance to play Superman."

"The fire department has been called," Trent said. "All radios are off. We're prepared to pull out. Ray has some demolitions experience, and he volunteered to examine the device. We need to know if it's real or not. If it's a fake, we could evacuate the estate and take Pugh right into an ambush."

Yossi nodded, but he looked worried.

"And if it is a bomb, Ray could get himself killed," the blond woman said. "And get all of us killed with him."

Mosier had stopped by the edge of the tank, and we watched while he pulled a penlight from his pocket. He shone the light over the cardboard, taking nearly a minute. Then he turned and gave us the hand signal to wait.

Natalie said, "Bullshit, this is all bullshit."

"Give him a chance," Yossi said.

"Yossi, I've been watching your perimeter for three days. It's next to impossible to cross the wall without getting a German shepherd up your ass. There's no way anyone could have snuck in here and planted a bomb. It's got to have come from inside the perimeter."

"I appreciate the compliment," he said.

"You know who I mean," Natalie said softly, and

looked pointedly in Mosier's direction. "There are easier ways to take out the tank. Why use a bomb? Why not park at five hundred meters and put a tracer round into the housing? It doesn't make *sense*. It's not *smart*."

Yossi shook his head, frowning. "Your father's correct. We need to be certain."

She made a noise, rolled her eyes at me. "I can't believe this."

I wasn't sure I could, either. Even if last night's encounter with Drama had been a sham, I still wasn't ready to believe that John Doe would plant a bomb on the estate that looked exactly like, well, a bomb. Why would someone who had replaced a section of a table to hide his last explosive suddenly go so low-tech as to use a cardboard box beneath a propane tank?

And there was no guarantee that the blast or ensuing fire would kill Pugh.

"Could be a decoy," I said. "Another device could be planted somewhere else."

"Convenient that it happened while we're here," Natalie muttered to me.

Mosier was backing away on his belly, preparing to crawl around the tank and approach the box from the other side.

The blond woman's jaw clenched, and she said, "Mr. Trent?"

"We'll wait. We could be heading for a trap. I don't want to take any chances."

The woman said, "I don't do the security, Mr. Trent. But if that thing goes, there won't be any help for me to give. We'll all be crispy critters."

"What do you do?" I asked.

She looked at me in disdain. "I'm the medic."

"Atticus," I said, offering her my hand.

"Karen Kazanjian," she said, ignoring my hand.

Mosier disappeared behind the tank until only his legs showed. We remained still and silent, waiting.

Natalie took a deep breath, then said, "Enough of this."

I saw what she was going to do, and I started to say her name, but she was already off and running, sprinting hard toward Mosier and the tank. Her father shouted something, and Yossi tried to grab her arm as she went by, but she was quick, and he missed.

I started after her, and Yossi spun and threw up a block, catching me on his shoulder. "Don't."

"She's going to—"

"We need to stay back."

Natalie had reached the tank, skidding to a stop and nearly losing her balance as the grass went slippery under her feet. She used the propane tank to right herself, and, with her right foot, kicked the box. It flew out from beneath the tank, tumbling across the lawn, bouncing, rupturing at its edges, and I could see the telltale white of plastique inside. Classic high-explosive.

Mosier had rolled out from under the tank, swearing, and Natalie stepped over him, nearly putting her Fila on his forehead, going after the torn box. Dropping to her knees, she plunged a finger through one of the tears. She waved a bit of the white matter beneath her nose, then touched it with her tongue.

We waited. Mosier pulled himself to his feet.

Natalie spat onto the lawn, looked our way. "Play-Doh," she declared.

I started laughing.

Trent found his breath. "Tell them to stand down," he ordered Yossi. "And find the goddamn guard who reported it, and start reviewing the logs. I want to know how the hell that thing got on the estate."

Yossi released me with a pat on the back. He was trying not to smile as he headed for the house.

Natalie was now sitting with the opened box in her lap. She held up a chunk of the clay and threw it at Mosier, saying, "Hey, Ray! Catch!"

Mosier batted the projectile out of the air, glaring at her. "Cut it out. You could have set it off."

"Take it easy, Ray," she said. "I didn't mean to steal your thunder. You can get the next fake bomb."

"Fuck you, you nearly got us all killed, fuck you!"

Natalie began mashing pieces of the Play-Doh together. "I'd forgotten how much fun this stuff can be."

Mosier turned to Trent in appeal. "She could have killed us all. She could have died. There was no way she could have known it wasn't a bomb. It's got to be Doe. He's fucking with us, trying to psych us out."

"Yossi will review the logs," Trent told him. "We need to find out how it got onto the estate."

"It was him," Mosier insisted. "He's testing us, trying to keep us off-balance."

"We'll see what we find. It's possible."

I turned and headed back to the house, wanting to talk to Yossi. I was at the porch when Pugh came out the front door, alone, blinking in the sunlight.

"A phony, huh?" There was perspiration on his brow, and there was relief in his voice. He'd been afraid for his life, and it showed.

I gave him a push in the chest, back inside. He stumbled, went down on his rear just as his guards

came down the hallway at a run. When they spotted
me, both guards looked embarrassed. I turned around
to close the door. When I faced them again, Pugh
was back on his feet, and his cheeks were coloring
up, fast.

"Son, you don't ever shove me again, you understand?" he snarled. "Don't you ever do that to me."

"You want to get shot?"

He jerked his head back. "What sort of damn asi-
nine question is that?"

"Then don't go outside without protection." I
pointed to the guards. "That's their job, they walk with
you. They give you cover. You don't go outside, ever,
without cover, understand?"

"It was a phony, for God's sake. It's not like I was
going to get blown up."

"So you come running out to look at a phony bomb
and a sniper picks you off. Easy."

His eyes widened in understanding. Then the real-
ization sank in. "Ah, hell," he said, breathless.

"Don't do it again."

He had brought his arms around to guard his
stomach as he tried to slow his breathing. Sweat shone
at the hollow of his throat. Fear plays with people in
funny ways, and for a moment I was afraid he would
hyperventilate and pass out. But Pugh remained steady
on his feet.

"I'm sorry I knocked you down," I said.

"I should have thought." His arms went back to his
sides. He dug out a grin, showed it to me. "Got to
make sure I do my job before the bastards put me
down. Can't fail on this one, right?"

"Right," I said.

He used the cuff of his right sleeve to wipe his forehead. "Let's go back to my room, boys. I'll buy you all some vodka."

"I'll see you Monday," I said.

"Damn straight you will." Pugh started up the stairs. To the guard in front of him, he said, "That boy down there, he's going to keep me alive."

CHAPTER NINETEEN

"Mosier planted it," Natalie told me. "Had to be him."

"Why you figure?" We were in a Chinese noodle house a block and a half from my apartment, talking over dinner. I'd suggested we dine at my place, but Natalie hadn't wanted a confrontation with Erika.

"He's the golden boy and we've been making him look ordinary. He had to get some stock back with Pop."

"I was thinking something similar. If we're running the close protection on Pugh, what's he supposed to do? Maybe he's out of a job."

"Yeah, that could be a part of it."

"We don't have any proof."

"It's just a theory, anyway."

"It's the theory I mentioned to Yossi."

"Oh, did you?"

"Just for the hell of it."

"And?"

"And he said he'll look into it." I reached for the teapot between us, refilled our cups, using the gesture as an excuse to scan the restaurant. There was a woman at the counter I thought I recognized, white, with straight blond hair. She wore dark business clothes, slacks and a blazer, and a pair of expensive running shoes.

Natalie was looking past my shoulder, as if she had forgotten I was there, so I said, "Marguiles wants us to send him a contract. We'll have to draw something up."

Her attention returned to me. "You have something at your place, don't you? Standard boilerplate?"

"Yeah, I'll get it after we eat."

"We're going to need some more help for this."

"Dale," I said.

"Definitely. Maybe Corry, too."

"Corry's on your father's payroll. That might pose a problem for both of them."

Natalie shook her head and then moved her ponytail back over her shoulder. "No, Corry quit, the day after the thing at the Orsini. Told Pop he wouldn't work for someone who figured his employees were cannon fodder."

"Have I told you how much I respect Corry?" I asked.

Natalie grinned. "Yeah, he's got the right stuff, as the test pilots used to say."

The bell hanging on the door jangled and the woman I'd been watching exited just as Chris Havel entered. Havel was wearing a sleeveless purple shirt and blue jeans, and she looked carefully around the restaurant.

"That's the reporter," I told Natalie.

Natalie turned her back to Havel. "She see you?"

I nodded. Havel was making her way to our table. I tried glaring at her to make her stop, but it had the opposite effect. She actually moved a little faster.

Natalie mouthed the word "shit."

"Hi, mind if I join you?"

"Yes," Natalie said.

"We were getting ready to leave," I said.

"Won't take long." Havel pulled up a chair. "Business dinner?"

"Social," I said.

"Really? I wouldn't think you'd have the time, what with the trial back on track and the bomb scare at the estate today." She shrugged. "Shows you what I know, I guess."

"You're remarkably well informed," Natalie said.

"Chris Havel," Havel said. "We haven't met, but I suspect that you're Natalie Trent."

"Who have you been talking to?"

"I've got a source."

"Inside Sentinel?"

"You know I can't possibly answer that."

"What do you want, Chris?" I interposed, trying to head off Natalie's temper.

"Can either of you confirm that a professional assassin has been hired to kill Pugh?"

"We were having dinner," Natalie said.

"Looks like you're finished. Neither of you is willing to go on the record about this?"

"You want a quote?" Natalie asked. "Is that what this is about?"

"I'd love a quote." Havel pulled a notepad from her rear pocket, twisted the end of a black Cross pen, and put its point to a clean sheet.

" 'Mind your own business.' "

"Is it something about me?" She flipped the notepad shut with an irritated flick of her wrist, then jabbed the point of her pen at me. "Why won't you let me in on this?"

"We don't know you," Natalie said.

"We don't need the publicity," I said. "We've got other things to worry about."

Havel leaned in, resting her forearms on the table. She had a tattoo of a wolf on her left shoulder, done in black and gray. It looked new. She said, "This is a big chance for me. Could be a good series of articles, could pan out into a hell of a book. Bodyguards, assassins, life or death, the contest of wills and skills, fucking classic stuff. Let me inside your operation."

I shook my head.

"I've been good to you," she said. "My pieces have been fair and objective, and, yes, a little tabloid. But I've reported the facts as best I could, and you're getting good press. I'm helping you. I can help you more. If you guys tell me what you want me to do, I'll do it. All I want in exchange is the chance to get inside your heads."

"No," Natalie said.

Havel looked intently at me. "I'm not going to quit the story. One way or another, I'll get it."

"I believe you," I said. "And that's why I'm trying to be cool about this, that's why I'm trying to not get pissed off. You smell a story, I understand. But we can't risk our work for you. You've got to back off and leave us alone."

"I can't let it lie."

"You're going to get nothing from us."

She got up, stowing her pad and pen. "Call me at the paper when you change your mind."

We waited until she had left the restaurant before

paying our bill and heading outside. It was dark, Friday night, and there were a number of people about. The woman with the expensive running shoes was three doors down, looking at the bottles displayed in the window of a wine shop.

Natalie slipped her arm around my waist and said in my ear, "We've got a watcher."

"Studying the chardonnay, three doors down. Female," I said.

Natalie moved in front of me, pretended to adjust the collar on my jacket, smiling. She shook her head very slightly. "Behind you, pretending to photograph the street. Male. He's moving this way."

I nodded and put my arms around her and Natalie rested her head against my shoulder. I could feel her body, the tension in my lower back, a ghost of the punch Mosier had landed. Nerves. We stood still, pretending to be lovers while the man pretending to take pictures walked by us, passing the woman who was pretending to contemplate wine. The man was at least half a foot taller than the woman, also in slacks and blazer, also with blond hair. The light on the street gave his hair a blue sheen.

When he passed the woman, he reached up and rubbed his neck with his right hand. That was the extent of their communication.

It was enough, though, because the woman stopped looking in the window, and headed our way. Her right hand disappeared into her coat, under her left arm.

I thought about Trent, and what he'd said about my history of gunfights in downtown.

"She's reaching for something," I whispered, stepping back from Natalie. I dropped my hand, ready to index my weapon. Natalie was turning, her right hand coming back.

The woman stopped, held out her left hand like a cop halting traffic. Her face was shaped like a cat's, plain features. She was smiling.

The man was nowhere on the street.

In my peripheral vision, a homeless woman in three different sweatshirts was pawing through the trash can on the corner.

The cat-faced woman slowly withdrew her right hand from beneath her blazer. Her left hand went back to her side. When neither Natalie nor I moved, the woman stepped forward again.

She was six feet from us when Natalie said, "That's fine."

The woman nodded and offered us the envelope in her right hand. Natalie took it without breaking eye contact.

"They're for tonight," the woman said. Her voice was just loud enough to hear over the traffic, and she hit the final *t* hard. "If you hurry, you'll make it by intermission."

That said, she turned and walked away.

CHAPTER TWENTY

I was staring at five hundred thousand dollars.

Two cashier's checks, one for Natalie, one for me. Crisp, clean, sharp on the edges. I could feel where the numbers had been punched in the heavy paper. The numbers seemed large. The zeroes were impressive.

Onstage, Velma Kelly was entreating Billy Flynn to get her out of a murder rap.

Natalie wasn't paying attention to the stage. She wasn't paying attention to the zeroes, either. She was paying attention to Claire Mallory, Neil Lamia's associate up from Atlanta, sitting opposite us in our box at the Shubert Theatre. Mallory looked relaxed, the checks resting on the handbag resting in her lap. The handbag was big, black leather, and expensive. It looked more like a Danish schoolbag than a purse.

"Two hundred and fifty thousand dollars for each of you, as a retainer," Mallory said for the second time. "Think of it as a signing bonus."

We watched her slip the checks back into her bag. Her fingernails were manicured, lacquered in a shade so light I'd thought at first they weren't painted at all.

She set the bag in her lap, holding it as if she was on the subway and afraid someone might snag it.

Billy Flynn began singing about how everything is just show business.

Natalie and I had opened the envelope the blond woman passed us to find two tickets to that evening's performance of *Chicago*.

"It's already started," Natalie had said, after examining the tickets and checking her watch. "Twenty minutes ago."

"Damn," I said. "I'll be totally lost."

"I'll fill you in. Saw it in May."

"Any good?"

"Worth seeing again." She raised an eyebrow at me and I nodded, and she stepped to the curb to hail us a taxi. There wasn't much point in talking about it; the tickets were an invitation, one that we couldn't really refuse. Whoever the messengers had been—John and Drama, Porgy and Bess, Mutt and Jeff—it didn't really matter.

The cab dropped us in front of the theater shortly before nine. The usher looked at our tickets and explained that he couldn't seat us until intermission, so we waited in the lobby, listening to the music from the stage. Natalie gave me the short version of the libretto while we waited.

Then the music had stopped and the audience had gushed forth, rushing to the rest rooms and the concession stands. The usher presented Natalie and me with copies of *Playbill,* then led us up a flight of stairs and past the lines of private boxes to one about thirty feet from stage left.

Claire Mallory had been waiting within, alone, looking much as she had the first time I'd seen her at
Pugh's initial deposition on Chambers Street. She'd
traded her business wear for a short dress with a round
neck and no sleeves. The dress was sage green, and its
hem ended just above her knee. She'd given us both
handshakes, told us that she was sorry we hadn't been
able to arrive sooner, and asked if we wanted a quick
synopsis of what we'd missed.

"What I want," I'd said, "is an explanation."

"It would be my pleasure."

And out had come the money, followed by the offer.

"I'm empowered to negotiate if the fee is an issue,"
Mallory said. I had to lean forward to hear her. Every
time she moved her head I caught a whiff of her per-
fume, a mix of fruit and flowers that was making my
chest tighten.

"Negotiate on behalf of DTS," Natalie said.

"Of course. This has nothing to do with Lamia and
Brackman." She opened her bag again, removed two
sets of papers. I caught a glimpse of the checks, a hairbrush, a compact. She handed a set of papers to each
of us.

Contracts. Fifteen pages long and effusively legal.

"Feel free to review them."

"Give us the short version," I said.

"Happily. These contracts retain you and Miss Trent
as exclusive security consultants for DTS Industries
for a period of one year commencing tomorrow morning at a salary of eighty-four thousand dollars a month.
That's in addition to the signing bonus, of course. The
contract assures full medical benefits for yourselves, as

well as any dependents, and covers moving expenses, incidentals, and any other fees that may be incurred during that year."

"In exchange for which, we do what, exactly?" Natalie's eyes were on the stage.

"You and Mr. Kodiak assume responsibility for the security of the DTS board of directors at home and abroad, both in domestic and industrial matters."

"Doesn't DTS already have a firm retained?" I asked.

"DTS uses three firms, actually. Anderson Vigilant provides plant security in Virginia and the Carolinas. Threat Defense 2000 handles office security in LA, Houston, and St. Louis. And Omega Technologies is contracted to provide counter-surveillance and electronic security to deter industrial espionage."

"Good firms," I said. All of them were, even if they had stupid names. They were also all big firms with legions of specialists in their ranks. Not only were Natalie and I outclassed by comparison, we weren't even attending the same school.

"They're extremely good," Claire Mallory agreed. "For what they're required to do. But you'll have noted, no doubt, that none of those firms specializes exclusively in personal protection."

"And that's why DTS wants us?" Natalie sounded skeptical.

"There is a concern that individual executives may be in danger," Mallory replied. "Certainly, incidences of kidnapping and extortion are on the rise. DTS would rather be safe than sorry."

I leafed through the contract. As far as I could tell, she was dealing straight. The monies practically jumped off the paper and into my brain.

The song onstage stopped, and the audience broke into polite applause. So did Mallory, though she didn't move her attention from us.

I folded the contract back up and looked at it in my hand. I'd done the math, as she'd known I would, but Mallory said it out loud just to make certain.

"Your individual salaries would come to one million eight thousand dollars a year."

"It's an odd number," Natalie said. I wasn't sure if it was mocking or an honest complaint.

Mallory took it as honest. "As I said, I am permitted some latitude in negotiating. Do you have a counteroffer?"

"Starts tomorrow?" I asked.

"Yes."

"And we're exclusive to DTS?"

"For a period of twelve months. Their feeling is that, for the amount of money they're offering, you should be available whenever they need you. For that reason, you're expected to relocate to Charleston."

I nodded, tried to look away from the contract. Singing from the stage had resumed, but I wasn't hearing it. I was thinking about Erika and college, about my apartment, about my bills. Beside me, Natalie was watching the show.

There was a whole different word for the kind of person who had the money this contract offered. That kind of person owned a home and didn't rent. That kind of person made certain dependents went to college. That kind of person paid bills on time and invested on Wall Street and didn't have to hit up friends for loans of equipment or cash. A millionaire didn't worry about hospital bills or incidental expenses or checks turning rubber or whether or not they'd make it until the next job came.

Natalie was waiting on me, and for a moment I resented her like hell.

"No chance they'd delay the hiring until after we've finished our current job?" I asked.

Mallory shook her head. "No, I'm afraid not. They were quite clear on that point with me. They want you both as soon as possible."

"How convenient," Natalie murmured. "Here we are on one job, and DTS appears with a juicy offer for another."

"You came to their attention as a result of your connection with Mr. Pugh's security," Mallory said. "I admit it puts you in an awkward position, but these aren't patient people. They prefer to move quickly whenever possible. Mr. Kodiak?"

"Hmm?"

"Is everything all right?"

I shook my head.

"Would ninety thousand a month solve the problem?" The innocence in her eyes was almost believable.

"Does Lamia know you're making this offer?" I asked.

She shook her head.

"I'm not clear on legal ethics, Ms. Mallory, but aren't you in breach of something? Acting in a conflict of interest?"

Mallory hesitated, then nodded, perhaps deciding she could trust us. "I was asked by DTS to make this offer."

"Puts you at risk, doesn't it? I mean, if we say no and Lamia finds out, he'll sack you."

"It's possible."

"Certainly remove you from the case."

"No doubt," Mallory said. "But that needn't happen. There's nothing sinister about this, Mr. Kodiak. It's simply a job offer. One that I would leap at, if I were you."

Natalie had her contract folded neatly in her lap. I looked at mine again. The edge where I was holding it was crumpled.

Mallory opened her bag one last time, and I realized she was positioning it so I could watch as she sifted its contents. I saw the checks again, and the compact, a hairbrush, a lipstick, and a string of condoms. She glanced up at me and smiled, then looked back to the bag and found what she was looking for. It was a thick Parker fountain pen, with a blue marble finish around its barrel. She uncapped it and offered it to me.

I am the stupidest fucking man I will ever know, I thought. "I can't accept," I said, getting to my feet. "Sorry."

Mallory scooted back in her seat to look up at us as Natalie rose to join me. She didn't seem anything other than disappointed. "That's for both of you?" Mallory asked.

"I wasn't going to be as polite about it," Natalie said.

I handed the contract back to Mallory, and she took it in her free hand while searching my face. "There's a lot to this offer," she said. "A great many perks. I think you should reconsider."

"Good luck in your new job," I said, and headed for the lobby.

.   .   .

Natalie caught up to me on the corner of Broadway and Forty-fifth, calling for me to slow down. I stopped and waited for her to reach me. A man wearing a sandwich board that read XXX ALL WOMEN ALL NUDE XXX stood handing out flyers in front of one of the last sex shops on Times Square. On the near corner, a middle-aged toad of a man was playing percussion on two upturned buckets, accompanied on harmonica by a Hispanic boy who couldn't have been past ten years old. The neon was bright, advertising shining down from all sides.

Natalie stopped beside me and put an arm around my waist, and for a moment I thought she'd spotted another tail, but she wasn't playing any games. She gave me a kiss on the mouth. The guy wearing the sandwich board hooted.

"Consolation prize," Natalie said.

"I'm always going to wonder what those perks would've been," I said.

"I can guess. Claire Mallory, for a start."

"Doubt that."

"She practically waved those rubbers in your face."

I started laughing, and Natalie did, too, and she kept her arm around my waist as we walked down the block. We hailed a cab, climbed in the back, and Natalie gave my address to the driver. It hit me that we'd not shared a bed since starting the audit. Of course the second I thought it, the tension returned, and when the taxi pulled up outside of my building, there was an awkwardness in the air. I got out my wallet and gave Natalie a five for my share of the fare.

"You want to head to the Sheraton in the morning?" she asked suddenly. "Or should we do that together?"

"I'm going to try and reach Lamia. I want to know

what changed his mind, why he's back on the case. The last attempt on Pugh was arranged through him, albeit unwittingly. He might know something that can help us."

"Ask him about Mallory, too."

"I will."

"I'll do the site check. Give me a call around noon, I'll have my cellular. We can work a time to meet Dale and Corry."

"All right," I said. "You have a good night."

"You too."

We looked at each other for a couple seconds longer, before I said "Good night" once more and got out of the cab.

"So my partner John is on his ass, and he's shouting, 'Behind you, behind you! She's got a gun!' I turn around, and there she is, all right, except what she's holding is this tiny little derringer-like thing. I shout at her to drop it, and she just stares at me. So I'm really scared, I've got my weapon out and on her, and I'm thinking I'm going to have to light her up. She couldn't have been older than you."

"And then?" Erika asked.

"And then she pulls the trigger, and this lick of flame comes out, and I realize she's not holding a gun, she's holding a lighter. She's got a crack pipe in her other hand, and she puts it in her mouth, and she lights the bowl, takes a big draw." Scott Fowler stopped, chuckled at the memory. "Then she drops everything, coughs, and says, 'I'm clean.' "

Erika laughed.

"Crime makes you stupid," Scott said, and then he saw me standing just inside the living room. "Atticus."

"Scott," I replied.

Erika waved at me. "He got here about an hour ago. I told him you'd be back soon. Where were you?"

"Imbibing culture," I said.

Erika stuck her tongue out at me, her response to my obvious fib.

"Wanted to talk to you," Scott said.

"Go ahead, talk," I said.

Erika jerked her head at my rudeness, looked at the two of us, and then got out of the chair that Drama had sat in the night before. "Think I'll just wait in my room," she said.

Scott waited until she had gone before reaching for the bottle resting on the floor. It was wrapped in white tissue.

"Peace offering," he said, holding it out to me.

I took the bottle. It was scotch, Glenlivet.

"I'm sorry," Scott said.

I looked at the bottle and felt myself shrinking, caught a glimpse of just how sour and small I could be when I put my mind to it. I shook my head, took a seat, and said, "You don't owe me the apology. I handled things badly. I'm just glad you haven't written me off."

"Jesus, give me a little credit. What'd you think? I was going to pull the plug on our friendship? Over that?"

"Yeah, I did," I said.

"You need a little more faith in the people around you, Atticus. Bridgett and I see each other about once a week, we have dinner. That's it."

"It's none of my business what you two do together."

"Maybe. You have any idea what we do over dinner?"

"Swap recipes?"

"She talks and I listen. She talks about you. She

talks some about Natalie. Occasionally she throws in something about her work. She's not interested in bedding me, and, frankly, as hot as I think Bridgett Logan is, I'm not interested in taking that trip, either. So, to me, she talks about her life. She can't go to Dale, and she absolutely can't go to Natalie. She goes to me. You need to call her. You need to reach out, to try to make things better."

"I slept with her best friend. You can't make that better."

"You hurt her. You were an asshole. And you're not making things better by continuing to sleep with Natalie."

"Erika told you that?"

"Are you going to say that it's none of my business?"

"No," I said. "But it's not as easy as you make it sound, either."

"All you do is pick up the phone and take it from there."

"I don't know what I'd say."

"You'll come up with something. You want to open that bottle and share some of the warmth?"

I got up and went to the kitchen, poured two glasses, and brought them back. Scott took his, saying, "How's work?"

"Out of control. DTS offered me a million dollars tonight."

"What'd they want in exchange?"

"My exclusive services. I'd always wondered what it'd be like to have someone offer to buy my soul."

"And?"

"It's strange. Made me feel old. You heard about the bomb?"

"Yeah. The U.S. Attorney tasked a couple of the agents in the office to look into it with BATF. Looks like tampering with a federal trial, among other things. Nothing yet."

"We've got another deposition scheduled in three days. No way Doe will let Pugh live to testify."

"Sentinel will do a good job protecting him."

"Not Sentinel. Natalie and I."

"Wear Kevlar," Scott advised. "We finally got an ID on the Orsini body, by the way. Canadian, member of the FLQ, name of Gaston Rafael. Royal Canadian Mounted Police have a thick file on him, several deaths in and around Quebec they've managed to tie him to. Don't think he was John Doe, though."

"He wasn't," I said. I didn't elaborate. I wasn't certain what I could say, and even if I did try to explain that Drama had paid me a visit the night before, I wasn't certain Scott would believe me. I almost didn't believe me.

"Interpol doesn't think so, either," he said. "They've got a couple of hard dates, something in Hong Kong a few years ago, and Rafael was in prison at the time. Sorry I don't have more to offer." He finished his drink. "Well, I'll be going. Give me a call sometime. We should get together for a meal, maybe go watch the Yankees."

"I will," I said, and walked him out. After I shut and locked the door, I started to head back to my room. Erika was standing in the hall.

"You should do it," she said.

"Eavesdropping again?"

"Call Bridgett," Erika said angrily, and she went back into her room.

CHAPTER TWENTY-ONE

The next morning I got Lamia's private office line from Marguiles and gave him a call. He took some persuading, but finally agreed to see me, so I took the subway down to Chambers Street and met him a little before ten. Lamia & Brackman took up floors one through nine. Lamia's office was on the eighth floor, far above where the bomb had gone off, and there was no way to tell anything had exploded anywhere in the building. He met me at the reception area, impatient to be done with the interview, tapping the toe of his Top-Sider on the terrazzo floor. I followed him to his office, passing another deposition room and a regal-looking law library. The halls were mostly empty. Not many people wanted to waste their weekend in the office.

"What can I do for you?" Lamia offered me a seat.

"I've got a couple of questions about Pugh's security for Monday's deposition. I need to know how many people you'll be bringing."

"Just Claire."

"Mallory?"

"Yes, Claire Mallory. Is that a problem?"

"Depends. Do you know she's running errands for DTS?"

His eyebrows came together. "I beg your pardon?"

I told him about the previous night's business at the Shubert, starting with the mystery couple who'd been following Natalie and me. I recounted the conversation with Mallory, showed him my ticket stub.

"Call Natalie Trent if you don't believe me," I concluded, giving him Natalie's cellular number.

He didn't write it down. "The man and the woman, what did they look like?" Lamia was examining my ticket stub, his thumb brushing the ripped edge.

"Both were white, in their thirties. The woman was five ten, slender. Blonde hair, plain face. The man had the same coloring. Big."

Lamia dropped the ticket stub on his desk, then pushed it back to me with his index finger. He still wasn't meeting my gaze. "Drakes," he said.

"Like the duck?"

Lamia shook his head, not bothering to elaborate. "Claire won't be at the depo Monday. She's fired. She just doesn't know it, yet."

I doubted that. I suspected that Claire Mallory was already in Charleston, cashing her first fat DTS check. "Who were the two tailing us? That what you mean by 'Drakes'?"

"I'm not certain who they were."

"Take a stab at it."

Lamia didn't like my tone on that. He folded his arms across his chest and revved up his glare. "Is that why you're here? I'm quite busy—"

"I'm here to talk about Pugh's security on Monday. With Mallory out, will you be coming alone?"

"I'll try to find a replacement for her. Don't know who it'll be on such short notice."

"But whoever the replacement is, he'll be present in the room?"

Lamia nodded.

"Our security will want to search both you and your colleague before beginning, and anyone else who will be in the same room as Pugh."

"I'd expected as much," Lamia said. His patience was wearing thin.

"Who else will be in attendance?"

"Aside from my associate and me, a court reporter, and a jams judge to decide on objections and motions."

"Jams?"

"Judicial Arbitration and Mediation Service. JAMS. Rent-a-judge. They'll send over a retired member of the bench to sit at the table and referee and charge us five hundred dollars for his expertise. It'll save time."

"We'll want to search him, too."

"Obviously."

"Who else in your office knows where the depo will be held?"

"Myself, Claire, Suzy—my secretary—but that's all. We've tried to keep it to a minimum."

"DTS has been notified?"

Lamia coughed. "William Boyer called, asking when we planned to proceed."

"Boyer. He's the one who testified before the Senate?"

"That's correct."

"What did you tell him?"

"I told him we were deposing Pugh as soon as possible. We hadn't decided where, so I couldn't give him the location."

"Did he ask?"

"No, he did not."

Not that it mattered. Mallory knew where the depo would be held, and that meant that DTS knew, too.

"Is that all?" Lamia shuffled some papers to emphasize that I was wasting his time.

"I'm curious why you came back on the case," I said.

"Changed my mind."

"You sounded pretty certain about dropping it when we last spoke. Looks a little strange, first you quit, then you come back."

Lamia glared at me across his desk. "What are you implying?"

"I'm not certain I'm implying anything. But I'm not the only one who can infer something from what's happened. Did DTS threaten you?"

"I don't know what you mean, Mr. Kodiak. Now, if that's all, I have work to do. You can show yourself out."

"Contact the U.S. Attorney's office," I told him. "Tell them what's happened."

Lamia shook his head. "Have a good day."

He opened a file and pretended that I wasn't there, began scratching on the page in front of him with a yellow highlighter. I rose, started to go.

"Thanks for your time," I said. "We'll see you Monday morning."

I was through the door when he said, "Wait."

I turned. The arrangement of files on his desk made him look like a machine-gunner in a foxhole.

"You can keep Pugh safe, can't you? You can make sure nothing happens during the deposition?"

I wanted to say that, yes, I could. I really did want to say that.

But I didn't want to lie to an officer of the court.
I closed the door after me as I left.

They were waiting in the big leather club chairs that ran like a border around the reception area. The woman had her feet up on the coffee table, and was slouched far enough down in her chair that it looked like she had no neck. She was wearing the same running shoes as the night before, but had switched into a pair of blue jeans and a black T-shirt. A leather jacket was bunched on the floor beneath her legs. She wore sunglasses, Ray-Bans.

The man sat beside her, also in blue jeans, but his T-shirt was white. His posture was better, straight back, feet on the floor, an open file folder resting on the table in front of him. I caught a glimpse of a photograph, black and white and eight by ten, as he slid it behind some papers streaked with photocopier toner.

She saw me first and straightened up. "Hunter," she said.

The man looked at her, then chased her gaze and saw me. He closed the folder quickly, brushed his palms on the thighs of his jeans, and rose. The woman didn't move.

He waited until I was turning for the elevator before saying my name. "Atticus Kodiak?"

"Almost always," I replied.

He was bigger than I'd thought at first, easily four, maybe five inches on me, a foundation of thick bones layered with muscle. Bigger than Dale, and perhaps stronger. Crow's-feet landed around his blue eyes as he examined me, head to toe. He took his time, and I didn't enjoy it. His gaze was reductive; I felt a mass of parts.

The exam lasted almost ten seconds.

"Would you like me to turn around?" I asked. "That way you can get the complete picture."

"I'll get it when you go." He leaned past me and punched the button on the wall with his thumb, as if gouging at someone's eye.

The woman got out of the chair. "You're being rude, Hunter."

The man grinned at me. "Sorry."

"All is forgiven." I looked for the indicator above the elevator. There wasn't one, just two arrows, up and down. Neither was lit. Either would do.

The woman was offering me a card, saying, "A more polite introduction than last night is in order, I think. I'm Chesapeake, this is my brother, Hunter."

I took the card. It was simple and classy. Printed in its center were the words "Drake Agency," and below, in the corner, "Chesapeake Drake." There was a phone number and no address.

"My long search is at last over," I told her. "I have finally met people with names stranger than my own."

Hunter Drake had moved around behind his sister, wrapping his arms around her shoulders. He wore a wedding band, thick white gold that would have been ostentatious on a smaller hand. His sister sank back against him, in his arms, and the gesture made her seem tiny, and Hunter enormous. Sort of like seeing a bear hug a raccoon.

"Parents with a sense of history," Chesapeake confided in me. Her hair was slicked back, and her ears were small. Pearl earrings sat on studs in each lobe.

"Or humor," I said.

"Our people helped found the Plymouth Colony," Hunter Drake informed me.

"Neat-o." I checked the arrows again. They still hadn't lit. The stairs would have been quicker. "So, are you working for Lamia or for DTS?"

"Afraid we can't divulge that," Chesapeake said. She was rocking back and forth on the balls of her sneakers.

"The Drake Agency," I said. "It's ringing a bell, now. You're private investigators."

"Maybe . . ." Hunter said.

". . . or maybe not," his sister finished.

I nodded, smiled, and fought down my urge to shoot them both.

"And you're Atticus Kodiak," Chesapeake said.

"You're a PSA . . ." Hunter said.

". . . a bodyguard . . ."

". . . a tough guy . . ."

". . . a hard case . . ."

". . . or so we've been told," Hunter said.

"Oh, stop, you'll make me blush," I said.

Chesapeake took a playful nip at her brother's right thumb, then took his hands in hers, tugging on them. He gave her a last squeeze before letting go. Chesapeake leaned forward and said, "Elevator's here." She smelled like the interior of Victoria's Secret.

"Thank God," I said, stepping into the car. "Strange meeting you both."

"Likewise, I'm sure." Chesapeake mocked a small curtsy.

"See you again, soon," Hunter said.

"Not if I see you first," I said.

"You won't," Chesapeake assured me. "You absolutely won't."

Erika was sitting on the stoop in front of our apartment when I got home, reading a library copy of *Henry and June*. She stood up and wiped her bottom with one hand when she saw me, saying, "Locked myself out."

"Why didn't you buzz Ortega or the super?"

"I tried. They're not in. Anyway, I wouldn't be able to get inside our place. Not the way you lock it up."

I opened the front door and waited for Erika to step inside. We got the mail, sorting it on the stairs. There was a letter from my brother, and I got a guilt spur as I realized I hadn't answered his last one. We were on the fourth-floor landing when I looked up and saw that the door to the apartment beneath ours was open.

"Somebody move in?" I asked Erika.

"No clue, Watson," she said. "Shall we investigate further?"

I went down the hall, knocked on the open door. Paint fumes billowed toward me. "Hello?"

"Moment!"

I looked at Erika. She shrugged and leaned against the wall, opening her book again.

A woman appeared, pulling the door the rest of the way open, smiling. She had the vestiges of a perm in her blond hair and a pouty doll's mouth, and glasses. Her hair was tied in a black and white bandanna. I put her around my age.

"Hello? Yes?" she said.

"Hi. You just move in?"

She nodded and offered her left hand, which was

marginally less painted than her right. "Midge. Pleased to meet you."

"Atticus," I said. "This is Erika."

Erika looked away from her book long enough to smile insincerely.

"Oh! You're the security guard," Midge said. "They told me you'd probably come by. Listen, the window off the fire escape, I don't like the looks of its latch. Can you do something about that?"

"I can take a look at it," I said. "Repairs need to go through the super."

"If you could, I'd really like that." She turned, leaving the door open, and led me into her apartment. Erika followed me in. The layout was identical to that of the floor above, and we went down the hall, passing boxes and cans of paint, until we reached what, in our apartment, we treated as the living room. Midge, it seemed, wanted to turn it into her bedroom. A drop cloth covered the wood floor, and she was in the process of turning the beige walls white.

She pointed to a window, saying, "It just doesn't look tight enough or something."

I crouched and examined the latch and the frame. "Looks fine to me."

"You sure? I mean, I think it's loose. Someone could just slide something in there and jimmy it open or something, maybe."

I made certain the window was fastened, then tried to open it. It didn't budge. "I don't think it'll be a problem. Just make certain the grate across the window is shut and locked, you should be fine."

"If you say so."

"That's my opinion."

"And that's what they pay you for, right?"

"Right," I said. "Well, welcome to the building. We'll see you around, I'm sure."

"Can I offer either of you something to drink? I've got some soda."

Erika, standing behind Midge but still in my line of sight, began shaking her head vigorously.

"I'm expecting company shortly," I said. "Rain check all right?"

"I'll hold you to it," Midge said, following us back to her front door. "You and your sister, both welcome anytime."

"I'm not his sister," Erika said.

"You're not?"

"No." Erika held her book to her chest, smiled like a schoolgirl.

"Oh," Midge said, and before I could explain her away from the obvious assumption, she had shut the door.

"Very nicely done," I told Erika as we headed the rest of the way up the stairs.

She was giggling. "God, did you see that? Her eyes bugged right out of her head."

"She's going to call the police."

"Would you stop worrying so much about what other people think?" Erika complained. "So what if she calls the cops. We explain the situation and that's that."

"You like making trouble, don't you?"

"I fucking live for it, bro."

Erika left right after Natalie arrived, saying, "You'll want the peace and quiet. I'll be back by eight."

I didn't retort. Peace and quiet were going to be

hard to come by, anyway; since we'd reached our apartment, Midge down below had ceased with the paint and taken up power tools. I only hoped the management knew about her redecoration ambitions.

Natalie took a beer and a seat at the kitchen table and watched me.

"You know anything about the Drake Agency?" I asked.

"Drake is to private investigation what Sydney Biddle Barrows was to prostitution. Think of them as the Mayflower Private Eyes."

"I've heard of the agency, but only in passing. Can't remember where."

"There was a small story on them in the *Times* last summer, when all of the tobacco stuff was first hitting the news. But that was the extent of their publicity, as far as I know. They're supposed to be extremely low-profile."

"How do you know about them?"

"Through Sentinel. Industry cross-chat. They're a family firm."

"Like a V. C. Andrews novel," I said.

"Scary?"

I described their behavior at Lamia's office.

Natalie shuddered. "Drake works predominantly for Big Tobacco. They get hired to dig dirt, find those sordid little secrets that discredit expert witnesses and keep people from testifying."

"Probably a growth industry." I finished wiping off the stove, rinsed out the sponge in the sink. The stove hadn't really needed cleaning, but it had kept my hands busy. I don't know why, but housecleaning helps me think. "When are the others getting here?"

"Dale said he'd pick up Corry on the way over. You

don't know why they were there, do you? The Drakes, I mean."

"I assume to report to Lamia. Hunter had a file that he was quick to keep me from peeking at."

"Smutty pictures, probably."

"And he was sharing them with his sister," I said. "That's sweet."

Dale and Corry arrived right on time, and after some small talk the four of us set down to work. Natalie had made her walk-through of the Sheraton, and had hand-drawn maps prepared. We looked at the possible routes of ingress and egress, spent almost five hours planning how we'd move Pugh, and where we felt the weak spots were. The power tools stopped around five, though Midge took up a hammer for a while after that.

"I want a room switch," I told Natalie. The idea was that, before we actually brought Pugh into the hotel, we'd move the whole deposition crew from one suite to another. Hopefully a last-minute change would throw a spanner into John Doe's works.

"That's a good idea," she agreed. "I'll take care of it."

Dale wanted a chance to check the route from the estate to the city before driving it, and Corry volunteered to take the trip with him the next morning.

"Maybe I'll see your father," Corry told Natalie. "Let him know that I've landed on my feet."

"I'm not sure that's what he'd call it," I said.

At nine we broke for the evening, and everybody split to head home. It had gone well, in my opinion, and I had some hope. The only hiccup had come when Dale asked if either Natalie or I had talked to Bridgett. There had been one of those horribly painful pauses.

"Never mind," Dale had said.

Erika got home just as everyone was leaving. She greeted Natalie pleasantly enough, perhaps because it was clear that Natalie wasn't staying. Nat was cordial in response, but I got the impression a lot of ice was moving under both of their surfaces.

The apartment emptied, and Erika and I watched a videotape of an old Gary Cooper movie. Erika told me that she thought Gary Cooper was the best.

"He's noble," she said. "Oozes from his pores."

"That's possibly quite disgusting," I said.

"I'm not saying I want to lick him," she said. "Are you having another meeting tomorrow night?"

"Yeah. I'll be gone most of Monday, too."

"That's all right. I'll be at Bridgett's tomorrow night, anyway. I can stay longer if I have to. She doesn't mind."

"All right."

"Yeah, you can tell Natalie."

"I may," I said.

"Knock yourself out," Erika said.

We had our final meeting at my place around eight Sunday night. Natalie arrived first, with her briefcase and her overnight bag.

"Put this in your room?" she asked.

I nodded and felt guilty. She wasn't talking about her briefcase.

Dale and Corry arrived together ten minutes later, and we gathered around the kitchen table to start our final briefing. Dale went over the routes he'd chosen, and we confirmed that a hardened vehicle, supplied by

Sentinel, would be waiting for us at the estate the next morning. The deposition was scheduled to begin at ten, which meant that we had to be at the estate, ready to move Pugh, no later than eight.

While Natalie double-checked our radio codes with Corry and Dale, I used the phone and called Trent.

"We'll be there between seven and eight," I said. "We'll do a final check and Dale will secure the transport vehicle before we move Pugh out."

"You'll have follow and lead cars on the route," Trent replied. "If that's all right?"

"That'll be fine." I ran down the other things we'd need, the postings we wanted, and he confirmed that everything would be in order. "We're going to refer to the principal as Trigger, so make certain your people know the codes."

"They'll know. You going to tell me your plan to catch Doe?"

"I'm dropping a trail of gingerbread crumbs that will lead into an oven. As soon as Doe enters, Natalie will slam the door shut, and I'll turn on the gas."

"You think this is a joke?"

"I think I've got other things to worry about besides catching Doe," I said.

"Understand me," Trent said. "You're out of your depth here, and way out of your league, and you're creating the exact situation you did when Rubin Febrcs died. If anything happens to any of your team, you're through, absolutely. I'll have your license burnt and shredded before your head comes out of the sand. And if anything, anything at all, happens to my daughter, I'll make you pay for it. For the rest of my life, I'll make you pay, and I swear that to God."

"Something for me to think about," I said, but he had already hung up.

Natalie was looking at me quizzically. "Problem?"

I shook my head. We could talk about it later, when we were alone.

"We're going over the final details. Who gets the long guns?"

"How are you with an AR-15?" I asked Corry.

"I can hit the target."

"Congratulations, you've just been nominated to provide covering fire if we get fucked."

"I second the nomination," said Dale. "All those in favor, say 'aye.' All those opposed, answer in the same."

"Aye," Natalie said.

Corry said, "Thank you, thank you all. I only hope I can live up to the expectations of the office, and perform adequately the duties assigned me. Most of all, I'm looking forward to busting a cap in the ass of whoever gets in our way."

Natalie, Dale, and I all clapped, and Corry wiped a fake tear from his eye.

"Very moving," Natalie said. "I want you to drop the AR-15 once we get to the hotel, switch to a shotgun."

"See, this is the part I love," Corry said, with his best NRA grin.

"Now, on to outfits."

"Fashion slut," Dale said.

She arched an eyebrow at him. "I'm assuming we're in professional attire?"

"I was thinking about that," I said. "It's a hotel, it's summer, it's Midtown. If we're all in a bunch of suits, we're going to look like bodyguards—"

"God forfend," Corry said.

"We'd have the deterrent factor working for us if we

look like people who don't want to be bothered. But the flip of that is, if we look like bodyguards, we're going to attract attention."

"Sentinel will be in suits," Natalie said. "They'll be looking the part."

"Then I'm inclined to think we should dress down," I said. "Let them attract the attention, let us do what needs to be done."

Everyone agreed that going in casual clothes would be preferable. It would also be more comfortable, and by the end of the day, that could make all the difference. Discomfort translates to inattention—instead of watching one's principal, a guard starts brooding about how much his shoes hurt—and inattention always translates into a mistake.

Mistakes tomorrow would be fatal.

That was it, and we said our good nights, and then Corry and Dale left, Natalie lagging behind with the excuse of, "I've got a few more things to talk about with Atticus."

When the door had closed, we stood in the kitchen and looked at one another. What we were doing together at night had started in this kitchen, almost ten months ago. It had been a cold night, late, and I had been alone and full of self-pity. Natalie had been a little drunk, and grieving, and looking for someone to share that with, someone who had known Rubin too.

Natalie and I had sat on my couch and drunk far too much, and we had commiserated about our shared loss, and we had become friends again. At the time, I'd been with Bridgett for less than a month.

And when we'd reached the long hours, I'd escorted her to the door, and instead of seeing her out, we'd gone to my bed.

I was thinking all of this when Natalie asked, "Should I stay?"

"No," I said.

"Probably not a good idea for tonight."

"You said it yourself; we can't keep doing this."

Natalie closed her eyes, and her body relaxed, and I realized she was relieved. I realized I was, too.

"I wasn't sure what you wanted," she said after a moment. "I wasn't sure if . . . this is going to sound so dumb, but I didn't want to hurt your feelings."

"Me too," I said.

Natalie laughed. "Christ, we've really screwed things up, haven't we?"

"Yeah."

"You know what I think? I think we should just wipe that slate clean. Forget the whole thing."

"Some of the sex is worth remembering," I said.

"Not lately."

"True enough."

"That's the part I meant."

"Then I agree."

"Good," Natalie said. "Anyway, I can't think of many partnerships that last when the partners are sleeping together."

"Marriage," I said.

"Don't take this the wrong way, but you're not my ideal mate."

"You wound me."

She laughed again, then stepped up and kissed me on my scarred cheek. "Have a good night, Atticus. I'll see you in the morning."

I watched her take her bag out of my room, then walked her to the door. She headed down the stairs without a look back, and I thought maybe her step was lighter. I certainly felt a weight had been lifted. For the first time since Friday, in fact, I felt optimistic. There was no guarantee that things would work out, no guarantee for Pugh, like I'd told Marguiles, but suddenly the chances seemed better.

I locked the door and checked the clock, then put the kettle on the stove. I had a new mint tea that I quite liked, and it was good for winding down, good for settling the head before going to sleep. I picked up the copy of *Harper's* I'd been working through and fought with the puzzle in the back while I made my tea. The tea turned out fine; the acrostic kicked my ass.

I had given up on the puzzle and started on Lapham's "Notebook" piece on the military-industrial complex, my tea almost gone, when the phone rang.

"Hello?" I answered.

"Hello yourself. So, what are you wearing?"

I dropped the magazine and just about burnt myself indelicately with the remaining tea.

"Awfully late to be up, isn't it?" Drama asked. "Busy day tomorrow. A big, busy day. I'd have thought you'd be getting some rest."

There was no way I could trace the call, and even if I could, it wouldn't do me any damn good. She was using a pay phone, or she was using a captured number. And in either case the call had probably bounced off six satellites before landing at the Bell Atlantic router and making its way to me.

"You're awfully quiet." Her voice was a little husky. Maybe it was the phone; maybe it was on purpose. "I'm just calling on his behalf to say good-bye. It's been nice. I wish we'd had more time together."

And she hung up.

CHAPTER TWENTY-TWO

Dale picked me up in front of my apartment at ten past six, saying, "You look like hell. Didn't you get any sleep?"

"Not much," I said.

"Nat spend the night?"

My look had teeth, and Dale quickly turned his attention back to driving. We picked up Corry and he climbed into the back of Dale's van with his gear and a paper cup of coffee, wished us both a good morning. Dale answered and I didn't.

Natalie had said she would meet us at the estate, so Dale turned us upstate, and we began toward York-town Heights at a good clip. There was a tape playing on the car stereo, Dire Straits' *Brothers in Arms*. Corry and Dale both sang along.

I had wracked my brains for most of the hours since Drama had called, and I just wasn't seeing it. If this was a joke, if this was Mosier or Trent yanking my chain harder, it wasn't funny, and it wasn't safe. If Drama was for real, and I was now almost sure she was, then we were being led down the primrose path right into the kill zone.

It was there, it had to be there, seeing it, and I was so frustrated I wan head against the dashboard until I could h block.

We had missed something. We had missed thing, and John Doe hadn't, and today Jeremiah Pugh was going to die.

We reached the gate around seven-thirty, and were checked through without a problem. Dale parked the van in the small lot. I didn't see Natalie's Infiniti. The doubt and fear I'd managed to keep just a seed so far began to sprout.

Mosier was nowhere to be seen. Yossi came out to meet us. He gave both Corry and Dale warm greetings, asking how they had been.

"It's only been a week and a half," Corry told Yossi.

"Yeah, but I missed you, you runt."

"Tall enough to kick your ass."

Yossi told me, "Trigger is waiting in his room. He's dressed, dined, and is enthusiastically awaiting you and your protective team's escort. Want to head on up?"

"Not yet," I said.

Dale looked a question at me. I just shook my head. I didn't want to have to repeat myself. When Natalie arrived, I'd break the news. I asked Yossi if I could use a phone, and he directed me inside, where one of the guards in the hall led me to the kitchen. It was a big kitchen, with an industrial-sized refrigerator and freezer, and an island in the center of the cooking area for food preparation. The phone was on the far wall, beside the microwave.

The guard left me alone while I tried to reach Marguiles. I called his home first, and either his young-sounding wife or one of his daughters told me that he'd

...ady gone to his office. I hung up, dialed again, and waited as the receptionist routed my call.

"Morning," Marguiles said.

"It's Atticus," I said. "I want to cancel the deposition."

"What's happened?"

"Nothing yet. But something will."

"You're certain?"

"Pretty certain. John Doe knows where and when the deposition is taking place."

"How'd he find out?"

"Probably through Claire Mallory."

Marguiles was silent for several seconds, before saying, "I can't accept that."

"Lamia's being blackmailed or threatened," I said. "DTS leveraged him back onto the case to force Pugh out in the open, to give Doe a free run at the mark. They bought off Mallory, they tried to buy Natalie and me. They're doing everything they can to expose Pugh so they can put him down. Lamia told me that William Boyer at DTS wanted to know the date and time of the depo. Once DTS knows, it's no stretch to get that information to Doe."

"But you've checked the security," Marguiles argued. "You've been working on this since Friday. Are you telling me that despite what I've hired you and Ms. Trent to do, Jerry's going to get murdered today?"

"There's a good chance that's what will happen."

"No," Marguiles said. "It can't be done. We must take this deposition today. Judge Halendall reopened discovery specifically to take this deposition. If I cancel, if Jerry doesn't show, discovery will be closed for good, and Lamia will see to it that Jerry never gets heard at trial. This is my last chance to get his testimony on record, and I have to take it."

"There's got to be another way."

"There's no choice, Atticus. Lamia needs a face-to-face deposition. He's allowed a written depo already, but it's not enough."

"We could video-conference," I said.

"I thought of that already, and suggested it. Neil turned me down. He wants to be in the same room as Jerry."

"Which means DTS wants Lamia in the same room as Jerry."

"Can you prove that?"

"No."

"I can't go to the U.S. Attorney with your suspicions. I need proof."

"Something will happen today, Mr. Marguiles. And I don't know if I or my people will be able to stop it before Pugh ends up dead."

"I have no choice," he repeated.

I stared at the phone on the wall, shut my eyes. I could see Drama, sitting in the shadows of my living room, laughing behind her two-tone mask.

"I'll see you there," Marguiles said.

"If we make it that far."

Natalie was pulling in when I came back outside. My watch read seven fifty-one. I didn't see Yossi. Dale and Corry were doing a weapons check by the van, loading the long guns. Corry was stowing spare clips in his pockets. Both he and Dale had dressed down, Dale in khakis and a white long-sleeve button shirt, Corry in jeans, T-shirt, and denim jacket. When Natalie got out of the car, I could see she was dressed much the same. We looked like a bunch of overage college students.

"Sorry I'm late," she said. "Pop called and kept me on the phone."

"What'd the puss-fucker want?" Corry asked.

"He is my father." Natalie said it sharply.

Corry went back to checking his rifle.

Natalie said, "Atticus, he asked me to pull out. Said you're going to get either Pugh or one of us killed."

"We need to talk about that," I said, and I motioned her over to the van, so Dale and Corry could be included in our conversation without my having to raise my voice.

Neither Corry nor Dale had heard about my first meeting with Drama, so I sketched that for them quickly. Then I said, "She called me last night, about an hour after you all had left. She called to say good-bye, and it wasn't because she and her perhaps-fictional employer are leaving town."

"Could be a bluff," Corry suggested.

"Why would she bluff?" Natalie asked.

"Why would she want to warn us?" Corry asked back.

Dale was scanning the perimeter. With his eyes on the gate, he said, "I assume the phone call you just made was to our employer?"

"Yeah," I said. "Marguiles says there's no way he can cancel the deposition."

Corry frowned. "Then we're really in the shit."

"I have been going over and over our prep work," I said. "We have missed something, but I can't see it."

"We haven't," Natalie declared. "Our prep has been one hundred percent solid. We've done everything we're supposed to do, we've done more than we're supposed to do. If there's a mistake waiting to happen, it's not ours."

"So you think Drama has breached Sentinel?" I asked.

"She's getting her data from somewhere."

"Maybe she's inside the op," Dale suggested. "Someone who's already here."

We all liked that thought so much, no one said anything.

"There's nothing we can do," I said. "We proceed as planned, and we take it as it comes."

"What the hell," Corry said softly. "Always wanted to go out in a blaze of glory."

Dale spent the next forty-five minutes with the drivers from Sentinel, going over the route with them, discussing contingencies. They would be driving the follow and lead cars. Corry liaisoned with Yossi, confirmed that the advance team, led by Mosier, had already arrived at the Sheraton and had completed their sweep of the assigned suite. The advance team had found nothing. Corry told Yossi that we would be switching rooms on arrival, and Yossi said he would pass that message on once we got moving, so a new sweep could be made.

Natalie and I went to check on Pugh, who greeted us at his door. He was wearing a slate gray suit, and it looked entirely wrong on him, sagging where it should have been tight, pinched where it should have been loose. The only thing about him that appeared comfortable at all were his shoes, the alligator cowboy boots.

He shook our hands briskly, his palm moist, then licked his lips. "Let's get this show on the road," he said.

"Put this on," I said. The Kevlar vest was heavy body armor, and it didn't pretend to be anything else. Wearing it, Pugh looked like he was wearing a life jacket. In a way, he was.

I made certain the Kevlar was good and snug, and that all of the panels overlapped. If they didn't and he took a hit, there was a chance that the bullet could pancake and slide around until it found a way into his body. Then we'd have the added problem of trying to get the vest off of him while he bled to death.

He experimented with movement after we'd fastened the last strap, swinging his arms about, twisting at his waist, all with a nervous smile. Then he held out his hands for Natalie. He was perspiring slightly, although the room was air-conditioned cool.

"What?" she asked.

"Give 'em here," Pugh said, and when he had her hands, he pulled her in against the vest and took her in a quick tango around his room that ended with a dip by the foot of the bed. "You dance divinely," he told her.

"Why, thank you, sir." Natalie straightened her hair, making certain her radio wires were still in place.

Pugh tugged the vest down once more, patted himself down. "It'll do," he told me. "It'll do. Makes me feel like the Man of La Mancha. Climb every mountain, all that, which reminds me, I did one for you. Over there, on the bureau, that one's yours."

"One what?"

He took a deep breath, but his words still spilled out rapidly. "A collage, son, art, whatever you want to call it. Told you I would and I always try to keep my word. It's sitting on the bureau, right there."

I took a look at it. For once, he had forgone the

cigarette theme, assembling the picture with clippings of architecture and nature. The composite was of a man. One leg was made from brick and cinderblock, another from concrete and marble. The arms were trees, California redwoods and Douglas firs. The head was encased in a helmet of steel, capped with a cowboy hat. A sheriff's star was on the left breast, assembled from slices of a western sunset.

"One suit of armor for another," Pugh said, rapping the Kevlar vest with his knuckles. His smile was thin.

"Thanks," I said. "I'll pick it up after we get you back here."

"You damn well better, or I'll think that you don't like it."

"No, I like it quite a bit."

"Can't stand that," he continued, not hearing me. "Hate it when people start lying to me. Destroys the whole relationship, annihilates trust. Learned that the hard way."

Natalie and I checked our radios, made certain that the units on our belts were fully charged and that the leads to the transmitters, earpieces, and mikes were tight.

"Dale?" Natalie asked her radio.

"Go ahead."

"Trigger's ready to run."

"All set to receive."

I turned to Pugh. He was holding on to the straps of his vest, as if to keep himself steady. "It's okay to be nervous," I said. "I am."

He blinked a couple of times, then licked his lips once more. "Jesus, Mary, and Joseph. My stomach's killing me, Atticus. Mouth feels like the Dust Bowl."

"You want some water?"

He shook his head.

"You'll be fine," I said. "We're going to go straight to the car now. When we reach the door, wait until we tell you to move. When you do move, do so quickly. Keep between Natalie and me. Go straight to the car, and once in the seat, put your head down. Keep your head down until one of us tells you it's safe to sit up."

Pugh swallowed hard enough I thought I could hear it. "Understood."

"Let's do it," I told Natalie.

"One minute," she told her radio.

"Confirmed," Dale said.

Natalie and I took Pugh down the stairs and into the front hall. Karen Kazanjian the medic, holding an orange jump kit, was there, with four guards. If there was a sniper, and if he didn't hit our principal with a head shot, and if Karen got to work fast enough, maybe Pugh would live.

We could see the cars lined up, three of them, black four-door sedans. Ours was the modified Mercedes-Benz in the middle. Ballistic glass, emergency lights, run-flat tires, fire suppression system. Gun ports in the sides of the doors. Not built for speed, but for strength. A genteel tank for urban survival.

Guards lined the walk to the Benz, four on both sides, an attempt to limit the field of fire. Three other guards in the hallway served the same purpose, and would walk out with us, in a tight diamond formation around Pugh. I'd stay behind him, off a little bit to the right, and Natalie would walk directly in front of him. At the end of the line of guards, nearest the car, stood Lang, awaiting our signal.

I keyed my transmit button. "Dale? You checked the cars?"

"All of them. They're fine."

Natalie said to Pugh, "Atticus hates cars."

"What?" Pugh managed a hoarse, nervous chuckle. "Son, that's practically un-American."

"Any time," Dale said in my ear.

"Trigger is go," I said.

We went out the front, the guards moving with us. Lang waited until we were halfway down the path, then opened the car door. Dale was already behind the wheel, Corry beside him, rifle held on the inboard side. At his feet, I knew, a duffel bag contained the shotgun, a couple canisters of smoke, and anything else Corry thought we might possibly need.

Natalie took the lead into the car, slipping in and across swiftly, and I pushed Pugh after her. Pugh made it to the center, and obediently ducked his head into Natalie's lap. I got in last; Lang shut the door. Kazanjian was heading for the follow car, along with another guard.

"Go," I said again, and Dale relayed the order into the radio on the dash, and all of the cars in our little convoy began to move out.

Natalie looked at me. "I think he's a dirty old man," she said.

"Dear, that's the best kind," Pugh said, into her lap.

Natalie thought that was funny. "You get fresh, you won't have to worry about an assassin."

" 'Fresh.' Now that's a word I haven't heard in a long time. You are clearly an elegant and well-bred lady."

We passed the gatehouse and pulled onto the road. The lead car kept five seconds ahead of us, not too far out, and not too close. My stomach was tying sailor's knots. The trees were thick and made good concealment on both sides of the road. If we got ambushed here, we'd have no warning, and almost no-where to go.

Natalie, Corry, and I kept scanning while Dale drove, and Pugh kept his head down, silent now. When we hit the Taconic, all of us relaxed slightly. The convoy accelerated to a little over sixty, all the cars holding their space.

"We're good," Dale announced.

"You can sit up," I told Pugh.

"Can I take this thing off?" he asked, tugging at his body armor.

"I'd say no," I said. "Ask Natalie, she's more chari-table towards automobiles."

"You can take it off," Natalie said. "You'll have to wear it again when we stop, and keep it on until we get you secured at the deposition. But for the ride, you should be okay without it."

Pugh twisted and bent, and with some help, man-aged to get the body armor off and onto his lap.

There wasn't much talking for the next several miles. Occasionally, Dale would say something to his radio, and the other drivers would respond. Slow down, speed up, watch the car on the right, watch the car on the left, careful of the bend. But that was it; the environ-ment wasn't really conducive to conversation.

North of Yonkers, Pugh asked Natalie, "You smoke, don't you?"

She looked surprised. "No, not really—"

Pugh punched her in the arm. "Don't. It'll kill you. It'll kill you sure as a bullet, and a hell of a lot slower."

"Don't you hit me." Indignation made her voice climb.

"You didn't like that?"

"No."

He socked her shoulder again. "That's what a cigarette does to your lungs, hon. That's the tar, that's the ammonia added to the tobacco to increase your nicotine intake, that's the acrolein. I could list a hundred other chemicals, all of them bad for you. Four hundred and twenty-five thousand people a year die from cigarettes, you want to be one of them?"

Natalie said, "I don't—"

"Jesus! Don't lie to me, girl! I was around the stuff for more than twenty years. I can smell a smoker at thirty feet. It's in your hair, it's in your clothes. Eau de Cancer, sweetheart, believe me, it followed you as we tangoed."

"I quit," Natalie protested. "I wasn't even really smoking. I had less than half a pack, for God's sake."

"Well, then, you *just* quit, because you had at least one sometime this morning." His hands were knotting the straps to the body armor now in his lap.

Natalie looked at me, and I didn't have anything to say in her defense, so she looked back at Pugh. "You're right," she said. "I had one this morning, before I drove up."

"Don't do it again," Pugh said, and turned to stare out the front window. We went a couple more miles, before he said, "I'm sorry, I shouldn't have punched you. That's not a way to treat a lady. I just kept smelling it, and I couldn't figure out which of you it was."

"It's okay," Natalie said.

"Hell, I've got no right to cast stones. I smoked off and on for fifteen years myself. Couldn't really work for DTS without sucking on a butt, could I? Billy and I used to sit in his office and sample different brands from different makers. We'd rate them, try to guess what blends they were using, how much fill they'd thrown into the mix. You know that between forty and sixty percent of your Class A cigarette is stuff that comes from the factory floor? They gather it up, pulp it, shred it, add it to the mix."

"Billy?" I asked. "William Boyer?"

"Billy, yeah. He didn't used to be E.V.P. He used to be VP Director of Marketing. Billy and his wife Rochelle, they'd come over to our house every week, stay for dinner, drinks with the wife and me. Smokes. We went fly-fishing a couple times in Montana, too, back before that damn movie came out and everybody and his sister figured that standing in water waving a stick was the neatest way to see nature since snowshoes."

"Have you talked to him lately?" I asked.

"Billy and I don't talk anymore," Pugh said curtly, and that was the last thing out of his mouth until we reached Manhattan.

The convoy arrived at the Sheraton without incident, and over the car radio we could hear the Sentinel security already on-site giving us updates. Dale brought us in and kept the engine running, and Corry opened the door almost before we'd stopped, starting to get out. He made a quick scan, checking faces, then higher, looking for sniper points. He didn't see anything, as I knew he wouldn't. In Midtown especially, but all throughout Manhattan in general, there are hundreds of thousands of places for a sniper to roost. If Drama or Doe were going for the long shot, they had their pick of sites.

Four Sentinel guards appeared from the lobby and headed our way. From the follow car another two guards emerged, and Karen Kazanjian. Kazanjian went straight to the lobby, the guards peeling off to join the detail assembling by our car. Corry opened the door on Natalie's side. She got out, Pugh right behind her, I again in the rear. The guards closed up around us, and we pushed into the hotel as Dale pulled the car away.

We were in the open, exposed, for less than fifteen seconds, and the time was elastic. I braced for the snap of bone, the sound of the rifle.

We made it just fine.

Mosier came on my radio, saying, *"We've secured second stairwell north, confirmed clear. You're good to eight."*

"Confirmed," I told him.

We marched over the carpet, passing the concierge and registration desks, scattering the people in the lobby. They stared at us. A chunky woman asked a clerk behind the front desk if Pugh was a politician. Corry fell into step to the right of Pugh, carrying his duffel bag with his left hand. His right hand was buried inside, around the grip of the shotgun. It wasn't subtle, but it was better than carting the weapon at port-arms.

Two of the guards separated and opened the door for us at the stairwell. Natalie gave a quick hand signal to hold up, and I reached for Pugh, ready to move him. He was breathing quickly, and he tensed when I put my hands on him. Natalie checked the line of sight, then motioned to continue, and we started up the stairs. Pugh was wheezing by the fourth floor, and I was afraid we'd have to stop for him, but he made it to the eighth without slowing.

"Coming out," Natalie radioed.

"Still clear," Mosier came back.

It was a hotel hallway like any other, decorated in Sheraton hues, and we moved without pausing down the corridor to the suite. Mosier and another guard were waiting outside, and they opened the door as we approached. I felt another surge of *déjà vu;* it hadn't been all that long since I'd secured a different principal in a hotel room while Sentinel security held the perimeter.

The open living room of the suite was empty. It was nicely furnished in that subclass of hotel fixtures where everything looks like an original, but is just a marginally accomplished knockoff. A flight of stairs ran to the second level above us, off to the left from the entrance, and Leslie Marguiles was looking down at us from above. His bow tie was red and white.

"Everything all right?" he asked. We ignored him.

Natalie made straight for the master bedroom on the right. Corry peeled off and took up post in the hall. The bedroom was clear, and Natalie spread out the guards while I helped Pugh out of his body armor. Once he was free, he bolted to the bathroom, muttering something about needing to wash his face. He shut the door after him, and almost immediately turned on the faucet. I could hear him gagging over the water.

Mosier watched the proceedings with his jaw locked and his mouth pinched closed.

"Who else is here?" I asked him.

He evaluated my worthiness before saying, "Lamia and some black woman, Breeden. She's his new assistant or something. Claire Mallory's here, too, with some guy named Boyer. Then there's the court reporter, same guy as before—Greer—and the judge. They're all on the second floor, waiting. We've secured the room they're going to use, closed the curtains, given it a triple-check."

"Why are Mallory and Boyer here?"

"You think they told me? They showed up fifteen minutes ago. There was some talking from the lawyers, but nobody left."

I didn't know what I thought of that. Someone in DTS, quite probably more than one person, had been responsible for buying the hit on Pugh, for hiring John Doe. I had no real reason to believe Boyer was calling John Doe's shots, but at the same time, I had no idea why the Executive Vice President of DTS would bother putting in an appearance at Pugh's deposition. Pugh had said they'd been friends, but that friendship was clearly over. I didn't imagine they would greet one another with flowers and hugs.

"And you searched everyone?" I asked Mosier.

He visibly bit back his first response. "They're clean."

"When did you switch the rooms?" Natalie asked.

"Got everyone settled ten minutes before you arrived."

"Good," I said. "Thanks."

Mosier said, "Yeah."

Pugh came out of the bathroom, drying his hands on a white towel that he tossed on the bed. It didn't land squarely, and slipped onto the floor.

"Ready," he said. His voice was raw. A wet spot showed on the collar of his shirt.

"Boyer's here," I told him.

Pugh's face went tight, the creases and lines in his skin etching deep. "Where?"

"Upstairs," Mosier said. "Stepped out on the balcony to have a smoke."

"Don't suppose he fell off?" Pugh asked.

"We haven't checked yet," I said. "You all right with this?"

"I'm ready," Pugh said, ignoring my question. He checked the knot of his tie, then wiped his mouth with the back of his hand. "Let's get this show on the road."

Most of the second floor mirrored what I'd seen of the first. Claire Mallory sat by the wet bar at the far end of the room, and she mouthed the word "hello" to me when I came off the stairs. Somehow, she made the silent greeting seem like a proposition.

A wall of windows looked out to the east, the curtains drawn except for one set, by the sliding glass doors. Outside on the patio, I could see a man lighting a cigarette. Opposite the bar was an open door, beyond which the court reporter sat fiddling with his laptop and steno machine. I caught a glimpse of Lamia and an African-American woman I assumed was Breeden preparing their papers.

Marguiles was waiting outside the room, another man beside him. The man had ten or fifteen years on Marguiles, and a face that looked as if it had been pressed down once too often by an anvil. He was dressed in a suit, banker's gray, and a pair of half-glasses hung around his neck. He watched our approach intently.

"Shall we get under way?" the man asked Marguiles.

"I just want a minute or two with my witness before we begin, Your Honor."

The judge nodded and gave Natalie and me another look-over before heading into the room to speak to the court reporter.

"This is going to be a little bumpy," Marguiles said softly to Pugh. There was an edge to the lawyer's voice I hadn't heard before, not just concern, but perhaps a little apprehension. "Lamia's going to run at you hard."

"Sure," Pugh said, but he wasn't looking at Marguiles. His eyes were locked on the man on the balcony.

"It's the same situation as before, Jerry," Marguiles continued. "Just like the first deposition. Slight change in personnel, but that's all. It'll be a cross-examination like we've discussed. Keep your answers short, clear, and precise. Let Lamia and his associate do the work."

Pugh nodded. The man on the patio, the man who had to be William Boyer, flicked his butt over the ledge and reached for the door to come back inside. He was big and white and stocky, a couple inches over six feet and large around the torso. His suit was expensive: you couldn't be sure if his girth was from fat or muscle.

Boyer slid the glass door shut and watched, bemused, as Mosier moved around behind him to adjust the curtains.

"Jerry," Boyer said.

Pugh stared at him.

Boyer coughed, then asked, "How's Helen? And Jordan?"

Pugh smiled crookedly, as if he had expected the questions, cast a sideways glance at me, and then launched himself at Boyer, arms out. He seized the big man before any of us had started to move, both hands around Boyer's throat, and was slamming him into the glass door when Mosier and I caught his arms.

"You don't speak their names, Billy-boy, you don't do that," Pugh hissed. "Not even a whisper, not even a mumble, you don't speak."

"Easy," I kept saying, trying to break Pugh's grip. Boyer's flesh slipped over the backs of Pugh's hands. Natalie had moved around behind, and was pulling Pugh back with a hand on his shoulder.

"Never again," Pugh said. But he let go, finally allowing us to pull him back a couple of steps. Mallory reached us, positioned herself next to Boyer.

Boyer coughed, reaching for a handkerchief. He used it to wipe his mouth, then his hands. "You're not a healthy man, Jerry," he said.

Pugh lunged for him again, but we had a good grip this time, and he didn't make it more than a step.

"Enough," the judge said. He said it evenly, and without raising his voice, and just the way he said it let you know he wasn't going to take any shit. "Mr. Marguiles, would you care to explain your witness's behavior?"

Lamia and Breeden had come out with the judge, and Marguiles turned to them. "Your client is antagonizing my witness," he said.

Lamia shook his head. He looked like he hadn't slept in a month.

"Your Honor," Marguiles said, "I would ask you to entertain a motion prohibiting Mr. Lamia's client from engaging in any communication with my witness, either verbal or non."

"Motion granted," the judge said, raising an eyebrow and directing his look to Boyer. "There'll be no more of this. Is that understood?"

"I don't have anything else to say to him," Boyer told Mallory. She looked at Marguiles and Lamia, and the three exchanged a silent communication.

"Claire," Lamia said, "I'd like a minute with you and Mr. Boyer, alone."

Mallory nodded. Boyer replaced his handkerchief inside his suit coat. We waited while Lamia escorted them down the stairs. They were gone for almost three minutes, and then Lamia came back upstairs. I hadn't heard the door to the hall open or close.

"Are they still here?" I asked.

"They'll wait downstairs during this proceeding," Lamia said. He didn't look happy about it.

I started to ask why Boyer hadn't left, but Lamia didn't give me a chance, continuing past us and into the room where the court reporter waited. Breeden followed him, and then the judge.

"Ten o'clock," Leslie Marguiles said.

Pugh sighed. He checked his necktie a final time, then hitched up his pants. He ran a palm over the top of his head, mashing down the white hair that stood like the bristles on a scrub brush.

"Ah, hell," he said.

And then, like the hero of a pulp serial marching to face a firing squad, Pugh walked into the room where his final deposition would take place.

CHAPTER TWENTY-THREE

"Counsel," Judge Flannigan said. "Before we begin, I am going to remind you that you have ceded to me the right to make all rulings in this proceeding, including on matters of findings and obstruction. I will brook no further outbursts of the kind I witnessed a few minutes ago. I don't like it, and I won't have it."

All three attorneys present nodded, chorused, "Yes, Your Honor."

The judge looked at Pugh. "Sir, I include you in this."

"I understand," Pugh said.

"Very good. Mr. Lamia, you may proceed."

"Mr. Greer," Neil Lamia said, "will you please swear in the witness?"

The court reporter nodded, turned to face Pugh. "Do you swear to tell the whole truth under penalty of perjury?"

"I do."

Lamia said, "Mr. Pugh, I assume that Mr. Marguiles has explained to you what a deposition is, but to make absolutely certain that there is no doubt in your mind, I want to go over some of the basic rules with you.

While this may be merely repetitious to you, it is vital that there be no misunderstandings." He cleared his throat.

"Here in this setting, with Judge Flannigan to rule on any objections, this procedure probably seems rather informal. But you need to understand that your testimony here has the exact same effect as if you were in a court of law testifying before a sitting judge and jury. Do you understand?"

"I do, sir."

"A deposition is a fact-gathering proceeding. I am entitled to, and expect, truthful answers to the questions I pose. Do you understand?"

"Yes."

"I want to make certain you also understand that you've taken an oath to tell the truth under penalty of perjury. This means that if you make a material misstatement of fact, it can and will be considered a crime. Do you understand that?"

"Yes."

"I'm entitled to your best answers. I am not interested in your speculations. Those things which you know in answer to the questions I pose which are based upon reasonable approximations, however, are not speculations. I'm entitled to such answers, as well. Do you understand?"

Pugh cleared his throat, then said, "Yes."

"Finally, since this proceeding is being recorded by Mr. Greer, the reporter for the Court, only verbal responses are acceptable. Do you understand that?"

"Yes."

"Good. Please give us your full name for the record."

.   .   .

I don't know what I thought it would be like, but I'm certain I didn't think it would be like this. And this is the truth, this is the honest-to-God truth about depositions.

They're boring.

Mind-staggeringly boring.

An example:

Q [Mr. Lamia]:   State your residence.

A: Richmond, Virginia.

Q: And your address?

A: 2543 Stanley Street.

Q: State your profession for the record.

A: I am a biomedical research scientist.

Q: Do we have his CV?

Mr. Marguiles: Your office received it Friday.

Ms. Breeden: I have it.

Q [Mr. Lamia]:   This is correct?

A: Yes.

Q: By whom are you currently employed?

A: I'm retired.

Q: By whom were you last employed?

A: DTS Industries.

Q: And for how long were you employed by DTS Industries?

And it goes on like that for another ninety minutes before Lamia starts asking questions that border on interesting, questions about the kind of work Pugh did for DTS, about the records he kept, and who he shared them with. It's like watching ice melt, except ice is moderately more entertaining.

The only person who seemed entirely alert and present was Jerry Pugh. This was what he'd been waiting for all along; for lack of a better phrase, his day in court. But his energy was nervous, and several times his voice caught, and he would cough, then apologize, then continue.

Around noon, Dale radioed me saying that Karen Kazanjian was wondering about lunch.

"Medic's saying that Trigger should eat. Wants us to order room service."

"Negative," I said. "Send two guards out to a deli, have them order and pick it up there, then bring it back. Don't use the hotel kitchen."

"Confirmed."

The food arrived almost an hour later, and a short recess was declared while everyone grabbed a sandwich and a drink. All of the attorneys and Judge Flannigan ate heartily. Maybe they hoped food would keep them awake. Pugh nibbled on the corner of a BLT, gnawing on the bacon and leaving the rest, then said he needed to use the rest room again. Dale followed him to the bathroom, and I took the opportunity to walk through the suite.

Claire Mallory and Boyer were in the sitting room on the first floor, dining from a room service cart.

"And how's it going?" Mallory asked.

I gave her my sweetest grin. "Swimmingly," I said, then stuck my head out in the hall, and nearly bashed into Corry as he was coming back inside.

"Looking for you," Corry said. "Come here."

"Trouble?"

He motioned me out of the room, shut the door. Three guards were posted in the hall, one at either end by the stairs—men I'd seen at the Westchester estate, but didn't have names for—and Pete White, standing next to the entrance to the suite. White greeted me with a nod.

"What's up?" I asked Corry.

"We're being followed. After Pete and I made the food run, he resumed post in the hall."

"And?"

"And this woman I'd seen at the deli just went into the room over there," White said. "Room 831."

"Alone?"

"Far as I could tell. Could be another person in there, though."

"Could be a whole bunch of people in there," Corry said.

"What'd she look like?"

White closed his eyes. "Five nine or so, blond hair, slim. Blue jeans, black shirt. Had a brown paper bag with her, no idea what was in it." He opened his eyes again.

"You're sure she was tailing you?" I asked.

"I wasn't sure at all until she came down the hall. But I hadn't seen her come out of that room all morning, and when she walked by, she didn't look my way."

That was odd. White was in plainclothes, khaki pants, loafers, a blue shirt with navy blue tie, and a blazer. He had an earpiece, a radio at his belt, and a gun. He looked like what he was, what he was supposed to look like; he looked like a bodyguard.

That should have earned him at least the first glance, if not the second.

"Who's the room registered to?" I asked.

White dug a piece of paper out of his sports coat, unfolded it to show me. With his right index finger he indicated 831, then ran an imaginary line across the page to the name in the far column.

"Drake," White said. "Party of two. Checked in last night."

"How do you want us to handle this?" Corry asked.

I felt the muscles along my forehead give birth to a bouncing baby headache. "Ask Ms. Mallory to step out here, would you? And have Dale spell me if the deposition resumes. I don't know how long this'll take."

"You want cover?"

I shook my head, crossed over to 831, and rapped on the door. White shifted behind me, to cover my back. It gave me unexpected comfort. I didn't actually *know* that the man and woman I'd met at Lamia's office on Saturday were the real Chesapeake and Hunter Drake; in fact, I didn't know if there really were Drakes, fake or otherwise, beyond the door.

The woman who had called herself Chesapeake answered, exclaiming, "Hunter! Company!"

"Hello again," I said.

"Hello yourself, man-who-is-named-after-sappy-book-and-a-big-Alaskan-bear. We were just playing Go Fish. Want to join us?"

I looked over her shoulder, saw Hunter sitting on the floor, holding a fistful of playing cards. He gave me a thumbs-up. A half-eaten sandwich sat on a folded paper bag beside him. I couldn't be certain, but it looked like pastrami on white. Probably with mayonnaise.

Chesapeake spun on her toe and pranced back to her brother, where she scooped up her cards and sat on the edge of the bureau. "I'll bet he's wondering why we're here," she said cheerily.

"I'll bet he is," Hunter replied. "You have any eights?"

Chesapeake examined her cards, then stuck out her tongue. "Go fish!" She made the word "fish" sound like a kind of exotic massage.

Hunter said, "Fuck," and drew from the pile.

"Well, come in, come in," Chesapeake told me.

I stepped inside. The room was smaller than the

suite we'd taken across the hall. The king bed was unmade, and a camera bag sat on the pillows by the headboard. A six-pack of soda was on the desk, two cans missing.

"Kings," Chesapeake said. "I want kings, all of your kings—diamonds, hearts, clubs, spades, all of 'em—gimme."

Hunter frowned and plucked a card from his hand and flicked it at his sister. She caught it. "Now I want queens."

"Go to the pond and dip your line, baby," Hunter said. "He still hasn't asked."

Chesapeake bent nearly double to reach the pile. "He's slow. Bears are like that."

Claire Mallory edged beside me, William Boyer following her. We were creating a bottleneck in the entrance of the room.

"Why are they here?" I asked Mallory.

She pursed her lips, then said, "You haven't asked them?"

"I'm asking you."

"Yeah, he's asking you," Chesapeake said. "Answer the man, already."

"Perhaps they're in residence," Mallory said.

I took two steps to the bureau, began pulling out the drawers. Chesapeake swung her legs out of the way to make room. But for the Gideon Bible, a copy of Bell Atlantic's Manhattan listings, and the assortment of Sheraton stationery, the drawers were empty.

"He should check the closets," Hunter said.

"They're empty, too," I said.

"Nope, wrong, incorrect," Chesapeake said. "There are *hangers*."

"And that little luggage thing, that stand, that's in there, too."

"Try again," I told Mallory.

"I have no idea why they're here."

"And you?" I asked Boyer.

He folded his hands, held them together in front of his belt. He looked bored, and perhaps contemptuous.

Hunter and Chesapeake had put their game on hold, and were now directing their attention to me. So was Mallory.

"Fine," I told her. "I want them gone. They work for you, I want them out of here. Tell them to leave."

"If they're in residence, I don't see why they should. They're not interfering with the deposition. The only problem here seems to be yours."

"Until I tell Marguiles. Then he tells Judge Flannigan that you and Mr. Boyer are conspiring to intimidate the witness."

"No, Mr. Kodiak, that won't happen. Pugh doesn't even know they're here, he's had no contact with the Drakes—at least, not directly. I'm afraid Judge Flannigan would find any such objection specious, at best."

"Besides, we've got the room until Friday." Chesapeake pouted. "You don't want to force us out into the hot, humid Manhattan wilderness, do you?"

"You'll find another room," I said. "There are plenty of places that rent beds by the hour."

Hunter went to his feet like his ass was on fire, putting himself between me and Chesapeake. "I don't like what you're implying about my sister."

"I'm sorry. I was implying it about both of you."

He pulled back to swing and I thought I had him, then, but Mallory shouted, "Don't hit him!"

Hunter froze, his balled fist looking like a flesh-colored brick. I didn't move.

"If you hit him, he'll call the police," Mallory said quickly. "You'll be rung up on assault charges."

Hunter wavered, the fist ready.

I blew him a kiss.

His fist opened and his hand banged down on my shoulder. He spread his lips in a smile and said, "That was pretty clever. That was a nice try." He gave me a not-so-friendly rattle, looked back at his sister. "I like this guy."

"I think he likes us, too," she said. "We're growing on him."

"Like mold," I said.

Hunter laughed, put his other hand on my other shoulder, and said, "Now get the fuck out of our room, or *I'll* call the police and tell them that *you're* trespassing."

"And won't that fuck your security but good," Chesapeake added.

I shrugged Hunter's hands off me, and he let his grip go. Mallory and Boyer preceded me out of the room, past White, who still stood in front of the open door.

"Have a funky day!" Chesapeake called after me.

I stopped, looked at where the siblings were smiling my way. I waved White back to post, then keyed my transmitter.

"All units, this is an SOP change," I said. "If you encounter activity from room eight three one, repeat, eight three one, during Trigger transport, you are to consider such activity hostile. Shoot to kill."

There was the briefest pause, and then the confirmations came back in my earpiece, one after the other.

The "shoot to kill" bit was pure theater, nothing more; I'd added it for the Drakes' benefit.

Chesapeake hopped off the bureau and came my way. "Tell Trigger bye-bye," she said.

Then she slammed the door in my face.

CHAPTER TWENTY-FOUR

Q [Mr. Lamia]: How many times have you been married?

A: Just once.

Q: How long have you been married?

A: Thirty-nine years.

Q: Are you presently married? Sir? I'll repeat the question. Are you presently married?

A: No.

Q: Did your marriage end in death or divorce?

A: Can he ask that?

Mr. Lamia: Your Honor, please direct the witness to answer the question.

Judge Flannigan: Answer the question, Mr. Pugh.

A: Death.

Q: Was it a sudden death, or did it occur over prolonged circumstances?

Mr. Marguiles: Objection.

Judge Flannigan: Overruled.

Q: Was it a sudden death . . .

A: It was sudden.

Q: I understand your wife committed suicide, is that correct?

A: You going to help me here or what?

Judge Flannigan: Do you have an objection, Mr. Marguiles?

Mr. Marguiles: Your Honor, this is a matter of privacy, clearly one that is painful to Mr. Pugh. . . .

Mr. Lamia: All of this goes to the witness's motivation for testifying, Your Honor. The Court has a right to know that motivation.

Judge Flannigan: Please direct your witness to answer the question, Mr. Marguiles.

A: Yes.

Q: Was your wife ever institutionalized?

A: No.

Q: Have you ever been institutionalized?

"Objection!"

"On what grounds?"

"Before I answer, I'd like to have a brief word with my witness, Your Honor," Marguiles said. "It won't take long."

Pugh sat perfectly still, eyes fixed on the pitcher of water that was sweating at the center of the table. Lamia leaned to a side and whispered in Breeden's ear. Breeden nodded and began scribbling on her legal pad.

"Considering that it's a question that can be answered with a yes or no, Mr. Marguiles, I'm not certain it's necessary," Judge Flannigan said. "But I'll allow it. You have three minutes."

"Trigger's coming out," I told my radio.

"Confirmed," Dale said.

Marguiles led Pugh out of the room. I followed, leaving Natalie to shut the door behind us. Dale was standing at the head of the stairs, keeping watch.

"I need to know the answer to that question, Jerry," Marguiles said softly.

"Why aren't you helping me in there?" Pugh tugged at his collar. The knot of his tie was slipping.

"I'm trying to, Jerry. But it's looking like they know something I don't, and if you don't bring me up to speed, I won't be able to protect you. Have you been institutionalized?"

"None of this has anything to do with DTS. They haven't asked me anything about what I know went on there." Pugh's voice was small.

Marguiles checked his watch. "Jerry, what are you going to say?"

Pugh looked at me for help, saw that I couldn't offer him any. "I institutionalized myself, five years ago. After my son died. Three weeks, that's all. Depression."

Marguiles frowned, then reached out and patted Pugh's shoulder. "It ain't gonna help us, cowboy, but we can live with it. Take a deep breath, and then follow me back in."

Pugh nodded, took the ordered direction, and I followed them back inside.

"Are we ready to resume?" the judge asked.

"We are, Your Honor."

Marguiles and Pugh took their seats once more.

"Mr. Greer, will you please read back the last question?" Lamia asked.

"Question, Mr. Lamia," Greer said softly. " 'Have you ever been institutionalized?' "

"Yes," Pugh said.

"Would you state for the record the reas—"

"Objection, Your Honor," Marguiles said.

Lamia threw up his hands. "What grounds?"

"Medical history is an issue of privacy, first of all.

Second, it's irrelevant. Finally—even if it *is* relevant—it is unduly prejudicial."

"We need to know the basis of Mr. Pugh's time under care," Lamia argued. "If he suffered a psychotic episode, for instance, his memory could be impaired. If there's another medical condition, we certainly don't want . . ."

Judge Flannigan held out his hand, and Lamia trailed off. For a moment, the tap of Greer's fingers on the steno machine continued, and then that, too, ended. Pugh was breathing quickly, guarding his stomach with his right arm, as if protecting his gut from repeated blows.

Judge Flannigan lowered his hand and examined each of the attorneys at the table. Then he said, "Gentlemen. Madam. This is clearly a point of contention for both parties, as well as one of discomfort for the witness. I'm getting the impression, also, that this line of questioning will play a major part at trial.

"For that reason, I am going to declare a short recess to refresh myself on the relevant points of law. I would ask you to return to the table in half an hour, prepared to argue to me the cogent points of your positions.

"Mr. Greer, we are in recess."

Natalie and I waited by the bathroom, listening to Pugh retch. Dry heaves, and they sounded painful. I knocked on the door.

"You need a hand?" I asked for the fifth time.

There was a pause, then a choked, "I'm fine."

Natalie sighed, leaned against the wall, frowning. "Poor guy," she said.

"He's tough," I said. "He'll make it."

Lamia and Breeden had stayed in the room while

Judge Flannigan had taken position on the couch opening a laptop of his own and searching a CD-ROM he'd loaded up. Marguiles had used the phone on the wet bar to call his law clerk.

"Evan, drop what you're doing and hop to on this," Marguiles had said. "I need everything you can get me in twenty minutes on privacy rights, specifically mental health history. Twenty minutes, twenty-five tops, that's it."

That had been thirty-five minutes ago. In that time, Marguiles had received his call back, jotting hasty notes about *Chnapkova v. Koh* and *Lewis v. Velez* while Judge Flannigan completed his laptop research. His Honor had decided Pugh's presence while the attorneys debated the objection wasn't necessary, and had told Natalie and me to wait. Flannigan and Marguiles disappeared back into the deposition room, leaving us to listen to Pugh being ill.

It made me feel helpless.

Dale came around the corner of the bar. "How's it going?"

"I think it's called taking it on the chin," I answered.

From the bathroom came a groan, the sound of the faucet being turned on.

"I'll get the medic up here," Dale said. "See if she can do anything for Trigger."

"Why don't you do that," Natalie said.

Karen Kazanjian came upstairs just as Pugh opened the bathroom door. She took one look at his ashen face and ordered him to sit down.

"You're not a well man."

"That's just what they'd like you to think," he told her. His chuckle was thin.

"Have you eaten?"

"I had lunch."

She rooted around in her jump kit, came out with a candy bar. "I want you to eat this."

Pugh rubbed his eyes. "I won't be able to keep it down."

Kazanjian handed it to me. "See that he eats this."

"He's right," I said. "He'll send it back up the moment he swallows."

She took Pugh's pulse, counted his respirations, then shook her head. "Get him a glass of juice or something. He needs to keep his sugar level up."

"I'll be fine," Pugh told Kazanjian, waving her off. "Almost done." He reached for my arm and I gave him a hand up.

Kazanjian poked me in the chest. "Call for me if there's any trouble."

"We will," I assured her, dropping the candy bar in my pocket. "Don't suppose you have anything for a headache in that bag of yours?"

"Tylenol," she said.

"That'll do. Natalie?"

"Yes, please," Natalie said.

Kazanjian rooted around, found a bottle and spilled out two gelcaps, then two more on my request. Natalie took three, and we downed them with a glass of water from the bar. Then the door opened, and Marguiles motioned us to come back inside.

"Overruled," he told Pugh.

It didn't look like anyone around the table had moved. I held Pugh's chair as he sat down, then stepped back. "Trigger's in place," I told my radio.

"Let's resume," Judge Flannigan said.

Q [Mr. Lamia]:   How long were you institutionalized?

A: I wasn't committed, I admitted myself.

Judge Flannigan: Mr. Pugh, please answer the
   question.

A: Three weeks.

Q: For what reason did you seek psychiatric care?

A: Depression.

Q: Is that all?

A: I was depressed.

Q: Before you entered treatment, had you contemplated suicide?

A: Yes.

Q: Was there a specific incident that led to your
   depression and your seeking psychiatric help?

A: Yes.

Q: Your son Jordan died, isn't that correct?

A: If you already know . . .

Judge Flannigan: Mr. Marguiles, would you please
   direct your witness to answer the questions
   posed directly, and to not editorialize.

Mr. Marguiles: Jerry.

A: Yes, my son died.

Q: How old was Jordan when he passed away?

A: He was thirty-two.

Q: How soon after Jordan's death did your depression reach such a level that you felt you needed
   psychiatric care?

A: Four.

Q: I beg your pardon?

A: Four months.

Q: How long after your son's death did your wife
   Helen commit suicide? Mr. Pugh? Sir?

Judge Flannigan: Would you like another recess, Mr. Marguiles? Your witness seems distraught.

A: Not . . .

Mr. Marguiles: Jerry, do you want to take a minute?

A: No, no. About then.

Q: Meaning about four months after your son's death?

A: Closer to five.

Q: Where was your wife's body found?

A: Excuse me . . . just . . . I need a minute. . . .

Mr. Marguiles: We can take a recess. . . .

A: No, I want to get through this. . . . She was found at home . . . in our bedroom.

Q: You were receiving treatment at that time, weren't you?

A: Yes.

Q: How did you find out your wife had died?

A: A doctor told me. One of the doctors at the clinic.

Q: Mr. Pugh, are you a smoker?

A: What? No.

Q: Were you ever a smoker?

A: Yes.

Q: Did your wife smoke?

A: Yes.

Q: Did your son? Mr. Pugh? Did Jordan smoke?

A: You son of a bitch.

Mr. Marguiles: Jerry, please answer the question.

Mr. Lamia: Unless your counsel has an objection . . .

Mr. Marguiles: No objection.

A: Yes.

Q: How much? A pack a day?

A: I don't recall.

Q: More? Less?

Mr. Marguiles: Asked and answered.

A: I don't recall.

Q: I just want to remind Mr. Pugh that he is under
     oath, Your Honor. This may be painful, but if
     he remembers, he has to answer.

Judge Flannigan: If you do not recall, sir, you may
     so state. But if you remember, you must answer
     the question.

A: A pack a day. Sometimes less.

Q: Ever more? Mr. Pugh?

A: I suppose.

Q: What did Jordan die from? Mr. Pugh, please.
     Answer the question. What was the cause of
     your son's death?

A: He had a brain aneurysm.

Q: Thank you.

Mr. Marguiles: Your Honor, I'd like a short recess
     to allow my witness a chance to collect himself.

Judge Flannigan: Granted.

CHAPTER TWENTY-FIVE

It was five minutes of five in the evening, and something was wrong.

Lamia had finally made it to his questions about DTS. Pugh, rattled and drained, was slowly coming back to life as he answered. Lamia wanted to know the circulation of Pugh's R&D reports while the latter had been in chemical analysis, and Pugh was trying to remember the list of names, who would have received his memos. Marguiles was scratching his beard.

Natalie caught my eye, and her look told me that she'd noticed it, too, and she tapped her earpiece.

The radio traffic had stopped. Silence in my left ear. Throughout the day, the earpiece from my radio had kept me informed of activity outside of the room. Corry and Dale, and, rarely, Mosier, giving me the hot wash.

Now it had gone silent.

Natalie pointed her index finger at me, then at the exit. I nodded and quietly stepped outside to find Dale and Mosier standing by the balcony door, whispering. They saw me exit the deposition and waited until I reached them before either spoke.

"We've turned the radios off," Dale told me, and he pointed out onto the concrete deck, at the small, almost perfectly square box resting on the ground. The box was flush against the wall of the room where the deposition was taking place, and had a green bow on it.

"Ah, Jesus," I said, and switched my radio off.

"Found it three minutes ago," Dale said. "Corry was making a round."

"I thought you said you swept?" I asked Mosier. I didn't ask nicely.

His cheeks pinked up. "I did sweep. It wasn't here when we started. It wasn't here when Boyer went out for his fucking smoke, and it wasn't here when you all took your last recess. It has to have been placed in the last hour or so."

"Could have been lowered from the floor above ours," Dale said. "Or placed by hand while we were downstairs and you were in there."

I had a sudden image of Drama, wearing her mask and her cat suit, rappelling down the side of the building like Spider Man, quietly setting her new bomb against the wall.

It wasn't a funny image.

No way to tell if it was real without opening it up.

The green bow was really pissing me off.

"You want an evac?" Dale asked.

If the bomb had been placed to kill Pugh, it had been placed poorly. Natalie and I had seated him away from the exterior wall as a matter of SOP. Drama would have known we would do that. If she had placed this package, then, it was either a decoy or an extremely powerful explosive. Neither option was good.

My stomach began to ache like my head. Too many possibilities, too many dangers.

"Atticus?" Dale asked.

"Get Boyer up here. I want to be damn sure that's not his present. And have White confirm that the Drakes are still in 831."

Dale headed for the stairs as Mosier became indignant. "I told you, it wasn't there when Boyer came back inside. It had to have been placed in the last hour."

"I heard you."

"I want to take a look at it."

"Don't move, don't fucking go near it," I said. "Just wait right here."

I went back into the deposition. Lamia was asking Pugh if he had ever kept a personal diary at his home which contained records of his work. I cleared my throat. Everyone looked at me. Judge Flannigan motioned for silence.

"We've found a suspicious package out on the balcony," I said. "We need to pull back while we take a closer look at it. Mr. Greer, Ms. Breeden, I'm going to have to ask you to save your work and shut down your computers."

Greer looked at Flannigan, and the judge nodded, saying, "This proceeding is in immediate recess until further notice. We will reconvene as soon as possible."

"I want you all to head downstairs," I told them. "If we can't be one hundred percent sure it's not a bomb, we'll have to evacuate and call the police."

"No," Pugh said.

"This is not subject to debate, Jerry."

Pugh jabbed his index finger at me. "I need to finish this, Atticus. Don't pull the plug, here. Don't do that to me. Not after everything we've been through today."

"Get him downstairs," I told Natalie, but she was

way ahead of me, and already had Pugh out of his chair. I moved out of the way as they went past.

"No, goddamnit," Pugh was saying. "Please. I need to finish."

The room emptied. I stepped back out to find that Dale had brought Boyer up to take a look, Mallory at his heels. Billy Boyer looked like someone had stolen his stock options, and Claire Mallory looked like she might emulate Pugh and head for the bathroom; neither even cast a glance at Pugh as Natalie hustled the old man downstairs.

I pointed at the box and asked Boyer, "Is that yours?"

He shook his head. Sweat was shining on his neck.

Dale raised an eyebrow at me and I nodded, and guided William Boyer back to the stairs as Corry came up them, three at a time.

"The Drakes aren't answering their door," he said.

"They still there?"

"White isn't sure. He didn't see them leave, and he was in the hall the whole time, but there's no answer. I can contact the management, try to get them to open up the room."

"No, don't bother. I'm calling an evac. Get Trigger ready for transport."

Mosier had crouched to his haunches and was staring intently at the box. The box hadn't moved.

"We're leaving," I said.

Mosier looked at me and I could read his thought; I just shook my head and went to tell the others.

Natalie, Dale, and Corry had everyone gathered in the hall by the entrance door. Karen Kazanjian stood beside Pugh, holding her jump kit. Boyer looked glassy-eyed, and none of the other attorneys looked much better. I couldn't blame them. I was scared, too.

But Pugh glared at me, his eyes red-rimmed and wet. "So."

"We're evacuating," I said. "Dale, take two guards in the hall and head down to the car, give us five minutes. We'll meet you out front."

"Don't do this to me, Atticus. It's just a damn box."

"This is not a drill," I told Pugh. "We don't know what's in that package."

"Hey, Billy-boy," Pugh demanded of Boyer. "You trying to kill me today?"

Boyer gaped, his mouth flapping for a couple of inarticulate seconds, before Mallory objected, "That's entirely inappropriate."

"I know," Pugh spat back. "Inappropriate. Just like you bastards have been all day today. They're not going to try to blow me to bits, Atticus. Not with Billy-boy here. You said so yourself, they could use a gun, just shoot me. It's another fake, son, it's got to be."

"We won't know that until we take a closer look," I said. "And we're not going to do that until you're out of here."

"Where's Mosier?" Pugh asked.

I looked around. Mosier wasn't behind me. "Dammit," I said, then added, to Corry, "Go get him."

Corry hadn't taken two steps when Pugh said, "When you find him, ask if it's the box with the green bow he had this morning."

"He had it this morning?" I felt my stomach turn from butterflies to knots. Pugh nodded.

"I'm going to kill him," Natalie said.

"Was Mosier upstairs anytime in the last hour?" I asked. "Alone?"

"After the last recess, Boyer went out on the balcony for a smoke," Dale said. "Mosier locked up after him."

"He had that bag of his," Corry said. "His tac bag."

"I'm going to kill him a lot," Natalie said.

"Go get him, bring him down here," I told Corry, but I needn't have bothered, because Mosier was coming down the stairs, then, holding the box. He was carrying it tenderly, the way one should carry a child, cradling it in both hands.

"Out of the way," he told me softly. "I'm going to put this in the tub, tamp the blast."

None of us moved. Judge Flannigan coughed once, and it wasn't to clear his throat.

Mosier said, "This could go off any second. I'd evacuate if I were you."

"I'll take it," Natalie said.

"Jesus, what's the matter with you people? Clear out of here!"

Natalie took a step and reached for the box. But Mosier pulled it back and out of the way.

"We know," I said.

"Know what? Would you fucking clear out? And for God's sake call the bomb squad. This is real."

"No," I told him. "It's a phony. And you know that because you planted it."

"That's a lie." It was an angry denial, and behind it was the humiliation, the knowledge that he'd been caught.

"Hand it over," Natalie said.

"Kodiak, get Trigger out of here. This could go off any second."

I shook my head.

Mosier looked us over, settling finally on me, and what he saw behind my glasses must have been enough. Some of the color faded from his face, and his eyes flickered dumb before he could find his mask again. But it didn't fit like it had before.

The seconds were depressingly awkward, and long, and then Mosier handed Natalie the box. He stared at me, afraid of backing down by looking away, afraid of what he would see in the other faces around us. There was water in his eyes, and he was fighting to keep the tears out, his mouth locked shut, breathing deep through his nose.

Humiliation does that.

Natalie removed the bow and slit the tape with her fingernail, then pulled open the flaps. She didn't say anything, just showed us the contents of the box.

More white Play-Doh.

"Corry," I said. "Spell me upstairs. I suggest the rest of you get back to what you were doing."

It took another second before people began moving, and Natalie led the group back to the second floor, passing Mosier on the stairs. Mosier never looked at any of them. I heard Dale guiding people back into the suite, Karen and Mallory and Boyer.

When we were alone, I said, "Get your gear and get out."

Mosier let his jaw slip enough to ask, "You going to call Trent?"

"Yes," I said.

"What are you going to tell him?"

"I'm going to tell him what just happened."

"You don't have to."

I didn't bother to respond. Mosier's look hardened. He came past me, off the stairs, and I followed him while he packed his gear back into his satchel. We went out the front door and down the hall, all the way to the elevator. White watched us quizzically, but he'd get his answer soon enough, as would the other guards; telling them now would only serve to humiliate Mosier further. I didn't want to do that.

Mosier entered the car as soon as it arrived, punching the lobby button. There was no water in his eyes now. His stare remained fixed on me as the doors swished together.

Then he was gone.

I headed back to the suite, was halfway down the hall when I realized my radio was still off. I switched back on and keyed the transmitter.

"Nat?"

"Go ahead."

"He's in the elevator, going down. When I get back in there, I'd like you to call your father, tell him what's happened."

"Better he hear it from me than from you?"

"That's what I'm thinking."

There was nothing in my ear for a moment, and then Natalie said, *"Well, I suppose it's one less thing to worry about, right?"*

I thought about the look on Mosier's face as he'd left, the last thing I'd seen in his eyes.

"Or one more," I said.

CHAPTER TWENTY-SIX

The deposition ended at eight fifty-five that evening, with Lamia declaring that he had asked his last question. "You've completed the written deposition I forwarded to Mr. Marguiles' office?"

"Yes, sir," Pugh said.

"Then I move we close the record," Lamia told Marguiles.

"I have no objection to that."

Judge Flannigan straightened in his chair and cleared his throat. The strain of the last eleven hours showed on his face: it had been a long day for all of us. "Mr. Greer, the record on this matter is closed. You are dismissed with many thanks."

There was a sudden burst of movement in the room, disorienting after so many hours of a sedentary proceeding. Breeden, Lamia, and Marguiles reorganized their papers, stowing them into their various briefcases. Greer popped a floppy disk out of his laptop, then began disconnecting the leads to the steno machine. Flannigan was on his feet, stretching. Natalie looked at me for confirmation, then went out to prepare our egress. Only Pugh remained seated.

"That's all?" he asked Marguiles.

"That's all."

"We're done? Really? They're not going to call me again?"

"Not until trial. You're clear." Marguiles stroked his beard, then added, "You should get some sleep. You look done in."

Pugh's face scrunched as he considered this, and then he sighed, rested his palms on the arms of his chair, and pushed himself up. I saw for the first time how this day had aged him. He leaned across the table, offering his hand with great formality to Lamia, then Breeden, then Judge Flannigan, and finally to the court reporter, Greer. Breeden and Lamia both looked surprised at the gesture, but all the same everyone shook his hand before leaving.

"I'm ready to go," Pugh told me.

"Dale's getting the car. We'll move when he calls."

He took another deep breath, shutting his eyes, and he seemed to double in age before me. "Dear Lord, I don't think I have anything left in me."

"I have a candy bar here, if you're hungry," I said. The day had done what time couldn't, and I realized that I was looking at an old man. The Pugh armed with play-vodka, rubber cement, and vitality had been replaced by the one before me. I couldn't remember seeing a man look so tired.

He opened his eyes again. "Stomach's still queasy. I'll have some toast when we get home."

We headed down the stairs, Marguiles leading. Lamia was speaking with Greer in the doorway, and the two guards in the hall were still on-post. Corry and Natalie waited by the foot of the stairs.

"Boyer and Mallory left?" I asked.

"About six," Corry answered.

"How'd they look?"

"I couldn't tell. You think something's up?"

"I don't know."

Natalie said, "The window of exposure just shut. Pugh's been deposed. Killing him now accomplishes nothing."

"We can relax," Corry added.

"When we get Pugh secured at the estate, then we can relax," I said.

"We'll be okay," Natalie said. She even sounded cautiously optimistic.

"It's a long drive," I told her.

We filled the car the same way we had come, Pugh scrunched between Natalie and myself, Dale behind the wheel, and Corry looking for trouble with his long gun at the ready. The lead and follow cars stayed with us for the drive. The traffic out of the city was nerve-wracking, heavy, until Dale broke out on the Saw Mill. I felt the tension sitting in my gut, squeezing at my temples. Pugh tried twice to start conversation before we reached the Taconic, and each time got silence in response.

"You all can relax," Pugh declared. He sounded both exhausted and exhilarated.

"Not yet," I said.

"What the hell can happen now? It's too late for them. The damage is done."

"There's still the trial."

"No, it's finished. They've got the deposition, they've got my testimony. I've done what I needed to do. I've spoken for the dead."

"You still have to appear in court, take the stand."

Pugh shook his head. "It's over."

Something in his tone demanded attention, and I turned from the window to see that Natalie had caught it, too. Pugh was staring straight ahead, at the taillights of the lead car.

"We were one big, happy family with ashtrays," Pugh said softly. "Lotta people don't know that you can get a brain aneurysm from smoking. They think it's all cardiopulmonary dangers and cancer. But cigarettes will give you blood clots, too. Plug the vessel good and tight until the pressure's just so great . . . it's so great that . . . it rips, you see? The vessel just . . . rips.

"And then you're bleeding inside of yourself. And that builds more pressure, all of the blood building up. Your own blood crushes your own organs."

Nobody in the car said anything.

"She didn't want to be without him," Pugh said quietly. "She didn't want to be alone. But I wasn't there when I should have been."

Dale signaled a lane change. The clicking of the turn signal was loud. Natalie had gone back to watching the road, and Corry was keeping his eyes forward, but we were all listening.

"You can know you're doing something wrong, keep doing it anyway. No faces attached to the deed, you can ignore it, forget it, rationalize it away. They're paying you a lot of money, after all, more than you'd ever thought you could make. Suitable financial compensation. Comes a time, though, when you look and the dead eyes are staring right back at you. And then you really have to ask yourself, 'So what are you going to do now?' "

He stopped himself, as if suddenly aware of what

he had been saying. Dale guided us off the Taconic and back towards Yorktown Heights. Over the radio mounted on the dash I heard the lead car transmit to the estate, giving them our revised ETA.

"Almost home," Pugh said. "Will you kids be sticking around?"

"I think we'll be heading back to the city," I said. "It's been a long day all around."

"Amen to that, son."

Yossi met us at the car, and he and I walked Pugh back to his room, leaving Natalie, Dale, and Corry behind to move our gear back to Dale's van. When we reached his room, Pugh went straight for the vodka and poured himself a substantial drink.

"Thank you, son. I appreciate what you did more than you know."

"It was no problem," I said.

"Bullshit," Pugh said softly.

"Sleep well."

He nodded and turned his back to us, and Yossi and I left him alone with his drink in his room. Only one guard was on the door, Lang. I waited while Yossi gave him the quick brief, and then we headed back downstairs together.

"Trent's coming up tomorrow," Yossi said. "Told me Mosier was sacked and that I was running the op from the field."

"He tell you why?"

"No, but I could guess. Raymond tried to make himself a hero?"

"Raymond stepped in it big time."

"Better that than you fending off an assassin."

"I'm not sure we have."

"In the absence of Pugh's cooling corpse, I'd say mission accomplished."

"I need to use a phone," I said.

Yossi nodded. "I'll be outside, making certain your partners don't mix it up with my crew. After taking on one of the Ten, they might be feeling invincible."

I made my way to the empty kitchen. Erika answered after a couple of rings, and I told her I'd be home in the next four hours, certainly after midnight.

"Cool," she said. "Will you have eaten?"

"Probably. Natalie and I will want to take Dale and Corry out for dinner, to celebrate not getting blown up."

"Is that a normal excuse for a free meal?"

"Today it works. Tomorrow, maybe not."

"Speaking of tomorrow, that Havel chick called again. Can you guess the rest?"

"I can and have," I said. "She left a number?"

"Yeah, two of them. You want them?"

"Absolutely not."

Erika laughed. "Enjoy your dinner."

Yossi, Dale, Corry, and Natalie were all joking around the van when I got outside, and I was greeted by a small round of applause that, honestly, made me a little angry.

"We're hungry," Corry said. "Feed us."

"And give us libation," Dale added. "For, with your leadership and the firm hand of the Lady Trent, today we have dodged John Doe's bullet, and we wish to rejoice with alcohol."

"And meat."

"Yes, much meat. Prime rib meat would be appropriate."

"We didn't dodge anything," I said. "There was nothing for us to dodge."

"He's testy," Corry told Dale.

"Alcohol and meat will fix that."

Natalie raised an eyebrow at me. "What's bugging you?"

"Nothing happened."

"Doesn't mean we didn't do a good job."

"No, it doesn't. It means that Drama was toying with me when she called."

"You know," said Dale, "it could be that we did such a thorough job that they had no opening."

"Do you really think we've outsmarted one of the Ten?"

"Well, clearly, you don't."

"No, I don't," I said as my pager went off. I heard the anger in my voice. I checked the number and saw that it was Marguiles.

"Can it wait?" Natalie asked.

"No," I said.

"Hurry," Corry said. "I might gnaw my own leg off if I don't get some sustenance soon."

I went back inside to the kitchen, heading for the phone. I dialed Marguiles. He answered immediately.

"Greer's dead," Marguiles said.

The phone was hard in my hand, solid resistance to the pressure of my grip.

Coincidence, I thought.

"Did you hear me? Greer's dead."

"How?" I asked.

"A coronary. While waiting for his subway train home. Died on the platform." There was strain in Marguiles' voice. "I've tried to reach Lamia, but I can't find him. Atticus, we have to depose Pugh again."

"You'd finished. I don't under—"

"We'd finished but it hadn't been filed. Greer was supposed to transcribe his notes tonight, print copies of the depo, then file them as official record. But his notes are gone, the disk the transcription was written to is gone, the cops can't find them. Legally, it means this whole day never happened."

"The notes, where were they?"

"The disk from his laptop should have been in his case with the hardcopy and the steno machine. They aren't."

"Doe," I said.

"There's no evidence of foul—"

"It's Doe, or Drama, or whoever the fuck it is who's playing with my head," I interrupted. "They never intended to get Pugh today. That's why Boyer was so frightened by the bomb scare. That's why Drama called me. They were after Greer the whole time. They wanted us looking the wrong way." I could hear my breathing on the phone, hot and fast. "And I fucking fell for it."

Marguiles said, "I need you to keep Jerry safe until his testimony is recorded."

"I can stay here," I said. "I'll send my other people home."

"Are you up to it?"

"More up to it than Greer," I said, and hung up, started back for the others, then ignored the front door and went upstairs, thinking that I should tell Pugh what had happened. Lang furrowed his brow when he saw me.

"Thought you were leaving," he said.

"So did I. He still in there?"

"Not a peep since you and Yossi left him."

I knocked on the door, reached for the knob, and

then the door flew open and Pugh pitched into me, his arms flailing, his eyes as glassy as a dead man's. The impact caught me off-balance, but I caught myself, then caught him as he dropped into my arms. His breath was coming fast, smelling of vodka, and his body was clammy, and as strong as hot rubber. He opened his mouth and said something that sounded like it included my name, but there was no sense, a word salad that meant nothing.

I started yelling for help, but Lang was already raising the alarm, and I wrestled Pugh back into the room, and he was fighting me like a violent drunk.

We'd blown it, he was dead, Greer was dead, the deposition was gone, we'd lost, and all I could think was how I'd done it again, how I'd tanked it again, how I'd lost another principal, killed another person who'd trusted me with his life for protecting. Doe, Drama, Mosier, somebody had gotten into the house, that was it, that was what had happened, and under my nose, Pugh was dying.

I stepped on something made of hard plastic, and it popped under my shoe, and I dragged Pugh across the littered carpet, knocking over the jar of rubber cement, knocking over the half-filled bottle of Stoli. Glossy magazine stock crumpled under my sneakers, suddenly and dangerously slippery.

"No no no no don't do this Jerry, don't do this to me don't go, don't go," I heard myself say. "Don't you fucking go."

Pugh flailed wildly, his arms and legs jerking, muscles locked. He was strong, made stronger by the unpredictability of his movement, and I kept losing my grip. He was still spitting gibberish. His wrist caught me hard in the chin, and I felt my teeth meet through the tip of my tongue, felt blood rush in my mouth. Somehow I got him on the bed, Lang helping me, and Pugh rolled to a side immediately, as if trying to get away, and we had to hold him down. Feet were rushing our way, people coming into the room, Yossi and others, and I heard one of the guards saying that Pugh was drunk, he was just a drunk.

Yossi stepped my way as Pugh jerked his leg up into my side, and I saw the broken plastic on the carpet, and I let go of Pugh.

"Where's the medic?" I shouted.

"She's coming," Yossi said.

"Get juice, get juice and sugar," I yelled. "Hurry!"

Yossi turned and I thought maybe he would delegate, but he didn't, he just bolted. A couple of the guards moved in towards the bed, trying to give us a hand, but it degraded into a furball of people, too close, trying to do too much, and Pugh kept twisting, slurring words at us. He slipped out of my grip, off the bed, his head bouncing off the nightstand. He hollered at the pain, kicked a leg out, catching Lang in the knee. I heard Lang curse, then Kazanjian's voice, ordering me to help Pugh up. We dragged him back onto the bed, tried to right him. Kazanjian tore through her jump kit, discarding gauze and tape, searching through the bag.

"Where's the fucking glucose?"

"Yossi's bringing juice," I told her, and spat blood when I spoke.

"Keep him up," she snapped. "Keep him up and steady."

Pugh's head pitched back and forth, as if it was too heavy for his neck. Yossi appeared with a glass of orange juice and a handful of sugar cubes. Karen held

Pugh's head as I tried to pour, but Pugh wouldn't take it, wrenching his head away, kicking out. Juice slopped out of the glass, onto my hands, onto the bed. Karen tried again, and Pugh pitched his head back and Lang caught hold. I poured. Juice spilled down Pugh's shirt, bubbled at his mouth, and then he took it, and he drank, and I emptied the glass.

"Let him down," Karen said.

We laid him back out on the rumpled bedclothes, and Karen went into her jump kit once more, coming out with her stethoscope and her BP cuff. Pugh's brown eyes were open, looking at the ceiling. The smell of vomit and orange juice was suddenly stronger, a smell I remembered, a smell that made me want to cry.

Karen put the stethoscope to Pugh's chest, and he whimpered. "That's cold."

"Jerry," I said.

He rolled his head to see me, and looked surprised that I was there. "I'm tired," he said.

"We're going to get you an ambulance," Karen told him. "Did you take your insulin today?"

Pugh shut his eyes, turned his head away from us.

"Mr. Pugh, did you take your insulin?"

"Leave me alone," he muttered. "Tired."

Karen took the pulse off Pugh's wrist, then nodded and waved us all back. Yossi began moving everyone out of the room. For the first time, I saw that Dale, Natalie, and Corry were present.

"You're going to be fine," Karen told Pugh.

"Eat shit, cow," he said.

Karen nodded again, as if she heard this sort of thing all the time. Her stethoscope and cuff went back in her jump kit, and she rose. I followed her to the doorway.

"We have an ambulance on the way?" Karen asked.

"Coming," Yossi said.

"What the hell happened?" Dale asked.

"He's diabetic."

"He's what?"

"You didn't know?" Karen canted her head to a side, surprised.

"No, we didn't know," Natalie said. "Someone must have neglected to tell us."

"He was in insulin shock," Kazanjian said. "Low blood sugar, not enough glucose to feed the brain. It's a dangerous condition. Leads to brain damage, then death." She looked at me. "You didn't make him eat that candy bar, did you?"

"If I had known exactly why you wanted me to feed him, I would have done so," I said.

"But you knew he was diabetic?"

"I didn't realize it until I got him on the bed, saw Yossi standing on the syringe."

"Had he taken his insulin?"

"I don't know. Not during the deposition, that's for sure."

"Did he actually eat his lunch?"

"Not really. Not much."

"He had a bite from a BLT," Natalie said. "And some water."

Karen Kazanjian looked back at Pugh. We were speaking softly, and he could probably hear us, but he was doing nothing to show it.

"Stupid old man," Kazanjian said. "If he hadn't been found, he could've been dead by now. He knows better."

Yossi's radio went off, the guards at the gate telling him the ambulance had arrived. He went to greet the crew, and Kazanjian stepped back into the room to look after Pugh. Two EMTs came up the stairs, and we watched while Karen helped them move him onto their gurney. Pugh didn't respond to their questions, and he didn't look at any of us as they wheeled him out, then carried him clumsily down the stairs.

My team and I followed the crew outside, watched them load the gurney into the back of the ambulance. Yossi had posted four guards to the immediate area, and the Cushman was parked just inside the front gate.

I waited until the gurney had been latched into place, then I climbed in the back of the rig with Karen and one of the EMTs.

"No room," the EMT told me.

I wedged myself in on the bench opposite where Pugh lay. He had shut his eyes, and there was water trickling down his cheeks. I could see where the tears had made spots on the sheet.

The EMT scowled at me hard and opened his mouth to try again, when Karen said, "He needs to stay with the patient. It's his job."

The EMT grunted, said, "Whatever," and then waved for the rear doors to be shut. Before they swung closed, Natalie leaned in, saying that she and the others would follow.

Then the doors slammed shut and the ambulance lurched forward, and we were moving.

Pugh kept weeping.

CHAPTER TWENTY-SEVEN

We spent the night at Northern Westchester Hospital in Mount Kisco, clustered in a waiting room on the fifth floor. Once I'd told them all about the phone call from Marguiles, the news about Greer's death, the unanimous decision was to remain on-post. Dale dozed in a chair, and Corry stretched out on the carpet. Natalie got the couch, and when she folded her jacket up to use it as a pillow, her pack of cigarettes fell out of a pocket. She threw them into the garbage can beneath the wall-mounted television without comment.

I couldn't sleep.

Pugh had been admitted without hassle, and Karen had given us the update as soon as the doctors had finished. He looked all right, she told us, but he'd have to stay under observation, at least until the hospital was certain his blood-sugar level was once again stable.

"They also want him to have a psychiatric evaluation," Kazanjian said.

"He underwent a voluntary evaluation after his son died," I said. "Depression."

"Had he tried to kill himself?"

"I don't think so." Lamia had run the field on the

institutionalization issue, but he'd mentioned nothing about Pugh attempting suicide.

"I've been working at the estate for almost three weeks," Kazanjian said, "and this is the first time his diabetes has been a problem. He hasn't had any trouble before. And it's not easy to go into insulin shock like that. Takes effort. Just one extra shot won't do it."

"I only saw the one syringe."

"There were another two on the bed, used. Found them when we were moving him to the gurney." Kazanjian brushed her bleached hair off her forehead, then narrowed her eyes at me. "You really didn't know he was diabetic? You're not just covering your ass?"

"We didn't know," I said.

"I thought Mosier had briefed you."

I'd kept silent. Either Mosier or Trent should have told us about Pugh's illness; neither had, and it made me almost sick with anger.

Karen left, returning to the estate, saying that Pugh was now in better hands than hers, and that she wanted to get some sleep. I took up post outside of Pugh's room, dragging a chair down the hall from the lounge. There was a window in the door, and when I stood I could see Pugh through it, lying in his bed, an IV running to his arm. He appeared to be sleeping, and on the bed he looked somehow diminished. The air smelled slightly of bleach and something that I thought of as sterile gauze. Sometimes I heard a voice from another room far away, or the sounds of footsteps on the pitted linoleum floor, but it was fairly quiet. Even the sick needed their sleep.

Yossi arrived at two with three other guards, and he and I argued about who would take the post on the door.

"You're beat," he told me. "Let one of my boys do it."

"I'm not heading home."

"Who told you to head home? Just lie down in the lounge."

"I'm not tired."

"You're a liar, then. You're going to need your strength, Atticus. Trent'll be here in the morning."

"Did someone call Marguiles?"

"I did. He'll be arriving with Trent. Go get some rest, my friend. I'll take over for now."

Pugh had shifted in his bed, and I could no longer see his face. I thought about stepping inside, asking if he was all right, but then I thought that was a stupid thing to do. Pugh was in a hospital, surrounded by strangers and guards with guns, he'd taken an overdose of insulin. He wasn't all right.

"Don't let anyone in to see him," I said.

"You know, I've been doing this job awhile. I think I can figure it out."

"It wasn't meant as an insult."

"Go and rest," Yossi said.

For an hour I sat at a table in the waiting room, watching a crappy print of *We're No Angels* on the television. The movie finished after three, and I had just realized that I hadn't called Erika when Dale suddenly sat up.

"What happened?" he asked.

"Nothing. The movie ended."

He looked around, blinked at the test pattern now showing on the television screen, then nodded. "Thought something happened."

"No change."

"What's wrong?"

"Nothing."

"I mean, what's wrong with you?"

"Nothing. Go back to sleep."

He grimaced, then nodded. It took a couple of seconds of shifting in the chair before he found a comfortable position for his oversized frame, and then he was asleep once more.

I thought about the people I should call, decided that it was too late for any of it.

Sometime after four, I dozed off, a deep drop into REM sleep, the kind that happens when you're too damn tired to actually rest. When my pager woke me a little after six, the only impressions my dreams left were of violence and pictures lost.

I'd slept with my cheek on my arm, and my hand had fallen asleep apart from the rest of me. It took some fumbling before I could silence my pager. I didn't recognize the number.

Dale was still asleep, Natalie, too. I didn't see Corry. I picked my way across the floor and found a pay phone, remembered that Erika had been in my dream, and Bridgett. The number on my pager was in Manhattan, and I didn't have the change for the call, so I used my credit card.

"Havel."

What a way to wake up, I thought. "It's Atticus. What do you want?"

"Same thing I wanted before, except this time I've got something to bring to the table with me."

I took off my glasses and rubbed the bridge of my nose. I'd woken up with the headache that had been born during the deposition, except it had matured, married, and now had children of its own. "How'd you get my pager number?"

"I'm an *investigative* reporter. You're not interested in what I have to say?"

"I'm interested in your leaving me alone," I said.

She made a disparaging grunt in my ear. I could hear a morning show in the background. Radio, not TV. Sounded like NPR. "You sleep alone a lot, don't you?" Chris Havel said, and when I didn't reply, she added, "Hey, no offense."

"I've tried to be polite to you, but you don't seem to have gotten it. So I'll try this—leave me the hell alone."

"I will, I promise, just hear me out. Listen, Atticus, I know about that court reporter, about Franklin Greer."

"He had a heart attack," I said.

"Yeah, that's what she'd like us to think."

I was awake, now. " 'She'?"

"Ah, I gather from the change in your tone that I finally have your attention?"

"Cut the crap. Why'd you say 'she'?"

"Because John Doe is Jane Doe, and I've got the eyewitness accounts to prove it. Been up all night chasing this down. I even have a description of her."

"Let's hear it."

Havel chuckled. "Give me some credit. You tell me where you are, I'll meet you and give you what you want. Then you let me tag along."

"I can't do that."

"Well, you aren't getting squat from me until we meet face-to-face. Those are my terms."

"I won't cut you out, Chris. I promise."

"Means nothing to me. We meet, then we talk."

I put my glasses back on, checked my watch. It was twenty-two past six. "This afternoon," I said. "I'll be home between three and four."

"Can't you make it sooner?"

"No."

She considered other arguments, then sighed. "All right. Where do you live?"

"I'm sure you've already figured that out."

"That a dare?"

"Good-bye, Miss Havel," I said, and hung up, turned around to find Natalie awake and watching me from the couch.

"What'd she want?"

"She says she has a description of John Doe, except it's Jane, not John."

"Not surprising, really."

I nodded my head in agreement.

Natalie got off the couch, looked at Dale.

"He'll never stand up straight again, sleeping like that," she said. "Where's Corry?"

"No idea. He was gone when I got up."

"Probably watching Pugh's room."

"For what it's worth," I said.

"Oh, you slept poorly."

"I must have. You're the second person to remark on it this morning."

"You need coffee."

"No, but it can't make me feel worse."

Natalie headed for the nurses' station, and I followed. We got directions from a man in his thirties with a pudgy, boyish face. He was cheerful, and spoke in a soft voice that required Natalie to lean across the counter to hear him. When she did, the nurse stared at her breasts, and, in fact, directed most of his conversation there.

"They're real," I told him.

The nurse turned pink, and Natalie shot me a look that was more amused than annoyed. We headed down the hall, took the elevator down to the ground floor, and found the cafeteria. It was mostly empty, some doctors and orderlies and nurses, and a handful of people all wearing the same strained look of not wanting to think about what was going on elsewhere in the hospital.

We got coffee and a seat by the wall and after a while Natalie said, "It's common to your gender."

"People staring at your chest?"

"Happens all the time."

"I'd hate it."

"Sometimes I do. Sometimes I ignore it. Not like you don't get objectified."

"I don't."

"No, you just don't notice," Natalie corrected. "Doesn't mean it doesn't happen. Now, what's eating you?"

I drank some of my coffee. Calling it bad would have been an insult to motor oil. "It's out of control," I said.

"Pugh's still alive."

"For how much longer? He's suicidal. You know it and I know it."

She sipped her coffee.

"Think about it," I said. "That monologue in the car said it all. He deliberately brought his blood sugar down, avoided eating. He knew what the insulin would do."

"I repeat," Natalie said. "Jerry is still alive."

"But Greer is dead. And who else is going to die on this one, Natalie? You? Dale? Corry?"

"Could be you," she mused.

"We can hope."

"Cut it out." Natalie brushed a stray couple of hairs back behind her ears. "It's not over yet. Lamia will take another deposition. We'll find a way to make it work. We'll keep Pugh alive."

"Even if he doesn't care to live?"

"We'll convince him."

"Up awful early, aren't you, son?"

I nodded and shut the door behind me. Corry, Natalie, and a guard from Sentinel, Fernando Picacio, were all outside. Corry had been sharing post with Picacio, and I'd asked Natalie to let me talk to Pugh alone. She'd grudgingly agreed.

I took the chair by Pugh's bed and looked him over. The fluorescent lights made his pallor look like a case of jaundice. The bleached pillowcase made his hair look like a mound of snow.

"Hell of a thing, huh?" he said cheerfully. "Can't believe I was so stupid."

"Were you?"

"Forgot I hadn't eaten."

"So you've said."

Pugh raised a bushy eyebrow. His feet made small peaks at the end of the blanket, and he focused on that. Finally, he said, "What if I did forget? If I thought I'd already taken my medicine? What would you think of that?"

"I wouldn't believe you."

"We all forget things, son. We all make mistakes."

"But you wouldn't make a mistake like that," I said.

"Maybe you give me too much credit."

"I don't think so."

"Well," Pugh said, as if we'd reached a shared conclusion. Perhaps we had. "Is that all you had to say?"

"Just tell me it was intentional, Jerry. No more bullshit, no more games, none of the fucking Will Rogers act. Tell me straight. Why did you try to kill yourself?"

His eyes locked on mine. "I told you already. I was done. I spoke the truth so it would be recorded, so that we could nail those whoreson pigs to the wall and cut out their cash-filled bellies. After that, there was nothing left."

"Trial," I said.

"You know as well as I do that the deposition was enough. You told me so yourself." He moved his left hand, rubbing his left eye. When he did, the clear IV running to his arm rattled. "I hear that sometimes it's even better than live testimony. Witness can't change his story, then, can't be battered in cross-examination or made to look an ass in front of a jury. After what Lamia pulled on me, I figure I'm doing Marguiles a favor."

"Hell of a favor, Jerry."

Pugh's hand went back to the sheets. "Don't smart-ass me, boy."

"You want me to say that I agree with you? That you were doing the right thing?"

"You don't have to agree with me, son. It's my life, it's my decision, and it's none of your damn business in any case. You're not talking me out of anything, and you're smart enough to know that you can't stop me."

I nodded. It didn't matter if the staff psychiatrist thought Pugh was suicidal or not; it didn't matter what anyone did. We could follow Pugh twenty-four hours a day, four seasons straight, and he would still find a time to take his own life, and sooner or later he'd get it right.

It was just another kind of assassination.

I sighed, getting back to my feet. "Greer died last night, Jerry, before his transcript of the deposition could be entered into the record. So you're going to have to hold off on your grand gesture, your penance, whatever the fuck you're calling it. You're going to have to sit for the lawyers again."

Pugh checked my face for the lie, and, not finding it, scrunched his eyes shut.

He was laughing when I left.

Corry handed us paper cups of coffee that he'd brought up from the cafeteria. According to the analog clock on the wall, it was eight minutes past nine. The elevators opened only twenty feet from the waiting room, and Trent saw us first, corrected his trajectory, and made straight for me. He was carrying a black leather portfolio, the one he used for operational notes. I couldn't read his expression. Marguiles was at his side.

The men reached us, and Trent put out a hand for Natalie, tried to give her a kiss on the cheek. She didn't resist, but she didn't bend to it, either, and Trent came away looking like he'd kissed ice.

"I'm glad you're all right," he told us.

"How's Pugh?" Marguiles asked.

"Stable, recovering," I said. "I can't speak to his state of mind."

"Why didn't you tell us he was diabetic?" Natalie asked her father.

Elliot Trent's eyes flickered. "I told Mosier *and* Kazanjian to notify you about Pugh's condition."

"Well, then, they forgot to share, Pop."

"I think we can put that down to Raymond," he said, turning to address Marguiles. "I apologize for that, Leslie. He was my man, on my payroll, and I read him wrong. I thought he was reliable."

"He's not my current concern," Marguiles said. "I'm more interested in hearing about how you're going to keep Pugh safe."

Trent nodded, shifted his portfolio from his left hand to his right. He had a Band-Aid covering the knuckles of his index and middle fingers on his right hand. The look that I couldn't read was still in his eyes.

"I was hoping that Atticus and I could discuss that," Trent said. "Would any of you mind if we spoke privately for a few minutes?"

"I would," Natalie said. "I'd like to be present."

Trent shook his head slightly. "It won't take long, Natalie, and I'd rather it were a private discussion."

Her look sharpened and turned to me.

"It's all right," I said.

"Where can we talk?"

"I managed to find the cafeteria once already. It'll do."

"Lead on," he said, and smiled.

I led on. He didn't say anything on the way, although he offered to buy me something to drink before we found a table. I declined. The cafeteria was busier now, filling with the sound of clanking crockery and conversation.

Trent got himself a cup of lemon tea, added two packets of artificial sweetener, and stirred. He'd set the portfolio on the table between us. It remained closed.

"I want you to withdraw," he said.

"Absolutely not, Elliot."

"You're running out of luck, Atticus, and luck's what's kept you going this far. If Doe had picked yesterday to take out Pugh rather than Greer, he would have succeeded."

"And Sentinel would have prevented that?"

He nodded solemnly.

"Whereas my people would have what? Held the target over Pugh's heart?"

"Your people would have created gaps that Doe could edge through. You don't have the manpower for this operation. You don't have the facility. It's only because of my support that you've made it this far."

"You're forgetting Mosier."

"I made a mistake. I'm big enough to admit that." He sipped his tea. The cup was plastic, the same color tan that's used on prosthetic limbs. "Now you need to admit you've taken on too much. So far, you've made it without major incident. But now somebody could end up dead."

"Somebody like Pugh?"

"Or my daughter. Or both, and more. Remember Katie Romero, remember Rubin Febres. Do you want that to happen again?"

"It won't happen again," I said. "I won't let it."

"Your arrogance won't keep Pugh alive."

"No, my ability will. Mine, and my team's."

"Not without my support."

I nodded. This was where he'd been heading all along, and I'd seen it the way a pilot sees the lights of a runway when coming in for a landing. "You're going to pull Sentinel out?"

"If I have to, yes."

"I'll call in stringers."

Trent almost laughed. "Who's going to work with you? Where are you going to find twenty guards on such short notice? What about their equipment? Transport vehicles? And how will you finance the operation?"

"I'll go to Marguiles, tell him what I need. He could co-sign a loan."

"You're determined to fight me on this?"

I smiled.

Trent pushed his plastic cup to the side of the table, flipped open his portfolio. He removed a stack of photographs, handed them to me.

"I didn't want to do this," he said.

There were twenty-four of them, eight-by-tens, black and white, surveillance shots. The focus on most was fuzzy, the result of massive magnification, but in all of them the subjects were clear.

"They were presented to me early this morning," Trent said. "As far as surveillance photos go, they're not the best I've ever seen. But they'll do."

"Who gave these to you?" I asked.

"Hunter Drake. He wanted to know if I was aware of your relationship with my daughter." Trent rubbed his bandaged knuckles. "I explained to him that if he or his sister ever tried to blackmail me again, I'd kill them."

I set the photos back on the table, facedown, careful about my movement. The rage hadn't reached my hands.

A couple of the captured moments were easy to figure out: the hug outside the restaurant before the meeting with Mallory; the kiss on the corner in Times Square. Shots of affection, only incriminating because of the suspicion they would breed.

But there were others, and they left nothing to the imagination. The sequence looked to have all been taken on the same night, shots stolen out of my apartment from across the street. The night I'd met Natalie at Paddy's, just before she had quit Sentinel and joined me on the audit. We had been wild, using each other freely, inspired by our anger. The memory of it came back with the images in front of me and made it all feel cheap.

"What do they want from you?" I asked Trent.

"They want me to pull Sentinel out, of course. To leave you high and dry."

I wasn't certain I'd heard him right. "And you're going to give them that?"

"No," Trent said. "Sentinel will remain. It's you who's going to pull out."

I was too stunned to speak.

"You've jeopardized the safety of the principal by becoming emotionally involved with another member of the protective effort," Trent declared. "You've broken one of the fundamental rules. The only thing worse would be if you were sleeping with the principal. There's no way you can be objective about your operation. You're distracted by the people around you, you're paying attention to my daughter rather than to the environment you're interacting with, rather than the safety of your charge."

"You do both me and Natalie a disservice," I said.

"If the Drakes had been shooting bullets instead of film, you both would be dead."

"But they weren't."

With great care, Trent said, "There is no way your relationship with Natalie cannot hinder the operation."

"We've done fine thus far." There was no point in trying to explain my relationship with Natalie, no point in telling him that we were no longer bedding down together. In his eyes, it would make no difference.

"Professionally, you're required to remove yourself from the operation," Trent said.

"No."

His fingers suddenly began drumming on the edge of the table as he realized I wasn't going to accept the argument. The tapping was like a burst of Morse code. Then it stopped as abruptly as it had begun.

"No father likes to know that his daughter is having sex," Trent said softly. "I suppose we all want our little girls to be virgins forever. It's vanity. But at some point one has to recognize that she's become an adult in her own right, free to make her own decisions and mistakes. One hopes that the man she's decided on is a good one, a man who deserves her, and treats her well."

"Elliot—"

"Shut up," he spat. "This has less to do with you than you think. I don't approve, but I've tried hard to let Natalie follow her heart, rather than follow my will."

"Then why—"

"Because her life is more important than her happiness, and the life of the principal is paramount in any operation. You may not care about the details of these photographs, you might be the sort who brags about your conquests, I don't know. You may not give a damn about the respect you receive from the people you work with, about their willingness to follow your orders."

He reached across the table, slid the stack together.

He made an effort not to look at them as he returned
the photographs to his portfolio.

"But Natalie does care about those things," he said.
"Her reputation, the respect she receives, they matter a
great deal to her. It would upset her enormously to see
those things suffer in the eyes of her peers. In the eyes
of Sentinel."

"You wouldn't," I said.

"To keep Natalie alive? To protect Pugh? It's what
you're forcing me to do."

I searched his face and saw only his intensity in
return, nothing to tell me the truth. He had to be
bluffing. No matter how badly he wanted me out Trent
wouldn't let the photographs of Natalie circulate. He
wouldn't humiliate her like that. He couldn't do that
to her.

But the mere fact that he would threaten to, that he
would use Natalie like a chip in a poker game, that said
it all.

I shook my head, got up from the table. "I used to
think that, in your own twisted way, you put Natalie
first. I was wrong."

"Tell Marguiles you're out," Trent said. "The pictures go up in smoke as soon as the trial starts." Trent
picked up his portfolio. He got to his feet. "You've left
me no alternative."

My hands hurt, and I realized I'd made fists. If I'd
been holding coal, it would have turned to diamonds
by now.

"What's it going to be, Atticus?" Trent asked.

I wondered what Trent would say to Marguiles,
what he'd say to Jerry Pugh. I wondered if he'd landed
a good punch on Hunter Drake when he'd first seen

the photographs. I hoped so. I hoped it had required stitches.

I said, "Pugh's diabetic, you know. Make sure he eats."

Then I left.

CHAPTER TWENTY-EIGHT

Midge in the apartment below ours caught me going up the stairs, and asked if I'd take a minute to check the locks on her front door. "I talked to your roommate about it, she said you'd be home last night."

"I got held up," I said.

"Do you have a minute?"

"Later would be better."

"It'll just take a minute. Please?" She smiled, and it occurred to me that she was used to getting her way. Suddenly, I hated her almost as much as I hated Elliot Trent. "Pretty please?"

I repressed a shudder, went to look at her front door. The locks were fine. A little scratched, maybe. I'm not a locksmith, though, and I told her as much.

"Really? Then what exactly do you do?" Midge asked.

"Protect my principals," I said.

The apartment was empty when I finally made it upstairs. I went straight to the phone, turned off the ringer, and played the one message waiting on the machine.

"Figured you got held up on business," Erika's

recorded voice said. "So I'm spending the day with Bridgett. Call if you want to. You know the number."

I punched the button to erase the message, turned off the answering machine, went into my room. I dropped my holster on the bed, my gun still in it, turned my pager off, then stripped down. I shaved in the bathroom, stayed in the shower until the hot water ran out, adding two more minutes under the cold stuff before shutting off the tap.

I wanted to climb into bed and sleep, and I tried it, and failed miserably. After an hour of tangling the sheets, I rose once more, dressed. I thought about putting on some music, some loud Lester Bowie, or maybe Charlie Parker. I didn't.

I sat in the chair by the window and looked out at the sliver of the city I could see through the buildings. It was another hot and humid day in hell. Cars and people dragged along the street below, as if the tar in the asphalt had melted.

The loneliness came and kicked my ass. I thought, this is the call you need to make, and it's a simple thing, really, just numbers and then voices, and what's so damn hard about that? What's so damn hard about saying, "Hey, it's me," and then taking it as it comes?

But I just kept looking out the window.

The intercom woke me with a sequence of barks. The barks kept coming, somebody rapidly pressing the button again and again. It was almost as pleasant as the staccato blast of an air horn.

I went down the hall, pressed the button to speak, praying that it wasn't Natalie, or Dale, or Corry. My prayer was answered.

"Hey, it's Havel. You going to let me in or what?"

"Go away," I told the intercom, realized that she wouldn't, and that I'd forgotten she was coming by.

"What the hell do you mean? It's three-thirty, it is exactly between three and four in the afternoon, when you told me to come by. Now let me in."

"Let's reschedule."

"No. Let me in or I'll buzz everyone in this damn building and tell them that the guy in 5D is selling kiddie porn from his apartment."

I buzzed her in, waited by my front door. She was fast on the stairs, and came onto the landing with a self-satisfied grin, taking off a pair of tiny sunglasses that she hung from her collar. She had a leather knapsack slung over her shoulder, and her blouse was almost the same shade of tan. Her pants were dark blue.

"You don't make things easy," Chris Havel said.

I shut the door after her, then pointed to the chairs around the kitchen table. She took a seat and said, "You got anything to drink?"

"How about water?"

"How about a beer?"

I checked the refrigerator and saw that I had a bottle of Anchor Steam remaining. There had been three bottles when I'd left the previous day.

"Where's Trent?" Havel asked.

"Natalie or Elliot?"

"Your partner."

I shook my head, said, "No idea."

She raised an eyebrow at me, took a swig of the beer, then said, "Let me give you what I've got, then you can bring me up to speed about what's happening on your end."

"Fair enough," I said.

"I talked to a bunch of people last night," Chris Havel began. "Everybody that I could find who was on the subway platform. Most can't say anything about Greer other than that he suddenly collapsed as the southbound 6 train was pulling in at Fifty-ninth Street. Rush hour was long over, not too many people around, but the station wasn't empty, either. Now, I haven't gone to the cops with this yet, so there's no medical evidence backing it up. There won't be an autopsy or anything like that unless it's declared a wrongful death. So, for all intents and purposes it looks like Mr. Franklin Greer had a fatal coronary, and that's it. You follow?"

"Right behind you," I said.

Havel took another pull from the bottle. "All right, then. This is, as they say, what went down.

"Greer was waiting on the platform, had his equipment with him, the black cases with his steno machine and his laptop, one of those carts you can bungee-cord everything to. Lot of people on the platform. This is between nine thirty-five, nine-forty.

"Now, there was a guy—says he's from Rio, but I think he's probably from Flushing—playing his guitar on the platform. He says that another man, young, pulling a similar set-up, stands in close to Greer, starts up a conversation. The musician sees the young guy gesture at Greer's steno case, he figures they're talking about their equipment, maybe. I can buy that."

"It's possible," I said.

"Now, there's also a couple of girls there, secretaries, they've had a few pitchers after work and are getting ready to go home. They all confirm seeing these two people talking, except that all three of them insist it was a man and a woman talking, not two men. They say that she's just wearing men's clothes."

"And?"

"And then the Number 6 starts pulling in, and people are looking at the train, and when the secretaries look back, Greer is on the platform, and this other person is on his or her knees next to him, checking for a pulse. People start noticing. This other person looks up and points at one of the secretaries, tells her to call an ambulance."

"Description?"

Havel looked uncomfortable. "Well, not really. Apparently her eyes were either blue or brown. Her hair was either blond or light brown, straight, not long. Slight build. Maybe five ten, maybe six feet tall. Nothing else, except that the Samaritan was wearing glasses."

"I see," I said.

"But you see what I mean, that it was a woman, right?"

"Sure."

She scowled at me before continuing. "Okay, fine. The Samaritan starts giving CPR, working on Greer, and she's at it for three, four minutes, working up a sweat, when the Transit Cops show up. They make a little perimeter, one of them comes in on the CPR with the Samaritan. This cop, his name's Holman, he's doing compressions while the Samaritan is breathing. Says that as far as he can tell, nothing's wrong, except that Greer isn't responding to the CPR. As far as he was concerned, the guy was already dead and gone.

"Another ten minutes, EMS arrives, they wave everybody off, get to work on the body. They pack him up, transport him, the MTA guys grab Greer's cart, start taking statements.

"And the Good Samaritan has vanished. So's Greer's steno equipment." Chris Havel looked at me as if I should be convinced. "There you are."

"Samaritans bolt all the time," I said. "They're afraid of getting sued for the good turn they've tried to perform. Or they realize too late they didn't want to get involved in the first place."

"And you think she just took Greer's case by mistake?"

"It's reasonable."

"Why are you suddenly being so thick?" Havel demanded. "I'd have thought you'd be right with me on this."

"You have no proof."

"Wrong." She flashed me her tight-lipped grin.

I waited.

"I couldn't figure out how she'd done it," Havel said. "If she'd used a weapon of some sort to bring him down, then there would be a mark, blood, something. But Greer was pronounced DOA at the hospital, and there wasn't a mark on him, far as anyone could tell."

"I'm listening."

"So she had to take him down somehow, right? I mean, once the guy's on the ground, it's a snap to kill him. All you have to do is perform the CPR wrong. If you landmark wrong for your compressions, you can end up shattering the xiphoid process, that bone that juts from the bottom of your rib cage. You shatter that, you've got a great big internal hemorrhage."

"Which would lead to a distended abdomen, which the doctors at the hospital would have noticed," I said.

Havel nodded. "Right, but if it was a result of CPR,

it's not out of the ordinary. There's nothing suspicious about it. It's a fatal mistake, but it's not murder."

After a second, I nodded. If you accepted that Greer's collapse was induced rather than accidental, everything Havel was saying made sense. The Samaritan didn't have to shatter the xiphoid, either, to do the deed. She would have had the whole body to play with.

But it was still just a theory. "Where's your proof?"

"Play along with me. If you were this woman, you wanted to kill Greer, how would you have taken him down? Without leaving a mark? Without leaving some sort of trace that you had made Greer collapse?"

"I'd use a needle," I said. "A straight jab to the thigh, perhaps. I don't know chemicals that well. There are plenty of drugs that would do it."

"But you could end up with bloodstains, puncture wounds. There'd be evidence of what you'd done, right?"

"Yes, but you'd have to know what you were looking for."

Havel reached for her knapsack, where she had set it beside her chair, and hoisted it onto her lap. She began unbuckling the top flap. "Suppose you didn't want to leave any marks at all? What then?"

I watched her hands play with the flap while I thought. "I'd use a stun gun."

"Give the man a Kewpie doll," Chris Havel said. She lifted the flap and came out with a paper bag. She dumped the contents of the bag on the table, and there it was, between the sugar bowl and the salt and pepper shakers, a stubby little black stun gun.

"It's rated at 250,000 volts," Havel said. "I went back down to the platform around midnight, found a bum who'd been sleeping between posts. He'd seen the whole thing. I gave him ten bucks, and he told me that when the train came in, he saw the Samaritan throw something on the tracks.

"I found it just beyond the third rail. Had to figh the rats for it."

I couldn't tell if the stun gun was the same one Drama had used on me or not. There wouldn't be any prints on it, I knew. There wouldn't be anything usable, anything that would help us find her. But it was very clever, the stun gun, and I couldn't help but be impressed. They're not a quiet weapon—in fact, they're designed to make noise, it's part of what makes them a deterrent—but by waiting for the train, Drama had ensured no one would hear the gun go off. It would have looked like she was reaching out to touch Greer's chest, nothing more. And then Greer would have gone down, suddenly, in pain, unable to move, and before he could speak, Drama would have gone to his neck, pretending to check his pulse, turned her cheek above his mouth, pretending to feel for his breathing.

With her fingers on his carotid artery, his face hidden by hers, she would have pushed down and in, and Greer would have been unable to make a sound while she began killing him. Once he was unconscious, she would have moved to begin CPR.

And the only mark left behind would have been a slight red discoloration where the stun gun had pressed against Greer's body, rapidly obliterated by the pressure of her hands on his chest during CPR.

"Pretty good, huh?" Havel asked.

"Brilliant," I said.

"Thank you."

I realized she thought I meant her. "You should give it to the police," I said, indicating the stun gun.

"They wouldn't know what to do with it. No crime's been committed, at least not as far as they're concerned."

"Call the Bureau, talk to Special Agent Fowler. Tell him you talked to me, tell him it's about John Doe. He'll hear you out."

"We had a deal, Kodiak, remember? You, me, Natalie Trent, the rest of your people, we're going to hunt down an assassin."

I used a napkin from the table to drop the stun gun back into the brown paper bag. Then I handed the bag back to Havel.

"I'm out," I said.

"Funny. Now, let's get started."

"No. I'm off the job as of this morning. You want to chase after Greer's murderer, call Elliot Trent."

The paper bag crumpled as she tightened her grip on it. "What the hell is with you?"

"Sentinel's taken over."

"Why?"

"I'm not at liberty to say."

"You son of a bitch, you drag me over here, I share what I've got, then you tell me you're not playing ball anymore? Fuck you!" She showed me her middle finger. "Fuck you!"

"If I was on the job, I'd let you in. Trent forced me out this morning."

"How? Why?"

I shook my head. "I can't go into it." She scowled at me, angry, and I took her empty beer bottle off the table, rinsed it out in the sink. I dried the bottle with a dish towel, then dropped it in the recycling bin.

In 4D, down below, Midge started hammering something into the wall.

"My agent has already talked to three publishers
about this," Havel said. "I've already started my background work on a book about Doe——"

"Call Trent's office, call Sentinel, see if they'll let
you ride along. They'll probably say yes. Trent likes his
publicity, as long as it's good."

Chris Havel stuffed the paper bag into her knapsack, cinched the flap shut with a savage jerk. She
threw the knapsack over her shoulder, getting up, and
headed for the door. "You suck," she said.

"Give Trent a call."

"He'll never let me in after the beating I gave him
in the paper, and you know that. Thanks a bunch,
Kodiak. Thanks for nothing."

CHAPTER TWENTY-NINE

Paddy Reilly's is divided into two rooms, really, the main bar that you enter into, with a little stage for the musical acts, and an open room in the back where a television hangs from the wall. The Yankees were on the screen, playing good ball against the Seattle Mariners. The Mariners were playing better ball. I got myself a Guinness and a seat, and watched. By the bottom of the fifth, the Mariners were up by three, Griffey coming in on a double hit by Jay Buhner. I liked Buhner; he reminded me of a Caucasian Dale, with less hair.

The bar started filling as the afternoon matured to evening, and by the top of the seventh the Yankees had closed the gap to one run, and enough people had arrived that I could no longer hear the babble of the game commentators. Small mercies. I'd had three pints, and I wasn't feeling any of them. Nothing quite matches the frustration of trying to get drunk when you can't do it.

Someone tapped my shoulder, and I turned my head to see Natalie.

"What a surprise," I said.

"Are you drunk?"

"Drunk?"

"Hitting the sauce."

"More broiling in my own juices. Giving it the old college try. Like that."

She waved a hand in the direction of the bar, and Dale and Corry came up from by the stage. Dale began gathering chairs, and they all took seats around me. I went back to watching the game, saw that Joe Torre had taken David Wells out and replaced him with Grahame Lloyd. I liked Grahame, too. Not as much as Jay Buhner, but I liked him.

"What happened?" Dale asked.

"I needed to go home," I said. "I had to examine someone's door."

"Pop came back from the cafeteria alone, and he told Marguiles, in front of all of us, that you had decided we were pulling out. Sentinel's taken over."

"Good luck to Sentinel," I said.

Dale murmured something I couldn't hear over the crowd buzz.

"Neil Lamia gave me a call after we left Pugh at the hospital, though," Natalie said. "Asked to meet with you and me. I told him we'd be at your apartment at eight. That gives us forty-three minutes."

"You shouldn't have done that," I said.

"You object?"

"Yeah, I object," I said, as Lloyd threw a slider to Joey Cora. Joey nailed it into left field, along the line and into the warning track, and got to second base standing up. "It's my apartment. You shouldn't volunteer it without consulting me."

"Sort of like you quitting without consulting us."

"That was my decision."

"No, it was our decision. If you're going to complain about my lack of courtesy, take a look at yourself first."

I looked away from the game, at her. She was sitting with her elbows on her knees, her face only a couple inches away, to make certain I could hear her.

"You've been elected group spokesperson, have you?" I asked.

"That's right. And the group wants to know what the hell happened. You gave my father exactly what he wanted, Atticus. Why the hell would you do that?"

"Your father was going to pull the Sentinel support, Natalie. He was going to leave us high and dry without the backup we needed on Pugh. How were we going to protect him? How were we going to keep a suicidal principal alive with only four people on the detail?"

"There are stringers we could have hired."

"Stringers who would be willing to work with me? Find me one in this city who'd take orders from me. Just one. Especially after Trent's smear campaign. You'll have an easier time finding an honest man."

"Oh, so that's it," Natalie said. "You're believing what my father has been saying."

"No," I said, "that's not it. I'm good at my job, damn good. But there are limits."

"We haven't hit them yet," Dale said. "I'll admit we're close to the wall on this one, but we're not up against it."

"That's a matter of perspective."

Natalie reached for my hand and I jerked away, grabbed my pint. Everyone caught the message in my movement, and for a moment there was an awful stillness. Then Natalie asked, "What did he say?"

"I told you."

"What else did he say?"

"What makes you think there has to be something else?"

"You wouldn't have backed down. You've never backed down in front of my father before. Why would you do it now?"

I drained my pint, tried to focus on the baseball game.

"What'd he threaten you with? Having your license pulled?"

The inning ended, and an ad for Chevy trucks came on the screen.

"Goddamnit, Atticus, answer me!"

Natalie had straightened back in her chair. Dale and Corry were leaning on the table, waiting. A waitress came by and took my empty glass and asked us if we wanted anything else. Corry told her no, thank you.

"The Drakes paid your father a visit," I told Natalie. "They came bearing gifts. Eight inches by ten inches, and glossy."

Her brow had barely furrowed before she filled in the blanks, and then her eyes widened. Her reaction was much like I'd imagined mine had been when Trent had handed over the pictures, but Natalie's skin is fairer, so it was easy to see her blush. She absorbed the knowledge, and then shook her head.

"So he knows about us, so what? It doesn't matter to me. It shouldn't matter to you."

"Knows about what?" Corry asked.

Dale wrapped an arm around his shoulder and whispered in his ear. Corry re-examined Natalie and me.

"How'd I miss that?" he asked.

"We tried to be discreet," Natalie said.

"You were successful."

"Not successful enough," I said. Now there was an ad for McDonald's. Lots of white people were happy about french fries.

"There's more, isn't there?" Natalie asked.

"The Drakes let your father keep the photos."

Nobody said anything for the next two minutes. The game resumed, the Mariners batting from the middle of the order.

Natalie said, "Dale, Corry, you two wait here until nine, then join us at Atticus'." I felt her take my hand. "Let's go, partner. We've got a potential client to entertain."

"Oh, joy," I said, but I followed her anyway.

Back at my apartment, I put on a pot of coffee, thinking that perhaps Lamia might like a cup later. Natalie hadn't said anything during our walk back. It was ten of eight.

"Did he say what he wanted?" I asked her.

"No, just that he wanted to meet me and my partner tonight at eight."

"He called us partners?"

"Yes."

"So did Havel."

"Maybe we should file the paperwork or something," Natalie said. "Come up with a name. Trent and Kodiak, perhaps?"

"Too many fricatives," I said.

She didn't grin. "Of course, it's going to be a pain in the ass, trying to start our own firm in the town my father owns."

"He won't like it."

"The hell with him," she said. "After using me as

leverage against you, he'll be lucky if I give a flying fuck about what he likes ever again. Part of me wants to go into business just to spite him."

"And the other part?"

"It's what I do, it's what you do. It's what we're good at. I've only had one other career, you know that, and at twenty-eight, I can't go back to modeling."

"You went to college, you've got a liberal arts education," I said. "A world of employment awaits you."

"A bachelor's in French literature. That's a growth market." She reached past me to the cupboard, got herself a mug, and poured herself half a cup of coffee. "Before we left the hospital, Marguiles told me that Lamia and he had already scheduled another deposition. Pugh is supposed to be discharged tomorrow afternoon sometime. Marguiles said they'd take his depo—again—the day after, on Thursday."

"If he doesn't get taken out before then."

"Sentinel's got a pretty tight lock-down on Pugh right now. I don't think he's in any danger for the immediate time being."

"Then Drama will have to take him at the deposition," I said.

"We're no longer entertaining the possibility that there's a John Doe, or even that Drama and Doe are a team?"

"Chris Havel presented me with some fairly persuasive circumstantial evidence this afternoon," I said, and then explained Havel's theory about the court reporter's death. "As of now, I'm thinking there's just one assassin, and that the killer is a lady."

"Well, a woman, at least."

"I stand corrected. Lady or not, though, she'll try to keep Pugh from speaking at the next deposition."

"Trial begins Monday. This is their last chance to depose Pugh before they start."

"Which means that it's Drama's last chance to complete her contract."

"Pure trap," Natalie said.

"What?"

She looked at me as if I should have understood her, then grinned. "Sorry. It's a sniper term. When you're trapping, you keep your crosshairs fixed and wait for the target to come to you. You pick your field of fire, and then you wait, and eventually, when their head moves into the zone, you pull the trigger."

"As opposed to?"

"Tracking. When you're tracking, you acquire your target, then follow it with your sight, giving it lead, and taking the shot as soon as you're ready. Most snipers prefer tracking to trapping. It's more active. When you're trapping, there's a chance your shot will never come to you."

"But if Drama knows when and where—" I said.

"It's a dunker. She'll just wait until Pugh puts his head in front of her bullet. Speaking metaphorically, of course."

"Or literally."

"She hasn't gone for the long shot, yet," Natalie mused. "Wonder why."

"Maybe she's saving it."

"Or maybe she has instructions to use a different method. You shoot someone in the head from five hundred yards, there's no doubt what the victim died from."

"And that's more subtle than blowing them up?"

Natalie shrugged. "Maybe DTS wants to send a message. 'Rat on us and we'll blow you to kingdom come.'"

"Maybe."

The intercom went off, and I checked it, then buzzed Neil Lamia through the front door. Natalie took another mug down while we waited for him to come up the stairs, and I opened the door immediately after he knocked.

"I have to make this quick," Lamia said without preamble.

"We were going to offer you coffee," I said.

"No. Thank you."

He waited impatiently while I shut and locked the front door, glancing around, then made his way to the kitchen, where he greeted Natalie. He was carrying a barrister's briefcase with him, and he rested it on the table before opening it.

"How many people know I'm here?" Lamia asked us.

"Four," Natalie said. "Myself, Atticus, Dale Matsui, and Corry Herrera."

"Those other two, they were the men with you at the Sheraton yesterday?"

"That's correct."

"And no one else?"

"That's it."

Lamia moved his look from Natalie to me. It'd been just over twenty-four hours since I'd seen him last, but he looked like the time had been spent on the rack. His eyes were puffy, black walnuts surrounded by irritated flesh. Lamia exhaled a burst of air, then opened his bag and brought out a thick manila envelope. He handed it to Natalie. She tore the flap open and pulled out the first sheet. I watched her face as she scanned the paper but couldn't track her reaction and then she handed the sheet to me.

It was a photocopy of a bank statement, the First

Bank Savings and Loan, in Georgetown, Grand Cayman. It was a numbered account, but someone's script on the original identified the statement as that of William T. Boyer.

I looked at Lamia.

"If anyone asks me, I'll deny ever being here," Neil Lamia said.

"You should have told me you wanted the meeting off the record," Natalie said. "I would have picked a different location."

Lamia shut his bag, picked it up. "I contacted you. I knew what I was doing then. I know what I'm doing now." The weight of his barrister's bag suddenly had turned enormous, although I knew that wasn't where his burden rested. He'd given us gold, and he'd crossed himself and who knew who else to bring it here, and the conflict over his actions was visible in his eyes.

"Why'd you come back on the case?" I asked.

Lamia looked at the envelope in Natalie's hands.

"I have a family, Mr. Kodiak," he said. "May you have a good night."

CHAPTER THIRTY

Dale had a cruller and a cup of coffee for each of us when I met him the next morning. He'd driven his van into the city, and I opened the garage for him, let him park it in my spot, next to the motorcycle. There was an oil stain on the pavement, left by some long-forgotten vehicle. I knew it wasn't from Bridgett's car; she'd never let her Porsche spring a leak.

We walked to the subway stop on Park, munching on our pastries and sipping at our coffees and not having a whole lot to say. It was eight o'clock on a Wednesday morning, and the weather was already oppressive, already hot, with the humidity hanging in the air like wet laundry drying on a clothesline.

We were going to see William Boyer. We were planning on applying a little pressure.

In the packet Lamia had left behind, there were almost thirty sheets. No originals, all bank statements, along with a typed piece of paper that gave William Boyer's New York City address. Three banks, two in the Caymans, one in Switzerland, all accounts apparently under the control of William Boyer. The documentation covered the last three months, back to April, and they were busy records with lots of transactions.

We knew what we were looking for, though, and it didn't take us long before we began getting hits, one after another. Fifty thousand dollars transferred here, seventy-five thousand there. April had seen wire transfers totaling one million and seventy-five dollars. May and June had each seen five hundred thousand and forty dollars moved.

"Why the odd numbers?" Natalie asked.

"Transfer fees," I said. "Figure he's moved two million dollars so far."

"I've got no less than fifteen accounts these transfers go to," Natalie said. "Ten in April, then another five in May."

"Add six more in June," I said.

"Twenty-one separate accounts?" Natalie said. "Jesus, where does she find time to kill people? She must be running around like a nut, opening and closing accounts."

I shook my head. "No, none of these are recent, and I'll bet you my left leg every account listed is now closed. Boyer transfers the money to bank A, bank A is under orders to transfer it immediately to bank B, and that's when Drama moves it to her account in South Africa, or wherever. Lots and lots of cut-outs, and no way to trace it back."

Natalie snapped the sheaf of papers in her hands, tapped their edges against my kitchen table. "But now we know for certain that Boyer bought the hit on Pugh."

"No, we don't," I said. "All we know is that he's paying for it. Doesn't mean he commissioned it. We'll probably never know who commissioned it."

"Two million dollars to kill Pugh," Natalie said with a sigh. "That's what DTS was prepared to pay us just to get out of the way. That's kind of flattering."

"Except that they're probably paying Drama more. Another million or two on completion. This is just her retainer."

"Nice work if you can get it."

"Maybe I'll go in for a career change," I said. "After all, Erika's going to need a college fund."

Natalie began to tell me how not funny I was when the intercom went off again. I buzzed Corry and Dale up, sat them at the table in the kitchen, and waited with Natalie while they played catch-up on the paper chase.

"Nice work if you can get it," Corry said.

"He's stealing my lines," Natalie complained.

"How'd you get these?" Dale asked. "Lamia bring them?"

"Lamia who?" I said.

"Can we assume that Boyer is Drama-slash-Doe's contact?" Corry asked.

"I think it's a safe assumption," Natalie said. "The assassin has to have some sort of protocol for contacting the contractor."

"That doesn't mean Boyer's got a way to contact her," Dale said. "Drama doesn't strike me as the type who'd take that sort of risk."

"She doesn't have a choice," I said. "Suppose DTS changes the terms of the hit, or suppose they don't want Pugh dead after all. They have to be able to call her off. They have to be able to contact her."

"So Boyer may know who Drama is," Corry said. "Maybe even be able to give us a description."

"I doubt they've ever had a face-to-face," I said. "If they've talked at all, it's been under that whole 'I work for John Doe' cover, and it was probably over the phone."

Dale rubbed his neck. "Which brings up another point. Are we really certain that John Doe doesn't exist? That there's only, as you've named her, Drama?"

"No," I said.

Corry laughed. "We are *so* fucked," he said.

"Yeah, this is where it gets good," Natalie agreed.

"It doesn't get anything," Dale said. "We're off the job, remember?"

"We can't just sit on this," Corry said. "We've got to do something."

"Dale and I will talk to Mr. Boyer tomorrow morning," I said. "We'll see if he can't be pressured into giving up what he knows about the assassin."

"Why Dale?" Corry asked.

"Because he's big and scary," I said.

"I can be big and scary."

"That's only before you've had your morning cup of coffee," Natalie said.

The train dropped Dale and me at Sixty-eighth Street, and we began walking west, toward where Fifth Avenue borders Central Park.

"What are you thinking?" Dale asked.

"Just making certain we haven't picked up a tail. Don't want anybody taking any more candid pictures of me."

"We're clear." He chuckled. "Don't suppose Trent would let me see those photos, do you?"

"You're queer, remember?"

"I understand you're in the pictures, too, moron. In all your unfettered glory."

"Forgive me, I was being unforgivably heterosexist."

Dale responded with something about the money to be made selling dirty pictures of Natalie and me, and by the time we rounded Seventy-seventh Street, both of us were laughing pretty hard. We headed down the block looking for numbers, staring at the façades on both sides of the street, so we didn't notice it at first. Then I saw the cars, and I stopped, and so did Dale.

Four sector cars from the Nineteenth Precinct were parked at the curb outside the townhouse we wanted. The townhouse was brick and bright, and a tree was growing on the sidewalk right out front. A CSU van had just cut its engine and was spitting out technicians. I didn't see anyone from the ME's office, but all that meant was that they hadn't arrived yet.

"Fuck me," I said.

"She knew we were coming," Dale said, after a second. "And she beat us here. She whacked him before he could roll."

A couple of uniforms were at the door to the townhouse, covering the entry. Two plainclothed detectives climbed out of their unmarked, stopped at the foot of the stairs to the entrance. They exchanged words with the uniforms present, and then they entered the house.

"We need to call Lamia, we need to warn him. He could be in real danger," Dale said.

"No, he's all right. Drama needs the deposition to hit Pugh, and she needs Lamia to get the deposition. He's fine."

"How'd she know we were coming?"

"We don't know that Boyer's dead," I said, and then the coroner's people arrived, and I shut my mouth. Dale gave me a look that took no joy in being proved correct.

We went down the street, close enough to mix with the ten or eleven other people who had clustered around the entrance to the crime scene. The gawkers were babbling and pointing, crime scene speculation, and it didn't take more than a minute to realize that they knew less than we did.

"What now?" Dale asked.

I saw Chris Havel on the far side of the group, a cellular phone wedged under her ear, pen moving over the pad she held in her hand. If we got out before she saw us, I wouldn't have to answer any damn questions, and just as I thought that, she saw me. She said a last word to her phone and turned it off, jogging out into the street to get around the vehicles to us.

"Hey, what're you doing here?" Havel asked me.

"Morning constitutional."

"You're fifty blocks from home."

"I have a hearty constitution."

"Uh-huh," Havel said, and turned her eyes to Dale. "You go all the way up," she observed.

"Dale Matsui."

"Christian Havel. Everyone calls me Chris."

I watched while they shook hands.

"You're the one who's making Atticus look good in the papers," Dale said.

"I was, until he froze me out." Havel glanced over at me. "You're not back on the job by any chance, are you?"

"Not exactly," I said.

"Here to see William Boyer?"

"That was the plan."

"Why?"

"He owes me money," I said.

"Get it from his survivors. Boyer is dead."

It wasn't as if I didn't know that it was true, but when she said it, I felt suddenly sad. Pugh had said he was married, I remembered.

"How?" I asked.

"Shot sometime this morning. Neighbor heard shots and called the police, there was a car only a block away, and it arrived in time to catch two suspects fleeing. They're already down at the One-Nine playing twenty questions with the detectives, but the three of us know they didn't do it, don't we?"

"Any details on the suspects?"

"Man and a woman, both white, both blond. The guy was big, like your friend here, or at least that's what I've heard. In their thirties. That's about all I've got. Mean anything to you?"

"Maybe," I said. "You're sure they arrested two people?"

Havel pointed her black Cross pen at a man in his late teens who was in among the spectators. "That kid there, lives down the block, saw the arrests. He's the one who gave me the descriptions. Said he heard the blond woman telling the arresting officers that they had no idea who she was."

Chesapeake, I thought. "You don't have the names?"

"I can find out, if you're willing to trade information. You're working again, aren't you? You going to protect Pugh at his deposition tomorrow?"

"She is remarkably well informed," Dale observed. "How does she know so much?"

"She claims she has a source inside Sentinel," I answered.

Havel grinned. "So why were you on your way to see Boyer?"

"Who's your source?" I asked.

"I can't give that up and you know it." Her grin turned sly. "You let me ride along, though, and I won't have to be so tight-lipped about how I'm getting my information."

"You tell me who's leaking to you, I'll let you ride along."

"And then you'll welch on the deal like you did before, and I'll have no source for my story. No dice, Kodiak. Let me in, I'll give you what I've got."

"She drives a hard bargain," Dale said.

My pager went off. I checked the number, turned it off, and said, "Got to go."

"You can use my phone," Havel said, offering me her cellular. When I hesitated, she added, "Don't worry, I won't eavesdrop."

I took her phone and thanked her, then pulled back fifteen feet or so. Dale stayed alongside Havel, chatting. I dialed Marguiles' office, got the receptionist I'd dealt with when I'd lied about Marguiles' family. Adrienne, that was her name. I told her I was returning Leslie Marguiles' page, and that my name was Kodiak, and if she recognized my voice, or knew who I was at all, I couldn't hear it.

"Atticus?" Marguiles said. "Glad you called."

"You paged me," I said. "Least I could do."

"I wasn't certain you'd answer the page. Jerry insists on seeing you, today. Would you be willing to go up and meet him?"

"Did he say why?"

There was the sound of the attorney settling his bulk back in his chair. "All he would say was that he won't testify at tomorrow's deposition if he can't speak with you first. I'm inclined to believe him. I'm willing to pay for your time, if that's what it takes."

"No, I'll see him. Is he still at the hospital?"

"Yes."

"I'll be there sometime between eleven and noon."

"I'll let him know. Thank you," Marguiles said, and he hung up.

I turned off the cellular, then turned it back on and dialed my home number, just to screw with the redial function. Then I turned it off again and brought it back to Havel.

"Business?" she asked.

"Personal," I said, then told Dale, "I need to head back home."

"I'll come with you, get the van."

"You have my number," Havel said. "My offer still stands. Call me. Let me in. Let me help."

In the cab back to my place, I told Dale about my conversation with Marguiles.

"Sounds like Pugh's got a crush on you," Dale said.

I shut and locked the garage after he left, and then headed upstairs, managing to make it past the fourth floor without Midge in 4D asking me to secure or examine anything. I scribbled a note to Erika saying that I was sorry I kept missing her, and that I'd see her that afternoon, and then I called Natalie.

"Wondering if I was going to hear from you," she said. "How'd it go with Boyer?"

"Great," I said. "He was dead when we got there."

"The fuck you say."

I told her what had happened, including my suspicion that it had been the Drakes who'd been arrested at the scene.

"You know just what to say to make me smile," Natalie said.

"They didn't do it," I said.

"You don't know that. Maybe they're John and Drama."

"John and Drama wouldn't get caught at the scene of the crime."

"There's a big difference between being caught and being convicted, Atticus. Could be an effective way of throwing off suspicion."

"I'm not even certain it *was* the Drakes who were arrested," I said.

"I can find out. Won't take long."

"Good, because I'm about to head back to West-chester. Marguiles paged me, says that Pugh's requested my company."

"You're going to the hospital now?"

"I owe it to Marguiles," I said.

"I'll pick you up," she said. "Give me fifteen minutes."

"Fine," I said, and hung up. There was a rattling at the door, and I went into the hallway in time to see Erika enter. She was wearing her Rollerblades, and was wobbling slightly. When she got through the door, I gave her a hug.

"Whoa, bro," Erika said. I let go of her, and she recovered her balance quickly, skated down the hall ten feet to her door. "You know better than to do that when I'm on wheels."

"I missed you."

"You missed me? I didn't think you'd have the time."

"It's been busy."

She shook her head, looking at me. "You sticking around?"

"I've got to go back to Westchester. But I should be free in the afternoon."

"Want to catch a movie?"

"That'd be great."

She dropped her left shoulder, let her backpack slip down her arm and into her hand. "I'll be around."

The phone started ringing. Erika skated into her room and grabbed the extension, then called, "It's for you."

"I'll get it in the kitchen," I said, and went back to pick it up. "Got it," I called.

I heard the line get quiet as Erika hung up the phone, and then Drama said, "Nice kid. Spunky."

My stomach did its best impression of a Bavarian pretzel. "I think so."

"Most kids her age, they're a holy terror. Adolescence. Sucks big time. Can't stand most teenage girls. But I like Erika."

From her room I could hear the sound of Erika taking off her skates, dropping them onto the floor.

"I can't believe you're out," Drama continued cheerfully. "Getting too hot for you?"

"The weather doesn't agree with me," I said.

She laughed. "Frankly, I'm glad. You could've gotten hurt."

"Like Boyer?"

"Like some people you know. As for Billy B., he was becoming a problem for my employer."

"So you eliminated him." I switched the receiver to

my other hand, wiped my palm on the thigh of my
jeans.

"John wanted him dead."

"You're full of it. You're so full of it your eyes have
turned brown."

"How do you know they're not blue?"

"There is no John Doe," I said. "It's just you, alone.
All by yourself."

"And certainly you understand the benefits of soli-
tude, Erika notwithstanding."

"I don't understand anything about you."

"I'm just a working stiff, like any other."

"Not like me."

"Perhaps just like you. But that doesn't matter. Jeremiah Pugh dies tomorrow, trapped and bagged. He
will become quite suddenly ill, perhaps from an insect bite, more likely from a touch he doesn't notice at
all. He'll start with sweats, then coughs, and then he'll
collapse. His respiratory system will crash. He'll go
cyanotic, and when his guards try to respirate him,
they'll come back with a mouthful of blood. He'll have
one last, sharp, shocking seizure, and he'll be dead.
And that will be all."

I was breathing too fast, or I wasn't breathing enough,
and I knew that I was letting her get to me, and I
hated that.

"I don't care," I told her. "I've been pushed out,
remember?"

She laughed again. It sounded as if she'd worked on
it, as if she'd studied how a laugh should sound, and
now was trying it out on a friend.

"You're lying," I said. "You're telling me this so I'll
hand it over to Trent. You're trying to manipulate me
again, like you did when you killed Greer. But I won't

play. I won't share this with Sentinel, and I won't influence their security."

"Of course you won't, Atticus," Drama said. "You've quit, remember? Pity I didn't find out sooner. No one needed to get hurt."

Ice broke in my chest, began whirling through my body. "What have you done?"

Erika came down the hall, stuck her head into the kitchen, looked at me curiously.

"I'm really sorry," Drama said. "Not for Pugh. For you, Atticus. I had become sort of fond of you."

And she left me listening to the dial tone, and my heart, pounding in my ears.

CHAPTER THIRTY-ONE

I began dialing as fast as I could. First Corry.

As the phone was ringing, Erika asked, "What happened?"

"Change of plans," I said. "I want you to call Bridgett, see if you can spend the rest of the day at her place, see if you can spend the night."

"What's going on?"

The phone was picked up, and I heard a woman's voice saying, *"¡Hola!"*

"Corry Herrera, *por favor*."

"Uno momento," the woman said.

"Atticus, what's going on?"

I shook my head, waved a hand at Erika to wait. Then Corry came on the line, saying, "Hello?"

"It's Atticus. Everything fine there?"

"Everything's good," Corry said.

"I just heard from Drama. She's coming after us."

He took a second, then said, "Shit. What happened?"

"She capped Boyer this morning. And she just called me. Natalie's on her way over, and I'm going to the hospital with her to see Pugh. I need you to check on Dale."

"Isn't he home?"

"No, he only left here ten, fifteen minutes ago. You and he need to get together, need to stay together, and need to get over to my place. Erika's here now. As soon as she lets you in, I want you guys to take her over to Bridgett's. Then come back here and wait for Nat and me."

"You think Drama's going after family?"

"I have no fucking clue what she'll do. She's killed twice already that we know of."

"I'm moving," Corry said, and the line went dead.

"I'm not going back to Bridgett's," Erika said. "I'm staying with you."

My intercom went off, and I headed for the grille, saying, "This is not open to debate, kiddo. Dale and Corry will get here in an hour. When they do, they'll drive you over to Bridie's." I punched the speaker button, confirmed that Natalie was waiting downstairs. "I'll be right there," I told the grille.

"You called her Bridie," Erika said.

I headed down the hall, began closing the curtains at the windows. "Call her, let her know you're staying at her place. I'll get in touch with you when I know it's safe to come back. And until you leave, stay away from the windows. Don't eat anything, don't drink anything, and try not to turn any appliances on or off. That includes the stereo and the television."

I finished covering the windows, headed for the door, Erika following me.

"Promise me you'll do what I ask," I said.

Her hand was at her ear, her fingers playing with the hair that covered her scar. She nodded.

I gave her a kiss on the forehead. "You'll be fine," I promised.

"But will you?" she asked.

. . .

Natalie drove fast, accelerating harder as I told her about the phone call.

"Bitch," she muttered. "Manipulative bitch."

"Absolutely," I agreed. "I ever get close enough, I'm going to shoot her on principle."

We were doing eighty. I decided I didn't want to look at the speedometer any longer.

To say I resented the way Drama was yanking us around was to say I was only a little worried.

Corry was fine. Erika was fine. Natalie was right beside me, pedal pressed to the floor, as close to fine as she was going to get.

Which left Dale. Dale was the only one unaccounted for, the only one I hadn't been able to contact.

And there was nothing I could do about it right now, except sit back, and cringe at Natalie's driving, and pray God that he was all right.

It wasn't that easy.

We reached the hospital at twenty to noon, and I waited with Natalie while she parked the Infiniti. We half ran, half walked to the lobby, to the elevator bank, waiting impatiently for the car.

"The Drakes," I remembered. "What did you find out?"

"They were taken into custody this morning at Boyer's townhouse," she said. "That's all I could confirm. Don't know if they've been charged, don't know why they were there, don't know what they did."

"If Pugh wants to talk to me alone, I'll need you to run interference," I told her.

Natalie nodded.

"Your father here?"

"I expect he's running the show personally."

The elevator doors opened, and we rode on up to the floor where Pugh was resting. Three guards had been posted in the lounge, in plainclothes, and one of them headed down the hall as a runner as soon as they saw us. The guards were men I'd seen on Mosier's detail, and they looked surprised to see me.

Trent came down the hall, the runner following him, walking briskly, jaw set.

"Pop," Natalie said.

"I don't know what bill of goods you sold Pugh, Kodiak, but he's given us no end of grief since he found out you left," Trent said, ignoring his daughter. "I can't keep a guard in the room with him. He drives them out. Keeps throwing things at them."

I tried not to laugh at the image of Jeremiah Pugh lobbing a bedpan at Elliot Trent's head.

"It isn't funny," Trent said coldly. "We all know what this situation has degraded to."

"Yes, we do," Natalie said, and her voice was even colder.

"The clock is ticking. The deposition is scheduled to begin at ten tomorrow. That's when Doe will make his move. And right now, thanks to you, Kodiak, I've got a principal who is actively fighting his protective team."

"What's he been saying?" I asked.

"Only that he wants to talk to you."

"Has he said why?"

"No. So, go talk to him. Talk sense. And make certain he understands just what it is he's doing. Behavior like this will get him killed tomorrow."

I nodded and headed down the hall, leaving Natalie

with her father. Picacio and White were on-post at the door to Pugh's room. Neither looked like they were having a good time of it.

"He wants to see me," I said to White.

"Yeah. It's been that and 'get the hell out' for almost twenty-four hours now."

Picacio had a slight bruise on his left cheek that was starting to swell. "Hit me with his water pitcher," he explained, opening the door. "Have fun."

Pugh was still in bed, but the back had been elevated, so now he sat almost upright. On the floor just by the door were a bedpan, a plastic vase, three plastic cups, and a pitcher. The plastic vase was cracked. The television was on, and Pugh was playing with the volume control when I came in, and the noise was loud, what sounded like a game show. He saw me and muted the television, and for a moment it went very quiet in the room. But the mute didn't work that well, and I could hear the televised voices whispering, like ghosts in the background.

"You wanted to see me," I said.

"Have a seat. Pull up a pew." He chuckled at his joke, motioned to the chair. He waited until I had moved it to beside the bed and parked myself, before saying, "What's this bullshit about you quitting?"

"No bullshit. I pulled out."

Pugh shook his head vigorously. He looked far heartier than he had the day before. "Don't do that."

"It's done."

"Then you'll have to undo it."

"Why?"

"I want you kids keeping me safe. You've done a bang-up job so far. I want you to go the distance with me."

"You'll have Sentinel. They're the best."

Pugh scratched his arm, at the bandage where one of his IVs had been inserted. "Son, I'll put it plain. You and yours cover me, or I don't attend the deposition tomorrow. Those are my terms."

"You won't have a choice. Lamia will subpoena you. They'll compel you to testify."

"Lamia will try. But there won't be enough time. The extended discovery ends tomorrow at five, and unless I sing before then, I'm not worth dick."

"They'll put you on the stand."

"I'll be dead." He said it matter-of-factly.

"There are easier ways to kill yourself," I said. "You don't have to goad people into doing it for you. Take a hot bath and slice your wrists—down your forearms, not across, it's more effective. Or there's the bullet in the head, through the roof of the mouth. As long as you don't try it with anything smaller than a .38, it's considered quite effective."

"I think I can find a method that will work."

"Then you don't need an assassin to do it for you."

"You misunderstand me, son. I have the highest regard for you, for Miss Trent and Mr. Herrera and Mr. Matsui. You all did a fine job at the deposition at the Sheraton. I'd like you to do it again."

"No."

"I'm going to die tomorrow," Pugh said. "Either by John Doe's bullet or my own hand. I figure that gives me some clout in the final wishes department."

I took a moment to absorb what he'd said. "Do you even realize what you're asking me to do?"

"I'm asking you to do your job, son. That's all."

"I will not put myself and my people into a certain free-fire zone just for your damn peace of mind." I said it a lot more angrily than I'd meant. "Not so you can just off yourself when the day is over, not so you can finish a job that may be left undone. No fucking way will I do that."

Pugh looked from me to his hands, frowning. The silence grew so I could hear the mumbling of the television again.

Pugh sighed. "I thought you understood the situation."

He wiped at his eyes with his hands, using the heel of his palms, pressing hard.

"I told you," Pugh said. "I've lost everything. I am guilty of murder. A hundred thousand times over, I am guilty of murder. All of those people DTS cut down, they're my bodies, too. There's only one way to fix that. Once I testify, once I tell them what I know and saw, I'll be done.

"It's not much of a redemption, but it's the only one I have. I failed my son. I let my wife die, I abandoned her when she needed me."

I got up and pushed the chair back to where it had been placed against the wall.

"It's my fault," he said.

"If we walk with you tomorrow morning," I said, "there's a good chance it won't be just you who doesn't make it home tomorrow night. Why should I do that? Why should I let my friends do that?"

"It's your job," Pugh repeated. "It's what you do."

I shook my head, turned for the door.

He cleared his throat. "If you don't guard me tomorrow, son, I won't testify. And those bastards will walk free."

It was a cheap shot. Part of me didn't believe the threat; he wanted his absolution too much to throw it away on this. But I understood that he wanted absolution on his terms, and if he couldn't have both, his testimony and his penitent suicide, he'd stick with the one that was certain to succeed.

I stopped and stood there, focusing on the door ahead of me. Pugh was waiting, silent. Picacio was watching me through the window in the door. I could see my reflection.

"You arrogant son of a bitch," I said. "Do you honestly think that the gestures you're so desperate to make can repair any of the mistakes you've made?"

"What else can I do?" Pugh asked.

"Learn humility." I faced him. "I will risk everything if what you're trying to do is the right thing *now*, Jerry. But if you're trying to undo the past, it's pointless. For both of us."

"I am doing this for them," Pugh said.

"Sure you are. And I'll do this for you, Jerry. I'm going to keep you alive. We all will. We'll protect you. We'll be sharp. We'll be frosty. We'll be on-the-fucking-ball. You want to know why?"

"You don't have a choice."

I shook my head. "Because we're going to keep you alive. We're going to keep you alive whether you want to stay that way or not."

CHAPTER THIRTY-TWO

"Dale's fine," Corry was telling me. "Knocked about a bit, but fine."

I relayed that much to Natalie, and she nodded, continued gnawing on her lip and watching the traffic. She was driving marginally slower for our return trip, and I was doing my best to ignore the road. It wasn't that she was a bad driver; I just was certain we were going to crash and burn.

"What happened?" I asked.

"Here, I'll put him on."

There was the jostle of the phone switching hands, and then Dale came on the line. "We just got back from Bridgett's. Erika's settled in."

"Good. What happened to you?"

"My van had a blowout on the BQE about half an hour after I left you. I was doing fifty at the time."

"Jesus, are you all right?"

"Corry called it, I'm fine. Tumbled the van, knocked me loopy for a few minutes, but other than that and some minor bruises, nothing. My belt held, and it's not like I've never had a blowout before."

"Praise the Army of the United States of America,"
I said.

Dale chuckled. "Maybe I should write Lieutenant
Horne a note, send it to him at Bragg. 'Dear Loo,
Remember all those uncontrolled skid drills on the
Crash Course? Well, you won't believe what happened
to me today. . . .' He'd love it."

"Probably post it in the Officers' Club."

"I could send a picture of the van with the letter. It's
in pretty sad shape."

"How sad?"

"Not-running-anymore sad."

"Rent a new one," I said. "And call Marguiles, find
out everything you can about the deposition site. I
want maps of the street, I want blueprints of the building, I want all of it. And tell him we need it today."

I could almost hear him cracking a grin. "Ah, so
we're back at work, are we?"

"Do you know how it happened? The blowout, I
mean."

Dale grunted. "I've got a couple of ideas. The tires
were all but new, got them replaced in May."

"Could she have caused it?"

"Drama? Sure. She knows where you live, and she
got access to your apartment once already. Getting at a
car in your garage wouldn't be hard."

"You're a lucky man."

"I'd say a skilled man, myself."

"Whichever you are, I'm glad you're okay," I told
him. "We should be there in about half an hour."

"Drive carefully," he said. I heard his laughter as I
hung up.

I turned off the phone and gave Natalie the conversation in brief.

"Kerosene?"

"Probably gasoline," I said. "Harder to detect. She probably injected it into the tire this morning, while Dale and I had gone to see Boyer. The gasoline would have pooled at the bottom of the tire, corroding the rubber just enough so that when Dale started driving, it would cause a blowout."

"So she was trying to kill him?"

I rubbed my eyes, then took off my glasses and cleaned the lenses on my shirt. "I don't know. Worst-case scenario, the gasoline would have eaten through the tire, Dale would have had a blowout at eighty and gone end over end through eight lanes of traffic. But Drama's been watching, she would know that Dale's our driver."

"If she really is working all of this alone, she must be stretching herself pretty thin by now."

I put my glasses back on. "She's a pro. If she wanted him dead, he'd be dead."

"So she didn't want him dead."

"Or she didn't care one way or the other."

"Why?"

"I don't know."

Natalie came off the gas a bit, and I realized what she was thinking, so I added, "I think we're safe." We'd already made it to Mount Kisco; if Drama had tried the same number on Natalie's Infiniti, we would have already learned it the hard way.

Natalie pursed her lips in an apologetic smile, more for herself than for me, and we resumed going too fast for my taste. She had me dig out a cassette of Sarah McLachlan's latest from her tape box, and I put it in the player.

Natalie hummed along with Sarah and I thought. I

thought about what I'd said to Pugh, I thought about what that meant I'd have to do, and I tried to come up with a way to do it. Unfortunately, the only solutions I found to our little problem all hinged on Pugh not attending his deposition. Somehow, I didn't think Marguiles would go for that.

We were dropping back off the FDR when my pager went off. Once again, I didn't recognize the number.

"Who wants you?" Natalie asked.

"No idea."

"You should get a service," she said, handing me her cellular phone. "That way you can call the service and figure out who's trying to reach you."

"You should keep both hands on the wheel while driving," I said. "That way we won't crash and die."

I punched the number on my pager into the phone. After two rings, Chris Havel said, "Yo?"

I almost hung up on her. "It's Atticus."

"Atticus, ah, Atticus," she said, dreamily. "Yes, the bane of my existence, the man who's daily dashing my dreams to pieces. Why the hell did you give Ray Mosier my number?"

"I didn't."

"Then who did?"

"I have no idea. I had no idea Mosier was in touch with you."

"He's harassing me. I've received two messages from him this morning, already, and a FedEx package of his previous publications. He included a note. Listen, 'Chris, I've been thinking about angles on our book, and I'm thinking a first-person sort of *nouveau* journalism approach would work well for us.' What the hell is he talking about? I've never even met the guy."

"Oh, fuck," I said, pulling the phone away from my

ear. I could hear Havel's voice, tiny now, asking what I was saying. "Pull over," I told Natalie.

"Pulling over."

"Chris, what's the return address on that package?" I asked the phone.

"It's, uh, hold on . . . here, it's in Brooklyn." She read off the address as I began rummaging through Natalie's glove compartment for a pen and something to write on. I found the pen. I wrote on my forearm. "There's a phone number, too. You want it?"

"Give it to me."

She did. Then she asked, "Is this what I think it is?"

"I'll call you back," I said.

Natalie had pulled us into a gas station on First Avenue, past the pumps, keeping the car idling. She watched while I dialed Mosier's number.

There was no answer.

"We've got to go out there," I said. "You know Brooklyn?"

"Not well. I've got a map." She leaned across me, pulled her borough map from the glove compartment. I gave her the address, and she used the index, then said, "That's near Prospect Park. I can get us there."

"Let's go."

She put the car into gear and pulled us back onto the street, swerved around a pickup truck with an advertisement for Dewar's mounted in its bed. Natalie jockeyed us into the fast lane of the FDR. It was almost one, and the traffic was thick, but moving.

"Drama's reached out to Mosier," I said.

"That much I had gathered. How?"

"She presented herself to Mosier as Chris Havel, told him that she was working on a book. Probably sweet-talked him into a credit for his help. Mosier bought it better than Drama had hoped, though; he tried calling the real Havel a couple of times this morning, sent her some of his previous publications."

"Jesus," Natalie said, and her voice turned thin. "If Mosier talked, if he thought Drama was really a journalist, he could have told her the whole Sentinel SOP. She'll know everything Pop's going to do tomorrow. She'll know everything they'll have planned."

"He couldn't have compromised that much," I said. "He had been fired."

"No, the SOP would be the same. The specifics would change, but she'll know the basics. She'll know all of it. Christ."

"Then let's hope he didn't talk," I said, knowing that he had, knowing that Natalie was right, and knowing that Mosier was already dead.

The building had gone up in the fifties and showed the wear of the last four or five decades, but it was clean inside, quiet, and cool. We didn't see anybody on the stairs, or up to the third floor. We didn't see anybody in the hall.

I knocked and we waited, and I knocked some more, and no one came, no one answered. Natalie tried the knob, and it turned, and we stepped in, shut it behind us.

The space was dark, all the blinds drawn, and cold. It wasn't large, a studio apartment with a Murphy bed, a small square table, a couple of chairs. There was a big-screen television and a laser disc player, a squat bookshelf, almost full. I could make out a couple of prints framed on the wall, including a great big one by Olivia DeBerardinis of a woman, mostly nude, a cross between a ninja and a samurai. She had a dragon tattooed on her body, its open mouth hanging down over one breast, scaled tail curling around the opposite thigh and disappearing between her legs.

Mosier had been left on the floor by the bed. The blood beneath him made the floor black, made him look like he was lying on a piece of midnight.

She'd used a knife.

"God," I said.

Natalie didn't speak.

She'd had the time and some privacy, and I could see where she had gone to his trachea, and I knew she had stolen his voice first. And then her mask had come off.

I counted almost twenty wounds before I gave up and turned away.

"Monstrous," Natalie whispered.

"Let's go."

"We should call—"

"We call the cops, they show up, they'll keep us for the next twelve hours at least, answering questions. We don't have the time, Nat. Pugh doesn't have the time. We've got to get out of here, and we've got to prep. Otherwise Pugh's dead, too. There's nothing we can do here."

Natalie looked from the body to me. "She destroyed him." She was having difficulty speaking.

I reached for her arm, but Natalie moved back on her own, turned, and I followed her. I shut the door, then used my shirttail on the knob while Natalie covered my back. The hall was still empty, and I thought that the apartments were probably all singles, all occupied by young, lonely professionals, hard at work on this Wednesday afternoon. Not a bad place to live.

A rotten place to die.

CHAPTER THIRTY-THREE

None of us liked it, and none of us knew what we could do to make it better.

"There are eight different points of fire," Corry said. "At least eight, and that's just in the atrium, here. God knows how many there will be on the street." He rotated the blueprints on my kitchen table, pointed with the red pen he had in his hand. Natalie, phone wedged between her ear and shoulder, glanced down and indicated another position, then went back to talking with her father.

"Make that nine," Dale said unhappily, rubbing his knuckle against his swollen lower lip. He had a nice lump on his forehead, too, from where he'd headed the steering wheel of his van. Neither seemed to actually be causing him pain, just annoyance.

"The whole lobby is a fatal funnel. And the rear's no better," Corry said. "Of all the locations in Manhattan, we're going to the one with an empty lot at its back."

"Who the hell picked this place?" I asked.

"Lamia. Which means DTS, which means Drama."

I took off my glasses and rubbed at the bridge of my nose, trying to knock back the eyestrain. When I shut my eyes, I hit a memory flash of Mosier's body, of the damage Drama had inflicted. It made me open my eyes again.

It was almost eight, and we'd been at this since Natalie and I had returned from Brooklyn, six hours earlier. After leaving Mosier's apartment, we'd made a stop outside a liquor store a good fifteen blocks away, and Natalie had dialed 911 and told them about the body. Then we'd headed back to the city, neither of us talking much.

Drama had taken Mosier apart like he was meat on a hook. Natalie had called it correctly; it had been the act of a monster. Whatever motivated Drama, whatever drive she had harnessed to become a person who killed for a living, it had broken free in Brooklyn. It had been the last thing Raymond Mosier had felt before he died.

We'd arrived at my place to find Dale and Corry already poring over the blueprints and maps that Marguiles had arranged to be delivered. The four of us had gone out again almost immediately, to make an on-site inspection of the terrain. None of us had liked what we had seen. Natalie had voiced it best, though. She'd called it "Sniper Country."

"Drama's going for the long shot," I told Dale. "It's the one tool she hasn't used, and it's the one thing this whole damn location has been made for."

We contemplated the blueprints once more, all of us trying to calculate angles, fields of fire. The building was fifteen stories, almost a perfect cube, with a glorious open-air atrium in the center of the space, filled with trees and plants and pools of water stocked with koi. Two sets of elevators stood at the north and south edges of the building, and stairs ran up at each corner. Most of the offices had windows, either looking out on the street or down into the atrium. A lot of glass, too much visibility.

"Outside or inside?" Dale asked.

Corry looked at me for confirmation, and when I nodded, said, "Outside, probably. But she'll have secondary and tertiary positions, you can bet on that."

"So the maximum exposure is when Pugh's exiting the vehicle?"

"Yeah. Then it drops at the entrance, spikes again in the lobby, drops again on the way up, and spikes a last time on fifteen, when Pugh travels down the hall to the actual depo."

"But with all the glass it's a fucking shooting gallery," I said. "And none of this means she won't try to hit us on the road. She could make her try before we even reach Manhattan."

"So, in essence, there's no place where exposure is limited."

"Not until we get him into the depo."

Natalie hung up the phone, redirected her attention to us. "Pop's got Pugh back at the estate, buttoned up. I told him we'd be calling again before midnight with the details on movement."

"Who's covering the advance?"

"Yossi." She examined the blueprints, then pointed. "I could take a counter-sniper position in the atrium, give cover during the ingress. There are plenty of places for me to roost."

"When would you need to take position?"

"Deposition starts at ten? I'd want to be in place and set up by five."

I shook my head. "You'd be exhausted."

"I could do it."

"Five hours looking through your optics, you're

going to be worthless," Corry said. "You'd need a
spotter with you."

"One of you could do that."

"So instead of being down one person we'd be down
two," I said. "No. Forget it."

"We need something to break the trap, Atticus.
Either a counter-sniper or something else."

It ran like a shock up my spine and danced on my
frontal lobe, and I dropped back in my chair, suddenly
aware of just how stupid I'd been. Dale was telling
Natalie that we weren't even certain Drama would take
the long shot, and she was telling him that either we
posted someone in the atrium, or we found a different
way to bring Pugh inside.

Trapped, I thought. Tracked or trapped, it's a sniper's
term, it's a word Natalie uses.

Drama had said Pugh would be "trapped and
bagged."

It didn't mean anything, it's a turn of phrase, it's not
person-specific. Drama needn't have heard it from
Natalie Trent's lips.

But it made such perfect sense, all of a sudden.

I grabbed the pen out of Corry's hand and scribbled
on the edge of the blueprint two words, IGNORE ME,
then tapped the table to make certain I had everyone's
attention. They all nodded and I got out of my chair
and onto the floor, and I started crawling. The linoleum was a little dirty, and I thought that I needed to
mop it, and I flipped over onto my back, and looked at
the underside of the tabletop, ran my hands over the
surface.

Nothing.

Corry had moved back in his chair and was looking
at me under the table, an eyebrow raised. I waved him

back. Natalie was telling Dale about the weapon she would use were she Drama. It sounded strained to me, but I couldn't say anything.

Paranoid, I thought, and went to get my tool kit. I had a set of small flathead screwdrivers that I kept for repairing my eyeglasses, and I took the largest of them, returned to the kitchen. All three kept watching me, still talking, now about what they wanted to get for dinner.

I unscrewed the phone jack, first, took it apart carefully. I should be talking, I thought. My silence incriminates me.

I said, "We could order from the Indian place down the block. They've got a good curry."

"Curry would be nice," Dale said.

There was nothing in the phone jack. I left it disassembled, and started working my way through the outlets. I just need to find one, I thought. Just one, and I'll know I was right.

Corry got up from the table, and I heard him walk down the hall, and a couple seconds later, a blast of Benny Green came from the stereo. He toned it down a moment later, but it was loud enough to fill the apartment. Maybe too loud to be inconspicuous, but I knew why he'd done it, and I couldn't fault him for trying.

It was in the second outlet on the kitchen counter, the one I used to power my coffee maker, nestled inside the lip of the hard plastic frame. It was perhaps twenty-five millimeters long, barely half that in thickness, with two leads running to the wires in the wall, feeding it enough power to transmit.

There had to be others, at least one, probably more, and something on the telephone, too. She would have gone for redundancy, just in case one of the bugs crapped out on her. And she would have wired the whole apartment. She'd had the time. Erika had been at Bridgett's, and I had been in the bush outside of the estate.

That was why she had been waiting for me when I'd returned home that night. She had covered her tracks by revealing herself—so what if the apartment had seemed a little mussed? I'd hardly been in any position to notice it, not after the way she had greeted me.

I stared at the tiny little mains-powered transmitter that had been spilling all of my secrets to Drama for the past week. How much of our prep had taken place in this kitchen? And she'd heard it all.

Mosier hadn't set us up: I had.

"Figure that she knows all of it," I said. "Everything that we've planned, everything that we've talked about. All of it's in the trash, now. We start again. We start from scratch."

They gave me nods.

I checked my watch. "It's eleven. We've got seven hours before we need to move, to get Pugh ready for transport."

Our waiter refilled our coffee cups, then asked Dale if he wanted anything else. Dale shook his head and pushed his empty plate off to a side. He was the only one of us who still seemed to have an appetite.

The waiter picked up the plate and moved away. The diner was mostly empty. We were near the back, a group of tired conspirators in a small booth, trying to make up lost ground.

"She's smart," Dale said. "She'll know we're onto her."

"Then that works for us," Natalie said. "She'll change her plans, too. Puts us on an even footing."

"Unless she was never intending to take the long shot."

"It doesn't matter," I said. "We're defending against all of it. Long shot, poison darts, exploding pencils—I don't give a fuck what she tosses our way. Pugh stays alive. We're going all the way, no half-measures, no regrets after the fact. I'm tired of this. I'm tired of being manipulated. Well, we can do use, too. Maybe not as well as Trent or Drama or DTS or Pugh, but we can do it, too."

It caught them off guard, and for a moment all of them looked at me with a little surprise. I was surprised, too. It had felt good.

Dale smiled and said, "That's the boy I remember."

"What are you thinking?" Natalie asked.

"We can't change the fact that we're walking into a trap," I said. "Maybe we can get her to walk into one of our own."

Christian Havel, it turned out, lived only a block from where Rubin and I had shared an apartment in Greenwich Village. We'd gotten her out of bed with our call, and she met us at her door in boxer shorts and a red tank top, and offered us coffee. Natalie and I accepted, took a seat side by side on the couch in her office-slash-living room. We'd come alone, sending Dale and Corry to rent the vehicle we'd need and to gather our gear.

Havel's apartment was small, cluttered, comfortable. Books fell off shelves and stood in stacks on the floor, and completely blocked the view of her television. Her walls were covered with clippings and photographs, taped or tacked into place.

We took our mugs, and Havel sat back in her chair and crossed her legs, and said, "Let's hear this offer, then."

"We'll let you in," I said. "Starting now. In exchange, you do what we ask you to do, and you tell us who your source inside Sentinel is."

"That's all?" she asked, sarcastically.

"It all comes down to tomorrow morning," Natalie told her. "Pugh's last chance to be deposed, Doe's last chance to stop that from happening. We're not just offering you a chance to follow us. We're offering you a chance to be a part of the action. To do the work alongside."

Havel ran a hand over her face, and I could see the wheels spinning, see her thinking it over. She cast a glance at her desk, where her portable computer rested.

"We don't have a lot of time," I said.

"Why do you need my source?"

"There's a chance that your source and the assassin may be one and the same," I said.

"Uh-uh," she said, shaking her head.

"We need to be sure."

"You're not fucking with me? You're not offering me this chance so I'll hand over the only trump I have?"

"We're dead serious," Natalie said.

Havel rubbed the tattooed wolf on her shoulder, her eyes moving from Natalie to me, her lips pressed shut, debating her decision.

Then she said, "Karen Kazanjian. She called me after I ran that first piece, said that she could give me the inside scoop on the Sentinel operation. I checked. Kazanjian is on the Sentinel payroll."

"The medic," I said. "Did she say why she was willing to talk to you?"

"Didn't like the way the show was being run. Thought it was putting people's lives in danger. She's the one who gave me that actor's name, d'Angelo."

"It's possible," Natalie said to me, but her tone matched my thoughts. Possible, but not probable.

"Drama," I said.

"She identified Kazanjian, then used her name for contact?" Natalie asked.

"Did you ever meet this woman, face-to-face?" I asked Havel.

"No, only the phone. She said she couldn't get off the estate except on business."

"Nice to know she's not selective about who she manipulates," Natalie said sourly.

"Are you saying that I've been getting my information from the assassin?" Havel asked.

"That's what it looks like, yes," Natalie said.

"Mother Mary," Havel said. "Why?"

"We don't know," I said. "Any number of reasons. Your articles created tension between us and Sentinel, that could have been one of her goals. Perhaps others."

"Are you sure about this?" she asked.

"I'll check on it tomorrow," I said. "Talk to Kazanjian, try to confirm one way or another."

"You going to tell me what you need me to do, now?"

I made for the exit. "Natalie will. I've got to take care of a couple more things. I'll see you in the morning, though."

She jumped up quickly when I did, but her suspicions fled when she saw that Natalie hadn't moved from the couch. Havel ran her gaze back to me, and her lips curled back in a self-satisfied little grin.

"I knew you'd come around eventually," Havel said. "If I bugged you long enough, I knew you'd let me in."

"Remember that tomorrow," I said, "when you're shouting at me to let you out."

The street was cool, light traffic. I had places to go, and not a lot of time, but I walked along Bleecker until I reached Thompson, turned south, and stopped outside of my old building. I looked up at it for a heartbeat, thinking about Rubin, about how he had been my friend and about how he had died.

For the first time, I didn't feel the guilt.

I continued down to Houston, hailed myself a passing cab, told him where I wanted to go. The driver didn't talk to me as he drove, and that was fine. I had plenty on my mind, thinking about the morning.

If I wasn't very careful, I'd lose Pugh. I'd get Havel killed. I might even lose another friend.

There was a good chance I'd pull the hat trick, and nail all three.

But this time, I'd go down swinging.

CHAPTER THIRTY-FOUR

Karen Kazanjian was double-checking her jump kit in the kitchen of the estate. She had removed the contents of the bag, stacked them neatly in piles, and was carefully replacing each piece of medical gear. She wanted them where she could reach them in an emergency; she wanted to make certain they would be there when she needed them.

I understood that behavior. I'd done the same thing with my equipment before arriving.

"I need to talk to you," I said.

She jerked her head back, said, "Fuck, you surprised me."

"Have a minute?"

"Shoot."

"Are you Chris Havel's source inside Sentinel?"

Her cheeks turned to scarlet. "You fucker. Where do you get off accusing me of something like that?"

"That's a no?"

"Of course it's a no, you idiot. What do you take me for?"

"Has Havel ever talked to you?"

"I don't even know who the fuck he is."

"Actually, he's a she."

"Chris? That's a guy's name. Her real name Christine?"

"Christian," I said.

Karen shook her head again, went back to loading her bag. "You have any other stupid fucking questions for me, or can I continue doing what I need to do here?"

"No. That was the last one."

I was almost out of the kitchen when she called, "You really think I'm the leak?"

"No," I said.

"Then why'd you ask?"

"I just want to be up-to-date on who's using who for what," I said.

White was on-post inside of Pugh's room, and he greeted me with a thumbs-up, then stepped out to give us time alone. The room was clean, almost spotless, nothing on the floor but the carpet, the bed tidily made. Pugh was wearing a blue suit, sitting on the edge of the mattress. The collage he had made me was in his lap.

"How you feeling?" I asked.

"Tired, son." He made half an effort at a smile.

"Probably shouldn't be out of the hospital."

"No choice, right?" He offered me the collage. "You forgot this."

"I'll get it from you tonight," I told him.

He set the collage beside him on the bed.

"Stand up," I said.

He got to his feet, and remained motionless while I

patted him down. I was thorough about it, though I tried to be gentle. Only when I was done did he ask, "What was that for?"

"I don't want you killing yourself on my watch." I handed him the body armor he had worn before. "You remember the drill?"

"Hard to forget it. Where's the elegant redhead?"

"Natalie's already on station."

I helped him into his body armor, cinched the straps. "This time, keep it on for the whole ride."

"Hope the air conditioner's working."

"It is. Ready?"

"Whenever you say so, son."

I pressed the button in my palm, said, "Three minutes."

"Confirmed," Corry told me.

White and I guided Pugh out of the room and down the flight of stairs to the entryway. The guards were waiting, as before, but this time, Elliot Trent was there, too. He waited until we had reached the foot of the stairs.

"I want to know what the plan is," he said. "I have a right to know. My people are on-site, Yossi is on-site. What are you going to do to bring down Doe?"

"Nothing," I said.

The disgust rode up his face like mercury climbing in a thermometer. "He's going to get you killed," Trent said to Pugh. "This is your last chance to reconsider. Let my people take you in."

"I'm happy with the security as it stands, Mr. Trent," Pugh replied.

"Ready for Trigger," Corry said in my ear.

"Stand by," I said. "And radio ahead, tell them he's wearing a blue suit."

"Got it."

"Once again, Jerry—" Trent tried.

"No, I'm sorry, but this is the way I want it. I appreciate your offer, but this is how it should be."

I moved in behind Pugh, motioned White to swing in at the front. "Going on my mark," I said to Corry.

"Confirmed."

I counted down, gave the word, and we poured from the house, a chute of people that ran to the back door of the waiting Benz. White climbed in, then Pugh, and then myself. Kazanjian and Trent both took seats in the follow car. Corry waited until everyone was loaded before radioing, "Move."

We pulled out, down the drive and past the opened gate. We were on the road when Pugh asked, "Where's Matsui? Isn't he the guy who drives?"

"Yes," I said, scanning the trees. There was a slight breeze blowing, and it made the branches sway, and created the illusion of a killer's motion.

"Where is he?"

"Wait and see," I said.

We were outside of Yonkers when I told Corry, "Now."

He keyed the radio on the dash and said, "Next left, pull off, first right, pull into the lot, stop."

There was a pause, and then the driver of the lead car came back with, *"Repeat?"*

Corry repeated it, then added, "Please confirm."

We were coming up on the exit.

The voice from the grille said, *"Confirmed."*

Trent said, *"What the hell are you doing?"*

"Please keep this channel clear," Corry said. I saw him grin in the rearview mirror.

Pugh and White were watching me. I kept scanning until the motorcade pulled into the parking lot. We were beside a small Sunoco station, and as the follow car came to a halt, Dale emerged from the driver's side of the service van he and Corry had rented the night before. The van was old and dirty, a workhorse of a vehicle.

"Stay put," I told Pugh, and got out of the Benz. Dale was halfway to me already. "All set?"

"He's just finished changing."

"Bring them out."

Dale turned around and waved at the van. Trent had exited the follow vehicle and was storming our way, demanding to know what the hell we were doing. Dale waited until the side door slid open, then turned back to me. "Now?"

"Now," I said.

Chris Havel came around the opposite side of the van, dressed all in black, and she looked unremarkable but for the red wig she was wearing. It wasn't quite Natalie's shade, but at a distance, it would sell. She was grinning like a nut, impatiently waiting for the other occupant of the van to emerge.

"What the hell are you doing?" Trent asked me.

"As much as I can get away with," I answered.

Nathan d'Angelo came out of the van. The actor had frosted his hair white, almost the same shade as Pugh's, but not quite. He was wearing the same make of body armor that currently enveloped Pugh, and a blue suit.

Trent saw d'Angelo and stopped speaking.

"Let's switch," I said.

Havel nipped to the Benz while Dale helped remove Pugh. I worked in next to them, and we hustled the old man the fifteen feet from one car to the other, shoved him into the back of the van.

"Lie down, don't move until I tell you to," I told him.

"Hiya, Dale," Pugh said.

"Hiya, Jerry. Be right back."

"No problem."

I slammed the door shut. Dale was climbing into the driver's seat, his shirt already half off. I ran back to the Benz, where Havel was waiting for d'Angelo to get into the backseat. Trent was shaking his head.

"There a problem?" I asked.

Nathan d'Angelo said, "I don't want to get shot at again, that's the problem."

"That's why you've got the body armor," Havel told him.

"We'll do everything we can to make sure that doesn't happen."

"I can't believe I let you talk me into this," he grumbled. "Coming by my home at two A.M., how am I supposed to make a rational decision?"

"Take a look at Trent," I said.

It took a moment, but a smile began to spread.

"That's why you're doing this."

D'Angelo nodded. "Hey, Trent? Blow me!"

Elliot Trent puffed himself up, then deflated without speaking.

I helped d'Angelo into the Benz, then stepped back to let Havel slide in beside him.

"How's your radio?" I asked her.

"Fine. We checked before you got here."

"You're okay with this?"

Her eyes were sparkling with glee. "You kidding? Quit wasting time."

I slammed the door shut and thumped twice on the roof of the car. Corry gunned the engine in response, and I started back to the van, but was blocked by Trent. He looked past me at the Benz, then back to me.

"Good luck," he said.

There was a duffel bag behind the front seat of the van, and as Dale began wending his way through Yonkers, I reached around and opened it up. I pulled out the bundles of clothes that had been stuffed inside. Pugh was lying on the floor of the vehicle, watching me.

"Time?" I asked Dale.

"Oh-nine-twenty-three," he said.

"Have you heard from them?"

"Natalie gave me a call, said that they've done three sweeps, it all looks clear. Yossi's secured the whole goddamn fifteenth floor."

"How you going to be with stairs?" I asked Pugh. "You going to be able to handle them?"

"I don't know," he said. "Fifteen floors? I'll need a breather."

"Better to take him up in the elevator," Dale said.

"Elevator to twelve, the rest on foot," I said. "Can you do that, Jerry?"

"Think so."

"Good." I got out of my seat, slipped into the back closer to Pugh, and began unfastening the body armor around his middle. "You can sit up."

He straightened and I helped him off with the body armor, saying, "Okay, get out of the suit, put this on."

I dropped one of the bundles in his lap, then began getting out of my clothes. It took us both about four minutes to switch into the coveralls that Corry had found us.

They were dingy and gray, and they had patches on the back that read "McMillan Heating & Air Conditioning." Nametags had been sewn over the left breast. Mine said I was Rip. Pugh's identified him as Earl. I couldn't see what Dale's tag said. We each had ball caps, too, with the company logo stitched above the brim.

"I think I'm beginning to figure this out," Pugh said.

"D'Angelo, the one who's pretending to be you, he's our entrance decoy. He and that group will enter through the back of the building, full formation, the whole song and dance. You, me, and Dale are going to walk in through the front door."

"Hate to break it to you, son, but that d'Angelo boy, he doesn't look a thing like me."

"That's fine," I said. "I don't want him shot at. I just want him to attract attention."

"Suppose he does get shot at?"

"Then I'll have gotten him killed," I said.

Dale parked us off Broadway, half a block from the building, just as the motorcade came to a halt. I could hear Corry over my radio, giving directions, confirming that the ingress was prepped.

"Atticus?" Natalie asked.

"Go ahead."

"We're clean and buttoned up. All parties present and accounted for, all routes secured. Ten on-post, plus two floating."

"Confirmed," I said. If all went well, that would be the last transmission I would have to make until Pugh was secured. I grabbed the two large toolboxes in the rear of the vehicle. One had duct tape around its handle, the other masking tape.

"Which one?" I asked Dale.

"Duct tape," he said. "It's got the smoke and the AR-15."

I hoisted the toolbox and used both hands to get it over and onto the seat beside him. The box was heavy and unwieldy, industrial size, and I could feel the canisters of smoke shift when I moved it.

Dale took it, and the three of us climbed out of the van. Pugh stood between us, Dale on his left, me on his right. With the toolbox, I only had one hand free, and I didn't like that, but didn't see any other alternative.

We started down the street, moving through the pedestrian field, staying bunched together. If Drama wasn't going for it, if she was onto us, there wasn't much we could do to deny her the shot. We stayed tight on Pugh all the same, and I forced myself to breathe. The air was heavy with exhaust and garbage, the smell of New York City sliding into deep summer.

"Trigger is debusing," I heard Corry say.

"Confirmed," Natalie answered.

There was some rustling on the radio, voices. We kept walking. An adolescent on a skateboard was coming our way, fast, making a furrow in the layer of pedestrians lining the sidewalk. Dale nudged Pugh, and all of us sidestepped right. The kid nearly wiped out on Dale's toolbox.

"Oops," Dale said.

We were almost at the entrance.

"Trigger is inside," Corry said.

"Confirmed. Southeast stairwell clear to top. Check through."

"Stand by."

Dale opened one of the doors to the lobby and I went through first. The shot would come any time now;

depending how far away she was when she pulled the trigger, I might even hear the bullet hitting before the report reached us.

Pugh remained upright, alive, right behind me.

The hallway opened into the atrium, and I could hear the sound of the atrium fountain immediately. At my left, I saw Havel, dressed as Natalie, disappearing into the stairwell.

One of the guards radioed, *"Coming up."*

"Ready," Natalie said. *"All posts, keep it sharp."*

"We've locked down the goal," Yossi said.

Elliot Trent came into the lobby, heading for the security desk. He bent over the counter and spoke rapidly, and I saw the guard at the monitors look our way quickly. But Trent reached into his suit pocket and flashed something, and the guard didn't ask what we were doing, didn't demand to see our work order.

Dale fell in again beside Pugh, and the three of us made it to the elevator bank. After a moment's hesitation, I leaned forward and pressed the button.

"I don't like this," Dale muttered.

I checked Pugh. He was wheezing, and had begun perspiring. "You ate today, didn't you?"

"Yeah," he said, trying to get his breath. "Just the walk. I'll be fine in a few seconds."

Dale turned slowly in a circle, watching for motion. My stomach felt wrapped in chains.

"Stopping at eight," I heard Corry say. *"Trigger needs a breather."*

"Make it fast," Natalie snapped.

Very good, I thought. They'd come up with that on their own. For a moment, it made me very proud.

The elevator chimed, and Dale and I closed in around Pugh, expecting an attack from inside the car,

but the doors slid apart, and no one was pointing anything our way. The car was empty.

We got in, and I put Pugh in the back, covering him
with my bulk. Dale punched twelve, and the doors shut,
and the elevator began rising.

"Moving again," Corry said.

"They're at nine," I said.

"Should we slow it down?" Dale asked.

I shook my head. Better to let things play out as they
were coming. So far, everything was working. So far, it
looked like we might get away with it. I didn't want to
jinx that with any sudden alterations in plan.

The elevator stopped at seven, and the doors opened,
and a man in his forties leaned in and asked, "Up
or down?"

"Up," Dale said.

"Sorry," the man said.

The doors shut again. Dale looked at me and took a
deep breath. When he did, I realized I needed one, too.
Get the oxygen, I thought. You're going to need it if
anything happens. Get the oxygen.

The elevator stopped on twelve, and we stepped
cautiously into the hallway. Offices lined both sides of
the hall, and I could hear the buzz of business machines,
the clacking of keys hitting paper. Many of the offices
had windows, through which I could see other offices, and more windows, and into the atrium.

We turned left, made our way down the hall to the
glowing Exit sign above the door to the stairs. A young
woman in a tight blouse and miniskirt hustled past us
carrying an armful of paper. Dale and I both brought our
free hands up to Pugh's back, preparing to move him.

"Hi," she said, and kept going.

I watched her, waited until she disappeared into one of the offices near the end of the hall.

We'd reached the door.

Corry, Havel, d'Angelo, and White were in the opposite stairwell on this side, should be passing our floor about now. A guard would have been posted at the top and at the bottom of each route.

Dale pushed the door back, checked, then nodded.

It was cooler in the stairwell, and darker, and for a moment I lost some of my vision as my pupils dilated. We waited until the door had shut before moving again, starting up. Pugh was walking slowly, using the railing for help.

We'd passed the next landing when I heard Corry say, *"We're coming out onto fifteen."*

"Looks good," Natalie said.

I could see the guard posted outside the door to the fifteenth floor. He was looking over the railing at the landing, watching us approach. He was smiling.

"Hold up, who's this?" I heard a guard asking. Lang, I thought. It's Lang, he should have been briefed.

"Havel," Corry said, and under his voice I could hear Chris Havel introducing herself.

"Christian Havel?" Lang asked. *"She was already here this morn—"*

"She's here!" Corry shouted. *"She's using Havel's ID as cover, she's in the build—"*

I lost the rest of what he was saying, because then the top of our stairwell blew up.

CHAPTER THIRTY-FIVE

Dale went backwards, into Pugh, and Pugh into me, and we tumbled down, suddenly in darkness, the smell of powder and smoke filling the stairwell. Dale got up quickly, grabbing Pugh, and I found my legs, got upright. There was mayhem on my radio, people cutting one another off.

I heard another explosion, farther away, probably the opposite stairwell.

"Down!" I yelled.

Dale had snapped open the toolbox and removed the AR-15, flipped the stock out. I popped the top of the other box, removed the shotgun, jacked a shell into place. There was a lot of yelling coming from the direction of the fourteenth floor.

"Status!" Yossi was shouting. *"All posts, by the numbers, status!"*

Dale took the lead, the assault rifle up and against his shoulder, and I covered our rear, trying to sort the jumble over the radio, the growing jumble in my head. We'd passed the landing at fourteen when there was another blast, loud, below us. Pieces of masonry and drywall blew up in the stairwell. The explosion echoed. Dale fell backwards, and almost knocked Pugh into me again, but I caught him with my free hand, and began backing up, back to the landing.

Pugh had lost his color, and I could feel his chest heaving for air. Dale pulled himself up again, wiping dust from his face.

"You all right?" I shouted to him. I barely heard myself, could barely hear the voices roaring in my ear.

Dale nodded. "Out on fourteen?"

"Don't have much choice."

He took the stairs back to the landing three at a time, brought the rifle up once again. I thought I could hear somebody calling my name, and I keyed my transmitter, said, "We're stuck, we're coming out on fourteen."

Dale shoved the door open, and the three of us went out into the hall, smacking into people, chaotic, yelling. Someone saw Dale's gun, or maybe mine, and screamed; most turned away, heading in panic for the other end of the hall. Dale began after them, dropping the barrel of his gun, holding one hand out and up, trying to indicate that he meant no harm. Pugh started after him.

A fire alarm was ringing, loud enough to override the buzz in my head. I knew Natalie was trying to raise me on the radio, but I couldn't hear her. The explosion in the other well had sealed us off, isolated Dale, Pugh, and myself from the rest of the guards. They were all above us, and once the fire alarm had started, the elevators would have been locked down. If both stairwells were blocked, there was no way they could reach us anytime soon.

"We're being herded," I realized out loud.

The throng had raced away from us, were forcing their way to the stairs. Even if the access from the fifteenth floor on that side was free, there was no way Natalie and the others could fight through the panic to our floor.

Dale had turned to me. "What did you say?"

Three people stood by the stairs, trying to keep the evacuation orderly. A woman, slacks and blazer, indistinguishable from the rest of the professionally clad, was helping them along.

When she looked at me, I knew.

The woman at the pool. At the Orsini Hotel. The one who had cued Natalie to the pool attendant, and had saved our lives.

"Cover," I told Dale. "We need cover fucking *now*, we need to button up until reinforcements arrive." My hearing was returning to normal; either that, or I was shouting very loud.

He had grabbed Pugh by the arm, and now began dragging him back in the direction we'd come. I brought the shotgun up to bear, leveled it at Drama, and she ignored me, kept getting the milling workers off the floor. She knew I wouldn't take the shot, and she was right. I'd hit half the crowd if I pulled the trigger.

Dale had kicked open the door to one of the offices, and we fell back into it, passing desks and PCs and laser printers and copier machines. Another door led to an inner office, and we went through that one, locking it as we passed, and found ourselves in a maze of beige cubicles. The klaxon was still sounding, and I couldn't hear anything else, no voices, no crowds.

We reached a final door, poured into an executive's office. I knew it was an executive's, because he had a

great big window that overlooked the atrium down
below, a leather couch, his own television and wet bar,
and three bottles of boutique water sitting on a coffee
table.

"We're out of space," Dale informed me.

Pugh was hunched over, hands on his thighs, gasping for air. I checked him quickly, and he caught my
eyes, gave me a nod.

Dale dropped his rifle, began muscling the couch in
one corner of the room over to the door. He groaned
and pushed and I gave him a hand, and the couch had
to weigh almost a ton, but we got it in place. Dale went
back for the coffee table, flipping it over and dumping
the bottles onto the carpet.

"Atticus! God fucking dammit, come in!"

"Nat?" I said. Dale was now knocking equipment
off the desk, telling Jerry to get out of the way.

*"Jesus, are you all right? We can't get to you. We
can't get down there."*

"We've fallen back to an office. She's here, she's
coming in after us."

"Hold on. We'll be there as soon as we can."

Having propped the coffee table against the couch,
Dale had now moved to the desk, and was straining to
lift it. He hollered and flipped it up, then onto its side. I
got out of his way, took Pugh by an arm and moved
him to the farthest corner of the room, away from the
door. He went down in the corner, wrapping his arms
around his knees, pressing his thighs to his chest. I
grabbed one of the bottles of water, popped it open,
pressed it into his hands.

He looked at the bottle, then at me. "Well," he said.
"You gave it your all, son."

I left him on the floor and helped Dale muscle the

desk against the couch. The desk was very nice, oak, maybe, and heavier than the couch.

There was a knock at the door.

Dale and I both dropped flat, began belly-crawling back to our weapons.

The knob rattled.

"I'll huff, and I'll puff, and I'll blow this door in," Drama said.

Dale brought the assault rifle up and sighted at the piled furniture. With what he was shooting and what I was shooting, we couldn't penetrate the door. The good thing was, neither could she. I hoped.

"Atticus?" Drama called. "Ready to call it a day?"

"Oh, yeah," I said.

"Then give it up and let's get this over with."

"Can't do that. Get out of here now. You've already lost."

"Not from where I'm standing."

"We're barricaded in here. By the time you get through the door and through us, the police and the fire department and all our backup will be here. You'll end up dead or in custody. You go now, you might just escape."

"But then you won't have caught me," Drama said.

"Trent wants you. I don't. I just want to keep my principal alive."

The knob rattled again, and then there was nothing but the sound of Dale breathing beside me, of my pulse thumping in my ears.

"Go," I said.

"Dead end," she said. "You're going to do everything you can to keep your principal alive, I accept that. But me, I've got to do everything I can to kill him."

The radio crackled in my ear. I ignored it. "Go," I said again.

She didn't respond, maybe thinking about it. I could feel my heartbeat against the floor.

"Ever been to Besquia?" Drama asked. "There's a place there, they make the best pineapple muffins you'll ever have."

There was the sound of something heavy hitting the door.

"My last try," she said. I thought I could hear her walking away.

I also thought I could hear the timer on the bomb ticking down.

"How long?" Dale asked.

I was already getting to my feet. "Thirty seconds?"

"Oh, fuck."

"Grab him," I said, and then I leveled the shotgun at the big, beautiful window overlooking the atrium, and I fired two shots into it. The glass broke like thin ice, turned to water as it fell out and away and down. I spun the shotgun and used the butt to beat away the shards, counting down in my head. Dale had lifted Pugh to his feet, was standing him beside me, and I dropped the gun and grabbed my principal, and I started forcing him out the window. A tiny ledge, not more than an inch wide, nothing more than detailing, than trim, was perhaps seven feet below.

"If you want to let go, you let go, you die," I told Pugh. "If you want to live, you hold on. Either way, it won't be her who killed you."

I pressed his hands against the sill as he went over, and he looked up at me, grimacing, his hands white from the exertion. I spun, dove for behind the bar and Dale was in the air, and then there was a crack, a burst, and a thunder. Everything flew apart, my head, the room, the walls, and I felt my body snap back, felt my back collide with something. My head turned off, and for a moment I was in nothing, the space between channels on the television.

Then I came back, tasting masonry dust and blood in my mouth, seeing that where there had once been a wall there was now nothing. Dale was only two feet away from me, but it took me a moment to remember who he was. His ears and nose were bleeding, and his left leg was bent wrong, and he had cuts from the flying glass all along his back. He saw me, and said something I didn't hear.

It took forever, and I was dragging myself to the windowsill before I even knew why, and I was face-to-face with Pugh's swollen knuckles, bone white and slipping. Dale dragged himself alongside, and together we reached over and grabbed Pugh's arms. I braced myself against the wall and heaved. My head was full of noise, and I could feel my nose bleeding, and something wet running down my neck.

Pugh came over the edge, flopped into the room like a landed fish.

Then Natalie was leaning over us, and I couldn't hear her speak, but I saw the word "deposition." Pugh was getting to his feet with Corry's help.

"His leg is broken," I told Natalie, pointing to Dale. I still couldn't hear myself.

Pugh was looking at me, and I reached out a hand and got his forearm. Corry helped us to the door, and together we made our way through the cubicles, to the hall, to the working stairwell. I saw four firemen rushing past, and a couple tried to stop us for medical attention, but Corry brushed them off, made certain we could make it to the fifteenth floor.

Marguiles was waiting at the door, Yossi beside him. They got out of our way to let us pass.

"Where's his seat?" I asked Marguiles. I sounded like I was whispering through a foam pillow.

Marguiles moved his mouth and indicated a chair. Pugh nodded and brushed with one hand at the dust coating his coveralls. He looked like an old, friendly ghost. He sat down, still gripping my arm.

Lamia, Breeden, and two faces I didn't recognize were looking at us. One of the faces sat behind a laptop.

"Swear him in," I told the face.

CHAPTER THIRTY-SIX

The deposition ran late because it started late, on account of Karen Kazanjian insisting on tending to Pugh. But by eleven-thirty it was under way, and by nine that evening it was over, and people were packing up their things and preparing for a chance to go home, to rest.

Dale had been taken to St. Vincent's by EMS, but he'd returned at six with an impressive cast on his left leg and a shiny pair of crutches, and he'd waited in the hallway outside of the deposition with the rest of us. I hadn't been back much longer than he had, dealing with the attentions of the police, the fire department, and the ambulance personnel.

There was still a lot to be done, but when Jerry walked out of the room, it didn't matter.

"You all taking me home?" Pugh asked.

"We'll take you as far as the car," I said. "But you're Sentinel's problem, now."

"Fair enough," he said.

The four of us rode down in the elevator with him, along with Lang and Trent and Yossi. One of the latter had radioed ahead, and the Benz was waiting out front.

Before he got in the car, Pugh offered me his hand. "I'll get your address from Marguiles, send you that collage," he said. "It hardly seems enough of a thank-you."

"You didn't let go of the windowsill. That's plenty of thanks."

Pugh released my hand, slid into the backseat of the car. Before Lang could slide in beside him, he said, "Probably should give my testimony in person, don't you think? At the trial?"

"Couldn't hurt."

"Those bastards'll probably appeal. I should be around for that, too."

"Probably."

"Something to think about."

I nodded, and Lang shut the door. Then the rest of Sentinel departed, and the four of us stood on the sidewalk on Broadway, watching the traffic flow past.

"You still owe us meat," Corry told me.

"And alcohol," Dale said.

"There's alcohol at my place. A good place to end the op," Natalie said. She held up a large manila envelope. "We can burn these."

Dale tried to grab for the photographs and missed. "Lemme see, lemme see."

"I'll have to be very drunk before you see them," Natalie said.

"A wrap party," Corry said. "I like that idea. I like that a lot. Let's celebrate, shall we?"

"We should call Havel and d'Angelo, invite them, too," Dale said. "They at home?"

"If the cops are done with them, and if Havel's filed her story, they should be," I said.

"We'll give them a call from my place," Natalie decided.

"I'll meet you all there," I said. "I've got to head home first."

"You better show up," Dale told me.

"It'd be arrogance for me not to," I said.

"Damn right."

We split, they retrieving the rented van, and I hailing a cab.

Erika was reading in the kitchen when I arrived, her feet on the table. From 4D below, I could hear what sounded like a drill, or perhaps a jigsaw.

"Why aren't you at Bridgett's? And get your feet off the table. We eat off that."

She didn't move her feet. "I wanted to be here. You look wasted."

"Had a hell of a day, kiddo." I reached and tickled the soles of her feet. She shrieked, planted them firmly on the floor. "You up for going out?" I asked.

"Depends. Where you thinking?"

"We're having a traditional end-of-the-operation party at Natalie's. Dale, Corry, Nat, me. A couple others. That's it. A quiet little get-together among friends."

"Let me get my shoes on," she said, snapping her book shut and sprinting to her room.

After a second longer to think about it, I did what I'd come home to do in the first place. I reached for the phone, and I dialed the number, and I told my stomach to settle down.

When Bridgett answered, I said, "Hey, you. It's me."

Then I said the rest.

ABOUT THE AUTHOR

Born in San Francisco, GREG RUCKA was raised on the Monterey Peninsula. He has worked at a variety of jobs, from theatrical fight choreographer to emergency medical technician. He is the author of *Keeper,* which was nominated for a Shamus Award for Best First Novel; *Finder;* and *Smoker.* He and his wife, Jennifer, reside in Eugene, Oregon, where he has just completed his fourth novel, *Shooting at Midnight.*

If you enjoyed Greg Rucka's third Atticus Kodiak novel, **SMOKER**, you won't want to miss any of this talented young writer's exciting thrillers. Look for **KEEPER** and **FINDER** at your favorite bookstore.

And look for **SHOOTING AT MIDNIGHT**, Greg Rucka's explosive thriller, coming in hardcover from Bantam Books in October 1999.

In the meantime, turn the page for a preview of **SHOOTING AT MIDNIGHT.**

For my thirteenth birthday, Da gave me a Midtown South sweatshirt that was too big for me, NYPD shorts, and a pair of running shoes.

It was just what I'd asked for.

The next morning, bright and early, I put them on and drove with my Da to Van Cortlandt Park on the north edge of Bronx County, just the two of us. He used orange traffic cones stored in the trunk of the car to set up a small obstacle course while I stretched. When he was finished, he showed me how I was supposed to run it.

"Is it like this at the Academy?" I asked.

"No, but this is a good place for you to start," he said.

I put everything I had into running that course, and when I had it mastered, Da made me run it in reverse.

I loved every minute of it.

From then on out, usually once a week, Da would take me to Van Cortlandt Park, and I would run whatever course he set for me. I'd run it in snow and rain, sunlight and humidity. Couple times his partner, Uncle Jimmy, would join us, and they would smoke and drink beer and watch and heckle and give me pointers.

Couple times that year my sister, Cashel, went with us, too, but she hated it and, after the third time, didn't come back. So Saturdays became days for my Da and me, for my Ma and Cashel.

Which I thought was just great.

For my fourteenth birthday, Da gave me a new pair of running shoes and a set of boxing gloves.

Just what I'd asked for.

We went out to Van Cortlandt Park and Da set up the same course as he had a year ago to the day, and he timed me as I ran it, and when I was done, he showed me the records he'd been keeping in his little notepad, showed me how much I'd improved.

"That's my girl," he said.

Then he put on sparring mitts, and he taught me how to throw a punch that would knock a man down. From then on out, we always ended our sessions with me wearing the boxing gloves.

"They'll make it hard on you. You're a woman, and they'll make you pay for it every inch of the way. But we'll fix it so they never know what hit them. You're smarter than me. You'll be tougher too. You'll get the gold shield I never got; hell, you'll get your own command. You'll have all the education and all the ability, and you'll have the heart and the strength, and that's the most important thing."

"Yes, Da," I said.

"That's my girl. Now . . . let's see that uppercut."

For my fifteenth birthday, Da gave me new shoes, a new MTS sweatshirt, new shorts, a sports bra, and a copy of the cadet's handbook. When I opened the sports bra, he blushed and said, "Your ma picked that out."

We went to Van Cortlandt Park and reviewed my progress, and Uncle Jimmy came along, and when I was done working out that day, Da and Uncle Jimmy gave me a beer. Then they gave me another one, and another, and I made it through most of a fourth before I got sick-drunk and passed out.

Da joked about how well I could hold my alcohol.

He hadn't figured out that I'd been sneaking beers after school for months already, drinking with friends.

He hadn't figured out that I'd begun smoking pot.

Even when I started missing my dates with him, either spending the night at a friend's he thought he could trust, or claiming I was sick because I'd caught a bad bug rather than a savage hangover, he didn't see it.

He was disappointed, but he never said so.

And by the time he suspected, by the time he was willing to admit what his eldest daughter had gotten herself into, I was gone.

I spent my sixteenth birthday living in an abandoned apartment in Alphabet City, trying to steal enough money to score.

.   .   .

Three months later it was over, Da and Uncle Jimmy bringing me back home to the Bronx at four in the morning, laying me in my bed. I was screaming and shouting and Da held me down while Jimmy got Ma and a basin of hot water and some towels.

"Jesus Lord," Ma said when she saw me, and she crossed herself.

"Jimmy, go sit with Cashel," Da said. "Keep her out of here."

"I'll be down the hall with her, Dennis," Jimmy said.

They waited until he had shut the door, and then Da held me still while Ma stripped and bathed me. When she saw my arms, she started to cry.

When they were finished, they left, locking me alone in my room.

Six days later Da woke me at seven in the morning, dropping my sweats and shoes on the end of the bed.

"I'll meet you by the car," he said, and left without locking the door behind him.

When I put on my sweatshirt, it hung looser than it had before. The shoes pinched at my ankles. When I came down the stairs, I had to use the banister for support.

Ma and Cashel were in the kitchen, having waffles for breakfast. They asked how I was feeling.

"Better," I lied, and went out to the garage, where Da was waiting by his Alfa Romeo.

We drove to Van Cortlandt Park without exchanging a word. It was winter and I was shivering, trying to keep my teeth from chattering. Da turned the heat up higher, but it didn't help.

He set up the obstacle course in the snow and told me to run it.

I put everything I had into running that course, and I couldn't do it. My legs wouldn't work, my coordination was shot. I could barely stand straight. I was sweating after only five minutes, my stomach cramping, my hands shaking. I tripped and fell again and again, and Da just watched.

I got sick, doubled over with dry heaves.

Finally he said, "Come here."

He put the gloves on my hands, the sparring mitts on his own.

"Jab," he ordered.

"Da . . ." I said. "Da . . . I can't."

"Don't cry."

"I'm sick . . . I can't."

"Jab."

"Da . . ."

"You throw that jab now, goddamn it, or so help me I'll make you fight back!" When he shouted his voice rumbled across the parade ground, echoing off the snow.

I tried to punch at his extended hand, and the glove on the end of my own felt like it was full of wet sand. There was barely a sound when leather met leather.

"Jesus Christ! Jab! *Jab!* Use your left, for fuck's sake!"

I brought my left up and missed. I was crying and the mitts were hard to see.

"Again."

I tried again. I tried every time he ordered me to. When I hit, it wasn't hard enough, and when I missed, he swore louder and louder. Finally he ordered a left cross that I just couldn't raise my arm to give him.

"I can't, Da, I'm sorry I can't do it." I was sobbing

when I said it, choking on tears and frustration. "I'm sorry I'm sick, I'm sorry I'm weak—"

Before either of us knew what had happened, the mitt on his right hand shot forward and caught me in the left eye, and I was on the ground in the frozen-sharp snow, feeling my sweats soak with icy water, my gloves hiding my face. I tried to swallow the noise I was making, tried to stand up, and I slipped and fell again.

Da took off his mitts and looked at me, his mouth half open and his eyes almost shut, his breath blowing away from him like steam from a train engine.

I saw what he saw, then.

There was never going to be a cadet's handbook or a command or a gold shield all my own. It was never going to happen.

Da crouched down in the snow in front of me, helped me off with my gloves. He took my face in one huge hand, and checked my eye where he'd punched me. Then he helped me up and put me in the car to wait while he stowed everything in the Alfa's trunk.

We never went back to Van Cortlandt Park.

That was thirteen years ago.

CHAPTER ONE

I woke up to find I'd been sharing my bed with Mr. Jones.

He fought me when I threw back the covers, and he fought me when I pulled on my sweats, and he fought me when I snapped on the light in the kitchen and turned the water on to boil. He whispered in my ear as I waited for the steam to rise, and he lurked behind me as I made my cup of herbal cures-what-ails-ya swamp water, and he mocked me as I sat in my easy chair and watched the sky debate color-coding with the coming dawn.

Mr. Jones is a smug motherfucker, and he wouldn't take the hint. So I spelled it out for him.

"I am not going to do it," I told Mr. Jones. "So you can just go fuck yourself with a fork."

Mr. Jones smirked and then slowly faded away, and as he went so did the memory and the ache and the itch. I caught my breath and waited for my heart to slow to normal, and when I felt safe enough, I checked my arms.

Clean.

Of course.

I was eighteen when I'd had the cosmetic surgery, expert skin grafts layered to hide my track marks. Good work, too, that had my father moonlighting at all the worst hotels to make certain we could pay for the operations. I've told myself a million times that it's impossible to know what the discoloration only I can see hides.

I toyed with going back to bed. Six minutes to five in the morning. I had to be at work at nine. What was the point? I could use my early hours productively; I could exercise, or read the *Times,* or listen to the entirety of *Morning Edition.* I could lay out my clothes and make my bed and act like the domesticated animal I now was.

And, of course, if I stayed awake, I'd be unlikely to dream another smack attack.

When I'd first kicked, my nights had been fast and furious with the dreams of using. As I've stayed clean and put more distance between my life and my habit, they've faded until, at times, I've almost forgotten I'd had them at all. Nearly five years had passed since my last run of drug dreams, but in mid-August they'd returned with a vengeance, two or three nights a week. Today's had been the worst in as long as I could remember.

My drug dreams are like sex dreams, and I'm talking about the really good ones, not the ones that fade by the time you hit the shower. No, these aren't so kind; these are sensory delights, filled with the memories of sight and sound and scent and most of all touch, the kind when, in the moment of opening your eyes, you can still feel the kiss on your lips or the hands on your hips.

Or, in this case, the needle in your arm and the rush of heat into your head.

These are the kinds of dreams that make me suspect
that there is, indeed, a good chance that the whole god-
forsaken mass called Humanity is, in fact the dream
of a Great Intergalactic Space Iguana. These are the
dreams that make me question reality.

Something like that, at any rate.

I hate them. They make me feel weak.

I finished off my herbal infusion and resolved that I
was now, in fact, officially awake, that there was no
going back, and that it was time to switch to coffee. I
filled the pot and looked at the phone and, even though
it was early, seriously considered calling the Boy Scout.
If I did, I'd wake him up. I wasn't certain how it made
me feel, knowing that he wouldn't mind. Atticus would
listen to what I had to say, and we'd talk, and then he'd
ask when could he see me, and I'd lie and say soon.

So when the phone did ring, I nearly started half out
of my skin.

But it wasn't him. It was Lisa Schoof, and she said,
"He found us."

"I'm coming over," I said.

She opened the door for me with one hand, her other
pressing a dirty pink dish towel filled with ice to her
bottom lip. Vince was a righty, and he'd worked with
that fist almost exclusively. Lisa's left eye and cheek
were swelling too. She was dressed in boxer shorts and
a tank top, and best I could tell, Vince had contented
himself with her face.

"Are you all right?" I asked before I'd even made it
through the door. "Is Gabe all right?"

She motioned with her free hand toward the kitchenette. I saw Gabe, in thin green pajamas, watching my arrival. He was wearing once-ivory colored sneakers.

"I made him hide in the bathroom." Lisa sounded like she was reading me a message from Western Union, still angry and still scared, and she spoke slowly to conceal it. "As soon as I knew it was Vince, I woke Gabe up and told him to hide in the bathroom."

"I had to lock the door," Gabe said. "I couldn't come out until he left."

"What'd he want?" I asked Lisa.

"Money." She put her back to me, went the eight feet across the apartment to the kitchenette, and reached for the whisk broom wedged between the refrigerator and the wall. A bright crayon drawing of an ambulance was stuck to the door with a magnet. Wedged between the magnet and the drawing were coupons from Fine + Fair.

I looked over the whole apartment, a process that took all of two seconds. Three rooms, counting the bathroom, and I almost didn't because it was so small the only person who could use it without asphyxiating was Gabe. Lisa was balanced on the poverty line, and closer to falling the wrong way than into money. The apartment mirrored that—a decrepit couch that served as her bed, a card table that was both desk and dining surface, two white plastic chairs that were reluctant to take on any weight other than their own. Gabriel had his own room, a real bed, even a particleboard bookcase.

What the apartment lacked in furnishings, it made up for in dignity.

Except that Vince had been through it, and done his best to cause as much damage as possible during his visit. There were shards in the kitchen, glasses that he'd shattered and two or three plates. The few pots and pans Lisa owned had been yanked from their shelves. Otherwise, most of the mess was paper, Lisa's text-books thrown from the table, Gabriel's homework scattered on the floor.

One of the benefits of not having much is that the mess is smaller.

"You're going to suck at that," I told Lisa, taking the broom from her hand. "Get the dustpan."

She let it go without comment, and Gabe moved out of the way to let us work, watching. When you see them together, it's clear they're from the same Scandinavian end of the gene pool, the straight blond hair and the almost gray eyes. But where Lisa's face is broad, with a wide mouth and a nose that's almost beaky, Gabriel's features are more condensed and narrow. He'd grown, too, maybe as much as an inch and a half, and I guessed that by the time he was done, he'd be taller than his mother's five six. Now, though, both of them were slender and small, and in comparison, I felt like a giant, especially in the claustrophobic apartment.

We finished in the kitchen and Gabriel and I set to work gathering the strewn books and papers. Lisa used the hand not holding the dish towel to convert her bed back into the couch, a process that consisted of folding a blanket that, once, had been gray. Now it was almost white.

Gabe and I replaced his collection of Matchbox cars in its blue and yellow plastic case. He showed me a tiny midnight blue Porsche and said, "It's not yours, but it's the closest I could get."

"Boxster," I said. "Not bad. Mine's better."

He looked at me thoughtfully. "Did you bring it?"

"How do you think I got here, buster?"

Gabriel considered, looking to where his mother was now sitting on the couch before he turned back to me. "I think you drove your car."

"You're a smart kid," I said, and dug into my jacket pockets. I had a roll of Wint-O-Green in my left, Tropical Fruit in my right. "Guess."

A smile crept onto his face, chasing Vince's shadow away. "Left."

"You win." I pulled the Life Savers from the requested pocket and pressed them into his hand.

"Thanks," he said with careful politeness, and began fighting with the foil.

"Don't open that," Lisa told him. "You can take it to school with you, have some after lunch."

Gabe stopped trying to unwrap the candy. His smile flickered out. "I'm not going to school. I'm staying with you."

"I've got to go to school too."

"I'll come with you. I won't leave you alone."

The ice had long since melted away, and when Lisa dropped the towel from her cheek, water trickled along her jaw. She wiped it with the back of her hand, then extended her arms to her son. He scrambled off the floor and went to her hug like he was being chased, and as soon as her arms closed around him, he began to cry.

I had no place in a mother-son moment, so I waited. Next door an alarm clock announced morning with a shocking blast of salsa music; the noise cut off as a fist slammed into a snooze bar. Walls this thin, the neighbors must have heard everything that had happened here, and yet there was not a policeman to be found. Lisa certainly hadn't called for one.

Instead, she'd called me.

First time we'd spoken in a year, and I began wondering what exactly she wanted me to do now that I was here.

Lisa rocked Gabriel against her, crooning in his ear, telling him that everything would be all right, that Vince wouldn't come back. Her eyes didn't believe a word she was saying, but Gabriel couldn't see her eyes, and he stopped crying and pulled back. She stroked his forehead, trying to calm his fear with her fingers, and it worked, because finally Gabriel nodded.

"Go take your shower," she said. "Get dressed. Then we'll talk about breakfast."

"I know a great pancake house," I said. "You want a ride in the Porsche?"

Lisa looked about to object but Gabriel asked, "Will you drive me to school?"

"It would be my pleasure."

He wiped a trail of shiny snot from his nose and went for his room, shutting the door quietly behind him. Lisa cocked her head, mother-radar sensing for misbehavior and, when the water in the shower came on, looked back at me.

"I can't pay for breakfast," she said.

"It was my invitation. I'll cover it."

Pride twitched at the corner of her mouth. "Thanks." She stood. "I've got to change too. I've got an EMS class at Fort Totten this morning."

"You want me to wait outside?"

"Nothing you've never seen before."

"True enough."

An old suitcase was wedged between the wall and the back of the couch. She crouched and flipped it open and revealed the entirety of her wardrobe. She pulled clean clothes and draped them over the arm of the couch. Tan slacks, blue blouse, bra, panties, socks.

She changed clothes while looking at her feet, and I suppose modesty should have kept my eyes off her, but it didn't. We'd first met when Lisa was fifteen and I was just-turned seventeen, and I'd easily weighed twice as much as she did even then, and not just because I was already six feet tall. All of her scars seemed to be the same, although it was hard to tell with her forearms, where the tracks were. But the cigarette burns still clustered at the base of her spine, and when she turned while slipping on her bra, I could see the thin puckered line where Vince, years ago, had run a knife up her left breast.

For a minute there, anger closed my throat like I was being choked.

When she was dressed, I asked, "Why did you call me? Not that I mind, but I'm not certain what you need from me, here. Moral support? Money? An extra set of hands?"

She used a blue barrette to clip her hair back. "Help."

"With what?"

She shot another look at Gabriel's bedroom. The door was still closed, but the shower had stopped.

"With what, Lisa?" I repeated.

"Killing Vince," she told me.